## PINNED DOWN . . .

Dobler looked at the men firing at his team. His six SEALs had cover of sorts, a narrow ditch that gave them some protection. Grenades hadn't done the trick on routing the Afghans. Only one way.

"Franklin, Khai, and Lam, on me. We're going to crawl around to the left and outflank them. Let's go, crawl, now."

Dobler wondered why he kept going on these fun-filled field trips. He was thirty-seven damned years old and hurting in most places the way a seventy-year-old does. Crawling wasn't as easy as it had been twenty years ago. He held the submachine gun across his arms in front of him as he dug in toes and elbows and powered ahead.

They were halfway there when he heard a motor start. Then one of their sedans moved slowly toward the enemy rifles. "Hold," he said into the radio. He watched, fascinated. Who? Oh, damn, that had to be Kat. What was she doing?

# SEAL TEAM SEVEN
# BLOODSTORM

## KEITH DOUGLASS

BERKLEY BOOKS, NEW YORK

*Special thanks to Chet Cunningham for his contribution to this book*

This is a work of fiction. Names, characters, places, and incidents are
either the product of the author's imagination or are used fictitiously,
and any resemblance to actual persons, living or dead, business
establishments, events, or locales is entirely coincidental.

SEAL TEAM SEVEN: BLOODSTORM

A Berkley Book / published by arrangement with
the author

PRINTING HISTORY
Berkley edition / March 2001

The Penguin Putnam Inc. World Wide Web site address is
http://www.penguinputnam.com

ISBN: 0-425-17881-1

BERKLEY®
Berkley Books are published by The Berkley Publishing Group,
a division of Penguin Putnam Inc., 375 Hudson Street,
New York, New York 10014.
BERKLEY and the ''B'' design
are trademarks belonging to Penguin Putnam Inc.

PRINTED IN THE UNITED STATES OF AMERICA

10  9  8  7  6  5  4  3  2  1

*Dedicated to those real-life*
*SEALs in Teams One, Three, Five*
*and Two, Four, and Eight,*
*who are out there on*
*the covert front lines doing*
*the dirty little jobs that must be done*
*to maintain our great nation.*
*They are the real heroes, the ones no*
*one ever hears about.*
*The silent ones.*
*The deadly ones.*
*The U.S. Navy SEALs!*

# SEAL TEAM SEVEN

## THIRD PLATOON*
### CORONADO, CALIFORNIA

**Rear Admiral (L) Richard Kenner.** Commander of all SEALs.

**Commander Dean Masciarelli.** 47, 5'11", 220 pounds. Annapolis graduate. Commanding officer of SEAL Team Seven and its 230 men.

**Master Chief Petty Officer Gordon MacKenzie.** 47, 5'10", 180 pounds. Administrator and head enlisted man of all of SEAL Team Seven.

**Lieutenant Commander Blake Murdock.** 32, 6'2", 210 pounds. Annapolis graduate. Six years in SEALs. Father important congressman from Virginia. Murdock recently promoted. Apartment in Coronado. Has a car and a motorcycle, loves to fish. Weapon: Alliant Bull Pup duo 5.56mm & 20mm explosive round. Alternate: H & K MP-5SD submachine gun.

## ALPHA SQUAD

**Willard "Will" Dobler.** Boatswain's Mate. Senior chief. Top EM in platoon. Third in command. 37, 6'1", 180 pounds. Nineteen years service. Wife, Nancy; children, Helen, 15; Charles, 11. Sports nut. Knows dozens of major-league baseball records. Competition pistol marksman. Weapon: Alliant Bull Pup duo 5.56mm & 20mm explosive round. Good with the men.

**David "Jaybird" Sterling.** Machinist's Mate Second Class. Lead petty officer. 24, 5'10", 170 pounds. Quick mind, fine tactician. Single. Drinks too much sometimes. Crack shot with all arms. Grew up in Oregon. Helps plan attack operations. Weapon: H & K MP-5SD submachine gun.

---

*Third Platoon assigned exclusively to the Central Intelligence Agency to perform any needed tasks on a covert basis anywhere in the world. All are top secret assignments. Goes around Navy chain of command. Direct orders from the CIA.

**Ron Holt.** Radioman First Class. 22, 6'1", 170 pounds. Plays guitar, had a small band. Likes redheaded girls. Rabid baseball fan. Loves deep-sea fishing, is good at it. Platoon radio operator. Weapon: Alliant Bull Pup duo 5.56mm & 20mm explosive round.

**Bill Bradford.** Quartermaster's Mate First Class. 24, 6'2", 215 pounds. An artist in spare time. Paints oils. He sells his marine paintings. Single. Quiet. Reads a lot. Has two years of college. Squad sniper. Weapon: H & K PSG1 7.62 NATO sniper rifle or McMillan M-87R .50-caliber sniper rifle.

**Joe "Ricochet" Lampedusa.** Operations Specialist Third Class. 21, 5'11", 175 pounds. Good tracker, quick thinker. Had a year of college. Loves motorcycles. Wants a Hog. Pot smoker on the sly. Picks up plain girls. Platoon scout. Weapon: Colt M-4A1 rifle with grenade launcher; alternate, Alliant Bull Pup duo 5.56mm & 20mm explosive round.

**Kenneth Ching.** Quartermaster's Mate First Class. 25, 6' even, 180 pounds. Full-blooded Chinese. Platoon translator. Speaks Mandarin Chinese, Japanese, Russian, and Spanish. Bicycling nut. Paid $1,200 for off-road bike. Is trying for Officer Candidate School. Weapon: Colt M-4A1 rifle with grenade launcher.

**Vincent "Vinnie" Van Dyke.** Electrician's Mate Second Class. 24, 6'2", 220 pounds. Enlisted out of high school. Played varsity basketball. Wants to be a commercial fisherman after his current hitch. Good with his hands. Squad machine gunner. Weapon: H & K 21-E 7.62 NATO round machine gun.

## BRAVO SQUAD

**Lieutenant (J.G.) Ed DeWitt.** Leader Bravo Squad. Second in command of the platoon. 30, 6'1", 175 pounds. From Seattle. Wiry. Has serious live-in woman, Milly. Annapolis graduate. A career man. Plays a good game of chess on traveling board. Weapon: Alliant Bull Pup duo 5.56mm & 20mm explosive round. Alternate: H & K G-11 submachine gun.

**George Canzoneri.** Torpedoman's Mate First Class. 27, 5'11", 190 pounds. Married to Navy wife, Phyllis. No kids. Nine years in Navy. Expert on explosives. Nicknamed "Petard" for almost hoisting himself one time. Top pick in platoon for explosive work. Weapon: Alliant Bull Pup duo 5.56mm & 20mm explosive round.

**Miguel Fernandez.** Gunner's Mate First Class. 26, 6'1", 180 pounds. Wife, Maria; daughter, Linda, 7, in Coronado. Spends his off time with them. Highly family-oriented. He has relatives in San Diego. Speaks Spanish and Portuguese. Squad sniper. Weapon: H & K PSG1 7.62 NATO sniper rifle.

**Colt "Guns" Franklin.** Yeoman Second Class. 24, 5'10", 175 pounds. A former gymnast. Powerful arms and shoulders. Expert mountain climber. Has a motorcycle and does hang gliding. Speaks Farsi and Arabic. Weapon: Colt M-4A1 rifle with grenade launcher.

**Tran "Train" Khai.** Torpedoman Second Class. 23, 6'1", 180 pounds. U.S.-born Vietnamese. A whiz at languages and computers. Speaks Vietnamese, French, German, Spanish, and Arabic. Specialist in electronics. Understands the new 20mm Bull Pup weapon. Can repair the electronics in it. Plans on becoming an electronics engineer. Joined the Navy for $40,000 college funding. Entranced by SEALs. First hitch up in four months. Weapon: H & K G-11 with caseless rounds, 4.7mm submachine gun with fifty-round magazine.

**Jack Mahanani.** Hospital Corpsman First Class. 25, 6'4", 240 pounds. Platoon medic. Tahitian/Hawaiian. Expert swimmer. Bench-presses 400 pounds. Once married, divorced. Top surfer. Wants the .50 sniper rifle. Weapon: Alliant Bull Pup duo 5.56 & 20mm explosive round. Alternate: Colt M-4A1 rifle with grenade launcher.

**Anthony "Tony" Ostercamp.** Machinist's Mate First Class. 24, 6'1", 210 pounds. Races stock cars in nearby El Cajon on weekends. Top auto mechanic. Platoon driver.

Weapon: H & K 21-E 7.62 NATO round machine gun. Second radio operator.

**Paul "Jeff" Jefferson.** Engineman Second Class. 23, 6'1", 200 pounds. Black man. Expert in small arms. Can tear apart most weapons and reassemble, repair, and innovate them. A chess player to match Ed DeWitt. Weapon: Alliant Bull Pup duo 5.56mm & 20mm explosive round.

# NOTE TO THE READER

Just wanted to warn you that this is an *interactive* book. You read it and then you write to me and tell me what you think about the story, the characters, and the SEALs. A kind of grown-up book report. How about that? You thought you were just going to have a couple of hours of good reading, watch the SEALs do their job, and then reach for another beer.

Tough luck this time. Well, yeah, it's a part of a bet I made with my writing buddy. I waged a small inheritance on the idea that I could get a thousand letters from you guys and gals out there who read these SEAL books.

Now, don't let me down. If you like them, if you don't, tell me to take a hike, whatever. Just figure on dropping me a quick line or two, and I can keep the ranch instead of letting this Simon Legree character foreclose on me because of a few lousy letters I didn't get.

Where? Oh, yeah. Send those cards and letters to:

Keith Douglass
8431 Beaver Lake Drive
San Diego, CA 92119

Hey, thanks a lot. Now you're cleared to go on reading this brand-new *SEAL Team Seven* book. Have fun.

—Keith Douglass

# 1

## Odessa, Ukraine

Chen Takung paused in the darkness next to a boarded-up building with peeling paint and graffiti-sprayed walls. To the left a woman screamed. Someone began sobbing. A baby cried. A cool breeze whipped a newspaper down the street. Chen stepped quickly into the dark alley and waited. He was good at waiting. This strange land was nothing like Shaanxi Province in China, where he grew up. Here it was dry, harsh, unfriendly, and even smelled bad. Not at all like the softness of a Chinese night with a pale moon riding high.

An older car with three colors of paint on it drove up slowly, stopped for a moment, then moved on. Chen was near the Odessa port district that fronted on the Black Sea. Odessa had once been the busiest port and main southern outlet for the Soviet Union in the glory days. Chen had heard that ships from all over the world had lined up to get dock space. Now the new nation that had split off when the Soviet Union fragmented was known as Ukraine, and it struggled to keep its economy going well enough to maintain its independence. Chen knew that ships still stopped here to discharge and take on cargo, but not in the volume they used to.

The smells assaulted him again. It wasn't the night soil odor of the Chinese country, but more a cloying smell of unwashed bodies and decomposing garbage. He hated it here in Ukraine. He hated any place that wasn't China.

Chen Takung had come to Odessa on board the *Star of Asia*, of Chinese People's Republic registry, a beaten-up and weathered freighter, which now sat at a dock awaiting its special cargo. Chen eased against the building, not letting the two-hour wait drag at his senses. He saw everything that went on in the

1

area, evaluated the actions, and determined that none of them held any danger for him.

He tried to relax tense muscles. His senses were on instant alert, searching for anything dangerous. He had made covert buys of sensitive goods from foreign nations before, but nothing of this magnitude.

Chen glanced where his backup crouched in the darkness across the street. The other man had a sniper rifle and was deadly accurate. No one would see him until they should see him.

Chen was highly trained in his field of international relations and secret operations. He was extremely efficient when dealing with those who worked outside of the law of their own countries.

He squeezed his left arm against his body and felt the reassuring bulge of the 9mm pistol. The two men he was to meet were late, which he had expected. He had played that role often in his dealings.

He faded to the left out of the mouth of the dark alley, and edged into the doorway of the run-down building. The door was inset two feet, giving him plenty of room to vanish completely in the shadows of the Ukrainian summer night.

The smell came again. Something dead, maybe a rat or a cat. He pushed it out of his mind.

Time dragged. Tension knotted a muscle in Chen's neck, and he rotated his head trying to calm it. Sweat beaded his forehead even in the cool night. Where were they? They should have been here a half hour ago.

He heard them first. Footfalls on the cobblestones coming from the right. Slowly two men materialized out of the darkness from the downtown direction, and paused at the side of the same building that shielded Chen.

"Nabokov?" Chen whispered the password. He felt better now, more sure of himself. Only two of them.

The men walked toward him slowly with nervous caution.

"Yes, I am Nabokov. Are you Chen?"

"Yes, I'm Chen." They spoke in Russian. Chen stepped away from the doorway. The two men stopped three paces from him.

"You are early," he said, still in Russian.

"Yes, we are ready to do business."

"First I need to inspect the merchandise. Then I'll show you the payment."

"You have the seventy-two million U.S. dollars we agreed upon?"

"Yes, the equivalent in gold bars, diamonds, and U.S. currency. I'll show you it after we see the goods."

"Yes, we agree. Come with us."

Chen had expected more than two of them. He made a curt motion, telling his backup rifleman to return to their headquarters.

Chen and the two Ukrainians walked down a block, where the three entered a ten-year-old Ziv auto.

A short drive later, the car stopped at a large run-down warehouse near the docks.

"The merchandise is inside," the taller of the square-cut Ukrainians said. "We have security. We tell you so you won't be surprised."

"I would wonder if you didn't."

Six Ukrainian soldiers stood just inside the warehouse's first door. They had the newer Russian-made AK-74 rifles. A Russian RK-46 machine gun stood on its mount of sandbags, and a soldier trained it on the door. At each of the next four locked doors there were three soldiers armed with the Portuguese-made stubby Lusa A2 submachine guns. They had an interesting closed configuration. Chen counted twenty-four guards before he came to the last locked door. They had worked their way to the far side of the warehouse. This last section was bathed with bright lights. Chen could smell a salty dampness in the air, so this area must be right next to the water.

When the door opened, he stared at the contents of the huge room. Chen caught his breath, but made sure the two Ukrainians didn't notice. The merchandise was as negotiated. Six of the Russian Satan intercontinental ballistic missiles. The six lay on shipping dollies with wheels for easier movement. All looked identical, painted brown and green in a camouflage pattern, eighty feet long, and should weigh a little over thirty tons each. Chen knew that when fired from a land-based mobile launcher or silo, one missile could travel over 6,500 miles and dump nuclear bombs on ten different independently targeted cities.

Chin shivered. Right in front of him were six of the large missiles waiting for him. They looked to be as ordered, with the correct Russian words and configuration. Ten nuclear warheads should be inside each of the sleek nose cones.

"I'll need to inspect each missile, to be sure there have been no changes, no sabotage," he said.

The two Ukrainians nodded. Chen crawled over and around the missiles for a half hour. The long-range ICBMs were in mint condition. He had trained at the Karkoff Institute of Scientific Research in Moscow for two years, specializing in the Russian ICBM system and its missiles. There was no evidence that any of the nose cones had been tampered with or the warheads removed. Good.

Back with the two Ukrainians, he nodded. "They appear to be in good condition and unaltered. We do not need the auxiliary launching and guidance systems. If we find any irregularities after we take possession, we'll come back and kill you."

"Have no worries. These missiles are as you ordered."

"Where do I go to make payment?" Chen asked.

"Do you have it in a vehicle?"

"Yes, a truck with the U.S. dollars, the diamonds, and the gold. Together it has a value of seventy-two million dollars."

"Bring it here."

"First our freighter must be under way so it can redock here."

The Ukrainian who did most of the talking smiled. "There is no need for that. Your ship, the *Star of Asia,* has been redocked just beyond those large doors."

Chen smiled. "Ukrainian efficiency. I'll go and bring the payment. We must have our ship loaded and be ready to cast off our lines before daylight."

"There should be no problem. Our harbormaster has been told of your departure."

"And compensated?" Chen asked.

They all laughed.

"I understand that not all levels of your government have been informed of this sale."

Nabokov, the larger man, chuckled. "This is a private sale."

"Good. If this works out, perhaps we can do business again."

Chen went with the other two back through the locked and guarded doors to the street. They loaned him a car and driver to take him where he needed to go. He had the driver drop him off two blocks from the small office he had rented two months ago when negotiations first began with Nabokov, director of the Nuclear Arms Arsenal just outside of Odessa. Chen knew that these were missiles that Ukraine had kept out of the inventory of the large numbers of nuclear weapons, missiles, and warheads that were transferred to Russia in 1994 and slated for destruction. That had been part of the disarmament accord between Russia and the United States. Chen had been told that now the hoarded nuclear weapons were orphans, known about only by a few men high in the government. Six of the missiles would not be missed due to the sloppy management.

Chen walked to the small office, opened the locked door, and turned on the lights. Everything must appear normal. He went into the back room and grinned at his six men. A chorus of questions greeted him. He saw his backup man had returned.

He held up his hands. "Yes, it is arranged. We take the money to them now. I know the way. Is everyone ready?"

The six men wore black combat uniforms, with vests and webbing hung with the tools of the elite Chinese military strike force specialists. All carried Russian AKSU-74 submachine guns with thirty-round reversible banana clips that had been taped together for fast reloading. All of the weapons were fitted with sound suppressors.

The truck was a 1974 Chevrolet half-ton pickup that had somehow found its way to Odessa. In back it held storage boxes filled with currency, gold bars, and boxes of cut and polished, brilliant diamonds.

"Let's go," Chen said. He drove the pickup, and the men stepped into an old van of mixed manufacture. Chen would pick up Nabokov and the other man at the front of the same warehouse. The Ukrainians would show Chen how to drive the small truck directly into the section of the warehouse with the missiles.

When Nabokov entered the pickup with his yes-man shadow, he frowned and looked behind them.

"There is a van following you," Nabokov said.

"That's my security," Chen said, and chuckled. "You didn't think I would try this transfer by myself, did you?"

Nabokov scowled this time. "I hadn't thought about that. Surely you must trust us as we trust you."

"My trust is the same as yours. You have twenty or thirty security men at the warehouse. I have my own security men. It is necessary."

"I want everything to go smoothly."

"We are paying you a great deal of money, Nabokov. I insist on my own security."

The Ukrainian licked his lips and took a deep breath. At last he nodded. He took out a small radio and spoke into it in Ukrainian for a moment.

"The rear guards will let us pass, both vehicles," he said.

After driving several blocks, they came around the corner of a building. It was right on the dock, and Chen saw his ship tied up at the adjoining pier. A large truck door rolled upward. Two guards barred their entrance until they recognized Nabokov. Inside, Chen saw the bright lights and the missiles. When both vehicles had driven in, the large door rolled down.

Chen nodded, and they left the pickup. Nabokov and the other Ukrainian went to the rear of the Chevy and examined the boxes.

The six Chinese Special Forces men left the van and fanned out inside the building. They had their orders. Two Ukrainian soldiers came through the door from inside the warehouse.

Chen shouted something in Chinese, and watched with satisfaction as both Ukrainian soldiers were shot by the Chinese commandos. They slammed backward with four submachine-gun rounds each in their chests as they stared in surprise at the black-clothed killers.

Nabokov looked up from the payment boxes in shock. "What are you doing?" he bellowed.

"Securing the area," Chen said. He held his pistol pointing at the Ukrainian. "I'll take your side arm and the radio now, Nabokov. You have no armed support inside. Let's not make this worse than it has to be."

Nabokov took out the radio, pretended to hand it to Chen, then pushed a button on it and shouted in Ukrainian: "Alert, alert, the missile room, now."

Chen shot him three times in the chest with his silenced pistol, then turned the weapon on the yes-man with Nabokov and shot him twice as he surged away. Both rounds took him in the back, one crushing his spine and dumping him into a death spasm on the concrete floor. Two Ukrainian soldiers burst through the small door at the back of the big room.

Chen saw them coming and shouted at his men, then dove behind the pickup. Both Ukrainian soldiers went down in a murderous cross fire of silenced submachine gun rounds. Two more soldiers raced through the inside door, and got off a dozen unsilenced rounds before the black-clothed Chinese specialists fired at them. The surprise entry caught the Chinese commandos by surprise, and two went down in the enemy fire.

Chen saw it all and jumped up, screaming and firing his pistol at the intruders. The other Chinese commandos cut down the Ukrainian guards.

"Lock that inside door that leads to the other rooms," Chen said into his radio. Two of the black-robed Chinese darted to the door, and closed it and snapped on two locks. A pair of shots sounded from outside the door, but the rounds didn't penetrate.

"The big doors, now," Chen said to the radio. "We must move quickly."

Two of the Chinese ran to the lift doors, looked at the row of buttons, and found the right ones. One of the twenty-foot-wide doors rolled up on greased tracks. Just beyond a thirty-foot-wide dock sat the *Star of Asia*. Deck sailors on watch took hand signals from Chen. A moment later a rusty-looking panel slid upward, revealing a thirty-foot-wide dock-level loading hatch. The interior of the ship looked like anything but a rust-bucket freighter. It was brightly lighted, and well painted. Quickly a loading platform bridged the three-foot gap between freighter and dock. A small tow tractor rolled over the bridge to the dock, and inside to the dolly holding the first missile. The tractor driver hooked up to the missile dolly, and then carefully towed it out of the warehouse, over the bridge, and into the hold of the freighter. It vanished somewhere to the left. Two minutes later the tractor came back for another missile.

A sudden burst of rifle fire came from the small door beside where the pickup had driven in. Two Ukrainian soldiers stood there firing at the Chinese Special Forces. One Chinese went down with a round to his chest. The other armed Chinese pounded the guard soldiers with thirty rounds of silenced death. They jolted backward. One man got off two more rounds before he died in another flurry of firing.

"Secure that back area," Chen shouted at his gunmen. One man ran to the door, and kept a watch outside.

Ten minutes later, five of the ICBMs were stowed in the decrepit-looking freighter. The Chevy pickup with the seventy-two-million-dollar payment for the missiles was driven across the bridge into the freighter. Then the remaining three Chinese Special Forces men carried the bodies of their dead comrades into the freighter.

While the tractor loaded the missiles into the freighter, Chen took a brisk walk down the dock. His destination was the sleek-looking freighter that was moored just in back of his down the pier. Its flag showed that it was of Panamanian registry. A sentry challenged Chen as he approached the gangplank.

As they talked, an officer came to the rail and saluted Chen. He quickly came down the plank, and they walked along the new, trim freighter. It was slightly larger than Chen's ship, but this vessel was in freshly minted condition.

"You have the goods?" the officer asked.

"We do. You have the payment?"

"Yes. Bring the missile here and we'll show you the payment."

"You have dockside-level loading?"

"No, we'll use two of our cranes. They are rated at over fifty tons."

"Good." Chen touched a button twice on a small radio he took from his pocket. "The goods are on the way."

Five minutes later, the small tractor towed the sixth ICBM from the warehouse to the Panamanian freighter. Now a stiff canvas covered the missile and shrouded its identity.

One huge crane swung out and down; then a second moved into position. Men attached cables to each end of the missile and the dolly. Winches ground. Slowly the thirty-ton missile and dolly lifted off the dock. It wouldn't fit into any of the holds on the ship, so they positioned it slightly aft on the main deck, secured it, and added more camouflage.

The Panamanian captain signaled, and a small crane swung down a pallet board with a wooden box on top of it. Inside the box were stacks of U.S. currency.

"There it is, fifteen million in hundred-dollar bills. Mostly used, but some with sequential serial numbers."

"We'll check it," Chen said. The tow tractor pushed its lift bars under the pallet board and carried the money back to the *Star of Asia*.

A few minutes later it was loaded on board. Chen stepped into the ship through the side loading hatch, and the tractor pulled the loading bridge inside. The heavy steel panels on the side of the freighter closed, and the rusty camouflaged plates slid down into place.

It took another five minutes for the crew of the Chinese ship to cast off its lines. Aided by a tug, it worked its way out of the dock area toward the channel that led to the open Black Sea. Within ten minutes they had cleared the port, paid the pilot double his usual fee, and put him in his small boat.

All of the regular clearances had been filed. They checked out with the port master's radio in faltering Russian, and were on their way.

For two hours, Chen stood in the bridge, listening to the radio and watching for fast-moving ships that might be overtaking them. He paced the small area, smoked one cigarette after another, and always looked to the rear. He saw and heard nothing unusual. Only when they were a half hour at sea did he take out a bottle of rice wine he was partial to and pass around drinks to the Chinese Navy captain of the ship and his executive officer.

"Due south?" the captain asked.

"Yes. Later we can change course to come to the Bosporus Strait."

The captain tipped his second small glass of the wine and lifted his brows. "All goes well. You will be a hero of China."

Chen's face froze into a steel mask. "Not yet. We have a long way to go. We have the greatest prize any warship has ever won. We have the future of the Chinese nation's place in history. We have fifty more nuclear warheads that we can retrofit and then use any way that we want to.

"They will give us flexibility. We have some nuclear weapons, but not as many as the Western nations believe. This will give us massive potential. They will fuel a power drive gobbling up nations and territories that no nation on earth will have the nerve to challenge.

"There will be no stopping this vessel in any port. We will .go through the strait, then on into the Sea of Marmara and out the Dardanelles.

"Once in the Aegean Sea, we will be able to relax and to meet one other ship. We must avoid any suspicion by any government. We are an oily old rust bucket of a Chinese freighter making for the Suez Canal on our homeward trip. Nothing we do can alter that image. We are the future of China.

"We also saved the seventy-two million dollars we were to have paid for the stolen goods. We have sold one missile for another fifteen million. We will go down in Chinese history books as the key men in jolting China into the forefront of the world powers and in carving up the Far East in any fashion that China wants to.

"I make a toast, Captain, to China, the greatest nation on the face of the earth."

"To China," the captain and Chen said together. Then they drank.

When the rusty old freighter was fifty miles south of Odessa in the Black Sea, sailors from the ship held a short Buddhist funeral service and slipped the bodies of the three Special Forces men into the Black Sea. Chen watched. The bodies sank immediately. They were good men, good soldiers of China.

# 2

## NAVSPECWARGRUP-ONE
### Coronado, California

Senior Chief Will Dobler grinned as his eleven-year-old son, Charles, stared in wonder at the "0" course while a squad of tadpole SEALs scaled the walls and walked the logs and powered over the obstacles.

"Wow, Dad, I want to do that. Please?"

Dobler chuckled. "Not quite yet, mister. You're not big enough to get halfway up that wall. When nobody is using it we'll go out and you can give one of them a try."

It was visitors' day at the Navy SEALs training facility on the strand at the south side of Coronado, and the senior chief of Third Platoon of SEAL Team Seven had his family on the tour. The Navy Special Warfare Section, Group One, was a secure facility. But the part of it that was the BUD/S training section and the home base for SEAL Teams One, Three, Five, and Seven was not actually a part of the secured area. It was a little more relaxed, and from time to time visitors were permitted to look over the training areas and the SEAL facilities.

Senior Chief Dobler's wife, Nancy, and Helen, his fifteen-year-old daughter, were along as well. It was to be an all-day family outing. First the base, then a picnic and surfing and swimming down at the Silver Strand State Beach on the ocean side.

Gunner's Mate Miguel Fernandez had brought his family along on this Sunday afternoon, and they'd teamed up for the tour. Maria Fernandez had been a help to Nancy, and now they were good friends.

At the fifty-foot-deep tower tank, Charles wanted to jump in, but his father gave him a curt no. The tank was little used now.

The waterproofing of the tadpole SEALs was done in a new pool.

Helen had asked to stay in the car during the tour, but her mother had persuaded her to come. "We want you to know where your father works and what he does here," she had said. Helen had pouted a little, but had gone along. She was tall, slender, and dark-haired like her mother. She had filled out during the past year, and Senior Chief Dobler had been worried about the boys who began to come to their house to talk to Helen. He knew they had more in mind than talking, and it bothered him. So far, no major problems.

The tour moved to SEAL Team Seven's headquarters and the Third Platoon office. Jaybird Sterling sat behind one of the desks, working on his machinist's mate specialty and getting ready for striking for first class. He stood as the civilians came in, then saw Senior Chief Dobler and relaxed.

The chief introduced his family and Maria and Linda Fernandez to Jaybird. While the chief told his family what he did in the office, Jaybird moved over beside Helen. Jaybird had felt his jaw drop in amazement when he saw the pretty girl.

She had to be eighteen, long dark hair, dark eyes, beautiful skin, and a face and figure that made him stop and look again. He grinned foolishly as he motioned to her.

"Hey, how do you like our digs?" Damn, what a stupid thing to say. She probably wouldn't even look at him.

She turned and smiled, and Jaybird almost melted into a puddle on the floor. "Jaybird. Yes, I've heard Father talk about you. He wonders how you got your nickname."

"That's classified. Sorry. You like the tour?"

"First time I've been here. Seen a lot of the Navy, of course. Ever since I could walk and talk."

Senior Chief Dobler looked at his daughter and frowned. He went on explaining what they did in the office. Then he looked at his daughter again.

"Jaybird, knock it off. I'm trying to talk up here."

Jaybird waved, and looked at Helen and grinned. "I'll get chewed out tomorrow," he whispered.

Helen laughed softly, and her smile brightened. "I hear there's a fish fry for the platoon coming up."

"Yeah, someone is always having one. Oh, you would come. Yeah, I'll look forward to it."

"That would be nice. I haven't made many friends here yet."

"Hey, I'll be your friend. Maybe I could call sometime."

"Jaybird, I hope so." Her smile was perfection.

Senior Chief Dobler growled at Helen as he led the group from the office. Jaybird stood watching. Helen was last to leave. She waved and gave him her best smile, then hurried out.

"Damn," Jaybird said softly. Now there was a girl. She had to be eighteen. He could check on the chief's personnel file. Hell, no. She was at least eighteen. He'd call her tonight and have a chat. The chief couldn't object to that. Jaybird snorted. The chief damn well would if he knew about it. He must protect Helen like he was a Doberman pinscher without a leash.

Later that afternoon Jaybird went to a movie by himself, had a beer, then from the apartment he shared with two other SEALs, phoned Senior Chief Dobler's home. Helen answered.

"Hi, this is Jaybird, hoped that you would be home. How was the swim?"

"Fine, but those breakers are so rough."

"I could teach you how to duck under them."

"That would be great. Only . . ."

Jaybird laughed. "Only your father wouldn't let you anywhere near me in your swimsuit. Hey, if I were in his place, I'd probably do the same thing. You have a boyfriend?"

"No. We've only been here a short time. I hardly know anybody."

"That will change. Are you out of school?"

"No. Soon."

"You'll probably go to college."

"I hope to. Did you have any college?"

"Just a few courses. No chance now that I'm a SEAL."

"Is it . . . do people shoot at you?"

He laughed. "Oh, yes. From time to time. But not when we're on base or in training."

"It must be hard. All that training. Then you go on the missions. Dad tells us a little about them, but not much. Mom goes out of the room when he starts talking about them."

"Good idea. Then she won't worry." He wanted to ask her if she would worry about him when they went on a mission, but he couldn't. "Hey, maybe we could go to a movie or something sometime."

"Maybe. Dad doesn't like me to go out on dates."

"You have been on dates?"

"Sure, not a whole lot."

"You ever go to the Coronado library?"

"Once or twice."

"Maybe you could go there to research something and I could just happen to be there. Your dad wouldn't know anything about it."

"We could talk?"

"For hours we could talk. How about tomorrow night, about seven at the library?"

"Yes. I'll be there. I better hang up. Bye, Jaybird."

Jaybird said good-bye and sat there grinning. He hadn't been so pumped up in years. A girl? He was getting this excited about a girl who was also the apple of the eye of his senior chief? He must be nuts. He laughed. Yeah, he was nuts, all right, nuts about this little lady Helen. Right then he couldn't wait for Sunday to end so he could wait for Monday night. If they had a night exercise or night training tomorrow, he was gonna kill somebody.

Monday came at last for Jaybird, and the training was easy, some classroom things about new weapons and then a ten-mile training run along the sand. He was tired, but so nervous he couldn't spit, as he walked up to the Coronado library. He was ten minutes early.

Jaybird found a table with no one sitting at it in the far corner of the reading room. He picked a book off the shelf and pretended to read. When he looked up from the book for the twentieth time, Helen stood across the table from him. She watched him as she stood there smiling but with her arms folded protectively across her chest.

"You came," she said, sliding into the chair opposite him. She reached out and touched his hand across the table. "I told Daddy that I wanted to bring home some mysteries. Let's do that first, then we can talk."

They found the mysteries, checked them out, then went back to the table and talked. Mostly she listened to him. He told her about his growing up in Oregon. She told him about moving from one Navy base to another. It was so comfortable, seemed so right to Jaybird. He'd never been this open with a girl before.

Helen looked at her watch. "Oh, dear. I have to be home by eight-thirty and it's almost eight already."

"I'll walk you home, almost all the way. First, let's look in the stacks."

They went into the long rows of books and stood close. When nobody was in the row, she reached out quickly and kissed his lips, then came away.

She sighed, her smile radiant. "Oh, my," she said softly.

He kissed her back and held it longer. They clung together.

"I think I love you, Jaybird," Helen whispered to him.

"Oh, yeah, I feel the same way. But you're my boss's daughter and he would kill me if he could see us right now. What the hell am I supposed to do now?"

# 3

## Tripoli, Libya

Three days after the *Benghazi Messenger* left Odessa, it docked in Tripoli. The port authorities knew it was coming. They had reported the time of arrival to the twelve-man Revolutionary Command Council and Colonel Muammar al-Qaddafi, the council head as well as Prime Minister, Minister of Defense, and Commander in Chief of the Libyan Armed Forces.

A huge celebration had been planned and exploded the moment the sleek, twenty-two-knot freighter touched the dock with its light cargo strapped down on the deck.

What few Western journalists there were in the capital had no idea what the celebration was about. There was no television or radio announcement about the landing. Nor when Qaddafi made a short speech at the site did he explain what was so important on board the ship.

Qaddafi had spoken from a low platform surrounded by two hundred of his elite personal guard. When he finished, he marched away in the center of this guard to his armored limousine, and it rolled away in a six-car caravan. The vehicles began changing places until it was confusing which one the Libyan leader rode in.

Two hours later, Qaddafi paced back and forth in a well-guarded warehouse near the waterfront. He watched his best engineers dismantling the nose cone of the Russian Sasin ICBM.

"Can't they go faster?" Qaddafi asked.

The man generally considered to be the number-two man in Libya had been pacing with his commander. They both stopped. The second man was Abdul Fantoli.

"Now is an excellent time to exercise some patience, Mr. Prime Minister. That way we don't rush the engineers so they make a mistake and ten nuclear weapons go off all at once, reducing our beloved Tripoli to an ash being washed over by the boiling Mediterranean."

Qaddafi stared at Fantoli for a moment and shrugged. "Just so the ten little packages are all safely inside and we can get them out and use them. For fourteen years I have been waiting for this day. So well I remember our blistering defeat in Chad back in eighty-seven when we had to pull out and leave a billion dollars worth of military equipment behind. That will never happen to us again. Never again.

"This time we will sweep in with power and speed that will make the Nazi Blitzkrieg look like a schoolboy game. This time we will overwhelm them and make them pay."

Fantoli nodded. "Yes, we are ready. Our special strike forces can be ready in three days, then move out to the assembly areas in the desert. One thing we need to finalize is the delivery method."

"Finalize it today, Fantoli. Test it tomorrow, alert the strike force the next day. Three days from then we strike."

Fantoli acknowledged the order and hurried away. In his own limousine, he phoned his top engineer. They met in his office, both arriving at about the same time in the bomb-proof structure four stories below ground.

The engineer listened to the timetable.

"I suggest that we use a MiG-23 Flogger jet to deliver the bomb," he said, "It will be recalibrated to detonate at ten thousand feet in an airburst. Our engineers know how to do this. Releasing the bomb from the hard point on the Flogger's wing will arm the bomb. It will be delivered over the target and descend from thirty thousand feet on a parachute to the ten-thousand-foot level, where it detonates.

"This will give our pilot plenty of time to get out of the way of the bomb blast itself or any effects of the radiation. He will circle thirty miles out, then return for a flyover for a report on the effect of the bomb. Pictures will be taken as well. When the nuclear engineers finish their work and give us the bomb ready to drop, we will be ready."

Fantoli drew diagrams on a pad of paper on his desk.

"You're sure that this will work?"

"The targetable nuclear warhead is relatively simple. We take off the guidance system and the small rockets, readjust the arming mechanism, and set them to detonate at ten-thousand feet of air pressure. Nothing can go wrong."

"I agree. That's why the Prime Minister and I and half of our staff will be in Benghazi for the next three days directing the attack from there. Good luck, and we'll see you when we get back." Fantoli chuckled. "That is, if nothing goes wrong, we'll see you when we get back."

Fantoli checked the target. It was just over the border into Chad a hundred miles, a small town called Yebbi Bou. None of the staff or the field commanders knew if they would actually drop the nuclear bomb or only threaten to. They would find out in three days. He had no current population figure for the town, but the estimate was about fifteen to twenty thousand people. It would be a wake-up call for Chad.

He made three phone calls alerting those who needed to know. Their troops would begin moving tomorrow, and would be in hidden camps along the border at the right time.

Fantoli knew it would happen. The engineers had researched this project for three months, had come up with their changes on the warheads and the propulsion systems and the arming device. They would have the bomb ready on time. The parachute had been tested a dozen times on a mock-up of the same weight. It had worked perfectly every time from thirty thousand feet.

He made one more phone call. Then was on his way to pick up the Prime Minister for their quick flight to Benghazi. It would be an interesting three days.

## NAVSPECWARGRUP-ONE
## Coronado, California

Commander Dean Masciareli slammed the flat of his palm down on his pristine-clean desk.

"Listen up, SEALs. There are going to be some changes around here. No more of this cowboy shit. You will go through channels of command. You will not bypass me or Admiral Kenner on any matter whatsoever. Is that distinctly clear?"

Lieutenant Commander Blake Murdock, his 2IC Lieutenant (J.G.) Ed DeWitt, and Master Chief Petty Officer Gordon MacKenzie all nodded.

"Gentlemen, I want to hear you say it," Masciareli barked.

"Yes, sir, clear, understood," all three said, and Masciareli snorted and sat down behind the large desk.

"All right. Any time this Don Stroh character contacts you,

he should be bumped up the chain to me and I'll tell the admiral. Then if there is an assignment, it will come down the chain from the Chief of Naval Operations to the admiral, not from some chicken-sucking CIA man."

Master Chief MacKenzie was the most relaxed man in the room. He had seen commanders come and go through this office. He cleared his throat, and Masciareli looked at him.

"Master Chief?" Masciareli asked.

"Sir. Let's say I get a phone call or a signal from the office of the Chief of Naval Operations. I am to buck that up to you?"

"Precisely, Master Chief. The admiral and I are tired of being bypassed and not even knowing where our Seventh Team Third Platoon is half the time. We have to be in the picture. Admiral Kenner just talked with the CNO this morning and ironed things out. The CNO will not be calling you, Master Chief, or you, Commander. This CIA man, Stroh, may be a problem. If he calls, tell him simply that he must get into the loop and go to the CNO, who will then contact Admiral Kenner and we'll get the word down to the concerned platoon. Is that all perfectly clear?"

Again the chorus of agreement came from the three SEALs.

"Good. Now sit down. We've had a tentative alert for sometime next week. It seems that the CIA has been monitoring a cache of former Russian ICBMs in the Ukraine. They all were supposed to have been returned to Russia years ago for their agreed-on destruction. Most were. Some were not. Now the CIA tells us that some of those missiles have been moved from the underground armory near Odessa, in what is now the independent nation of Ukraine, and put on board a Chinese freighter.

"The satellites have lost the freighter, but the CIA believes it to be somewhere in the Aegean Sea. It's moving at only ten knots and the freighter is said to be an old rust bucket. The CIA thinks it's on its way to China.

"Those ICBMs are the type that have ten independently targetable nuclear warheads in each nose cone. If the Chinese get three of them, that's thirty more nuclear bombs they can add to their arsenal. If they get ten missiles, it's a hundred more nukes for them.

"There is a chance that your platoon may be asked to intercept that freighter and take it over to destroy the warheads, or simply sail the ship into a neutral port where U.S. forces could take control of the nose cones of those missiles. Comments."

"Why would the Chinese use an old rust bucket to haul out such a valuable cargo?" DeWitt asked.

"We don't have an answer."

"How fast is the ship traveling?" Murdock asked.

"That we do know," Masciareli said. "Ten knots. Which seems strange when most freighters can make from eighteen to twenty-three knots. Comments why?"

"A ploy to throw us off the scent," Ed DeWitt said. "Nobody would put all those missiles in an old scow that could make only ten knots. They hope to slip through the net."

"Why didn't they fly them?" Murdock asked. "Be a lot simpler and faster."

"Probably too hard to get a Chinese transport plane large enough to take the type missile we're talking about," Masciareli said. "Then getting clearances in and out of an airport in Odessa would be much harder than slipping away from a dock at midnight."

"So we could have a wet takedown on the scow if we can find her," Murdock said.

"About the size of it," Masciareli agreed. "The admiral will keep us up to date on matters. He said Don Stroh will still be a field rep for the CIA, but official action will go through the admiral."

"Yes, sir," Murdock said.

"That's it. I would guess you might have some wet training to do about now."

"Yes, sir," DeWitt said.

The three stood.

"You're dismissed," Masciareli said. The SEALs walked out the door and left the building.

"Good-bye, Don Stroh," DeWitt said.

"Not a chance," Master Chief MacKenzie said. "Oh, he'll pull back, send requests through, but there will be a time when it just won't work through channels and he'll jump the CNO to call me direct and get things moving. Won't be long. Kenner and Masciareli had their big shot, moved things to Navy time, so they'll be happy for a while. First thing you know they won't want to take the time to keep tabs on us, and we'll be back to business as usual."

"Hope to hell you're right," Murdock said. "Stroh has been a pain sometimes, but he gets the job done. Now, for some training. Take down a freighter at sea. Ideas, 2IC?"

"Yeah, a couple."

They stopped at the Quarterdeck, where Murdock put in a request with the master chief for the use of a destroyer for two days for sea training. The request went to Masciareli, who asked for Murdock on the phone.

"A destroyer for two days? You know what that's going to cost the Navy?"

"A few hundred gallons of diesel fuel and some tired sailors. We need the actual at-sea training going up the side of a ship. Hone our skills on daylight practice, then chasing down the ship at night and doing the same thing. Think what it will cost if we can't do the job and that freighter gets through to China."

An hour later they had the authorization through Admiral Kenner. By 0935 Murdock was on the phone with Commander Zertiz, CO of the *Donald Cook*, DDG 75, ported at the 32nd Naval Pier for some minor repairs.

"You want to do what?" Zertiz asked.

Murdock explained it to him.

"Whatever the admiral says," Zertiz replied. "My crew is on board. We were due to sail in the morning on a training run. We'll just jump it a few hours. We'll see you five miles off Point Loma sometime after fifteen hundred."

"Right, Commander. Once on station, set a two-mile-box course at ten knots. That's the speed we need."

Third Platoon of SEAL Team Seven had been scheduled for a five-mile run and a five-mile ocean swim that afternoon. Ed DeWitt made the needed arrangements. They took a bus to nearby North Island Naval Air Station, with a flatbed truck right behind them holding two fully inflated IBSs. The Sea Knight chopper sat on the flight line warmed up and ready to move. The Sea Knight is a workhorse medium assault helicopter with two contrarotating, three-blade main rotors fore and aft on the fuselage. It can haul twenty five fully combat-ready troops or fifteen litters on a hospital run. It is armed with two .50-caliber machine guns, and can use door gunners with freewheeling machine guns. It has a maximum speed of 165 mph, with a maximum range of 420 miles.

The sixteen SEALs, wearing cammies over their wet suits, loaded on board the helicopter and pushed the two IBSs and their special equipment inside through the aft hatch. All the men wore their usual combat vests and carried their assigned or selected weapons with full loads of ammunition.

The chopper's pilot checked with Senior Chief Dobler, who gave him a thumbs-up, and the bird lifted off just after 1435.

"How many of you have done this before?" Dobler asked. He had a response of twelve hands out of the sixteen. "Nothing to it. Just follow orders, work slowly and carefully, and it will go off like clockwork. Any questions?"

"We're going to run down a destroyer in our IBS?" Tony Ostercamp, Machinist's Mate First Class, asked.

"The destroyer will be making only ten knots. That's the speed this rusted-out freighter is supposedly doing. We'll drop in ahead of the ship, power over to her and match speed, then latch onto the side of the destroyer with our magnets. We've been over the procedure a dozen times."

"Jump time in three minutes," the speaker in the chopper said. The men stood and began checking each other's gear, then lined up with one squad on each side of the big bird waiting for the aft swing-down hatch to open.

A minute later it yawned downward. When the red jump light came on, the first two SEALs pushed the two IBSs out the rear, picked up their flotation drag bags, and looked at Dobler.

"Go, go, go," Dobler shouted to be heard over the sound of the chopper. The SEALs ran to the back of the CH-46 and stepped into space. The craft was only ten feet off the water. They hit almost at once, went underwater, came up grabbing at their flotation bags, and swam toward the floating IBSs.

Once all the SEALs were on board the two rubber boats, the engines were started and the small craft began nosing to the left to meet the path of the destroyer about a mile behind them. They plowed through a medium sea at the assigned ten knots.

Murdock watched his men. Jaybird would be the first one up the side of the destroyer. Out of the other boat it would be Fernandez, Gunner's Mate First Class, who had done it before. Murdock judged the angle of the destroyer and motioned for the two boats to move ahead another hundred yards. Then they waited. The men on the destroyer were supposed to ignore them.

As it came up, Murdock thought that the five-hundred-foot-long destroyer had never looked larger. He watched as it sliced through the water fifty yards to the left. Kenneth Ching, Quartermaster's Mate First Class, who was on the motor, revved it at just the right time and moved the rubber boat ahead at nearly full speed as it ate up the distance to the big ship and came alongside amidships. Holt and Bradford slammed the strong magnets against the side of the destroyer and tied them off to the side of the IBS. They were latched on. Behind them he saw the Bravo Squad boat miss the tie and surge away from the destroyer. It powered back to the side of the craft, landed the strong magnets, and tied the IBS to the mother ship.

At once Jaybird and Fernandez began to work their way up the sloping sides of the destroyer. They had strong hand magnets and smaller ones on their boots. They lifted the hand magnets off the side of the ship, extended their arms as far upward as they would go, and let the magnets clamp tight as they took a step upward. Each man trailed a strong woven nylon line behind him.

The side of the destroyer was maybe a quarter of the distance from water to rail that a freighter would be. The two SEALs worked upward quickly, and were soon over the rail.

On the deck of the destroyer, Jaybird ignored six curious seamen, and tied off the nylon line to the strongest rail support and gave it two quick tugs. Below, Joe Lampedusa, Operations Specialist Third Class, grabbed the rope and began to climb upward, walking up the ship as he heaved his body upward hand over hand on the strong line.

Murdock was the last man up from his boat. He left Vinnie Van Dyke, Electrician's Mate Second Class, to stay with the boat. On the actual operation all eight men would go topside.

On the destroyer's deck, Murdock gathered his men around. "That's how we'll get on board. It will be a lot tougher climb than that. We'll go back to base tomorrow and work on the rope climbs. Now everyone over the side on the rope in reverse order from the way you came up."

They all went down the rope. In a real operation they would leave the nylon line attached. On this training exercise one of the destroyer crewmen was asked to untie it once the last man was down.

They unlatched from the destroyer, surged away from it, and went to the other side, where they worked the climb again. By that time it was turning dusk. They stayed on board this time, had chow with the crew, and got ready for their night exercise. It would be much the same, only without any lights. The destroyer would be in combat mode showing few lights.

Captain Zertiz came down on deck and watched the SEALs go over the side. He found Murdock.

"You guys always have this much fun?" he asked.

Murdock grinned and shook the commander's hand. "Usually it's best when nobody is shooting at us. Thanks for your help. We needed some polishing."

"You do this at night?"

"Right. Easier to hide in the dark so we don't get shot. We'll do the climb twice in the dark, then we'll ask you to call in our Sea Knight for a night pickup. We'll leave the IBSs with you and retrieve them when you get back into the bay."

The night climb proved to be little different from the daylight one. They did have more trouble estimating the speed of the destroyer and finding the right path to motor alongside it. Then it was routine.

Topside after the second climb, Murdock asked one of the chiefs standing around watching to have the captain radio to North Island Naval Air Station that it was time to send the chopper out for a nighttime pickup with the ladder.

A few minutes later Captain Zertiz came down to the SEALs.

"You going to do this night pickup from the water or the deck?"

Murdock laughed. "Hey, Captain, anybody can board a chopper off a destroyer deck. We won't have that option on a mission. The dark-water pickup is more dangerous for the chopper crew as well as us, but it's the only way we can exfiltrate on some missions."

"Going to jump in?"

Murdock shook his head. "Nope, we'll ask you to come to one knot forward so we can go down the lines and stay together with glow sticks. We've done it before."

A seaman came to the captain and talked a moment.

"Commander," Zertiz said, "looks like the chopper pilot wants a word with you. He's on his way."

Murdock went to the communications center and took a mike.

"Yes, CH-46, this is Murdock."

"We'll be landing on the destroyer, correct?"

"Negative, Forty-six. We're SEALs here. We want a water pickup with your ladder out the rear hatch. You've done it before."

"Never at night, Commander."

"No sweat. Turn on your down landing lights, keep six feet off the water, and let out the ladder. My boys do the rest."

"Do I have an option? If I think this will endanger my helicopter and my crew, I will refuse to do it."

Murdock waited a minute to let the pilot think it over. He came back on the air.

"What the hell, Commander, let's give it a try. If it doesn't work we can always get you off the rear-landing pad on the destroyer. Out."

It went by the book. The destroyer slowed to one knot forward. The SEALs went down the lines, tied them to the IBSs to be hauled on board, then congregated around light sticks to wait for the chopper. It came in high the first time, went around, and came in at six feet with the ladder trailing in the water.

Jaybird went up first, followed quickly by three more SEALs. Then the fifth man lost his footing and fell off the ladder. He hit his head on one of the swinging steps. Murdock saw it, and dove to where he figured the SEAL could be. He bumped into something in the dark water, and grabbed hold of cammies and kicked for the surface.

Two more SEALs were there to help. It was Van Dyke, the new man, who had fallen. Murdock slapped him in the face gently until he came around. By then all but the four at the ladder had gone up. Murdock put Vinnie over his shoulder and with Bill Bradford, Quartermaster's Mate First Class, right behind him holding the man in place, the three of them went up the unstable rope ladder to the end of the hatch, where six hands grabbed them and pulled them inside.

Kenneth Ching, Quartermaster's Mate First Class, followed them up the ladder quickly, and the chopper crewman pulled in the ladder and closed the hatch.

"Home, James," somebody said, and half the SEALs hooted.

Vinnie shook his head. "Hey, I don't know what happened. I slipped, I guess, and that damn ladder slammed into my fucking head."

Jack Mahanani, Hospital Corpsman First Class, and the platoon corpsman, knelt beside Vinnie and checked him out. He used his pencil flash and had Vinnie lie down on the floor of the chopper.

"You'll be fine. Stay down until we land."

Murdock let out a held breath. He looked at DeWitt, who sat nearby. "Second, have we ever made a nighttime ladder pickup like this before?"

DeWitt grinned. "Not that I can remember. May be sometime before we try another one, unless we're getting away from a hot firefight somewhere."

# 4

## Baninah, Libya

Not far outside the limits of Benghazi is the regional airport at the small town of Baninah. The international airport serves many airlines, and at the far side, well away from the civilian terminals, sit four large hangars that are patrolled by Libyan soldiers.

Inside one of the hangars final preflight checks were made on a MiG-23 Flogger E, Russian-made and one of the best aircraft of the aging Libyan Air Force. Major Akbar Andwar sat in the cockpit fighting himself. He knew the mission. He knew that he would be closely monitored by three other MiG-23's. He must perform flawlessly.

Akbar also knew that today within a few hours, he would kill thirty thousand people—not soldiers, but civilians, men, women, and children. Even small babies who could not yet speak.

He slashed at sweat beading on his forehead. His colonel climbed up the steps to the cockpit and smiled.

"Today, Major, we make military history. We use a nuclear weapon as an instrument of peace, not war. We use the bomb to avoid killing many thousands in an all-out ground war to rid the world of the cancer that is Chad.

"Our children and our grandchildren will forever be in our debt for this glorious act of honor and justice."

"Yes, my colonel. It is time. I should order the doors rolled up and get my engine started."

"Do it now," the colonel said as he saluted Major Andwar and stepped down from the plane.

Before he wanted it to happen, Major Andwar realized that he was rolling along the access route to the main takeoff runway. In minutes he and his three buddies would be in the air, working up to thirty thousand feet and ripping almost due south toward the Chad border.

In an hour's flying time at Mach 1, the planes would cross the border. Then, a hundred miles on south, they would be at the small town of Yebbi Bou. It would take only ten minutes after crossing the border. Then, at the correct point, he would release the nuclear bomb and he and his wingmen would swing round and blast north until they saw the flash behind them.

Major Andwar checked his controls. They were almost at the border. The land below looked the same, the unending Sahara Desert. Not even a fence showed where the border was. There were no roads, no towns, only sand and more sand.

Even as he thought that, he had slammed through another ten miles.

No. He was closer. His radio chattered, but he didn't understand. The transmission came again.

"Just checking, buddy. We're three minutes from release point. Wind drift has been noted and punched into the computer. Now we are two minutes and forty-five seconds from release. You read?"

"Ah, yes, I read. All is good here. Ready for release. I make it slightly over two minutes, at thirty thousand feet. I'll tell you release time and then we turn right and get out of here."

He waited a minute.

"One minute to release. Is everyone on board?"

He listened to the three radio check-ins. Then one of the men began a countdown on the radio.

"Retribution Leader, I have forty-five seconds to release." There was a pause. "I now have thirty-five seconds. By five second intervals: thirty . . . twenty-five . . . twenty . . . fifteen . . . ten, nine, eight, seven, six, five, four, three, two . . ."

"Release!" Major Andwar said, his voice rising with the emotion. "I have release, showing a clean separation from the aircraft. Do you have visual?"

"Yes, visual, it's on its way, let's do our right turn now."

The four Libyan jets turned to the right 180 degrees and slanted north at thirty thousand feet.

Twenty seconds later a brilliant flash filled the cockpits of the four jet aircraft, slashing at them from the rear and blasting forward to the horizon. A few seconds later a shock wave jolted the four planes sideways through the sky as if they had been swept away by a giant hand.

"Hold on to the controls," Major Andwar shouted into the microphone. "It's the shock wave, it will be gone quickly, don't lose control."

The planes did a little dance in the sky, but because they were a half mile apart, did not slam into one another. Then the shock wave was past and they flew straight and level again.

"Turning ninety degrees left to look to the rear," Major Andwar said. The four planes turned. The giant mushroom cloud towered well over their thirty thousand feet.

"Confirmed," the major said.

"Confirmed," the other three said.

"We just killed thirty thousand human beings," one of the pilots said.

"No," the major shouted. "Don't ever say that again. We did our duty and now return to base. On my signal we turn due north. Now."

The planes dropped down to ten thousand feet to watch history in the making below on the desert. Thousands of wheeled and tracked vehicles charged across the desert heading south.

Thousands and thousands of troops rode forward, ready for battle if there was one. Major Andwar knew that the diplomatic channels were crackling with charges and countercharges, and from Libya there would be an ultimatum to Chad. He would hear it later on television and radio when they returned to their base near Benghazi.

In Benghazi, al-Qaddafi took the cue from the television director and began to speak.

"To the people of Chad. Libya bears no malice toward you. It is your leaders and your corrupt form of government that we abhor. We have today vaporized the town of Yebbi Bou in northern Chad with a nuclear weapon. This is our message to your leaders.

"Our Armed Forces are even now overrunning the northern boundaries of your country. The Chad military must lay down its arms at once and surrender the country to Libya. You have twenty-four hours to do this and to cease any and all forms of resistance from both military and civilians.

"If any Libyan Army or Air Force units are fired upon or attacked, dire retribution will be meted out to the guilty.

"If your leaders do not believe us, or think that we are not in earnest about our annexation of Chad, we will drop another nuclear bomb on a much larger Chad city exactly twenty-four hours from when the first fell.

"Urge your leaders to capitulate and to broadcast such a message to us within the hour.

"The target for the second nuclear bomb will be your capital, N'Djamena. We have no wish to vaporize your capital city. We will want it to be flourishing as one of our show points when we control the ex-nation of Chad. Demonstrate to us and to our Army units that your leaders are sincere in their capitulation, and your historic capital city will be spared.

"We come not as conquerors, but as brothers too long separated, so that we may now complete this part of our family circle. We look forward to hearing your answer."

## CIA Headquarters
## Langley, Virginia

Everard Sylvester scowled at the printout where he sat at his desk in the A section on the fourth floor. Less than an hour ago Chad had been hit with a nuclear bomb, a small town wiped out, and an immediate ultimatum of surrender issued by al-Qaddafi.

Response.

What was the U.S. going to do to nip this sort of nuclear-blackmail aggression in the proverbial bud before it came to full flower and engulfed half of Africa?

Don Stroh dropped into the visitor's chair next to Sylvester's desk.

"So?" Stroh said.

"I don't know. The chief gave me an hour to come up with my recommendation and I don't have a clue. Step in with a broadcast nuke threat of our own to al-Qaddafi? Pull his forces back and cease and desist on the use of any more nuclear weapons or one of his own towns would be vaporized? Will the big stick work anymore? He would broadcast a counterwarning that a named U.S. city, say Portland, Oregon, would be blown off the map by nuclear bombs if any U.S. aggression took place on Libya soil. Threat and counterthreat. I don't think that's the way to go here."

"So?" Stroh asked again.

"My other plan takes longer. Find out where he bought the nuke he used and quash his supply. Eliminate any more nukes he may have, and then turn the economic screws on him, even going so far as to blockade his oil export ports of as-Sidar and Marsha al-Burayqah."

"An act of war," Stroh said.

"So is A-bombing a Libyan city."

The two men stared at each other.

Stroh broke the stalemate. "First we find out where they bought the bomb and shut off that supply. The only nukes we know of for sale on the open market have been in Odessa, Ukraine. We have been following some activity there lately. We can check the ship movements from Odessa and see if any went directly to Tripoli."

"We can do that?"

"A computer scan of the satellite photos of the past week to ten days. If the satellite shows it, we'll find it. I better move."

Stroh talked with the CIA director for five minutes and had approval for the search. A half hour after it started, the satellite analysis specialist came in with the report.

"Two ships, both freighters, left Odessa within minutes of each other six days ago. One meandered around a general route toward the canal. The other, much faster, plowed straight through to Tripoli."

Stroh hurried up to the director's office with the report. "We know the one ship is of Chinese registry, an old rusty freighter making only ten knots. We've been watching it, but the faster ship we haven't tracked."

It took the CIA only an hour to dig out the name of the two ships that left Odessa on that day. One or both of them could have carried ex-Russian ICBMs from the Odessa hideaway.

"Track that fast ship and see if it's still in Tripoli harbor," said the director. "If it is, we need to know if there is a missile there, or part of one, and we need to know if the missile was one of the ones with ten independently targetable reentry warheads. The warheads could be yanked out of a Satan and used as single-shot weapons such as was dropped on Chad."

"You want the SEALs to go in and check out the ship and destroy or capture the remaining nukes if they are on board that ship?"

"That's why you're here, Stroh. I'll have to get approval from the President, but that shouldn't take more than an hour. Alert your SEALs for the mission and keep them on standby. Oh, be sure to go through the CNO. Some of the sailors out there in Coronado are getting touchy."

"Yes, sir. I'll call the Chief of Naval Operations and get the operation set and we'll trigger it when the President gives us a thumbs-up."

## NAVSPECWARGRUP-ONE
## Coronado, California

Master Chief MacKenzie took the phone and identified himself.

"Yes, Master Chief, good to hear your voice."

"Mr. Stroh. How are you these days?"

"A bit different. We had our asses chewed by the Navy, so now we're going through channels. Wanted to warn you and give you a time line on these guys. See how long it takes to get the word to you.

"About a half hour ago the President authorized my boss to take some direct covert action on this Libya situation. You'll get official word through channels. Just wanted to see how long it takes. Mark down your time now and let me know when your team commander gets the word to you."

"Will do, Mr. Stroh. Good to hear from you again. Will you be along on the mission?"

"Probably. Somebody's got to keep your boys out of trouble. You take care, Master Chief."

MacKenzie took a piece of paper and put on the top the name of Don Stroh, then behind it he wrote in the time, 1042. He would see just how efficient the Navy was in an emergency order transmission.

It wasn't until almost 1345 that Master Chief MacKenzie took the call from Commander Masciareli.

"Master Chief, where is Third Platoon right now?"

"On the strand taking a hike, then a swim," MacKenzie said.

"Send a Hummer out there and bring back Murdock and DeWitt. Then show them up to my office as soon as possible. Something is cooking."

"Aye, aye, Commander. Right away."

Fifteen minutes later, the two SEALs, in their wet, sandy cammies, and MacKenzie, in his pressed and spotless uniform, stood at attention in the SEAL Team Seven commander's office.

"At ease, but don't sit down, you're still wet. We've got an assignment for you. Just came from the admiral's office the way it should. He received it from the CNO, who had the order directly from the President.

"You know about the nuclear bomb that Libya dropped on

Chad early this morning. For sometime the CIA has been monitoring the ICBMs left over in Ukraine after the breakup of the USSR. They all were supposed to go back to Russia for disposal, but not all made it.

"Last week the CIA found out that some were sold or stolen and taken out of Odessa on a ship. We believe, but are not certain, that one or more of the Russian Satan ICBMs were on that ship, which went directly from Odessa to Tripoli. The CIA believes that one of the multiple independently targetable reentry-vehicle warheads was what Libya dropped on Chad.

"Your platoon has been authorized to conduct a covert operation to determine if the ship did have one or more of the Russian Satan missiles, and if so, to destroy the remaining warheads so they can't be used as independent bombs. Either that or capture the remaining warheads and transport them out of the country for U.S. control."

"Simple," DeWitt said.

Commander Masciareli glared at him a moment.

"The only easy day was yesterday, J.G." He looked down at some notes. "You will operate from an aircraft carrier in the Mediterranean which will move up from its position off Lebanon. Don Stroh will be your on-board contact and you will work out your strategy and operation en route and on board the carrier. Transport for your platoon will leave North Island in three hours. Is your platoon operational, Commander?"

"Yes, sir. We've had almost two months since our last fling and our wounded are healed and tough. Our one replacement man is integrated into our group and can function." He paused. "Is there anything else, sir? We need to get our men out of the ocean and into some dry clothes."

Two and a half hours later, the properly cammy-clad Third Platoon of SEAL Team Seven stepped off a Navy bus at North Island Naval Air Station onto the edge of the taxi strip. A sleek Gulfstream II, which the Navy designates as VC-11, sat on the taxi strip warmed up and waiting for them.

They had flown in the business jet before. It was usually reserved for VIPs, and called a large executive jet by the Navy. It was made by Grumman Aircraft, later called Gulfstream Aerospace, carried a crew of two or three, and could transport nineteen passengers.

It has a maximum cruising speed of 581 mph at 25,000 feet, and can cover 4,275 miles between fuel drinks from a tanker or on the ground. It has airline reclining-type seats, and facilities for meals and refreshments for the passengers if the flight plan calls for that.

The SEALs settled down in the comfortable seats and relaxed. They knew what their job was; they just didn't know how they would handle it. That would be worked out on board the carrier in the Mediterranean Sea.

Stroh had called just before they left their quarters. He said he'd meet them on the carrier.

"I'll probably get there first," he said. "I have a three-thousand-mile head start."

Murdock, DeWitt, and Senior Chief Dobler conferred near the front of the double row of seats.

"So we don't know how many ICBMs there could be in that ship just in port from Odessa?" DeWitt asked.

"We don't until we open the door and look," Murdock said.

"These are the MIRV babies with ten warheads in each nose cone?" Dobler asked.

"Right," DeWitt said. "The CIA thinks they took out one of the independently targetable warheads and turned it into a drop bomb and blew half of that region in Chad into Bolivia."

"Then their Army charged across the border," Murdock said. "Which might help us since most of their good troops will be out in the field, not guarding that ship."

"How do we know it will even still be there?" DeWitt asked.

"Priorities," Murdock said. "If I was Qaddafi, I'd get that first bomb out and ready to go before anything else on that ship moved. First jobs first."

Dobler looked at Murdock. "Anybody in our platoon know how to defuse and destroy a nuclear warhead?"

"Not that you could count on," Murdock said.

"Our orders were to capture or destroy the warheads, as I heard," Dobler said. "We going to pack them out of there on our backs with a ten-mile swim, or what the hell?"

"Mostly the latter," DeWitt said.

They looked at each other.

"So?" Dobler asked.

"So we play it by ear until we can get some on-site intel and then plan out damn carefully just what the fuck we're going to do," Murdock said. "Right now I'm ready for a nap. On this one we better sleep when we can. It's about a three-hour run to D.C. Then we'll probably get some juice in the air or on the ground. After that I'd bet we'll drop in on Lisbon, Portugal. That should take another seven or eight hours."

"What do I tell the troops about chow?" Dobler asked.

"Supposed to be something on board, box lunches, and we hope, better than MREs."

An hour later, Ed DeWitt was still wide awake. He poked Murdock in the shoulder and weathered the growl.

"Hey, Boss, I keep thinking about the destroy part of that mission description. I'd bet you know who I'm thinking about."

"True, true as blue, J.G. We were lucky once, why tempt fate? This one looks just nasty as all hell. No reason to expose that person to all the shit we're going to run into."

"Yeah, you're right." DeWitt grinned. "Okay, you can go back to sleep now."

An hour later the crew chief came back from the cockpit. He had a printout of a radio message from Washington, D.C. Murdock rubbed the sleep out of his eyes and focused on the paper and the stark black print.

"Thursday, September 12.

"From the Office of the President.

"To Lieutenant Commander Blake Murdock, Commander SEAL Team Seven Third Platoon.

"Commander Murdock: The President has assigned a special agent to assist you in your destruction of the warheads we suspect are on a ship in the Tripoli, Libya, harbor. That person is someone you've worked with before, Katherine Garnet. She will travel with Don Stroh and meet you on the carrier. Good luck." It was signed by the President's administrative assistant.

Murdock showed the paper to DeWitt, who read it.

"Not again," he said.

"Again," Murdock said. "Just like in Iran on our death race. At least the lady knows her business. All we have to do is keep her alive, do the job, then get her home in one chunk without a lot of bullet holes in her pretty little hide."

# 5

## USS *Franklin D. Roosevelt*, CV 69
## In the Mediterranean Sea, Off Libya

Third Platoon of SEAL Team Seven came off the COD plane on the deck of the *Franklin D. Roosevelt* carrier tired and grumpy. Most of them had slept little on the fourteen-hour flight. They had crossed so many times zones that they had no idea what time it was other than it was still daylight.

They were shown to their quarters and a nearby double-size compartment where they could stash their gear and weapons and work on them when they needed to. Murdock called them together in the assembly compartment. Jaybird struggled in the door, the last man to report.

"I haven't had any new signals on our mission," said Murdock. "For those of you who want to set your watches, it's now thirteen-fifteen. You have lost seven hours, we had a thirteen-hour flight, and you're all assigned to your bunks until eight hundred in the morning. Senior Chief Dobler will tell you where your chow is and will boot you out of your bunks in the morning. Any questions?"

"Yeah," Jaybird asked. "I heard something about a civilian with us again. To do the destruct on the warheads. Is it that pretty Lieutenant Gurnet again?"

"It is. She knows her job and as I remember, Jaybird, she can outswim you and outrun you."

That brought a chorus of catcalls from the SEALs.

"Yeah, but . . ." He stopped. "Hey, I'm glad she's gonna be along. Gives us a little class."

Murdock dismissed the men, and found Don Stroh coming in the compartment door as the men filed out.

"Well, Stroh, I hear the Navy chewed your CIA ass," Murdock said.

Stroh came up and shook hands with Murdock, DeWitt, and Dobler.

"Not true. A mild reprimand, and that from some lower-half admiral I've never heard of."

"We have," DeWitt said. "He signs our paychecks."

"So, the Navy chain of command communication works. The master chief and I checked. It took the Navy three hours to get word to you after I had the go-ahead from the President to the CNO."

"That's good for Navy time," Murdock said. "Where's Kat?"

"She's resting. It was a long flight. The three of us have a conference with the XO and the CAG in fifteen minutes. You don't need to shave. These men know your schedule."

"Let's get to it," DeWitt said. "We need some more input about the target ship and the port there and just where that ship is."

They met in Commander Engle's quarters. The XO was a short, thickset man with a windblown complexion, intense brown eyes, and a demeanor that showed all business.

Captain Prescott, the CAG, nodded to the SEALs and Stroh, and pointed them toward a map on a table hinged to the bulkhead.

"Gentlemen, I'm Prescott and this is Commander Engle."

Murdock introduced himself, then the other two, and they all looked at the chart of the Tripoli harbor.

The carrier's executive officer pointed to a spot about a third of the way into the harbor.

"The satellite picture shows the target ship at this pier, which is reported to be a secure area with armed patrols. There is a warehouse directly across from the ship, which also now has armed patrols around and inside it. We do know that security around the building has been reduced somewhat today. We think that's because some of the troops have been sent into Chad on the invasion."

"How big is that harbor?" DeWitt asked.

"From the harbor mouth to the ship is about a third of a mile," the XO said. "No more than that."

"The swim from offshore to the ship will be no problem," Murdock said. "We have any human intel from an in-country man?"

"No agents in that area, as I understand," Stroh said.

"So, we'll have to do it ourselves," DeWitt said. "That's going to take longer. We recon, study, then attack."

"Do we know if the missile or missiles are still on the ship, or are they now in the guarded warehouse?" Murdock asked.

"We don't know where they are," Stroh said.

"Timing?" the CAG asked. "We could do something with a fake air raid on Tripoli, never getting inside their airspace," the Commander of the Air Group, now called an Air Wing, threw out.

"You'd need Presidential approval for that," Stroh said.

"No, I meant a training flight into the immediate area," CAG Prescott said.

"Couldn't hurt," Murdock said. "Timing? My men need some rest time. We can go in with first dark tomorrow night at the earliest."

"Won't do," Stroh said. "We need you in there with first dark today."

"We just arrived," DeWitt said. "We need to do our planning, our alternative operation, what weapons to take."

"Murdock, can you have your platoon and Kat ready to go on a chopper from here at seventeen-thirty?" Stroh asked. "The President said if you didn't move fast, there would be nothing there to find when you arrived."

"He's right, Stroh," Murdock said. "We can be ready. Ed, go get the troops moving. They have three hours to sleep, half an hour for a special chow, and another hour to get gear ready and to transport. Go."

Ed left the compartment.

"Captain, can you loan us a Sea Knight for transport to within a mile of the harbor entrance?"

"Yes."

"We'll have a SATCOM with us. We'll need a Pegasus on call from the beach at anytime before dawn. If you can keep him around the three-mile mark offshore, he can get to us quickly. We'll swim out a half mile when we know he's coming in. We'll use light sticks for contact."

The XO made a note. "Yes, we can have a Pegasus at that point two hours before dawn waiting your call on the SATCOM. Use TAC Two."

"Roger that, Commander," said Murdock. "Now, we'll need a facilitator to draw ammunition, arms, and explosives from your stores. Can you name us a man and have him here quickly?"

The XO nodded. "He'll be at your assembly compartment as soon as we break up here."

"Stroh, is Kat up to speed on the project?"

"She is. She knows what I know."

"Does she have her special tools and equipment for the job?"

"She does. Everything except the explosives she said are vital."

"Get some cammies cut down for her and have her at the assembly compartment in three hours. She'll probably want a sub gun, and I want her to have an ankle hideout."

The XO pushed another stick of gum into his mouth and chewed with vigor. He stopped and looked at Murdock.

"That's all the planning you can do?"

"We don't have the intel to do any more. This is a play-it-by-ear kind of mission, the deadliest kind, Commander. I wish we had all the intel we need. We don't, so we have to generate it near-site, or blast in and see what we have to do on-site and react with deadly force. Usually it works."

"Let's play what-if," Stroh said. "What if you find the missile, it still has nine warheads in it, but you can't get to it to destroy them due to the overwhelming forces of the Libyan Army. What's Plan B?"

"Then we would call in four Tomcats from the CAG to blast the warehouse with four Phoenix missiles, hoping to rip apart the missile and destroy all of the warheads. I'd suggest you put through a request like that to the President and get preapproval of it, so if we need to, we can SATCOM Captain Prescott. He will have his planes in the air ready for a five-minute strike on the warehouse, or the ship, wherever we locate the missiles and can't reach them."

"That would be no problem from this end," Captain Prescott said. "I would need an absolute go-ahead from the President for such a strike, and it must come through channels as well."

"I'll get on that," Stroh said. "Now, any Plan C?"

"My Plan C is to leave Kat on board here and have her tell my people how to blow up those warheads," Murdock said. "We were lucky getting her out of Iran. It worries me having a civilian along, even though she can out-SEAL some of our SEALs."

"That's not a plan. Kat is on your team by order of the commander in chief, and it went through channels. Forget Plan C."

"Anything else?" the XO asked. "Commander Murdock, in effect this ship and its crew and planes are yours to command. Anything you want, you get. We are now about two hundred miles off Libya's port of Tripoli. Before you leave on the Sea Knight, we'll be about fifty miles offshore. Your mission is our mission."

"Thanks, Commander. I feel blind on this one, like both of my flanks are open just asking for an attack. It's on missions like this one where we lose some of our men. I don't like that. We'll get the job done. I just hope that all of us will be coming back on the Pegasus."

"Looks like we're done here, gentlemen," Captain Prescott said.

Murdock stood. "You're done. I'm just getting started."

At 1630 the SEALs were back in the assembly compartment, fed and working on weapons and equipment. The armament specialist from the carrier had been with Dobler, and had brought up everything the SEALs and Kat had asked for in the way of ammunition and explosives.

Kat arrived with Stroh, and the SEALs cheered.

"Good to see you again, Lieutenant," Jaybird screeched. The others whistled and hooted as Kat walked in wearing cammies that had been tailored to fit her. She grinned and waved at the men. She knew most of them.

Kat walked up to Murdock and saluted. "Lieutenant Garnet reporting for duty, sir," she said.

Murdock chuckled. "Your salute is terrible, Lieutenant." He grinned and shook her hand. "Good to have you on board." He meant it. She looked the same: five feet eight and slender. Short brown hair, deep brown eyes. She had a Ph.D. in nuclear physics from MIT and a GS-15 rate in the civil service. That was as high as the ratings went. He knew she was a Scuba diving instructor, had made more than forty parachute jumps, and had won the second Ironman Triathlon in Hawaii when they let women participate. Now she ran marathons for fun.

She took a deep breath. "Murdock, I'm not sure if I'm glad to be here or not. From what I hear, this is a chancy mission. We don't know enough about where the missile or missiles are in Tripoli."

"True, Kat. We follow orders. We go in and see if we can find the warheads and blast them into kindling and scrap metal, then swim for home. Simple, really. I checked out an H & K MP-5 for you. I remember you like the sub gun."

"Yes. It can come in handy."

"Like saving somebody's life. I thank you again for that, young lady. You do good work. How about a hideout for your left ankle, a fine little six-shot revolver?"

"Will I need it?"

"If you do, it will be too late to get one. I suggest you take it. Senior Chief Dobler has your weapons and combat vest."

She watched him, then smiled and nodded. "Yes to the hideout. You're welcome about the little Iran shoot-out. I'm glad that I was there at the right time and place." She frowned. "Is this one going to be as tough as it looks like?"

"Probably. We do what we can. We don't sacrifice half our platoon to get it done. We're getting approval from the president to bring in missiles on the missile site if we can't get the warheads destroyed."

"Oh, yes, I like that."

Murdock lowered his voice. "I don't see any rings, so I'd guess that you aren't married."

She laughed, and it reminded him of earlier times. "No, not married, and I see you aren't either. Hasn't Ardith trapped you yet?"

"Not yet. Have you eaten?"

"Yes, and I even got three hours of sleep. I'm ready. My tools are packed, we have the right explosives all packaged ready to push fuses into. Now, I want to get off this ship and get moving before I start to get nervous."

A half hour before takeoff, the SEALs and Kat waited on the flight deck. Their gear, in waterproof tote bags, was all stowed on board. Each bag had a SEAL's name on it. They carried their weapons ready to be strapped over their backs on rubber tubing, and all had on camouflage makeup smeared in jagged patterns on their faces and noses, and their ears were blackened out.

Murdock came out of the Sea Knight chopper and waved the platoon forward. "Let's get out of here," he said. "We've got places to go, and warheads to blast into shards of worthless junk."

# 6

## The Mediterranean Sea, Off Libya

The Navy Sea Knight skimmed the small chop on the Mediterranean as it bored through the just-dark sky less than fifty feet off the water. The pilot told Murdock the low course would help prevent any new Libyan radar from spotting them.

The flight from the deck of the carrier would be less than twenty-five minutes to the drop-off point a half mile offshore. Murdock had his platoon as ready as they could be. He had given Kat a quick refresher course on the Draegr LAR V, the bubbleless rebreather, then taken her on deck and she'd fired two magazines through her submachine gun.

"Oh, yes, I remember," she'd said as she quickly dropped out the empty magazine and slammed in a full one and chambered a round.

In the big chopper, Murdock checked his watch. "Time," he shouted at the troops. They lined up on each side of the helicopter and waited for the aft hatch to open. The craft slowed, then hovered ten feet over the water. The hatch swung downward forming a ramp, and the SEALs ran forward, stepped into space, then almost at once plunged into the cold water of the Mediterranean.

They surfaced quickly, gathered in their two squads, and Murdock led them in their underwater swim toward shore. They dropped down fifteen feet and kicked through the dark waters. Murdock used the compass board, a plastic device about a foot square with a large lighted compass in the center and handholds on both sides. Using it, SEALs can follow a direct course while underwater to their target position.

Murdock surfaced for a quick peek after a half mile. They

were still offshore, and needed to correct to the left to come to the harbor entrance.

Murdock had Kat on his buddy line so he could keep track of her. There was no question about her swimming ability. She also had held up well under fire, killing at least three of the enemy on their trek into Iran several months ago. Still, he knew that he and every SEAL in the platoon would be protective of the pretty lady.

Murdock surfaced again just inside the harbor entrance. Another half mile to the ship. He could see piers along both sides of the port. He angled to the left and looked for a pier they could hide under until their recon had been completed.

They stayed underwater for another quarter of a mile, counting swimming strokes to determine the distance. Then all the SEALs surfaced. Each one had been pulling a drag bag that had a flotation device in it to make it easier to move.

Murdock pointed at a pier that had a freighter tied up to it and was in a night-loading operation. There was room beneath the pier, and the SEALs slipped under and found soggy timbers from a previous wooden pier. They hauled out of the water and rested, sure that the activity overhead and the noise of the loading would cover any sounds they made.

Murdock pointed at Jack Mahanani and Joe Lampedusa, Operations Specialist Third Class. "We'll go recon this freighter and the warehouse. See if there are any holes in their guards and just how good they are. DeWitt has the con. We should be back in forty-five minutes. If we're not back in two hours, DeWitt will continue the operation without us."

The three recon men left their drag bags and slid back into the water. They were still a hundred yards from the bright lights that marked the ship and warehouse targets. Murdock led the trio five feet under the water. When they came to the lights, they broke the surface to sneak a peek.

Lights bathed the side of the ship and the pier and the warehouse front. It was two minutes before any of them saw a guard. One man came around the side of the warehouse, marched down the length of it, and vanished at the other end.

As soon as he saw the sleek freighter up close, Murdock discounted her as holding the missiles. She was in the process of being loaded, but there was no night crew. Cranes stood at the side of the big ship, and dozens of trailer containers and piles of goods sat on the concrete dock to be loaded.

The SEALs looked back at the warehouse. It had huge doors, all down the front. All were closed, and probably locked, Murdock decided. They swam to the edge of the pier, and found a ladder going up a concrete pier support that vanished into the water.

The SEALs were in the darkness here, but twenty yards ahead the floodlights took over, turning the night into noon. The three men climbed the ladder, edged onto the pier, and hid behind some stacks of wooden boxes ready for shipment.

After five minutes they found out there were three guards circling the warehouse. A small jeep rolled up and two men in it talked to one of the guards. Then the rig drove back the way it had come.

"Every two minutes another guard comes around," Murdock said. "Does that give us time to grab one of them, strip him, and put Lam in his uniform and insert him into the guard rotation?"

"Damn short time," Lam said. "I could have my Draegr and combat vest off and put his clothes over my cammies."

"Where?" Mahanani asked.

"Closest stack of goods, those cardboard boxes just at the end of the warehouse," Lam said.

"Worth a try. That would give us four minutes to get to that first small door, bust it open, and get inside."

"What if I meet those guys in the jeep?" Lam said.

"You take them out silently and we go hard if we have to," Murdock said. "It would take them some time to miss the jeep guys. Then to get some men here. Maybe in that time slot we can open the cones and set all the charges."

"Then run like hell," Lam said. "I'm game. Hell, I like walking guard duty."

"Not now. You two stay here and watch for anything new. I'll go bring in the troops and your drag bags. Stay out of sight."

It took Murdock ten minutes to swim back to where the SEALs hid and get them moving toward the warehouse.

"We'll put Bravo Squad on the pier with Kat. Alpha stays at the foot of the pier in the water. When Bravo gets inside the warehouse, we'll see what we have. Probably Alpha Squad will come on the pier and deploy defensively protecting this end of the warehouse. We hope to keep this silent until we get the charges set and we're back in the water. If it doesn't work out

that way, we play it by ear, defending with all our weapons until
Bravo Squad gets out of there with Kat."

The SEALs swam.

Murdock went topside and watched the rotation of the guards.
Lam picked out the one he wanted to take out. He'd use his
KA-BAR fighting knife for a silent kill.

"See those boxes nearest the warehouse?" Lam asked. "I'll
get behind those in the first gap between guards, then take out
the one I picked as soon as he turns the corner and has his back
to me. I'll have twenty yards to cross as quickly and silently as
I can. Then I drag him back to the boxes and change clothes."

Lam had stripped off his combat vest and his Draegr, and put
down his Colt Carbine. He waited. When the next guard vanished, Lam sprinted for the boxes. He made it without a cry
from any stationary guard.

The targeted guard came past and turned. Lam left the boxes
at full stride, his rubber boots making almost no noise on the
concrete. The Libyan guard must have heard something. He
turned a second before Lam hit him from the side. Lam's hand
went over the soldier's mouth. His other hand drove the KA-
BAR blade into the guard's side and slanted upward so it penetrated flesh and then lanced into his heart. He died a few
seconds later.

Lam dragged him by the hands back to the boxes, leaving
only a thin trail of blood to show his passage.

Murdock couldn't see Lam stripping the uniform shirt and
pants off the Libyan and pulling them on over his cammies.

Quicker than Murdock expected, Lam, in the Libyan uniform
and floppy hat, ran back to the warehouse, picked up the guard's
automatic rifle, and began his slow walk around the warehouse.

Murdock called up Bravo Squad with Kat. They climbed the
ladder and hid behind the boxes.

"Kat, on the next round by Lam, Mahanani and I will run
over to that small door and get it open. We'll check inside and
see if there are any guards. If there are, we take them out. Then
I'll come to the door and wave. You wait until you see Lam
coming. When he shows, he'll wave at these boxes to let you
know it's him. When you see him, you and Bravo Squad dash
across the concrete and get inside the door within a minute.
Then you go to work."

He crawled to the ladder and talked to Dobler. "Chief, you
have command of Alpha Squad. As soon as you see Bravo

Squad get inside, you bring up your men and deploy them for protection, but keep hidden from the guards. We'll get out as soon and as soundlessly as possible."

He got back to the freight boxes just in time to spot Lam on his rounds. Murdock and Mahanani sprinted to the regular door on the end of the warehouse.

"Locked," Murdock said. He put his sub gun on single-shot and fired three silenced rounds into the door-lock area. The door swung open.

Murdock listened. He heard nothing. He slid through the half-open door. The inside of the huge warehouse was as bright as the outside. He saw four guards pacing around an eighty-foot-long missile that sat in the middle of the otherwise empty warehouse. They were forty yards away. Three tables sat near the missile. On it Murdock saw four shapes of what could be nuclear warheads. Murdock went silently to the floor.

Mahanani crept in beside him and went down, his Alliant Bull Pup with its 5.56 underbarrel already tracking the guards.

"I've got two on the right," Murdock whispered. Then he fired the submachine gun on a three-round burst. Two of the 9mm singers slammed into the guard who had just patted another soldier on the shoulder. He slammed backward from the force of the rounds and jolted to the floor. Before the man he touched could turn to see where the rounds came from, he took one of a three-round burst in the throat, and died in seconds from a shooting spray of blood spurting with heartbeat regularity from his carotid artery.

Mahanani's first round caught the left guard in the chest and drove him backward into the fourth man, who stumbled and fell. Mahanani pumped three rounds into the crawling man, who seemed to be trying to get behind some wooden boxes.

"Clear right," Murdock said.

"Clear left," Mahanani said.

They all had put on their personal radios as soon as they were out of the water. Murdock and Mahanani stood and checked the rest of the building quickly. There were no more guards inside.

"DeWitt, get your men and Kat in here when you can when Lam comes by again. We're clear in here. One missile and some items on tables. Move it when you can."

Murdock and Mahanani checked the four guards. Three were dead, but one was still moving. Mahanani put a silenced round into his head, and they pulled the bodies away from where Kat would be working on the warheads.

"Those little things are nuclear bombs?" Mahanani said.

"These are good-sized ones. We have them so small they'll fit in a suitcase."

Ed DeWitt and Kat came through the door. Then Kat ran to the table.

"Yes, four of the warheads. Are there any more in the missile nose cone?"

Murdock and Kat hurried to the big ICBM, and saw where the nose cone had been opened. Four more missiles remained in place.

"Will they have to come out of there?" Murdock asked.

She shook her head. "No, I can set the charges right where they are, but we do have a problem."

"What?"

"We have eight warheads here. They exploded one in Chad. Where is the tenth warhead?"

"Shit. I knew this was going too easy. What would they do with it?"

Kat went back to the table and examined the four warheads. She opened a drag bag and carefully took out four large charges of TNAZ, a plastic explosive fifteen percent more powerful than C-5. She placed the charge at an exact spot, then wrapped it in place with sticky green ordnance tape. After that she took out her tools and worked silently over the warhead for three minutes. Then she nodded and moved to the next one.

Murdock pressed his throat mike on the Motorola.

"Holt. Get your ass over here into the warehouse when it's clear. Bring your boom box with you."

Holt came in a few minutes later and looked at Murdock.

"Wind up that thing and see if you can raise the carrier on TAC One. Big Daddy is the call sign."

Murdock helped Kat with the third warhead on the table, putting on the green tape when she had the charge placed.

"I need fifteen minutes more," Kat said.

Holt came up holding out the handset. "I have a Captain Prescott on the horn, Skipper."

"Captain, Murdock here."

"Yes, Commander."

"Small problem. We have located eight of the warheads. One is missing, one was shot off over Chad. We're going to try to find the missing bomb, but right now don't know how or where to look. Any suggestions?"

"It could be refitted and ready to drop on another city," Captain Prescott said. "Check out that facility. It might be best to take eight out of nine and haul ass."

"I read you, Captain. One more observation. We have only one missile here. The ship that brought it is in the process of on-loading freight. We don't think it ever contained any more missiles or they would be in this warehouse. You might relay this to Stroh, who will be vitally interested. We'll keep you advised. Out."

Murdock watched Kat work, then moved along the table, looking for any paperwork. There could be something here to give them a clue where the other warhead was taken. He found nothing. He looked in the open nose cone, hoping someone had dropped a map indicating where the other warhead would be.

Nothing.

He was about to use the radio again when a bell rang, then one of the huge warehouse doors fronting the pier began to roll up slowly. When it was head high, a tracked vehicle clanked its way through the door. Murdock scowled as he and the rest of the SEALs and Kat dropped into hiding places.

"It's a damned Russian armored personnel carrier," DeWitt whispered on the Motorola. "Looks like a twenty-millimeter cannon on front."

"It's the APC-nineteen model," Holt whispered in the mike.

"Not a chance," Fernandez said. "The Ruskies didn't make a nineteen. Could be the thirteen."

"Whatever it's called, it's trouble," Murdock said. "On the other hand, what a good rig to transport a nuclear warhead."

By that time the APC had rolled to within fifteen feet of the silver-tipped missile. The big door had rolled back down behind the machine. A forward hatch opened and an officer with braid on his shoulders pushed up and out of the APC.

The officer frowned at the table with warheads with green tape on them, and shouted something in Arabic. He reached for a pistol at his hip.

Murdock's silenced round hit him in the right shoulder.

"Move in," Murdock said to the mike. The closest two SEALs grabbed the officer before he could shout again, stripped away his pistol, and covered his mouth. Murdock ran from the side and aimed his submachine gun down the hatch.

"Train, get up here," Murdock shouted. Train could speak Arabic. The slender SEAL hurried up.

"Tell the driver to surrender. We have captured his officer."

Train shouted into the open hatch, then repeated the words.

"Order him to come out without a weapon or we'll drop in a grenade," Murdock said.

Train gave the message, and a moment later a soldier came out with both hands over his head.

"Ask him why the rig is here," Murdock said.

Train asked twice, then slashed him across the face with his hand. The man jolted backward, surprised. Then he wilted and began talking. When the Arab finished, Train turned.

"This one says they came in to pick up another nuclear warhead. He said they are to take them to a secret place where they are to be stored."

"Ask him if they have already taken one there."

Train asked him. The APC driver said that they had. He wasn't sure where it was. The officer drove the last few miles.

Murdock and Train went to the officer, who had been trying to yell at them through the hands that held his mouth.

"Ask this one where they took the other warhead," Murdock said.

Train did, and the officer laughed. "He said he will never tell pigs like us. He would rather die first."

"Sounds reasonable. Tie his hands and feet with plastic strips. Then lay him down next to the rig's tracks and tie him to the tracks so he can't roll over."

It was done quickly. Then Murdock took Train up to the Libyan officer. Murdock pulled a hand grenade from his vest. The officer's hands were free, but his wrists were bound securely. His arms were then bound tightly to his body with green tape so he couldn't move them, only his hands.

Murdock put a grenade in his hands and had Train explain.

"This is a hand grenade. Soon we will pull the pin and you will hold it. Hold down the arming spoon so it won't go off. When you get tired, you will relax your hand and the bomb will go off on your chest, sending you quickly into your meeting with Allah."

The officer screeched something in return. Murdock took the hand grenade from him and pulled the pin, then holding it carefully, he wrapped the Libyan's hand around the grenade to hold the spoon. Murdock surged behind the APC and waited.

• • •

He put Train where he could hear anything the officer said but still keep away from any shrapnel.

"Now we wait," Murdock said. He put Kat back to work on the warheads. She had four of them done, then went into the nose cone to take care of the other four.

"All we do is wait," Murdock said.

The Libyan officer stared at the deadly hand grenade. He knew what they could do to a man. He would die surely. Maybe he could hold out for five minutes. Sweat beaded his forehead and ran down his cheeks. Truly he did not want to die. He felt the cramps coming on his hand. It wouldn't be long now. What should he do?

# 7

"Yes, I'll tell you," the Libyan officer screamed. "Help me. Help me. Come get the grenade. I'll tell you where the warhead was taken."

Tran Khai, "Train," charged from his safe spot behind some boxes and slid to the concrete beside the officer. Carefully he gripped the grenade and slid the man's fingers from the spoon. He held the spoon against the small bomb and yelled for some green tape. A moment later he caught a roll and taped the spoon tightly to the grenade's body, preventing it from exploding.

Murdock knelt beside the Libyan captain. "Train, ask him where he took the other nuclear warhead."

Train did, and the Libyan answered in a low voice that Murdock knew was brimming with disgust at himself for being so weak. Train looked up.

"He says he took it to a special building about three kilometers away. It has four scientists there working on it to convert it into a drop bomb."

"Can he take us there?"

Train asked, and the officer said he could.

"Untie him from the track but keep his wrists bound," Murdock said. He hurried over to the nose cone. Kat was working on the last warhead. She bound it with the green tape and looked at Murdock.

"Done. All we have to do is set the timers and get out of Dodge."

"Good. Hold on the timers. Let's see if we all can fit into this Russian personnel carrier." He examined it. It was much like the U.S. APCs, but was designed to carry only fifteen fully armed troops. They had to get seventeen inside, eighteen counting the officer. Ostercamp could drive the thing. Murdock called to Tony Ostercamp, who checked the driver's position.

"Piece of cake, Skipper," Ostercamp said.

"Jaybird, get out to the door and grab Lam on his next round. We're about ready to get out of here."

Five minutes later Murdock had Alpha Squad inside the building and all the other SEALs crammed into the APC. He and Kat set the timers for five minutes on the eight charges, then ran for the carrier and jumped on board. They had left the driver bound and gagged in the far section of the warehouse, which shouldn't be damaged too severely by the bombs.

The door swung up, and Ostercamp drove the rig onto the pier, and soon into the streets. Four minutes away from the dock, Kat called for them to stop. They looked behind them toward the top of the freighter, which they could see over the buildings.

"Four minutes and thirty seconds," Kat said. Less than a minute later the sky over the docks turned a bright red and a loud clap of thunder rolled toward them. The shock wave bounced the APC a foot down the street, and they could see windows shattering all around. The first explosion was followed by another, which Kat said must be three or four more of the charges going off at the same time.

Another shock wave battered them. Then the sound came and rolled over them with a roaring blast. To the rear they could see flames and smoke coming up in the red glow.

"Yes," Kat shouted, and pumped her fist in victory.

"Eight down, one to go," Murdock said. The rig moved ahead. Train translated as the officer told them where to go.

Murdock warned him that if he led them into a trap, he would be the first to die. They passed a squad of eight soldiers running toward them, then past and on toward the fire. Soon they met two trucks heading for the docks, both loaded with soldiers. They saw little other military force.

A short time later the APC came to a compound with guards and barbed-wire concertina along the top of the fence.

An officer waved them through a gate, and almost at once through a truck door and into a building much smaller than the one they had come from. When the outside door closed, Murdock popped open the rear hatch, and the sixteen SEALs poured out with their weapons ready to fire.

They found four men in white lab coats working over a warhead on a table. Already they had stripped away the rocket thrusters and taken off the guidance system.

Train shouted at them in Arabic to raise their hands and to be quiet. Colt Franklin, Yeoman Second Class, another Arabic speaker, repeated the message and waved his Colt M-Al at them.

Murdock and Kat ran to the table. He pushed the men away and turned to Kat.

She frowned, then shook her head. "This isn't a real warhead from the missile. This is a copy. It looks like a replica they made to practice on. We're at sea here. We have to find out what they did with the real missile warhead."

"Colt, on me," Murdock called. Colt ran up and looked at the warhead.

"This is a practice bomb," Kat said. "We need to make these guys tell us where the real one is."

Colt growled at the four men in white lab coats. He lined them up and brought up his Colt, as if to spray them with bullets. Then he began shouting at them in Arabic. All looked frightened. One man began trembling, then gave a short cry and crumpled forward in a dead faint.

"You are all dead men in ten seconds if you don't tell me where you sent the live nuclear warhead," Colt bellowed at them in Arabic.

Another man wavered, but retained his feet. The man beside him lifted one hand. Colt moved in front of him, thrust the muzzle of the silenced carbine into the soft tissue under the man's chin, and pushed upward.

"I know where the bomb is," the Libyan said. "I am in charge here. I can tell you. These men know nothing." He spoke in Arabic. Colt translated for Murdock.

The rest of the SEALs had scattered out, covering the three doors into the building and working as security on the place.

Murdock stared at the tallest of the Arab scientists and waved his submachine gun.

"Tell me where the bomb is and how to get there, or all four of you are corpses," Murdock barked. Colt translated.

The tall Arab frowned, then spoke rapidly. Colt waved at him to stop as he told Murdock.

"He says another APC like this one came an hour after the bomb arrived here, and a colonel took control of the bomb and left with it. He said he was taking it to the headquarters of the Fourth Tank Battalion at the edge of town. I know where it is."

Murdock held up his hand. "Dobler, tie up these three, save the tall one for the APC. Put the Libyan captain from the APC with these three and tie him. Then load up. We're going for a ride."

The scientist used a hand beeper and opened the door as they approached it in the APC, and then they were out and through the ring of soldiers around the place. Now there were more of them. It looked to Murdock as if they were standing shoulder to shoulder around the facility.

Now they met more military cars and trucks heading for the docks and the fire there. Train did the translating and gave the directions to Ostercamp.

The APC would do thirty miles an hour down the open streets. Ostercamp wound it up to top speed. It took them over an hour to work their way through the jumble of streets and cars and carts. The capital city had almost two million people, a third of the population of the whole nation. At last they came out of the city to a coastal plain, and soon saw the flags of the tank battalion ahead.

Murdock stopped the rig. "Ask him if he knows where inside the camp they would have the warhead."

Train did the questioning. "He's not sure. He was here twice, and both times they took him to a building near the back gate. It was guarded and held sensitive material for their nuclear program, which was in its extremely early stages."

"Let's give it a try," Murdock said, and the rig moved forward.

It didn't even stop at the guarded gate, just clattered through and took the first right, then a left down a street filled with more than a dozen tanks. Murdock couldn't see them well enough through the firing slot to know what kind they were. Russian most likely.

They came to a small building with barbed wire, concertina, and razor wire on the fence around it. Six soldiers walked in front of the building and down one side. There was only a small drive-in door here.

On the trip, Murdock had had Colt put on the Libyan Army fatigues and the hat. They still had the rifle as well, and now Colt pushed open the rear door and stepped out, followed by the scientist in his white lab coat.

Colt jabbered something at the guards, who parted at the front gate and opened it for the two to walk inside. As soon as the two were out of the line of fire, silenced weapons opened up on the guards, dropping all six of them before they could get off a shot. The SEALs swarmed out of the rig, dragged the guards past the fence and behind cover, and then drove the APC inside the building.

Colt held two men under his gun as the scientist looked at the device on a table under bright lights. He nodded. Kat hurried over and checked it.

"Got it, Commander. This is the real thing. They have stripped off the guidance and propulsion, must be ready to reconfigure it for an aerial drop."

"Do it," Murdock said. Kat went to work on the warhead.

"Trouble," DeWitt said from his position at a small window at the front of the building. "About twenty men moving up on the front of the place. They are in an attack mode going from cover to cover. They'll be at the fence in a few minutes."

"We need two minutes more on the device," Murdock said. "Take five men and open up on them. We want to keep the APC. It's the best transport we've ever had to move around with in enemy territory."

Ed took five men, jolted through the front door and to cover inside the fence, and began firing at the approaching Libyan soldiers.

Vincent "Vinnie" Van Dyke set up his H & K NATO-round machine gun and covered the street itself. Anything that moved caught his attention. Lampedusa trained the laser sight on the Bull Pup rifle and sent two aerial bursts from the 20mm rounds over the troops moving up. Five or six of them turned and charged to the rear.

Paul Jefferson, Engineman Second Class, used the 5.56 barrel of his Bull Pup and began picking off the Libyans as they tried to move forward.

Ed DeWitt's sub gun was outranged, so he had taken Fernandez's sniper rifle, and now made every round count. Within three minutes of their first rounds, the SEALs had stalled the attack from the front.

"Keep up the pressure," DeWitt said on the Motorola. "Don't let them get the idea they can move an inch forward."

Inside the building, Kat hesitated before strapping on the explosives. "Maybe we should take this one with us," she said. "We've never had one of these and our nuke guys would go nuts over taking this one apart."

Murdock decided at once. "We can't take the risk. Too damn

heavy to carry if we have to ditch the vehicle. Blow it up here. Let's see if there's a rear door to this place."

There was: two doors that opened outward, large enough to let the APC squeeze through.

"Get everything on board," Murdock said. "Kat, set up a blast for inside here with a five-minute timer. Give them something to think about."

Two minutes later the rig was loaded except for the five SEALs out front.

"Ed, bring them home," Murdock said on the personal radio. "Time to haul ass out of Dodge."

Murdock cracked the back doors and looked through an inch-wide space. He scowled and eased the doors closed.

"I want all of the Bull Pups up here right now, and get out your twenty-millimeter. We've got a fucking tank staring down our drawers back here."

Lampedusa, Ron Holt, Jack Mahanani, and George Canzoneri trotted up to the back door.

"The tank out there is at a forty-five-degree angle to us so we can see his treads. I want four rounds on the front of those treads to try to blast them off. The twenties are contact detonation, so belly down and as soon as I open the doors, blast that damn tank."

The men loaded a round in the chambers of the 20mm barrels and flattened out in front of the door.

"Now," Murdock barked, and pushed open the doors. Almost at once the four twenties fired, and then in ragged order they fired again and a third time. By then the tank had begun to turn, but before it had moved a foot, the front of the left track curled off and the big tank spun round in a circle facing away from the SEALs.

Murdock closed the door before the tank's machine gun could be brought to bear on them.

"Everyone in the rig," Murdock bellowed. "We'll head out the front door and take our chances with the riflemen."

Kat set the timer on the bomb for five minutes, and they pushed the scientist toward the front door. Then they all squeezed into the APC, barreled through the front door, and raced away, then took a hard right down the street. In seconds they were away from the riflemen, who had begun to move forward again.

They took some rifle fire on the armored rig, but the rounds bounced off.

"Where the fuck to?" Ostercamp called from the driver's seat.

"No damn river here that we can jump into and swim right past them at the port," Murdock said. He tried to remember the maps he had looked at. Then he had it. The coast wandered a little south to the east of Tripoli. If they headed due east they should be able to find the water, jump in, and call in the Pegasus well before daylight.

"East, Ostercamp," Murdock said. "We want to head east and maybe a little north to find the wet."

"Great, Skipper. Which way is east?"

"Lam, ride shotgun with Oster up there," Murdock said.

"Black as the inside of a whore's heart up here, Skipper," Lam said a moment later. "Hey, got a clue. We take a hard right at the next road. Looks like it goes to the east. Some traffic, so that's a good sign. None of them are tanks hunting us, which is a better sign."

"Anybody wounded?" DeWitt asked. Nobody responded, so DeWitt relaxed a little.

"Bunch of lights up front a mile or so," Ostercamp said. "My guess is it's a roadblock."

"Move up until we're sure," Murdock said. "Then we take it out with the twenties. Ed, work the top hatch with your Bull Pup. That scope should help you ID the roadblock if that's what it is."

The Bull Pup was the SEALs' latest weapon, still under development for the Armed Forces by Alliant and not set to be issued to the military until 2005. The SEALs and Don Stroh had talked the company out of six of the weapons and the needed ammunition.

The top barrel of the weapon fires a 20mm round that can come in armor-piercing, ball, or with a proximity fuse for airbursts. The weapon has a laser beam that, when fixed on a target, sends back the range data, then fuses the round for the number of rotations needed to reach that target and explode in the air. The rounds also will detonate on contact. The weapon comes with a six-shot magazine. The 20mm rounds cost $30 each. The bottom barrel on the weapon is a standard 5.56mm kinetic round with a thirty-shot magazine.

DeWitt pushed back the top hatch and leveled in the weapon, which was lighter than the old M-16 Army rifle. He checked through the six-power scope and video camera, but couldn't be sure what the lights were. A quarter of a mile later he had it. Two trucks parked across the road.

"We have a roadblock," he shouted to the men below, then aimed with the laser and when he had a spot on one of the trucks, fired, then adjusted his sight and lasered the second truck and fired. They were three quarters of a mile away.

He saw the first hit over the truck. The round exploded twenty feet in the air, blasting shrapnel in all directions. He saw two men go down, and two more dead on the ground. The second round hit in the same general area and exploded in the air.

Then he concentrated on hitting the trucks. His first round slammed into the engine and it exploded, setting the truck on fire. The second truck was driving away from the first one. DeWitt's third round jolted through the rear of the truck and exploded in the driver's compartment, shredding the soldier and dumping the truck into a ditch well off the road.

Ed dropped down into the APC. "Looks like we have a clear path ahead through the roadblock."

When they drove through the roadblock, Ostercamp had to make a small detour around bodies in the road and the still-burning truck. If any of the men manning the spot were still alive, they had fled in terror.

"Still heading east?" Murdock asked Ostercamp.

"Yes, sir, if my small pocket compass is working and not picking up too much metal. At least we're getting out of the clumps of towns. These Libyan suburbs?"

"Must be. Keep us moving."

Ten minutes later Ed dropped down from the open hatch. "I've been scouting ahead with the scope. Looks like we have some real trouble. Two tanks are rumbling along toward us. No way we can hurt them head-on with the twenty. Might be time to give up our horse and get back on our feet."

"Anywhere we can pull off the road and let them go by without their seeing us?" Murdock asked.

DeWitt shook his head. "Not around here, Skipper. No trees, no brush, no ravines. We're into flat almost desert country."

"How far away?" Murdock asked.

"I'd say a mile and we're closing at about sixty miles an hour. Thirty theirs and thirty of ours. That gives us about a minute until we slam into each other. What the hell are we going to do, Skipper?"

# 8

Murdock heard DeWitt's warning and shouted at the driver. "Stop this thing and put it crossways in the road. Everybody out, take your gear.

"Kat, set your timer on a bomb for three minutes and let's all haul ass. Move, move, move. We've got about forty-five seconds left. Go to the left of the road. Move."

Ostercamp stopped, then pulled the APC crossways in the narrow road. The back hatch on the APC burst open and bodies flew out of it in all directions. Kat put a timer/detonator in three charges of TNAZ and set the timer for three minutes. Then she jumped out of the rig, charged across the road to the left, and kept running. Most of the SEALs were fifty yards ahead of her.

Jaybird had slowed, and waved as she came up. They sprinted together the hundred yards to where the SEALs had all gone to ground behind whatever concealment they could find.

Behind them on the road, the two tanks lumbered forward in the darkness. The lead tank came within thirty yards of the APC and slowed, then stopped. The top hatch opened and a man leaned out, staring ahead.

Slowly the tank crept forward until it nudged the Russian-built APC.

Three minutes on the timer elapsed. The TNAZ blew with a resounding crack like an artillery shell going off. The APC shattered into scrap metal flying in all directions. The lead tank jolted backward from the blast, then tipped to one side until it rolled over.

"Let's move, people," Murdock said into his Motorola. The SEALs stood and jogged away from the blast at a right angle, putting all the distance they could between them and the pools of fuel burning in the roadway where the APC used to be.

A mile from the blast, Murdock called a halt and looked at his compass. "East is to the right," he said. "Lam, out in front fifty, keep us to the east, and we should find the wet."

"How far?" somebody asked.

"From five to fifty miles," Murdock said. "Your guess is as good as mine. We'll never get there just talking about it."

They moved out in their usual diamond formation, with Lam in front by fifty yards, then Murdock and his Alpha Squad, with DeWitt and Bravo right behind them. Ron Holt, with the SAT-COM radio, walked behind Murdock. The SEALs maintained a five-yard distance between each other in the best combat tradition. A lucky grenade, mortar round, or burst of enemy fire would get only one or maybe two men. If they were bunched up, shoulder to armpit, a lucky round could wipe out a whole squad.

They were in the country now, with few buildings. It was the coastal plain, and semiarid, but here and there they came to cultivated fields. Murdock could not figure out what they were growing. It looked like some kind of grain, but he wasn't sure. They swung wide past a village that was dark and quiet. Only two dogs greeted them as they hurried by.

They had lost the blacktopped road, and now they found few others. They were mostly dirt and gravel tracks that had no traffic this time of night. For more than two hours of hiking they saw only one motor vehicle, an old farm truck of questionable vintage parked beside a weather-worn farmhouse.

Murdock stopped the men. "Lam, you hear anything?" he asked on the radio.

"Yeah, for the past five minutes. We're moving right toward the sounds. I'd say about four heavy trucks on a road ahead somewhere."

"Military?"

"My guess. Who else would be out this time of night with four heavy trucks in the country?"

"We're still heading east and a little north. Any sign of the coast?"

"Nada."

"Figures. Let's move up until we can see what those trucks are hauling."

"Hey, Skipper, the trucks stopped. Dead ahead, maybe two miles."

"Exploding that bomb was a signpost pointing directly at us, but it had to be done," Murdock said. "We live with it."

"Want me to move out and see what those trucks are?" Lam asked.

"Yeah, Lam. Go. Double-time it and let's see what this is all about. We'll come along at the usual pace."

"Roger that, Skipper."

Kat moved up beside Murdock. "At least this is easier than last time."

"So far. We're not out of this one yet. Then what about finding those other missiles? Say China grabbed them or bought them. They sold this one to Libya. Maybe they sold another one to Iraq and one to Iran and one to Afghanistan. Are we going to have to chase down all of them?"

"Never thought of it that way," Kat said. "I figured that if China was the buyer from some lowlife in Ukraine, they would keep most of the warheads for themselves. They could chop out the nukes and dump the missiles in the Mediterranean and make it a lot easier to get the bombs back home. Fly them even."

"Now you're getting me worried," Murdock said. "Thanks a lot. So we either have to take down that Chinese freighter or find out who the Chinese sold the other missiles to."

"We'll have some help on that one." She took a deep breath, and Murdock looked over at her. "At least I haven't had to kill anybody on this mission."

"Not yet," Murdock said. "You're not quite recovered from that walk in Iran, are you?"

She looked at him and shook her head. "No, I don't think I will ever forget it, forget how I felt right afterwards."

"You did what you had to do, what we had trained you to do, and it worked. Saving my life was a bonus—for me."

She flashed him a smile. "That was what helped me get through the first month or so."

Murdock's radio earpiece came on with a whisper.

"Skip, I'm here and I don't believe it. They are Army trucks and six or eight soldiers. They seem to be in charge of more than a hundred civilians. All have some kind of a firearm, an old rifle, a pistol, a carbine. Looks like a home guard of some kind. They have spread out in a line of skirmishers maybe a half mile wide."

"So, we go around them," Murdock said.

"Not that easy, Skip. There's a bluff on one side here and on the other side a good-sized village. The valley we're in now funnels in here. Nowhere to go around."

"Are they moving forward or in place?"

"They seem to be just sitting here, waiting. A blocking force. Do we have to shoot up a bunch of civilians? I mean, Skip, these are old men and boys, and I'm sure I've seen a dozen or so women in the group, all with guns."

"Hold there and we'll be up to you soon and figure it out. Any trees around there?"

"Yeah, some on the bluff and around the town. Not much in between."

"Roger. We're moving."

Kat shivered. "Civilians up there? Murdock, I don't like the sound of this. Are we going to have to shoot our way through them? Old men and boys and women?"

"Not if there's another way. Come on, Kat. Stay hard for me here. We're going to need you."

Five minutes later Murdock and DeWitt crawled the last fifty feet on hands and knees to a small rise. Ahead of them, less than half a mile, they could see three Army trucks and a line of people. Both officers used binoculars.

"Civilians, all right," DeWitt said. "In a good blocking position."

Lam lay in the sand beside them. "Since we talked, another truck came, a civilian one, and dumped out twenty more old men and boys with weapons, then headed back to the village."

"The soldiers, are they spread out to command the troops?" DeWitt asked.

"That's what it looked like."

"Diversion," Murdock said. He turned his binoculars, and then used night-vision goggles and checked the bluff to the left.

"Yeah. We'll have three of our Bull Pups put airbursts over those trees on the end of the bluff. Four rounds per gun and keep the muzzle flashes hidden so the people out front won't know where the rounds came from. That could pull a bunch of the civilians and soldiers out of the line and moving that way to reinforce."

"Might work," Lam said.

"Ed, get back to the men and put those rounds into that bluff. Then bring the rest of the people up here."

Four minutes later, Murdock heard the first explosion over the bluff and saw the rounds going off. He could hear chatter below as the civilians and their Army trainers talked it over. One section of the line directly in front of the SEALs swung to the left, moving toward the bluff. Another section of the line jogged in the same direction.

Murdock grinned as the rest of the SEALs ran up beside them.

"We have everyone?" Murdock asked. The men checked in on the radio network.

"All present," Ed said.

"Let's move down there through that gap," Murdock said. "Everyone with suppressors put them on. We don't want to let them know we're here if we don't have to. Move out."

They jogged forward in a line twenty yards wide, ignoring the five-yard rule this time. Murdock was slightly ahead, and as they came to the spot where the Libyans had been, he checked the area carefully. He spotted the trucks and a driver leaning against the fender. Murdock lifted his submachine gun and put three rounds into the man, who cried out and fell to the ground.

Just to Murdock's right another figure lifted up and fired a shot. It missed Murdock. Before he could swing his weapon around, he heard the *pffhitts* of three rounds from a sub gun, and the Libyan shooter spun around and sprawled on the ground in the faint moonlight.

Murdock looked to his right and saw Kat lower her weapon. In the moonlight her face showed as a mask of tension and terror. He grabbed her by one arm and they ran forward.

"God, did you see that?" Kat asked, her voice raspy, and she sounded almost in tears. "Did you see that? The shooter back there was a woman. That woman tried to shoot you, Murdock. So I killed her. I shot her three times and she looked up at me. I'll never forget that expression of anger, and pain, and terror. I just reacted. I saw her shoot at you and I didn't know it was a woman and I fired. Oh, God, I never wanted to kill anybody else. Damn you, Murdock!"

"Good, yeah, my fault. Now let's move our asses or one of us is going to get hurt out here in the dark."

The SEALs charged on through the spot, and were a quarter of a mile away before the civilian army realized it had been tricked and began working forward after the SEALs.

It was no contest. Murdock told Lam to head the SEALs due north. The Mediterranean had to be up there somewhere.

Murdock kept watching Kat. She stayed up with them. She looked angry, yet resigned. It was another traumatic shock for her, but she'd come through it. He checked with Lam on the Motorola, but there was no sign or indication they were any closer to the water than they had been two hours ago.

He checked his watch. It was 0220. They had another four hours, maybe five to dawn. Was there time enough to get to the water and be picked up?

The SEALs jogged again. They had systematically lightened their drag bags when the need for the equipment was gone. After they found out the missile was in the warehouse, not the ship, they'd dumped the heavyweight limpet mines they had for the ship. Later they'd dropped the extra explosives and gear they had brought in case they had to open a missile. Now they were down to their combat vests, usual personal weapons, and regular issue of TNAZ.

Twenty minutes later they came over a small rise and saw a road ahead with moving traffic.

Murdock sniffed and grinned. "I can smell salt air. Can't be far now."

They moved down to the road and ran across it when there was no traffic, and just beyond some dunes they could hear the light surf of the Mediterranean slapping the Libyan shore. They could see no troops or transport for troops up or down the beach.

"Holt, crank up that SATCOM, let's do some Navy business."

It took three tries to contact the Pegasus offshore. The boat had just arrived on station. The time was 0315.

"What's your position, SEALs?"

"We have no idea. No road signs. Wait a minute. Ed may have a Mugger."

He did, and they used the locator device to talk to four satellites and give them their location by coordinates. Ron sent the coordinates to the Pegasus.

"How did you get twenty miles down the coast from Tripoli, SEALs? We'll be off your location in ten minutes. How far out will you come?"

"Ten minutes' worth, or enough for a half mile," Murdock said.

The SEALs stowed their Motorolas in their waterproof pockets, slung their weapons over their backs, and walked into the Mediterranean.

Murdock tied his buddy cord to Kat. She looked up and took a deep breath. "Murdock, we've got to stop meeting this way.

Every time that I'm around you I wind up killing somebody. I don't like this one bit."

"Let's go for a swim and forget about it. I promise you won't even have to fire your weapon again." Murdock frowned when he looked away. He sincerely hoped that he was right.

# 9

## USS *Franklin D. Roosevelt,* CV 69
## In the Mediterranean Sea, Off Libya

Jaybird, Dobler, DeWitt, and Murdock sat around a small table in the SEALs' assembly room on the carrier staring at Don Stroh.

"You saying that Chinese freighter is a floating garage sale for nuclear warheads?" Murdock asked, the first to get his voice after Don Stroh's quick briefing.

"We're not sure, but we've had the old scow under AWACS scrutiny the past three days. There have been helicopter landings on the Chinese freighter twice. The choppers moved to land sites where there were international airports."

"Our best guess is that the Chinese are stripping the nuke warheads out of the missiles and selling them on the open market?" DeWitt asked.

"Possibly. They are easy to move. You could have carried one for ten or fifteen miles in that APC, you told me."

"So we take out the freighter before they distribute any more nukes around the world," Dobler said.

"That's been our recommendation to the President and my chief," Stroh said. "We're also trying to track those choppers and what they did with their cargo. We've got one of them tied down as to who picked it up and where it was left and the route the plane took that picked it up. We're working on the second one."

"Where's the ship now?" Murdock asked.

"That's another curious development. The ship is wandering around the Greek islands in the Aegean Sea. One chopper went to the boat and then back to Athens. Sometimes the ship is making only five knots."

"Waiting for more customers," Murdock said. "My bet is that the brass will decide to take out the ship next, then try to find any of the warheads that are still missing. How far are we from the freighter?"

"Too far, almost eight hundred miles," Stroh said. "We have a cruiser in the Athens harbor now. It can be pushed out toward the freighter to give you a platform to work from in case we go after the Chinese ship next."

Jaybird scowled. "Most cruisers carry a Seahawk chopper. It's smaller than the Sea Knight and can haul only twelve men. We need sixteen. We'd have to use a Sea Knight and squeeze it on the cruiser. It should fit. The Sea Knight's rotor blades are only fifty-one feet in diameter. The Seahawk's blades are two feet longer, so the larger bird should be able to land and take off from the cruiser."

Stroh looked at Jaybird with surprise.

"Jaybird remembers those kind of things," DeWitt said. "Now, when can we get some word about this new mission?"

"When I hear, I'll call you. I don't know how the Navy will put this through channels, but it should get here eventually. In the field we'll go with the first word we get and let channels catch up with us. Okay, troops?"

The four SEALs nodded. They had been on board the carrier only an hour, and hadn't eaten, showered, or slept yet. They were headed in that direction when Stroh nailed them.

"I'll get clearance for a Sea Knight on board the *Cowpens,* CG 63, in Athens if this one goes down the way we think it will. Now, why don't you guys get some food and some shuteye. I might be calling you before you know it. The chief is hot on this one. Nobody in Washington wants these warheads charging around the world like loose cannons."

It was only a little after 0830, but Murdock and DeWitt both ordered up steak dinners at the dirty-shirt mess.

Later they found Kat sitting in the wardroom, staring at her hands and sipping coffee. She nodded a grim welcome.

Murdock and DeWitt watched her a moment without speaking. She looked up and set her mouth in a firm, hard line. "I'm so damn mad that I could spit," she said. Her eyes were furious brown holes hidden by lowered brows.

"I don't think I'm going to do this anymore," she went on. "I just might call the President and tell him to get another player. I'm used up."

"Kat, I'm no shrink, but I've sent more than one of my men

to take a few sessions with the psychos. If you don't want that, how about a talk with the chaplain."

She looked up at Murdock and nodded, her brows raised in surprise.

"Yes, now why didn't I think of that? I can't get that woman's furious expression out of my head. She knew she was dying and she looked right through me. I shivered then, and I'm shivering right now remembering it.

"I killed her, Murdock. I shot her three times and she died right there in that field. How can I ever accept the idea that it is all right for me to kill someone when I'm wearing this uniform? Even when I'm on a mission to save hundreds of thousands of lives? It doesn't make sense to me. How do I get in touch with the chaplain?"

Captain Ira Ralston, senior chaplain on the carrier had learned years ago that being a Navy chaplain was a lot more than holding services and listening to complaints. He found himself to be father confessor for the Catholics, and oftentimes psychiatrist in uniform for many of the Protestants and Jews. He had been listening to this young lieutenant for a half hour now, and knew more about her and her life than he wanted to.

"So, how can I justify killing another human being?" she concluded.

"You simply reacted to the situation. You responded as you had been trained to do. You also fired in an attempt to save the life of a teammate. Those are all good and worthwhile motives. I've talked to a lot of men in combat. They say that they are always reacting before they can think. In a split second your mind must order your body to do something, in this case to aim and fire to protect another member of the team.

"Kat, you were in a combat situation. You've been there before, you told me, and you've killed before. This is no different. The fact that the victim was a woman is a coincidence. It more than likely would have been a man with the ratio of men to women in the defense force.

"This all goes way back in man's development to the cave man when he fought huge ferocious beasts. He did it for food and to survive.

"Today some of us have to do the same thing. We fight to survive. Now we often call it 'him or me.' In the heat of battle, even if it lasts only a few seconds, the basic primal urge of fight to survive surfaces. If it's a confrontation with another person, then it all comes down to who kills who. It's him or me who will live. We always strive our best to be sure that it's the me who survives and not the him."

Captain Ralston watched the young lieutenant. He knew about her civilian status and the temporary rank for convenience. She looked up at him, but didn't say anything.

"How did you handle this when you came out of Iran?" he asked.

"Not well. I cried a lot. I took a month off work and tried to get myself settled down. I kept having a dream when I relived the whole damn thing. Then I went into denial, and that almost worked. One day I woke up and realized that I had to face it, confront the fact that I had killed four or five men in Iran. Yes, part of it was a him-or-me syndrome. I never sought any professional help. I can see now that I should have."

He waited. She looked at him, then at the bulkhead, then back at him. "So?"

"Did you throw up after the incident?"

She smiled. It was the first smile he had seen from her. "Incident? I kill a woman and you call it an incident?"

"Yes. Those warheads that you destroyed could have killed up to a half million each. That would be four and a half million lives that you saved in the world. The loss of one woman's life against four and a half million makes it a ridiculously small incident."

"Oh. I never thought of it that way before." The smile came again. "All right, let's summarize: I didn't throw up after the . . . incident. I have not gone on any crying jags since that time, now almost five hours ago. I feel fairly well adjusted, but I think that I can now grieve for the woman I killed, without ruining my life. I'm ready to move on. Also, I want to call the President and resign from this special assignment and ask him to send me home."

Captain Ralston smiled. "Good, good. I think this little talk has been of some benefit for you. I'll call the communications center and have them set up a call with the White House. As you know, there is little chance you'll talk directly with the President. But he will get the message."

Twenty minutes later, Captain Ralston left the communications center when Kat picked up the handset.

"I'd like to speak with the President, please. This is Katherine

Garnet on the aircraft carrier *Franklin D. Roosevelt* in the Mediterranean."

"Yes, Miss Garnet. Congratulations on your successful mission on the nine warheads. I'm the President's personal secretary and he knows about your good work. He left an hour ago for Europe and can be reached only in emergencies."

Kat stared at the handset.

"Miss Garnet, are you still there?"

"Yes."

"The President tried to call you, but we couldn't get through to the ship. Some mix-up somewhere. He'll try to call again tomorrow. May I offer you my congratulations on saving the world from nine more nuclear explosions and the millions of lives you saved."

"Thanks, but the SEALs did most of it. I . . . I'll wait for the President's call. Thank you."

When they first arrived in the assembly compartment, the SEALs had dropped their gear, had a big supper-type breakfast, and fallen into bed in their quarters. Mahanani had taken care of any scrapes and scratches. Ching had had what they decided was a sprained finger. They'd taped it tightly to the finger next to it.

Murdock showered after his meal, and dropped into bed, one of a six-pack officers compartment. DeWitt was in the bunk over him.

Three hours after he got to bed, Murdock came awake with a start. Don Stroh was shaking his shoulder.

"Okay, sailor, up and at 'em. You've had more than enough sleep for one day. The captain wants to see you."

Murdock came awake instantly. It was a skill he'd had to develop in the SEALs the first month he'd arrived, and he had maintained it.

"Captain? The ship's captain or the CAG?"

"Yeah, the fly guy. He says he just received some messages from Air Force One and from the CNO. Sounds like they have made up their mind about the next move."

Murdock decided to let DeWitt sleep. He dressed, and Stroh led him to the carrier's Combat Information Center. It was the heart of the ship's battle capability. All combat information came in there, and most of it showed on a large display of screens.

Captain Prescott nodded at the two and led them to a screen.

"This is a feed from our AWACS plane monitoring the Chinese ship. At the moment, she's almost dead in the water. A small ship of some sort is approaching her, and it looks like some kind of a meeting or a mid-sea transfer. Either way, we don't like it. Wanted to let you see this so you know that we know what the Chinese are doing all the time."

He took two sheets of paper from a small desk area and waved them. "The gist of this signal from the President is that we have a green light to go ahead and stop, board, take control, examine, and generally satisfy ourselves that there are or there aren't any of the former Soviet Satan missiles on board.

"The only vessel we have in the area is a missile cruiser at Athens. She's been alerted, and has left one of her helicopters onshore. She will be ready to receive a visiting Sea Knight, if that is what we decide. She is now steaming in the general direction of the Chinese ship, the *Star of Asia,* a freighter in poor condition."

"You also got the signal through Navy channels?" Murdock asked.

"Yes, from the CNO through channels. It took a little over an hour more than it did for the message to come from the President. At least we're legal."

"So we figure out how to take down a rusty Chinese freighter on the high seas?" Murdock asked.

"That's the size of it, Commander. I understand your men have done this before."

"We have. How big is this freighter?"

"About the size of our combat stores ships. Five hundred and eighty feet, about sixteen thousand tons. That's a generality, but that's the signals we get back."

"So, we go from here to Athens in a COD. Pickup the Sea Knight in Athens and join the cruiser in the Aegean Sea. That's the easy part." Murdock paused. "Anything about timing of our attack? My men just came off an all-night mission."

"The President mentions that in the signal. He said if you could get to the freighter sometime tonight, it would be the best scenario."

"Tonight?" Murdock looked at his watch. It was 1206. "So we're still nearly eight hundred miles from Athens. The Carrier Onboard Delivery planes make about three hundred and fifty miles an hour. A two-and-a-half-hour flight. Then make connections at the Athens municipal airport, or do we have some military in Greece?"

"We have some military. Athens is about seventy-five miles from the Chinese freighter. We have a COD on board here that you can use anytime."

"It sounds possible. My men can sleep on the trip. Not more than a half hour on the Sea Knight to the freighter. Then we go out the hatch with our IBSs and go up the freighter's rusty side and take her down. We'll need hand and foot magnet climbers, the kind our men use when working parts of the exterior hull."

"I'm sure we have them. When do you want the COD to be ready for takeoff?"

Murdock looked at his watch again. "We'll plan a midnight attack. Gives us twelve hours. Let's let the men sleep two more hours, then we'll get them up and moving. We'll need breakfast and box lunches. Also a resupply on ammo and explosives. Oh, do you have two IBSs? Inflatable rubber boats?"

"One of our support ships has some. We'll get two of them on board within an hour."

"Good. You'll clear this with the XO and the captain? I'm getting bugged about going through channels."

Captain Prescott grinned. "I know the feeling. Yes, I'll inform them of the plan."

Murdock stood. "I better get my second up and briefed. You'll alert the kitchen crew we'll need breakfast in three hours?"

"Right. Our cooks can come up with any kind of meal any time of the day."

Murdock grinned, waved, and headed for his compartment. He had to get DeWitt up and moving and briefed. DeWitt knew where Senior Chief Dobler bunked. Two hours' more sleep for the men, then they would be up.

Murdock wondered how Kat was doing. At least she wouldn't be along on this run. He poked DeWitt on the shoulder.

"Hey sailor, get up. Time we do it again."

DeWitt came alert slowly. He sat up, shook his head.

"We're going after the damn freighter?"

"Roger."

"Wonder if they have any Chinese troops on board. Ah, probably not. It's just an old rust-bucket freighter."

# 10

The SEALs were ready when the COD rolled up. They had spent an hour checking gear, getting weapons cleaned and oiled, and making everything ready. Kat had come down and sat watching them. Murdock had phoned her earlier and told her that they wouldn't need her on this mission.

"Kat, our first job is to take down the ship, seize control. Then we can spot a place on the deck, clear it out, and have an LZ for you to step into from a hovering chopper. When we need you to look over the warheads, we'll call you in. I'm not about to mess with that kind of nuclear power myself."

"I can go up the side of that ship as well as any of your men."

Murdock chuckled. "Hey, Kat, I know it. But somebody might start shooting, and that's *our* strong point. So let the guys do their thing, and then we'll use the SATCOM and get you on board quickly."

"This is assuming that there are missiles and warheads on board that Chinese ship."

"Assuming, yes, Kat. But there's not much of a choice where they can put them. They could have ferried them all to land for a trans-Siberia plane ride, but I don't think so."

"I'd still like to be with you guys."

"Well, we're flattered. You want to go even after what happened early this morning back there in Libya?"

"Yes. I'm working through it. I decided not to tell the President that I wanted to quit."

"Good. You have a nap and some dinner and if all goes well tonight, we just might be calling you for a helicopter ride come daylight."

"I'll be ready." She paused. "Murdock, thanks for hanging in there with me when I was coming apart at the seams."

"Hey, nice lady. We all have our seams. See you tomorrow."

A half hour later, the SEALs trooped into the COD. It was exactly like the ones they had used around the world. A workhorse for a fast ride onto or off an aircraft carrier.

The flight to Athens was routine, well within the range of the C-2A Greyhound. They landed on what looked like a military airstrip, but nobody explained to them where they were. A Navy Sea Knight dropped down within thirty yards of the COD, and the SEALs left one plane for the next. In the interim they moved their uninflated IBSs into the chopper and inflated them, positioning them at the rear of the craft next to the aft hatch. First they would push out the boats, then jump in after them all from about ten feet off the water if they were lucky. Just the way they had practiced that day off San Diego in the Pacific Ocean.

The pilot came back and checked with Murdock after the sixteen SEALs had settled into the bird.

"Commander, we have a little over a half hour flight time. The target ship is steaming at ten knots again in a generally southern direction. As I understand it, you want to jump out about a mile to the front of the freighter and on its line of travel."

"Right, Lieutenant, and we don't want the Chinese to know we're there. We stay a mile away, they won't hear us. If that old scow has the kind of radar on it I expect it to, they won't have a prayer of spotting the chopper."

"That sounds good to me. I don't think I'll ever trust those damned Chinese to do or say what we expect them to. We're out of here in about three minutes."

The crew chief buttoned up the craft and went with the pilot back to the small cockpit.

Murdock took advantage of the quiet before takeoff to talk to the men.

"We're about half an hour to getting wet. We get out, get in our boats and wait for the freighter. One man will go up the side from each boat and they'll use two drop lines for the rest of us. Any questions?"

"What if the old tub is so rusty that our magnets don't hold?" Jaybird asked.

"Then the climber will detour to another area where the magnets will hold. The boats in the water will follow the climber wherever he goes."

Then the big rotor cranked up, the engine howled, and they lifted gently off the ground.

Jaybird Sterling sat on the floor of the chopper beside Senior Chief Dobler. He leaned away a little so he wouldn't touch the chief. He had been trying his best to avoid talking to the chief lately. Ever since he'd kissed the chief's daughter, he had been so mixed up he could hardly breathe.

He shook his head remembering. Ke-reist, no girl had ever set him off the way she did. The soft little way she had of moving her hands when she talked. The easy-to-get-along-with conversations they had. Then that kiss in the stacks. He shook his head again. It had never happened that way before.

He didn't know how old she was. She had to be seventeen at least. Hell, he could wait a year—if he could see her now and then. The library was the best bet. Yeah, first thing they got home, he was going to call her when he knew her dad would be at the BUD/S. Yeah. That would work.

What if when Helen was eighteen, Chief Dobler still objected to Jaybird seeing her? What then? Hell, he'd cross over that minefield when he came to it. Carefully, but he'd get across. Hell, he was a SEAL. That should count for something with her old man. Saving his ass a time or two under enemy fire would help. Yeah, and not fuck up between now and then. That was the big one.

Jaybird had played football and baseball in high school. He was good, but not good enough to get a scholarship anywhere. Like so many players, his folks couldn't afford to send him to college. He didn't want to go to some rinky-dink junior college or a state college, especially in Oregon where he grew up. So he cut out for the Navy when he was just over eighteen.

It took him three years to get into the SEALs, and he'd been slaving in Third Platoon now for another three years. Hey, there was almost nothing that would get him out of the SEALs.

The new guys to the unit kept asking him how he got his nickname. They knew it meant naked, as in naked as a jaybird. He had told so many different stories now that he hardly remembered how it actually happened.

His best story was that he had this dish down at the beach and it was late and nobody was around. They went skinny-dipping just before dark, and when they got back to shore, saw a group of twenty or so had parked right beside their clothes and towels, set up a volleyball net, and had a game going. Others had started a fire in a fire ring, and they all appeared to be settled in for the evening.

That left him and his girl both naked and getting cold. She cried and yelled at him to go get her clothes. He tried, but one of the men spotted him and chased him back into the water. After that they decided he should go back to the car for a blanket and use that to go get their clothes and towels.

Of course his keys were in his pants pocket on the blanket. Still, he said he could break in. He had a secret way. He ran up the cliff to the parking spot, and had almost succeeded in prying loose the driver's side door when two cops grabbed him. Next thing he knew he was in the county lockup wearing jail clothes. The cops wouldn't believe his story. They impounded the car. He had to call Murdock to come bail him out.

It was two weeks later before a package came for him with his clothes, his wallet, and his car keys. The girl who mailed the bundle back to him refused his phone calls and he never saw her again.

Jaybird grinned. That was one of the best ones. Yeah, those stories wouldn't help any with the senior chief. He'd have to start toeing the line, doing everything right.

Damn it to hell, he wondered just how old Helen was.

The chopper's radar picked up the freighter when they were five miles off, flying at a hundred feet over the dark waters of the Mediterranean. The *Star of Asia* had not changed course, and had slowed to seven knots. They were still well ahead of the freighter. The pilot reported that they would move up to within a mile of the craft, check the course again, and drop the SEALs off.

At the one-mile mark, Murdock went up and looked through the cockpit window. He could see the running lights of the freighter. It didn't have the look of a ship trying to hide.

"Listen up," the crew chief shouted. "In one minute the aft hatch will open. Then you're on your own. Dump those big rubber boats out of my chopper and jump in after them. Good luck."

The SEALs came to their feet, checked each other's gear, then lined up with a squad on each side.

The aft hatch swung down, making a ramp.

The SEALs pushed the first raft out the door, then the second one. The bird had come to a complete stop, and hovered about fifteen feet over the water.

"Go, go, go," Murdock bellowed. The two lines of SEALs ran forward and jumped off the end of the ramp. Two seconds later they were wet and clawing for the surface, their heavy combat load dragging them down.

It took them almost five minutes to get the IBSs righted, and for the SEALs to climb into them. Murdock made a vocal check to be sure all sixteen men were on board. The two boats were tied together with a twenty-foot cord.

"Directly to our rear you can see the lights from the freighter," Murdock said. "The pilot checked with the plane overhead and we know this is the right ship, the *Star of Asia,* of Chinese registry. We'll both stay on the same side, the way we practiced it. Keep the boats tied together and latch them onto the hull. As soon as we touch, I want the two climbers moving up with the pull cord attached. Everyone get out your Motorolas and let's get on the net. Questions?"

There were none.

"We're drifting off the ship's course," Lam said. "About a three-knot drift."

"Start the engines," Murdock said. "Let's keep as close to that course as we can. The ship should be here in nine minutes."

The SEALs shivered. They had done this a hundred times before, but they never became used to the cold. They had elected not to wear their wet suits. They wouldn't be in the water long enough to justify them, and the suits would slow them down once they made it up the ropes to the deck.

The time dragged. Someone told a dirty joke. That triggered a dozen more.

Murdock hushed them after three minutes. "Coming up on us. Hold it down."

Now they could see the ship better. They could make out the different-colored navigation lights standard on all vessels. Then a minute later they could hear the growl of the diesel engines inside the big ship, and the gentle hiss as the bow parted the waves.

The ship would miss them by forty yards.

"Let's move up on her," Murdock said. "Match her speed, then we edge in beside her amidships and latch on with our magnets. Go."

The twelve-foot-long-by-six-foot-wide rubber boats moved

closer to the ship, matched its speed, then angled toward the hull that soon towered over them. Murdock guessed it would be a forty-foot climb. This part they hadn't practiced.

Ching perched on the edge of the IBS nearest the big hull and held the powerful magnet. It had a line tied to it and looped around a rope tie-down that circled the top edge of the small craft.

"Closer," Ching whispered. The small boat edged in again, countering the soft wake of the large craft. Then Ching lunged to the side, planted the magnet on the side of the ship, and at once tugged the line tight, holding the IBS against the large freighter.

As soon as the tie-down was completed, Jaybird put both hands against the side of the ship, testing the magnets strength. They held. He put one foot against the ship's hull, then the other one, with the magnets grabbing the metal. Then he began the slow work of going one hand and one foot at a time as he worked his way up the side of the ship. A thin nylon line trailed from his combat vest.

"Cover him," Murdock said. The same thing happened at Bravo Squad's location, where Colt Franklin went up the side of the ship. Murdock could see Jaybird. He was halfway up. Then two jerks came on the line, and Jaybird tied off the climbing rope. A few moments later, two more jerks came on the climbing rope.

The SEALs in Alpha Squad were lined up at the side of the ship. They allowed ten feet of free rope, then another man started up the rope. Four men would be on the rope at once before the first one reached the top.

After Jaybird tied off the climbing rope to a sturdy stanchion, he faded into the shadows of some machinery at the side of the deck, eight foot from the rail. He waited. Ching came over the rail, swung his weapon off his back, and moved beside Jaybird. They were to move to the bridge, take down any civilians there, and take control of the bridge.

This was the dicey time, when half the squad was on the rope and only two of them were on the deck. Jaybird heard something, a motor grinding. Suddenly the metal he leaned against vanished into the deck, and when he looked around he found himself staring at a pair of missile firing tubes. Directly in back of that a false cover swung back to reveal a machine gun aimed directly at Jaybird.

Jaybird hit his Motorola. "Abort, abort. This thing is no rust bucket. Missile tubes, machine guns, and that's just so far. This tub is a Chinese man-of-war, either a destroyer or a frigate."

"Confirmed?" Murdock asked.

"Fuck, yes!" Franklin shouted into his throat mike. "I've got all kinds of firepower staring at me from a hundred-and-thirty-millimeter guns to torpedoes. Abort."

Jaybird dove for the rail. The machine gun chattered and rounds slammed into the area where he had been. He rolled twice, hit the rail, and went overboard. Ching was right behind him. Ching felt a hard blow to his back, but didn't drop his weapon. He slid under the rail and jumped feet-first into the Mediterranean below.

The men on the ropes dropped off, hit the water, and swam for the IBS. Three men remained on each of the small boats. They cut the lines holding their craft to the side of the freighter.

Murdock saw muzzle flashes from the rail above. The overhang meant the gunners had to lean out over the rail to get a shot at the side of the ship where the boats were. Murdock slammed three three-round bursts at the muzzle flashes above, and felt his craft slide away from the freighter. Somebody on the motor kicked it over, and they swept farther away from the freighter. It would take the big ship a half mile to stop.

Even now the ship slid away from them.

"SEALs," Murdock bellowed. "Find your boats. We're here waiting for you."

Murdock's earpiece buzzed. "We've got four in our boat," DeWitt said on the Motorola. "One more coming on board. I'm still light by three. Use light sticks?"

"Not yet. They could have machine guns aft. Make a lovely target. Hold. We just got one more. I'm four short here."

Murdock kept calling. Two more of his squad found the IBS and were dragged on board.

When the big ship was only a shadow in the distant darkness, Murdock broke out two light sticks, the kind you bend to break an internal barrier letting two chemicals come together and glow. He had two red ones.

"SEALs," he bellowed again. "We're here. Find us." He turned to Senior Chief Dobler. "Who are we missing?"

"First two men up, Ching and Jaybird."

"Anybody get shot on the deck?" Murdock asked.

Ed DeWitt came on the radio. "We are still missing one man.

We think he was hit when he was on deck. The number-one man up the rope after Franklin. It's Canzoneri."

Holt came up with the SATCOM ready. "Call, sir?"

Murdock took the handset. "TAC Two?" he said. Holt nodded. "This is In the Wet, calling Knight One. Can you read?"

No response.

Murdock waited a minute, had two more glow sticks activated, and then tried again.

"This is In the Wet. Knight One, can you read?"

A response came back at once.

"Wet, this is Knight One. Trouble?"

"Right. Can you reverse that thing and come get us?"

"That's a Roger. We're at land base, but can be moving in five. Give us a Mugger location."

DeWitt had been listening to the talk over the Motorola. He read off a series of coordinates to Murdock, who passed them on.

"See you in thirty-two. A parachute red flare would be helpful."

"Can do, Knight One. In thirty-two."

Murdock signed off, told Holt to keep the channel open to receive, and looked out at the gentle Mediterranean. He was glad there was no bad weather.

"Call out, you guys, make some racket. We have thirty minutes to find our last three men. We will not leave anyone behind."

# 11

Murdock took out his night-vision goggles and kept scanning the swells around them. Dark water that looked green in the night viewing. He thought he saw something to the left. No, only a swell that formed a small whitecap on top. Just what they didn't need, a rising sea.

He quartered one area, then another, working all the way around the IBS. The two boats were still tied together.

"We've found a man," the Motorola said. It was DeWitt. "Not sure who it is yet."

Murdock kept looking. Every man in the boat checked harder to find any sign of their two lost men.

"It's Ching," DeWitt said on the radio. "He's got a wound in the upper chest. Not sure how bad it is. We'll stop the bleeding. We still need two men."

"Jaybird and Canzoneri," Murdock said. Both had been on deck of the craft when the shooting started. Sitting ducks. Jaybird had said the ship was a Naval vessel? Franklin said there was all sorts of firepower around, including a 130mm gun and torpedoes. Jaybird had mentioned missile tubes and machine guns.

"Better tell somebody that ship is a Chinese destroyer," DeWitt said. "She's camouflaged, but now her cover is blown."

Murdock used his binoculars and stared the way the Chinese ship had vanished. "If she's a destroyer, she'll be coming back to clean up," Murdock said on the mike. "Let's get those two men."

"The men we've recovered so far have all been ahead of us, down the path of the freighter," Senior Chief Dobler said. "Let's power up and move that way a hundred yards."

Murdock nodded. "Do it. Tell the other boat."

They motored ahead slowly, watching new territory.

"Swimmer to port," somebody called. DeWitt's boat was leading and he powered that way. A moment later he reported.

"We've got Jaybird. Looks like he's got a dislocated shoulder. No gunfire wounds."

"Good. Now let's find Canzoneri."

They kept moving slowly forward. Then a light stick in green glowed just over the swells well ahead of them, vanishing now and then, but soon showing again.

"To starboard, light stick," Murdock shouted. The boats motored that way, losing the light stick, then finding it at the top of the next swell. Murdock's boat got to him first. They dragged Canzoneri into the boat, and then saw that the light stick was jammed in the shoulder section of the combat vest. Canzoneri was not breathing.

Mahanani laid him as flat as they could get him in the craft and did mouth-to-mouth CPR. Three minutes, then four, Mahanani kept it up.

Then Canzoneri heaved upward as vomit and seawater exploded out of his mouth, drenching Mahanani.

"Yeah, you fucker, you can throw up on me any time," Mahanani said. He wiped Canzoneri's mouth, lifted his shoulders a little, and put Canzoneri's head in his lap.

Murdock turned to find Holt. The radioman held out the SAT-COM handset. "You want to make a call?"

Murdock grinned. "How in hell do you do that, Holt?" He took the mike and talked to the chopper coming for them.

"Relay to whoever you can that the Chinese rust-bucket tanker is actually a destroyer in disguise, with full arms, torpedoes, and missile tubes. That's all we saw on our quick tour of the main deck. It's no rust bucket, and should be able to make at least twenty-two knots if it wants to. So far it hasn't come back to finish us. They knew we were coming, which means they have excellent radar."

"Copy, In the Wet. Will forward your report to my CO. Our ETA your last coordinates is fifteen minutes."

"We'll have all sorts of light sticks for your welcome," Murdock said. "No sign of the Chinese warship." He signed off and tried to relax. Half of the Motorolas were not working due to a sudden swim.

"Skipper, Jaybird is in a lot of pain over here," DeWitt said on the box. "Can Mahanani pull an arm back in its shoulder socket?"

Murdock pointed at Mahanani. "Never done it, J.G., but I've seen it done. Want me to come over there?"

"Jaybird says it's worth a try. He says his shoulder can't possibly hurt any more."

"It will for a few seconds. We'll pull the boats together."

Two minutes later, Mahanani stared down at Jaybird, who sat on the bench. "You ready for this, SEAL?"

"Just goddamn do it, or give me a .45 with a round in the chamber."

"I'll do it." Mahanani put his foot in Jaybird's right armpit and took hold of his right wrist with both hands. He had felt the dislocation and figured which way he had to pull. He increased the pressure with his foot, then suddenly pulled out and down.

Jaybird let out a bellow of pain that they must have heard in Athens. "You killed me, you sonofabitch. Why the fuck did you have to do . . ." He stopped. "Hey, the hurt is not as bad, it's fading away."

Jaybird yelped in delight, then faced Mahanani. "Hey, don't you never die, you motherfucker. We need you in this outfit." It was the highest praise one SEAL could give another.

The chopper showed up a quarter of a mile from where the two IBSs bobbed in the Mediterranean, which was now showing routine whitecaps. The big bird did a circle, spotted the half-dozen light sticks, and came in slowly.

Murdock had been on the SATCOM.

"Yeah, funny bird with propeller on top. Come in right over the first boat. We'll try to go up the ladder from the boat. Should work. In any case we dump the boats. They are expendable."

"That's a Roger, Wet Ones. Be right there."

Ed's boatload went first. He had the two wounded. Ching swore at them.

"No sling for me, you shitheads. I can climb the fucking ladder. Done it a thousand times."

"You're shot up, Ching."

"I go first just to show you lowlifes how to do it."

Mahanani had stayed in DeWitt's boat. He signaled to the J.G. that he would be right behind Ching.

The bird came in slowly, positioned directly overhead, and turned on the landing lights. Ching grabbed the trailing wooden and rope ladder, and got his feet on the bottom rung. He was two grabs from the top when his left hand slipped off the rung. Mahanani was a step behind him, and went up beside him and hoisted the 180-pound Ching up the last two steps, where two men in the chopper grabbed him and boosted him inside.

After that it was routine. Jaybird needed help on the last rung. The chopper moved to the second boat. Canzoneri had recovered, and went up the ladder quickly. The rest of Alpha Squad made it inside.

Murdock climbed the rope and rungs as the last man, and at the hatch turned and fired six rounds into each of the two IBSs. They wouldn't sink quickly, but over four or five hours they would take on enough water to sink so low in the water they would be hard to spot.

The hatch swung upward, and the SEALs slumped on the floor of the chopper. The crew chief called Murdock to the cabin, where the pilot gave him a throat mike and earpiece to the radio.

"Yes, sir, Admiral, you heard right. That Chinese rust bucket is a disguised and camouflaged Chinese destroyer. Those panels swing back to show missile-launching tubes, a 130mm cannon, machine guns, and deck torpedoes. That was all our men saw in the short time they had before they aborted our mission and dove overboard. We have one man wounded and another one hurt and we almost lost one man. Yes, I'll talk to the President and tell him the same thing. If those other missiles are on board that Chinese man-of-war, it's going to be damn hard to take a look at them."

Murdock listened on the earphones.

"Yes, sir, we'll be in Athens in about half an hour and we'll be glad to bring our eyewitnesses to a debriefing with anyone you choose. But first I have two wounded I need to take care of. What kind of medical do you have there?"

"Just a small clinic with one doctor," said the admiral. "We often use a hospital in Athens that is excellent."

"Could you have an ambulance waiting for my men? One has been shot in the upper chest. Not critical but serious. Another man was revived from drowning with CPR, and I want his lungs checked over."

"Yes, Commander, we'll have medical waiting, but we request that you put him in the medics' hands and come to our debriefing as soon as you set down. There could be a lot riding on this debriefing."

"My wounded come first, sir. If you can assure me they will be in good hands . . ."

"They will be, Commander. I've seen these doctors in action. The hospital is as good as most in the U.S."

"Fine. As soon as my two men are in that ambulance, we'll come to the debriefing."

"Thank you, Commander."

Murdock handed the mike and earplug back to the pilot.

"Thanks, Lieutenant, for the ride. You held this chopper as steady on our pickup as I've ever seen it done. You do good work."

The pilot slipped on the radio gear and nodded.

"Debriefing in Athens?" DeWitt said. "They want to talk to our men who were on the deck?"

"About the size of it. A pair of admirals have flown in from somewhere, and somebody from NATO. They said they have already brought Kat over from the carrier. Big party."

When the chopper landed, an ambulance was waiting. A doctor checked Ching.

"The bullet that hit him is still inside. We'll need to operate and find it." He listened to Canzoneri's lungs and shook his head. "His lungs don't sound right. He'd better come to the hospital as well. They will be in good hands, Commander, I guarantee."

A bus took the rest of the SEALs and their equipment to a NATO facility where they would be debriefed. Jaybird, Franklin, DeWitt, and Murdock reported to the meeting room as soon as they arrived. They were told not to change clothes or even wash up. Time was vital.

The debriefing went about as Murdock figured it would. The two admirals were joined by a general from Germany and two nuclear experts, as well as Kat from the carrier. The panel of debriefers sounded more like a courts-martial panel. They grilled the two SEALs who had been on the Chinese ship's deck.

Jaybird and Franklin reported what they had seen on board the Chinese ship.

"No, sir, I didn't see any Chinese personnel," Jaybird said. "I did see a machine gun firing at me and four missile-firing tubes. She's a destroyer or a frigate and definitely military."

By noon the debriefing was over. Murdock and DeWitt were

asked to stay, along with Kat, to talk to the debriefing team. A civilian entered the room. He introduced himself as Horner from NEST. Murdock remembered that was for Nuclear Energy Search Team. What was he doing here? That team was called in on a broken arrow, a radiation spill, or a leaking warhead.

Now the tone of the meeting changed. Admiral Tanning spoke first. "We now have intel that shows us almost one hundred percent that five of the six Satan missiles taken from Ukraine are on this Chinese ship which you now claim is a warship. Our problem: How do we confront the ship and the Chinese government? How do we stop and search the ship without causing an international incident? How do we get the missiles out of Chinese hands?"

"Some more information for you," General Archibald said. "We have intel from our people in the Ukraine that the two managers of the secret missile storage area outside Odessa evidently were the traitors who sold the missiles. The price tag was something over seventy million dollars.

"However, both the managers were found shot dead in the warehouse where the missiles were stored before on-loading on the Chinese ship and the Libyan-bound freighter. Traces of nuclear leakage were found on the floor of the warehouse. There was no trace of any payment money, so the Chinese probably faked that or took the money with them."

"So, how do we treat this ship?" Admiral Tanning asked.

Murdock looked around and saw no one ready to comment, so he did. "We treat them the same as we did in Libya. Just because China is already a nuclear power should not make any difference. We committed an act of war against Libya by going in with our military and destroying the remaining warheads that they had purchased on the open market. We felt in the name of international peace we were justified. We should treat the Chinese ship the same."

"Are you suggesting that we attack her, maybe sink her?" General Archibald asked.

"As a last resort," Murdock replied. "There are many ways we can slow, harass, even stop the ship in mid-Mediterranean. One example would be to disable the ship, force it into port for repairs, and then take it over by force. Along that line, SEALs can plant a pair of limpet mines on each side of the hull aft and flood some of the holds. This would require some quick porting."

The admirals and the general looked at each other. "An act of war now could save millions of lives if these warheads went to the wrong parties," Admiral Tanning said. "We realize that. The President and NATO are extremely concerned. If we do anything to that Chinese ship, it will be under NATO auspices, a spread-the-blame procedure."

"What ever happened to the *Cowpens,* that U.S. cruiser that was in Athens when we began this?" DeWitt asked.

"Plans were changed when we found out the Chinese ship was so close to Athens," Murdock said. "Forget to tell you that. I understand that the *Cowpens* is playing a role."

Admiral Tanning nodded. "Indeed. She sailed as soon as we were sure the Chinese ship had the missiles, and has been shadowing her about ten miles off. The *Cowpens* would be a good platform for any SEAL operation, or any other move on the Chinese."

The quizzers talked to Kat then, asking about the type of warheads she had worked on, how they were set up, how she deactivated them, how long it took. And what she suggested they do if they did capture the five remaining missiles with the fifty warheads on board.

Admiral Tanning shook his head. "As for our next step, we don't know. We'll talk with the President within the hour. He will consult with NATO. Anything we do must be authorized by the highest authority, as well as NATO. But this does not mean it will take weeks to happen. I expect that some decision will be made within three or four hours. Until then, we hold fast."

Then the session was over and Murdock tarried, so he could ask Admiral Tanning if he had any orders for him and his platoon.

"No sense your going back to the carrier. We'll have our other carrier in the Mediterranean that's a lot closer come up to this area. In the long run, we may have to push a battle group around the Chinese ship and make her show her true colors or get blown out of the water by any one of fourteen ships or eighty-five aircraft."

He stared at Murdock for a moment. "Commander, I admire what you and your men do. See to your wounded and I'll get orders cut so you remain here on this NATO base until we figure out what to do. That's not going to be long. That Chinese ship could kick up to twenty-five knots and be in the Suez Canal within a day or two. We can't let that happen."

At the temporary quarters the SEALs were assigned, they settled in and cleaned their weapons and oiled them. They always had to clean them well after a dunking in salt water.

Murdock called the hospital where his men were. After several tries with operators, he got one who spoke English and was connected to the nurse who was attending his men.

"Commander, your one man with the lung problem is doing fine. A week's rest here and he'll be good as new. Your other man with the bullet wound . . . He's in surgery right now and the doctor told me, if you called, to urge you to get over here as fast as you can. The operation isn't going well."

Murdock grabbed his clean cammy shirt and pulled it on as he ran out of the officers' quarters looking for some transportation to the Athens hospital. Damnit, he wasn't about to lose Ching.

# 12

## Athens, Greece

The driver of the NATO sedan who took Murdock to the Athens hospital told him the Greek name of the hospital meant mercy. Murdock hoped the name was accurate. He talked to two people at the front desk before he found the English-speaking nurse who had talked to him on the phone. She met him in the lobby and took him to a waiting room just off the operating room.

"Mr. Ching is still in the OR, but the operation should be nearly done. I'll go and check. He has improved since I spoke to you last. One doctor said that they had found several fragments of the bullet, and that no vital organs had been hit; however, there has been serious damage to his upper body and one shard penetrated his left lung. It has been removed, and the lung is back to normal functioning."

"Good. Let me know when I can see him." The nurse nodded and went through a door into the operating room area.

Murdock sat down, and couldn't stop thinking about the Chinese ship. She had to be a destroyer, camouflaged and outfitted to look like a freighter. They must have changed all of the antennas, or fixed them so they could be raised when needed.

He'd seen the book on Chinese destroyers. They were loaded with highly efficient missiles, torpedoes, and all sorts of firepower. He was certain that the admiral would ask him how the SEALs could disable the ship and force it into a nearby port, where the national port authorities could take over, seize the ship, and confiscate the nuclear warheads. Great idea if it worked. It would depend on how much damage the SEALs could inflict.

It couldn't be so much that they would sink the craft. No real chance of that with limpet mines. Just damage her enough to make her go into port. He wished he had a schematic of the ship showing its structure. Somewhere aft would be best. Not the engine room.

He was still trying to work out a plan when a doctor came through the OR doors and walked up to Murdock.

"Your sailor is alive. Getting better. My English poor."

The nurse who had talked to Murdock before hurried up and spoke with the doctor, then translated.

"This is Dr. Arjarack. He was the surgeon who worked on Mr. Ching. He says that all of the metal is removed and Mr. Ching should be fine in two months. No strenuous exercises from now to then. He'll be in the hospital here for a week to watch for infection and any other developments. Then he'll be released."

Murdock thanked the nurse, shook the doctor's hand, and headed back to the NATO compound. The driver and his car were waiting for him in a VIP spot just outside the hospital doors. Nice to have a little clout somewhere.

"So how the fourteen of us gonna knock down a fucking destroyer?" Ostercamp brayed. "We just got our asses kicked out there in the briny deep, don't forget."

"Attention on the deck," Senior Chief Dobler barked, and the SEALs jumped to their feet.

Murdock came in the door and grinned at the regular Navy discipline. It didn't hurt now and then. The SEALs didn't make a habit of it.

"As you were," Murdock said.

"How are the guys?" Jaybird asked.

"Canzoneri should be back in two or three days. Observation. That slug that ripped into Ching shattered and went all over his chest. They think they got all of it, but had to do some cutting. He won't be with us anymore on this mission. In a week or so I'll get him flown back to Balboa Navy Hospital in San Diego."

"So we're down to fourteen," DeWitt said.

"We get a mission yet to take out that destroyer?" Franklin asked.

"Not yet, but we can always plan what we would do, what we can do, and be ready when the word comes down."

"Why not our biggest limpets?" Holt asked.

"Maybe wrap cable around her screws. When she winds in

the last of the cable, there's a contact-bomb attached that blows her screw in half." It was Paul Jefferson's idea.

Murdock looked around. "Only two ideas? Come on, you guys, we need eight or ten."

"Against a fucking destroyer?" Ostercamp asked.

"How about a few RPGs into her bridge?" Khai asked. "That should slow her down and get her into a port for repairs."

"Yeah, but who wants to get within two hundred yards of her in an open boat?" Lampedusa asked.

"How about a sea-skimmer missile from a ship?" Vinnie Van Dyke asked. "They could take out half the warhead so it wouldn't sink the sucker, just blow a hole in her hull."

Senior Chief Dobler had a notebook out, and wrote down each idea as it came along.

"Ed, any suggestions?" Murdock asked.

"How about a Stinger missile?" DeWitt asked. "Hand-held, five feet long, up to three miles of range, and travels at Mach 1. Two-point-two pounds of high explosives with a penetrating design."

"That's a ground-to-air missile," Mahanani said. "Don't you need an IR source for it to lock onto?"

"Not sure," DeWitt said. "The RPG sounds possible, maybe a combo limpet and RPG. What's the best range for an RPG anyway?"

Nobody knew.

"Bradford," Murdock said. "Get on a phone and find out the maximum and best range for the regular RPG."

Bradford ran for the door.

"My guess here is that the President and NATO will give us one shot at getting that rust-bucket destroyer into port," Murdock went on. "If we can't damage her enough, then the Navy's task force with that second carrier will bear down on the Chinese and threaten to blow her out of the water if she doesn't submit to a Greek inspection. She's in Greek territorial waters with all these Greek islands. Then it will be up to the Chinese, to give up the missiles and warheads, or get their ship blasted into compliance without sinking her. Either way they lose."

"Let's hope," DeWitt said. "Anybody hear what's happening in Chad? Has Libya taken over the whole country? Is there any more fighting?"

Mahanani had a small powerful standard-band radio he carried, and he'd been listening to the Armed Forces Radio station.

"Chad at first capitulated," Mahanani said. "But when they heard about the rest of the Libyan warheads being destroyed, they began fighting back again like the other time Libya invaded. Neither side has a huge army, maybe sixty or seventy thousand men. Last I heard, Chad was making slow progress in blowing Libya out of their country."

Dobler came up and talked to Murdock. "We've got bunks for the men and know where the chow hall is. I hear there's some kind of a PX, but we don't have any money so it doesn't matter. Maybe we should let the men get some sleep."

"Good idea, Senior Chief."

"Hey, Chief Dobler, is there any place around here that I can get Internet access?" Fernandez asked. "I want to send a long E-mail back to my wife."

Dobler said he wanted to send a couple himself, and they went off hunting a computer with on-line access.

Murdock checked his watch. It was only 1309. Felt like 2200. It had been a long day and night and day. Sleep. He needed some. He found his quarters and tumbled into the bed. It was a real room with a door and just two single beds. BOQ quarters of some ilk. He didn't fight it or even question it. He just went to sleep.

Murdock woke up at 1635 hungry as a cootie bear. He saw DeWitt sleeping, and left. The officers' mess was not crowded. Murdock saw Admiral Tanning at another table with two men. The admiral nodded, Murdock nodded back. The food was better than he expected. He had his usual after-mission steak dinner, and went back to his quarters and rolled into bed.

## Star of Asia
## In the Aegean Sea

The most difficult work lay ahead.

Chen Takung watched the engineers work with increased respect. It was just past 0800, and with the new day the engineers had removed the nose cone from one of the Satan missiles in the hold. Then the first warhead had been extracted and carefully separated from the rest of the elements.

Now the engineers had to disassemble the receiving elements of the guidance system from the warhead. Chen had never seen one before. It looked like a small rocket to him, with a propulsion system and guidance controls.

The captain of the ship had asked him why they hadn't made

the Ukrainians do this work. Since what they wanted were the warheads, why not simply buy them and not the whole rocket? There were several reasons, but they all had to do with time and secrecy. Chen explained that it would not have been possible to do the breakdown of the missiles and take out the warheads in the missile storage area near Odessa.

Someone would have seen it happening and report. Neither could they take the time in the warehouse at the port to do the same job. It could be done leisurely at sea, the rest of the missile parts and body dumped overboard when the nose cone came off.

Chen checked his watch. Nearly 1400. Their radio communication with the visiting ship had been affirmative. It would rendezvous with the *Star of Asia* promptly at 1500. The first warhead was ready. He had been authorized to sell one missile and one warhead from another missile. The price for the single warhead was the equivalent of ten million dollars U.S.

It was the same boat that had met them two days ago. At that time the sale had been agreed to. Now the ship would bring the payment and take delivery.

Then it would be full speed toward the canal. Chen laughed softly, full speed at ten knots. He still wondered who the attackers had been during the night. His men on the deck said they were dressed in camouflaged uniforms, and had good weapons. Pirates of some ilk, ready to take down a rusted old scow of a freighter?

That was the only scenario he could think of that made sense. They had been scared off quickly. One or two had been wounded or killed. His men had made a mistake by firing too quickly. They should have waited until all of the pirates had been on the deck. None of his men had been scratched.

For a moment he wondered what his reception would be in China. He would be met in port, or perhaps well out in the Gulf of Bo Hai, with a Naval escort. There would be bands and a parade, and perhaps even President Jiang Zhemin himself would be there to pin the medals on him. Oh, yes, what a glorious day that would be.

One more sale, then the ship would head directly for the canal.

He tired of watching the engineers, and returned to the bridge. They were making five knots in a generally southern direction. Never had Chen seen so many islands. They were the Greek

islands, and many of them were populated. It must be a head-
ache to govern. He would rather have his country all in one
piece with water only on one side of it.

"Sir," one of the officers on the bridge said. "We have a ship
coming up from the port side at fourteen knots. She has the
radar appearance of a small freighter. Range is ten thousand
meters."

"Thanks, Commander. You better let your captain know."

Moments later the ship's captain came on the bridge.

"Not visual yet, sir," the commander said. "Range now a little
under ten thousand meters."

"Try a hailing frequency," the captain ordered.

A few minutes later the radio man returned to the bridge.

"Sir, she responded, she's the *Faizabad Roamer*. That's the
same ship we contacted two days ago. She gives you her com-
pliments and says she will be alongside shortly for a transfer of
the package by high line."

The captain shook his head. "It's too choppy out here today
for a high-line transfer. We'll do it with a small launch. Get my
gig over the side at once, Commander."

An hour later the transfer was complete. The warhead had
been cushioned with insulation inside a wooden box, then
swathed with flotation blankets. Next they'd wrapped the box
securely.

The money came over in the captain's gig first; then the warhead went back. The two boats were within a hundred yards of
each other for about fifteen minutes. With the safe transfer, the
two boats turned heading in opposite directions.

Chen nodded. Yes, the last contact with the Western World
before he headed for Mother China. He lit another cigarette and
chain-smoked for an hour. All the time he thought about home,
his wife, and their small son. He would be home soon. Again
he wondered what his reception would be when he returned to
China with forty-nine nuclear warheads. Glorious, it would be
glorious.

# 13

Murdock and DeWitt had been summoned to a meeting at what looked like a corporate boardroom. It was 0720 the morning after their failed attack on the Chinese ship, and Murdock and Ed DeWitt both had been roused from a dead sleep. The oblong table in the large room was of dark wood Murdock figured was something better than mahogany. When they arrived, Admiral Tanning was waiting. So was Don Stroh.

"You boys move faster than I do," Stroh said, "but I always catch up. The admiral needs some input before he makes a decision. Admiral Tanning, I believe you've met these SEALs."

The admiral nodded, and looked up from some papers he held.

"We have a change of direction," he said. "I thought we'd be going for the freighter/destroyer, but not now. Less than an hour ago, a ship approached the Chinese vessel and steamed alongside for some time not a hundred yards from the destroyer. We're not certain, but we think that there was an exchange of some kind between the two. After fifteen minutes the ships parted, going in opposite directions.

"We've had information from our satellite trackers and the AWACS plane in the area, that the smaller freighter is moving along at fourteen knots and heading generally southeast, which would bring it out of the Greek islands and position it for a run through the Mediterranean toward the Arab nations of the Middle East."

Murdock frowned, bringing three deep creases to his forehead.

"So the thinking is that there could have been a transfer of a warhead or two from the Chinese ship to the second one. Do we know the registry of the second ship?"

"No. We're trying to determine that. It may take a flyover by a jet to establish the name."

"So we have a second ship at sea," DeWitt said. "This one probably isn't a destroyer. We could do the same thing we tried to do with the Chinese warship."

"Another chance for a really bad international incident, attacking an innocent ship on the high seas," the admiral said. "Is there a better way?"

He looked up as a Marine came in with a folder. He gave it to the admiral and retreated. Admiral Tanning looked at the papers a moment, then shook his head.

"Changes, gentlemen. The latest word from the AWACS is that the smaller freighter has changed course and is now steaming at fourteen knots back toward Athens."

"Where she could connect with a plane to take a small package with a nuclear warhead to any country in the world," Murdock said. "The new freighter has to be our first priority. We know where the rest of the warheads are. Where could the new one, or two or three, be going?"

"How heavy are those warheads?" DeWitt asked.

The admiral looked up. "Could be anywhere from fifty pounds to three hundred. They could carry three or four in a small boat from the destroyer to the merchantman."

The same Marine came in with more papers. He gave them to the admiral and left.

"Uh-huh. Yes. The AWACS reports that there is a helicopter approaching the small merchantman headed back toward Athens. There is a landing pad on the freighter. If the bird lands, AWACS will tell us and then follow it to wherever it goes."

Don Stroh headed for the door. "I'm getting on my SATCOM and calling my chief and the President. They need to know about this."

"Admiral, can NATO take a squad of men and surround that chopper when it lands?" Murdock asked.

"Not a chance. By the time we told the Greek officials what we wanted to do and had approval, it would be next Thursday. They don't work quickly here, and we have no authority otherwise."

Murdock scowled. "That's bad. Hey, how about a gaggle of civilians, say fourteen, all men, storm that chopper when it lands thinking there is a famous movie actress on board."

"Might work," the admiral said. "You men do a kind of sit-in while I get the Athens airport police to seize the chopper for possible smuggling."

"Time?" Murdock asked.

"The chopper has over a hundred miles to go. Could take him two hours. It's a small civilian bird. Let's get to the PX and get you some clothes. You can change on the way."

A half hour later the fourteen SEALs, in various kinds of civilian clothes and without a weapon among them, headed toward the Athens airport on a NATO bus. The SEAL SATCOM hooked up with the AWACS plane, and it told them precisely where the chopper was about to land, at the far end of the airport near a little-used gate.

The bus charged through a gate that said no admittance, and hurried down a half mile to the chopper. Both arrived at the same time. The SEALs boiled out of the bus and charged the chopper.

Already they could see they were too late. A small pickup truck had been in position where the chopper landed. A large box had been pulled out of the chopper and hoisted into the pickup, which promptly smashed through the back swing-out gate, breaking a lock and slamming open the steel and wire barrier. The pickup raced off down a dirt track and into a light industrial area.

"No way our bus can stay with that light truck," Murdock said, not even breathing hard after the thirty-yard sprint. "Let's grab the pilot and the second man in the chopper for a little informal grilling."

The two men spoke only Greek. By that time airport police had boiled up in a pair of cars, and the police rushed up to the chopper. One of the officers spoke English, the second language of Greece.

"This helicopter landed without clearances," the policeman said. "They will be held and charged. Looks like they also broke the fence. Another charge for that."

By that time another official car had pulled up. It was the airport police chief. Beside him was Admiral Tanning.

"If we'd had our weapons we could have stopped them," Murdock told the admiral.

"Yes. But this isn't our country. I've told the chief the problem. He says he has men watching all air freight areas and all private planes leaving. If they try to fly the box out of here, he will catch them and seize it."

"Lots of luck. It could slip through a hundred different ways," DeWitt said.

"I'm going with the chief while he questions the two chopper pilots," said the admiral. "If they know where the box was heading, we'll find out."

"Anything on the name or registry of the freighter?" Murdock asked.

"Yes, something here, Satellite photo, I think. Here it is. She's the *Faizabad Roamer*. My guess, Panama registered. Seems that ninety percent of all ships are registered there. It's easy, quick, and cheap. No safety regulations."

"Could our men help watch the air freight areas?" DeWitt asked.

The admiral asked the chief something in Greek, and had an answer.

"He said yes. They will give you jackets to wear at the main building. He's sending two of his men along to get you suited up and positioned."

The SEALs spent the next six hours patrolling the air freight areas. They watched shipments being loaded; they checked on the carriers that had loads in place. They all wore jackets with airport security logos, which gave them license to go anywhere.

Once they found a box that seemed familiar. When they checked it, Bradford said it was too big. He lifted one side of it and shook his head. It was bound for New York.

"Whole thing can't weigh more than thirty pounds. Too light."

They kept looking.

Admiral Tanning sat in his car nearby watching and talking on his SATCOM. Murdock checked in with him every hour.

"Might have something, Commander," the admiral said the next time Murdock stopped by. "One of the pilots of that chopper said the word Kabul. The only Kabul I know of is the capital of Afghanistan."

"That is bad news, Admiral. That's where Osama bin Laden had his headquarters for years. I hear he may be moving his operations back there and that he's on good terms with the government there again."

"We ran the name of the ship through our sources, and it came back with a Panamanian registry, but also that it is owned by a shipping company from Afghanistan and with a home port in Jask, Iran."

"Have you checked any aircraft leaving that have filed a flight plan for Afghanistan?"

"Not yet, but I'm about to. Just hope that we're not too late."

Ten minutes later, the admiral honked the horn on his sedan. Murdock ran over to it. The admiral was grim.

"Report just came in. A private transport craft left an hour ago bound for Kabul. It carried over twenty thousand pounds of freight, and all of it had export tags passed by the customs department. I'd say we missed the box with the warhead in it."

An hour later, the SEALs had returned the civilian clothes, put on their cammies, and relaxed in their quarters at the NATO compound. Don Stroh showed up with a SATCOM slung over his shoulder.

"Hey, Stroh, you joining up?" Ron Holt yelled at him.

"Should. I've been spending enough time on this radio. I love it. I can call anyone I want anywhere in the damn world. Where's Murdock?"

"Officer country."

"Right behind you," Murdock said, coming through the door.

"Change of plans," Stroh said. "Came through channels. The admiral wants to talk to you. We're not tracking the plane heading to Kabul. The powers figure that can wait. We need to take down that damn destroyer first."

"Where is it?"

"Still inside the Greek islands and making ten knots."

"How do we stop her?"

"Murdock, my friend, that's up to you and Admiral Tanning. He wants to see you, Ed, and your senior chief right away in his office."

"We're on our horse."

When the SEALs arrived, Admiral Tanning looked grim. "We're back on the damn Chinese freighter/destroyer. I've had this through channels. The President wants your Third Platoon to slow or stop that destroyer. It has to look like an accident, so we can't use any overt military action. What are your ideas?"

"We mentioned limpet mines before, Admiral," Murdock said. "They could be planted covertly. If both were on one side, it could appear as though the ship hit a floating mine left over from World War II."

"A possibility. What other ideas?"

"Sir, one of the men suggested that Stinger missiles might be used. They have a three-mile range, two-point-two pounds of high explosives, and Mach 1 speed," Senior Chief Dobler said.

"No. That's an air-to-ground or air-to-air missile and it's IR-guided," Admiral Tanning said. "No infrarred to latch onto on that destroyer. Anyway, that would make it too much of a military hit."

"If we wanted to board her, we'd need two hundred men and a complete sweep-down by twenty-millimeter rounds by helicopter gunships," DeWitt said. "We know that's one that won't work."

"One of my men suggested we dive and throw a line around her screws," Murdock said. "When the last of the line wraps around the turning screw, it has on the end a bomb that blows off the screw, putting the ship dead in the water."

"That one sounds good," Admiral Tanning said. "What else do you have?"

"We considered RPGs," Murdock said. "But that would put us within two hundred yards of the ship and their radar would undoubtedly pick us up. Such an attack could be blamed on terrorists or maybe modern-day pirates, but the destroyer would have no problem with a small attack like that."

"The President and his advisors didn't say how we were to stop the ship, just that it had to be stopped without the use of any obvious military action," Admiral Tanning said. "Commander, what's your best shot at this job?"

Murdock looked at his two fellow SEALs. "We think it should be the limpets and the bomb on the propeller. Both could be blamed on old mines. We could use some kind of weathered cable, a quarter inch or so, to reinforce the idea that it was an old tied-down mine that broke loose."

The admiral took out a pipe, cleaned it, and put in fresh tobacco. He lit the pipe, then blew out a cloud of blue smoke and waved at the SEALs.

"I'm giving you a go on this, SEALs. It's within the parameters. Then we'll let the top brass figure out what to do with the destroyer once she's dead in the water." The admiral pumped out more smoke. Then he nodded.

"Yeah, I thought of what was bothering me. About two months ago somebody came to us with a larger-sized limpet mine. Twice as big as any I've ever seen. He wanted to put on a demo for us. Had to turn him down, but he left some for us to experiment with. Would you like to take a look at them?"

"Yes, sir."

Twenty minutes later, in the NATO ammo bunker six feet underground, the admiral showed the SEALs the limpet mines.

"Still magnetic and with a simple detonator," the admiral said. "You can take them if you want to."

"Yes, let's use them," DeWitt said. "Two of them on the stern of that destroyer should make an impression on the Chinese mind."

"How many?" Murdock asked.

"We should have two to use and two for backup in case we lose one," Senior Chief Dobler said.

"Then we'll need some TNAZ or some C-4 to make our prop bomb," DeWitt said.

"And the cable," Murdock added. "Something used and old if possible. The Chinese will send divers down to check out a blown-off screw."

"Our top ordnance man here can fix you up with whatever you need," the admiral said. "What's your timing?"

"Have to be at night. It's now almost 1600. Too late for tonight. Is that cruiser *Cowpens* still shadowing the destroyer?"

"Yes."

"We could use her for our launching pad," Murdock said. "Chopper us out there and we push off at first dark. It would help if the cruiser could move in another five miles toward the destroyer just before we launch. We can go in tomorrow night. Give us all day to get set up."

"That sounds good. I'll order the cruiser to move in to five miles from the target tomorrow when you're ready to launch at first dark, and I'll get that Sea Knight authorized and ready. My ordnance man can fix you up with the rest."

"Oh, we'll need two IBSs. The cruiser might not have any."

"That's the small inflatable boats you use. I'll get a pair flown in from somewhere. Talk with ordnance here and get this part worked out. Good luck, Commander."

Back in their quarters at the NATO compound, the SEALs began going over their equipment. Both squads would make the trip. Two boats, four limpets, two as backup.

Heads turned as Kat Garnet walked into the room wearing a trim Navy officer's blouse, jacket, and skirt.

Somebody whistled.

Kat grinned and waved at Murdock. "Hi, guys. I hear that I'm going to be going with you on this limpet-mine attack on the Chinese destroyer."

# 14

Senior Chief Dobler looked up from where he worked on his weapon, and did a double take.

"Say what, Lieutenant? You're going along with us on our limpet hit on the Chinese destroyer?"

"That's what I heard," Kat said. "Do you want to outfit me with gear or wait until it's official?"

"If it's all right with the lieutenant, ma'am, I think we better wait."

Kat grinned. "That's fine, Senior Chief. There isn't any hurry. I'll just talk with the guys. Sorry you got blown off that rust bucket of a freighter that turned out to be a destroyer. Do we know that for sure yet? Maybe it's a frigate."

"Either way we got stomped on good. We didn't expect it, Kat. We were looking for about forty merchant seamen and a pistol and one rifle on board. We got surprised. But we were lucky to get away with just one wounded."

"Ching. How is he?"

"He'll make it, but he's out of action for a couple of months, I'd think." The chief paused. "Kat, you really hear something about going along on our limpet run?"

"Not a chance, Senior Chief," Murdock said as he came up behind Kat. "She's just trying to stir up some trouble. Right, Miss Dressed All Up Garnet?"

Kat laughed and tipped her head from side to side. "Well, it was a quiet day, and I've been bottled up over there in that funny BOQ all day and all night, and I was getting antsy. Okay?"

"Fine by me. Hey, you can come visit us anytime. Brass wants you to hang around here in case we get anymore warheads. Or if we do take down that destroyer and need to do some close disassembly work on the missiles and the warheads."

"Admiral Tanning told me. But for now, what am I supposed to be doing? There's that strange little PX here, but no movie theater, and no library. I'll go crazy in a week."

"Won't be here a week," Murdock said. "Things are moving too fast. Hey, this would be a good time for you to write your memoirs, *My Days As a Navy SEAL*. Should be good for at least a bestseller. That is, if you could get permission from the Navy to publish, which you can't."

"Thanks for the help," Kat said.

"Hang around a while so I can get some things straightened out and I'll take you to dinner."

"Where? Some fancy Greek restaurant downtown?"

"How about the officers' mess?"

"I was afraid of that." She paused. "Yeah, why not?"

An hour later, Murdock picked Kat up at her BOQ. He surprised her.

"Hey, you're dressed all up yourself," Kat said.

He had borrowed some khakis and some insignia and wrangled a sedan and a driver who knew Athens. The driver took them to what he called one of the best restaurants in town. He had even made reservations.

It was sleek and modern and classy. Murdock felt underdressed, but enjoyed himself. He found one waiter who spoke English, and had him order for them. When the waiter left and they tasted their drinks, Kat yelped.

"Hey, I don't have any money. I know you never carry any money on a mission. How are we going to . . ."

Murdock held up his hand. "I borrowed a hundred-dollar bill from Don Stroh. So don't worry."

"Oh, good. I have this dream every once in a while about eating a big meal at a fine restaurant and finding out I lost my billfold and my money and my credit cards. It always ends as I start explaining and the manager is calling the police."

"Not this time. Now, about you. What have you been doing since we met like this before in Iran?"

"Working. But I'm not in disposal anymore. I'm working on how to establish a really safe nuclear waste site. It's a big problem with all the medical hot waste and some from the military and from nuclear power plants."

"How is it going?"

"Mostly NIMBY."

Murdock frowned, trying to remember the word. "What?"

"Mostly the reaction is NIMBY, Not In My Back Yard. We find a great site and the local population vote it down. The government is getting more sensitive to the people's views nowadays."

"So how is your love life?"

"Don't ask."

"But you had been seeing someone."

"None of your business." She frowned. "How did you find out that?"

"Remember, Don Stroh is CIA. He can find out anything about anybody. The President asked him to do a screening on you before he talked to you about the Iran caper."

"Oh, that's what those guys were about. One man kept hanging around. He wasn't very good if he was CIA."

"If you saw him, you were supposed to. That way, if you had anything to hide, you might freak. You didn't."

"What else did Stroh find out about me?"

"Everything. I don't remember the list. He knows what you like to eat, where your favorite restaurant is, what movies you see, your brand of toothpaste, and the color of your underwear."

Kat laughed. "I bet the underwear was a disappointment."

"Stroh didn't say."

The dinner came and they ate. Murdock didn't have the slightest idea what kind of meat it was. He was afraid to ask. The vegetables and the salad and the dessert were all delicious.

They lingered over another bottle of wine, and Kat said she hated to leave.

"You'll need a good night's sleep for your jaunt tomorrow," Murdock said.

"What? You said I wasn't going on the mission."

"You're not. One of the NATO officers' wives has arranged to take you on a sightseeing and shopping tour tomorrow. It will last all day and then you'll go to a stage play or an opera, she wasn't sure which."

"Great, no money."

Murdock shoved a new one-hundred-dollar bill across the table to her.

"You can go a little wild, because Stroh is good for another tap. He says it's expense money, so use it in good health."

Kat's brown eyes glistened for a moment until she brushed away the moisture. She shook her short brown hair and leaned

over to kiss his cheek. "I think you guys are trying to spoil me."
She frowned. "Either that or you're softening me up for tonight
when you try to take advantage of me."

"Nice try, SEAL. Good defensive move. An attack is always
the best defense. Keep up the good work." She stared at him,
scowling. Then gradually the look eased and turned into a smile.
A moment later they both laughed.

"Hey, we better get out of here," Kat said. "You have to work
tomorrow."

At the sedan they found their driver finishing a Greek take-
out dinner and a large container of Coke. He put it all away,
held the door open for Kat, and drove them back to the NATO
headquarters in Greece.

At the door of the BOQ, Kat paused. "You know, I'm the
only person in this wing. Six rooms and all vacant except mine."
Kat reached up, caught Murdock's face with both her hands,
and kissed him on the lips. It lingered and then kept going. She
moved away and took a long breath.

"Oh, my," she said. "I really hadn't planned on doing that.
But I'm glad I did." She smiled. "One more?" The kiss was
more intense this time, with their mouths opening and tongues
working. Murdock was the first to ease away this time.

"I think you better get yourself into your room. It's that Greek
wine, I think."

"Really? Next time I'll get two bottles." She smiled, touched
his face with her hand, then eased through the door and closed
it.

Murdock stood there a minute. No, he told himself. He had
a commitment and he was standing by it. He had a lady back
in Washington, D.C. One lady was plenty for him.

The next morning was a whirl as the SEALs drew the ordnance
they needed, including the four large limpet mines and explosives and more rounds for their personal weapons. The two IBSs
were flown in from the closest carrier task force and dropped
off at the NATO compound.

Dobler checked them both to be sure they were working properly, then deflated them and checked for new canisters to inflate.
When all was right, he marked them off his list.

Kat swung by in her sedan that morning on the way to her
shopping trip. She wore her Navy uniform, and wished the
whole platoon good luck. She had taken special care with her

hair and makeup and looked delicious, Murdock decided. He walked her back to her car.

"You okay?" he asked.

She nodded, but didn't look at him. Then she turned. "Last night I wasn't drunk when I asked you to come inside. I was lonely and overwhelmed by your charm and your delightful body and I wanted you. I'm not sorry. Yes, I remembered about Ardith Manchester back in D.C. But I took a chance. So, still friends?"

"Absolutely. I shouldn't tell you how close you came to getting your wish. Now, get out there and be a tourist, view and sightsee and shop. Go."

She laughed, and ran for the sedan. He watched it head for the main gate.

The SEALs had an early lunch, and flew off the base at 1320 for their two-hour ride in the Sea Knight. Most of them slept on the trip. Senior Chief Dobler read a war paperback. Murdock thought about the mission. It was a no-see mission. They would have to be careful attaching to the destroyer this time. They would have to come in ahead of it, power their boats over to it, and with small hand magnets hold their place on the side of the ship until they could get the limpets attached and the timers set.

Working on the screws would be more difficult. They would have one or two tries at each of the destroyer's two shafts. Even if they could get clamped on to the very end of the destroyer, it would be a tough throw to get the light line that was attached to the cable into the area where the propeller was sucking in water before it blasted it out to the rear.

At ten knots it wouldn't be such a task as it would be at thirty knots. Murdock worked it over and over in his mind. He didn't have any better plan by the time they landed on the cruiser *Cowpens*. He decided not to send a swimmer under the hull with the cable and bomb. There was a big chance the swimmer would be sucked into the propeller blades and be chopped to pieces.

Murdock knew the mission had the highest priority when the XO of the *Cowpens* met them at the chopper pad.

"I'm Marshall," the commander said, holding out his hand to Murdock, who was first off the helicopter. "Captain Casper wants you to know that this ship is yours. Anything you want, you get. It isn't often we get a direct order from the CNO."

"Murdock," the SEAL said, taking the other man's hand. "We

won't need much. Just want to be seven miles ahead of that Chinese destroyer just after dark. That way you should be able to stay out of his radar pattern and still get us in position."

"No problem. Let's get your men off here and into some quarters. We'll feed you before you go. I see you have the IBSs. We can launch you off the fantail and put the men down on ropes. You have some ordnance?"

"Yes, heavy limpets. They can be stowed close by."

Murdock had already assigned the attack teams. The IBSs would be tied together with a sixty-foot line. He again went over in his mind the assignments and how it would work.

The SEALs gathered in an empty compartment amidships and Murdock rehearsed the actions again. Four men had the limpets as their duties, and four more would work the propeller throw, two on each shaft.

"You other six men will be security. Watch the rail for any kind of action. Listen for any whistles or shouts from above. I don't think they can detect the magnets on this rusty outside hull, but they just might have some sort of device to measure the jolt."

They had chow at 1700, then cammoed their faces with black, green, and blue greasepaint, and went up to the helicopter launch pad at 1800. It was just starting to go dusk. The men wore their jungle cammies and floppy hats. A short time later the cruiser took a 45-degree turn to the left.

"We're moving closer to the destroyer," Murdock told the men. "We should be seven miles ahead of it. The cruiser will drop us off on the direct course of the destroyer. All we have to do is lay low and let the big bucket come to us. Then we motor up to her, clamp on our magnets, and lash up.

"The first boat has the limpets, the second the prop men. That line connecting us should be sixty feet long. First boat latches on about fifty feet from the bow and plants the limpets there. If you have time, attach three of them.

"Second boat, we latch on as close to the stern as possible. We'll try throwing our lines under the end of the boat. It's going to be tougher than I had figured. We try until we loose the last of our six lines.

"We'll use the Motorola. Give me a call, Ed, when you're done. But don't detach until you get the word."

A short time later the XO appeared. "We're on course and should be seven miles ahead of the Chinese ship in two minutes.

We'll cut power and let you off directly on the destroyer's course. Your men can go down rope ladders?"

"Yes, sir."

"Fine. As soon as we cut power, we'll drop the tethered IBSs over the fantail. Good luck, SEALs."

Two minutes later the big ship cut power and slowed in its forward progress. Another minute and the XO pointed, and sailors put the IBSs over the fantail so they would trail the ship. The crew snugged the IBSs up tight against the back of the ship and dropped rope ladders down. The SEALs went into the boats by squads, with the officers last to go down the ladders.

"Bravo Squad, you ready to cast off?" Murdock asked.

"Motor started and ready," DeWitt said.

Murdock nodded to Lampedusa, who started the motor on Alpha Squad's small boat.

"Cast off," Murdock said, and the two small boats coasted away from the slowly moving cruiser. A minute later the cruiser powered up and moved to the side to get back in a ten-mile tracking position.

"We hang around right here and see what shows up," Murdock said. "We have that sixty-foot tether binding us together?"

"On here," Lam said.

"Tether on," DeWitt said.

"So, we dick around here for a while," Murdock said. "At ten knots it should take that Chinese destroyer thirty to forty minutes to come to us. Each boat needs a lookout."

They waited. There were almost no waves, just a gentle swell that lifted them about four feet and then lowered them again. Mahanani called in.

"Hey, Skipper. I figure we have a current running here of about four knots almost at right angles to that destroyer's course. Shove us a lot farther than it will that big junk pile."

"Roger that, Mahanani. He's coming SSW at us, so we need to do about two miles at a right angle to that. Let's try it now and wait. We should be able to see his lights at three or four miles. We've been waiting for ten minutes now."

Lampedusa called to his CO. "Skipper, we have a problem back here. Somewhere we have a ripped panel. I can hear air hissing out, then it bubbles, and then hisses. The boat must have snagged on something when they launched it off the cruiser."

# 15

Murdock moved to the side of the IBS where Lampedusa sat.

"A leak? No lie, Lam? Where?"

"Not sure, Skipper. Listen, you can hear it." The men in the boat stopped whispering and listened.

"Yeah, I heard a hiss and then bubbles," said Murdock, "so it's somewhere on the side or bottom, and we can't get to it for repairs."

"We going down?" Van Dyke asked.

"Hell, no. These little boats are built in something like fifteen to twenty compartments, airtight compartments. They simply won't sink. Remember how they never really collapse all the way? That's so one lucky rifle shot into an IBS won't sink it. She has a lot of other watertights to hold her up. So, no sweat. We continue on as usual. Anybody see any lights yet?"

No one responded. Murdock checked his watch. They had motored at a right angle to the path of the destroyer. That should take care of the current drift. Almost no wind to deal with.

Ten minutes later they spotted lights moving toward them.

"She's still two miles off and I can see some of her side lights, so we're not on her line of travel," Lam said.

"We'll wait until we're closer to move up," Murdock said.

"I'd say we're a quarter of a mile off her course," DeWitt said on the Motorola.

"Should be. Ed, you ready?"

"All set soon as she comes up to us. No way they can have radar that can find us. Important point is, they won't be looking for something this small."

They waited.

"Holt, crank up the SATCOM," Murdock said. Holt had to hold the antenna. The small dish might not be stable enough in the tiny boat, which bobbed around in the light sea. It could have trouble holding onto the satellites.

Murdock took the handset and used voice.

"Sardine, this is Floater, come in."

No response.

He had to make the transmission four times before he had a return call.

"Breaking up, Floater. Try again."

"Sardine, the can approaches. We'll make contact in ten. Call you when we're done and give you our coordinates. Over."

"Read you. Soon as you're done you contact Sardine. We'll figure out what to do then. Roger."

"Button it up, Holt. Keep the spray out of it. We can't afford a breakdown on our commo gear."

"We better choggie in on her," DeWitt said. "Near a half mile off her course and a mile upstream. Pick up our speed to ten?"

"That's a Roger, DeWitt. We're right behind you."

The little rubber boats moved quicker through the silent sea then as they angled toward the destroyer, which they could see now with navigation lights all on and glowing.

A short time later the radio came on again. "Cutting throttle," DeWitt said on the radio. "Estimate we're about fifty yards off their course and we're still a quarter of a mile ahead of her. Be here shortly. We latch on sixty feet from the bow, you hit the stern. Right?"

"Right," Murdock said. "Tell us when you power forward to meet your buddy."

Murdock checked. The six lines and cables were laid out across the back of the IBS. Ready for throwing. The more he thought of it, the worse his job sounded. He had no idea how far the screws were from the stern of the ship. He had no idea how far underwater they were, two feet or fifteen feet.

"Now, we're powering up," DeWitt said. The tether cord tightened; then the second IBS moved ahead. The big ship lunged at them through the sea. It looked huge from this viewpoint. They were fifty feet off the course line and the ship was coming toward them. DeWitt moved his boat faster, then worked through the slight bow wave and contacted the big ship. He bounced off, then came back again, matching speed with the freighter/destroyer.

Then Khai planted one magnet against the massive hull, and it held. He tightened up the cinch line, and the boat was latched to the Chinese craft. At once Mahanani moved to the side with the extra-large limpet mine, and let the strong magnet pull it against the side of the ship.

Ostercamp placed the second one two feet away, and Jefferson attached the third one. Immediately the men moved the fusing system to On, and waited for DeWitt to call the time to program the detonator to set off the high explosive.

The big limpets were set two feet above the waterline. With any luck they would blow a hole big enough to let water pour into the hull.

On the other boat, Murdock saw DeWitt attach his boat. Murdock cut power and let the tether line swing him around until he touched the big ship gently. Will Dobler attached a magnet to the boat, and latched it to the line that ran around the top of the IBS.

"Now," Murdock said.

Bradford had the first line and cable in hand with the charge set on the end of it. He threw it down into the water at the side of the big ship with the hope that it would swing under the boat and be sucked into the powerful pull of the screws.

Bradford threw three of them, and then Van Dyke threw the last three. They heard nothing.

"Done here," DeWitt said softly into the mike.

"Done here," Murdock said. "Cast off." Both boats snapped loose the lines that held them to the big boat, and it jumped away from them as it slanted past at ten knots. The SEALS all crouched low in their boats as the big ship plowed ahead. Any watch on the stern would have an impossible job to try to spot the SEALs or their boats in the dark water and the blackness of the moonless night.

Murdock waited until the sound of the big ship faded. Then he called DeWitt.

"I could use some Mugger coordinates, Mr. DeWitt."

"Roger that, Captain. Be a shake. Yes. Now I have them."

"Hold until I get that cruiser."

The second call produced an answer, and Murdock gave the cruiser the coordinates where they bobbed along in the Mediterranean Sea on a three-knot current.

"How long?" Murdock asked on the SATCOM.

"How long did you set those fuses for?"

"Fuses set for fifteen minutes. That's another six minutes to the blasts," DeWitt told Murdock, who repeated it into the SAT-COM.

"Let us know when they go off and we'll start moving your way. His radar can nail us as soon as we come over the horizon."

"Roger. We're not going anywhere. We have a three-knot drift to the SSE."

"We hear you."

They waited.

"Two minutes," DeWitt said.

Almost at the same time a brilliant flash erupted in the darkness in the direction the Chinese ship had sailed. Then another one and a third one on top of it. A glow showed in the night sky for ten or fifteen seconds. Then it died.

"Three big bangs," Murdock said on the SATCOM mike.

"He's not much more than three miles from you," the man on the cruiser said. "Suggest you rev up your engines and motor away from him at your top speed. We need at least seven miles to be on the safe side."

"That's a Roger, Sardine. We can do eighteen knots. Give us twenty minutes and we'll be six miles more to the NNW."

"Understand. Twenty minutes. We have heard no distress call from the Chinese. Nothing on the international hailing frequency or any SOS. You didn't sink her, did you?"

"Not a chance. They are playing it cagey, as I would. See you in twenty."

Later Murdock checked his watch. It was almost two hours before they saw the cruiser bear down on them. The SEALs had out light sticks so she wouldn't run them down. They had made three more Mugger location checks. Now the small boats powered up, and moved to the fantail of the cruiser and tied up to lines.

Jaybird bleated in pain as he went up the rope ladder to the chopper landing pad. Lampedusa helped him up the last three rungs.

"We need a corpsman over here," Lam called out.

"I'm fine," Jaybird said.

"Yeah, I always carry you up a rope ladder," Lam said, and kept Jaybird on the deck until two corpsmen hurried up. They talked to him a minute, helped him stand, and hustled him down to the ship's sick bay.

"On the chopper," Murdock bellowed. "We'll leave the IBSs for seed. We might be back."

The XO was there before they finished loading. Murdock waved at him. "Commander, one of the IBSs has a leak in one of the chambers," said Murdock. "Can you have it repaired?"

The commander nodded, and Murdock stepped on board the chopper and the crew chief closed the hatch.

This time all of the SEALs slept on the two-and-a-half-hour ride back to Athens.

The last time Murdock checked, the cruiser's radio had still not picked up any kind of distress call from the Chinese ship.

It was 0240 when Murdock and his charges, less Jaybird, stepped off the NATO bus in front of their quarters. Don Stroh came out of a sedan grinning.

"Shit a bucket full of cookies, you boys have done it again."

"What?" Murdock said, jolting himself fully awake. "The cruiser didn't hear any distress calls."

"True, neither did anyone else in the Med. But our AWACS plane shows that the *Star of Asia* is now dead in the water, and has been for the past three hours. That old tub ain't going nowhere. Now all she has to do is ask for assistance and we can board her and take over, get the damn warheads, and then tow her into port."

"You wish. Her captain won't allow a boarding party within ten miles. He'll break out his big guns and challenge you."

"Challenge the whole damn 14th Fleet task force now steaming within eighty miles of his position?"

"Hell, yes. What does he have to lose? He's stopped, but he isn't done. He's within chopper distance of Athens and lots of places. Choppers can pack a dozen warheads a trip."

"Oh, damn, I didn't think of that. So we shoot down the choppers. It was an accident."

"Hard sell on the international news scene. Hey, your problem. Our work is done. Now I'm trying to decide if I should get breakfast or a shower, or just drop into my bunk and sleep for twelve."

"I'd suggest the bunk first. The brass has been up all night working on this. They have firm intel that the plane that left here with the warheads has landed in Afghanistan. If I'm any gauge of what comes next, it's that the President and my boss will both want you and your men to get into Afghanistan and blow that nuclear warhead into tiny, tiny pieces that nobody can put back together again."

"Not even Humpty-Dumpty?"

"Especially not him."

The SEALs dragged themselves off the bus and grouped around Murdock.

"So, did we nail that bastard?" Ron Holt asked.

"We did. He's dead in the water, not going anywhere. But he won't put out a distress call. Which I can understand. He's probably waiting for some kind of instructions from his furious friends in Beijing. Now, hit the sack. In seven hours we go see what the top dogs want us to go bark at next."

"Seven hours? Damn generous of them. I just voted for the sack. I may not even take my shoes off."

Murdock didn't have time to. The moment he opened the door to his small two-man room he sensed somebody else was there.

"Well, its about time you got back. Afraid I dozed off there for a minute waiting for you."

Murdock laughed. What else could happen today? He held out his hand to the middle-aged man who stood up from his bunk.

"Hi, Dad, how is everything back in D.C., and how in hell did you find me this time?"

# 16

## Star of Asia
## In the Greek Islands

Chen Takung was in the Combat Direction Center talking to the radar operators about a mysterious ship that had been appearing on and off the screens for the past two days.

"Sometimes it looks like an American cruiser," the technician said. "Other times it fades away. Sir, if we could put up our top antennas, we could get a complete surface scan and a much better picture."

"We can't do that. Your job is to keep a log on this mystery ship," Chen said. "I want a detailed record of when it appears and how far away it is."

At that moment the 511-foot ship jolted to the left, pitching Chen against the radar operator, dumping both of them to the floor. They came up on their hands and knees. Then the next explosion smashed them to the left again, against the stools in front of the various screens.

The third detonation came, but this time Chen grabbed hold of the console base and rode out the leftward surge.

An alarm bell sounded as the ship heeled over to a ten-percent list to the left.

A speaker over Chen's head began spitting out commands.

"Battle stations. Battle stations."

"I want a damage report now," an officer shouted into his microphone. "Where have we been hit? Damage control, come in, damage control."

Chen surged to his feet and out of the combat center, and onto the bridge. The ship's captain was already there.

"We've been hit at the waterline in section fourteen. That's

115

about a third of the way back from the bow. We're taking on water and have sealed off three compartments."

"The missiles are forward of that point?" Chen asked.

"Yes, they have not been harmed. We are attempting a complete damage assessment. We have cut our forward speed to three knots."

The Chinese Navy captain stared hard at this civilian he had to take orders from. It rankled him, but he was Navy and would obey his orders. "Sir, I suggest that we fully extend two of our radar antenna so we can do a complete surface search. We need to know who is out there and who might have fired a torpedo or missile at us."

"Denied. We don't want to give away our real identity until we have to, if we indeed must at some point do that. It wasn't a missile that hit us. It came in too low, so it had to be a torpedo or a mine of some kind. Weren't there a lot of mines planted here in World War II and never recovered?"

"Yes, sir. A continuing drive to find and destroy them has been highly successful. Most of the usual shipping channels are now free of these mines. But a few break off now and then. Haven't heard of any problems with them for six months."

"Can you put a diver down to be sure it was a mine?"

"Yes, right away."

"For just a moment Chen wondered if this was an attack by the same forces that had hassled the chopper transfer of the package from the freighter to the helicopter and then into the Athens airport. How could anyone know? He had silenced the only two men he had worked with at the source.

Chen went down to the rail over the damaged area and watched. The captain had sent down men on lines to assess the damage. One reported on a handheld radio.

"Captain, we have what looks like three holes blasted into the outer skin and then through the hull plates and into the hold. Two of the explosions meet to form the most dangerous hole. Not enough penetration damage to be a torpedo."

"A mine, or three mines did it?" the captain asked on his handheld radio.

"Yes, sir, mines. The damage extends below our waterline. An engineer with me says he'd be against any forward motion of more than five knots."

"Five knots?" Chen exploded. "At that rate it will take us months to get home."

"We can go back to Athens, find a dock, and have emergency plates welded over the holes, then pump out the water and repair what interior damage we can."

"Then can we make twenty knots?" Chen asked.

"Possibly. But we could run into trouble in port if the authorities insist on an inspection."

"We are violating no international or maritime law by masquerading as a merchantman," Chen said. He frowned at the sea, and for the first time sensed that the whole mission could be in jeopardy.

"How long on the missiles?" Chen asked.

"Our special engineers are working around the clock. So far we have the warheads separated from one of the missiles and the warheads prepared for shipment. They will need another week to complete the work."

"We don't have a week, Captain. Have the engineers pull the warheads out of the missiles. Tell them not to detach them from their rocket motors or their internal guidance systems. They will make a larger package that way, but still be workable. Get the emptied ICBM bodies out the loading hatch and overboard as soon as possible. We can hide the warheads if we must make a port. See how quickly the task can be done.

"During this time attempt exterior damage repair with welders over the side. We'll turn and head back for Athens at four or five knots, whatever is practical."

"Aye, aye. It will be done." The captain hesitated. "You said you had a fallback plan."

"Not yet. We aren't out of options yet. Anyway, for the other plan, all of the warheads would have to be stripped of all rockets and guidance systems. We may not have time for that. Captain, let's get moving with those engineers and turn the ship around for Athens."

## NATO compound
## Athens, Greece

"Blake, good to see you too. Yes, I'm fine and your mother is fine and Ardith sends her love. Now, how the hell is this floating nuclear warhead salesroom problem coming along?"

Murdock grinned as he looked at his father, Charles Fitzhugh Murdock, ranking Congressman from the great state of Virginia.

"About the same," Murdock replied. "Dead in the water. We don't know what they'll do next. Did they tell you, it's a camouflaged five-hundred-foot destroyer of the Chinese Navy?"

"I heard that, yes. How did you let that one shipment of warheads get away to Afghanistan?"

"Sloppy work, I guess. How is Mom?"

"She's fine, and busy. Well, not all that fine. We have her on some new arthritis medicine that seems to be helping. But she's still working six to eight hours a day on her charity circuit."

"Come on now, Dad. Tell me how you found me."

"Easy. I called Don Stroh. He still owes me a few favors."

"That's cheating," Murdock said, grinning. "I just wish I knew what kind of blackmail you have on Stroh. I could use it sometimes."

"On the House National Security Committee we do have some clout. Then, too, I play some golf with Stroh's boss at the Agency. One hand washes the other, you might say."

"You must be here on a Congressional jaunt of some kind. Are we taxpayers getting our money's worth out of this one, Dad?"

"Most certainly are. These warheads are a prime concern of the National Security Committee. We also advise the National Security Council in the White House. We want to be sure that this threat of nuclear blackmail is snuffed in the bud as fast as we can get the job done."

"Now you're even sounding like a Congressman, Dad. How long will you be here?"

"A couple of days. Came with two on my committee and three from the Senate Armed Forces Committee. We're tremendously concerned."

"So are we. We took care of the nine warheads in Libya. Now we've got fifty more to worry about."

"You busy? Let's go have dinner. I've been in Athens before and can show you an authentic Greek restaurant I think you'll like."

"Dinner? Dad, do you know what time it is?"

"Nope. My day clock is a bit disoriented after the long flight. Is it still dark outside?"

"It usually is at three A.M. I've got an 0930 meeting, which is about six hours from now. That's exactly the amount of sleep I hope to get before I have to go talk with the admiral."

"Yes. I understand deadlines. You need your sleep. I'll catch a nap. We'll talk tomorrow."

Murdock found his father an empty room, and the man

dropped off to sleep before Blake had the door closed. The SEAL took off his shoes and shirt, then dropped into his bunk and slept.

The next morning, Murdock had a farmer's breakfast, then made it to the meeting at the admiral's office ten minutes early. He hadn't seen his father. He shouldn't have worried. His father was already talking with Admiral Tanning.

The meeting started precisely on time.

"Gentlemen, we have with us as an observer, Congressman Charles Murdock, who just happens to be Commander Murdock's father, and also a ranking member of the House National Security Committee. Let's proceed. The photos."

An officer brought in grainy $8 \times 10$ photos of the side of a ship.

"This is the Chinese ship. She has three holes in her hull well toward the bow. Right now she's dead in the water. This morning we have a new report from our AWACS plane. She has lifted her masts and antenna and is no longer trying to hide as a freighter. We don't know what that means."

"Is she still dead in the water, Admiral?"

"No, she's making about five knots, and evidently is heading back toward Athens. We don't know why."

The admiral looked around the room. "Mr. Murdock. Evidently blowing off the screws did not work."

"No, sir. Not when the ship kept moving at ten knots. Too dangerous."

"What's our next step?" the admiral asked.

General Archibald, who had been in on the first debriefing, was back again. He peaked his fingers, then ran them through his graying hair. "We watch her, of course. Can we challenge any ship that attempts to contact her to pick up a package?"

"We can, but international laws would be violated," Admiral Tanning said. "We're on the open sea here, even if it is in the Greek islands. Tricky on the legal angle."

"Couldn't we simply refuse to allow any helicopter to land on her deck?" Murdock asked.

"We have the choppers to chase them away, but that's another act of war," Admiral Tanning said. "If we do that we might as well go in with all of our assets and blow that destroyer out of the water. The international fallout would be the same."

"They must not be ready to make a move yet," Murdock said. "It takes some time to rip those nose cones off and take out the warheads and detach them from their rockets and guidance systems. That's what they want, just the rawboned warheads."

"How much time would that take?" Congressman Murdock asked.

"Depends how many engineers they have who know how to do it."

They all looked at the admiral. He had the most clout of anyone present. Don Stroh coughed. The Congressman cleared his throat. Ed DeWitt stifled a yawn.

"We've talked a lot about what we can't do," the admiral said. "Who has a suggestion what we should do?"

"Sir," Murdock said. The admiral looked at him. "I suggest we put a twenty-mile-diameter picket fence around that ship. Move when it moves. Use four destroyers with choppers to monitor the area. If a strange chopper comes toward the Chinese destroyer, it will be turned back by firing across its bow if necessary."

The admiral lit his pipe and puffed a moment. No one else said a word. "Yes, it should work. A minor international violation of airspace, and almost impossible to prove. Yes, I like it. That task force is within hailing distance of the area. I'll get four destroyers headed over there. In the meantime we'll have the AWACS folks warn us of any choppers approaching, and the cruiser *Cowpens* now on station can launch its chopper and warn them away. Yes. I'd say we're done here."

Everyone but the admiral stood. "You're dismissed. Oh, Congressman and Commander Murdock, would you both stay a moment?"

When the others had left, the admiral cleaned out his pipe and put it away. "I'd like both of you to be my guests for lunch. There's a great little restaurant in town I think you'll like." He paused. "Commander, you better have your men rest up. There is something cooking that may boil over any moment. I think it has to do with Kabul, Afghanistan. I'll send a car to pick you up at 1130."

Back in the quarters where the men had left their equipment, and now worked over cleaning and oiling it, Murdock talked with his father.

He called the cruiser and found out that Jaybird was cleared for duty by the medics and screeching at everyone to get him back to Athens. Murdock called Stroh, who authorized a chopper ride for Jaybird. He'd be back in the platoon by three that afternoon.

"Now," Murdock said, looking at his father. "What is Ardith up to since I'm not there to watch her?"

"She's doing just fine. Ardith told me to tell you that she's had two more job offers. She calls them positions. Big steps up the ladder, but they are in D.C. She says she hasn't said yes or no and wants to talk with you first."

"That woman is going to drive me out of the Navy yet."

"Couldn't happen at a better time. The Twenty-first District in Virginia is opening up for a special election next June. Crawford is resigning. He's not in good health and says he can wrap up his projects by May. Since a slot has to be open before a special can be held, it will be in June. You could move into that district and run."

Murdock laughed. "Dad, I'm not a politician. I don't even know what diplomatic means. I take direct action. Couldn't you just see me putting a stranglehold on some Congressman right on the House floor until he voted my way?"

They both laughed. The Congressman went serious first. "You think about it, Blake. Might not be a chance like this for several more years."

"I'll think about it. But first I have forty-nine nuclear warheads to worry about, and some of them probably are in Afghanistan right now. My guess is that we'll be on our way over there within twenty-four hours. One big drawback: Only one of my men speaks Persian, nobody knows Pashto."

# 17

"There is no good way to get into Afghanistan," Murdock said as he faced the gathering in Admiral Tanning's office in NATO headquarters in Athens at a 1600 meeting. "The country is landlocked, so we can't swim in. She's in the middle of unfriendly countries. Commercial air might work for three or four of us, but not fourteen."

"So you parachute in," General Archibald said. "Do that long free fall and get down quickly."

"Say it works," Ed DeWitt said. "How in hell do we get out?"

"And whose airspace do we violate flying in there?" Murdock asked. "You have your choice of Pakistan, China, or Iran. None the most friendly."

"How about the Russian breakoff nations to the north of Afghanistan?" Admiral Tanning asked. "That would be Turkmenistan, Uzbekistan, and Tajikistan. Yes, I just looked them up on the map. Would they be more friendly for an overflight?"

"We're not on the best of terms with the three," General Archibald said.

"Where does that leave us?" the admiral asked.

"At thirty-three thousand feet over Pakistan," Murdock said. "That sounds like the best we can do."

"The President wants you to take the lady nuclear warhead specialist along with you, Commander," the admiral said. "Is that going to be a problem? Does she parachute?"

"With all respect, Admiral, I don't see how we can take her. She can parachute, but we have no exfiltration route. We'd have to play it by ear and we could lose half our men. We can blow up a few nuclear warheads when we find them."

Don Stroh coughed and got some attention. " 'Find them' are the key words here, gentlemen. Afghanistan is almost as big as

Texas. Lots of places to hide. We damn well better know where those warheads are before we drop in on that country."

"How?" Murdock asked.

"The Company has some friends left in Kabul. My suggestion is that we talk with them, then we drop in two men to check out the information, and if it's good and we can find the location of any warheads, then we send in the platoon to take the place down."

"So that gives us some time for Kat to train four of us how to blow up a nuclear warhead without scattering the radiation over half a country," DeWitt said.

"Not a lot of time," Stroh said. "We've had our man in Kabul looking for that plane and where the goods went ever since we knew the warheads were going that way. He's making progress. Actually, the agent there is a woman and extremely good at her job. She has a tentative, but nothing firm. She says within twenty-four she should be able to nail it down for sure."

"I'll go in," Murdock said.

Stroh shook his head. "You're too damn big. Should be the smallest men you have, especially if any speak Farsi, Arabic, or the two crazy Afghanistan languages.

"Franklin and Khai," Murdock said. "Both speak Arabic and Franklin has Farsi."

"What ships do we have in the Arabian Sea right below Pakistan?" General Archibald asked.

Admiral pointed to one of his men in the room. "Find out," he ordered. The man left at once.

"Do we still have landing rights at Muscat City in Oman?" Murdock asked. "Used it during the Gulf situation. Might be a spot we could take off with a high-flying plane."

"Once you fly to the Pakistan border you'd have three hundred miles due north to Afghanistan," Admiral Tanning said. "Anybody know what kind of air defense Pakistan has? Then what about Afghanistan? Do they even have an air force?"

"We've got some homework to do," Stroh said. "I'll get on the horn and ask the home office about the fighter capability of those two countries."

"Why not send our two men in on commercial air?" Murdock asked. "Stroh can get them travel papers, local documents, everything they need. Money and a fake company they work for. His meat. Then they meet his lady inside and find the nukes. Maybe the two of them can blow up the warheads and fly out.

Be a lot simpler that way. We can give them the skin color they need and they go in as Arabs looking for business."

"That sounds best," Admiral Tanning said. "I'll call my people and the President. Stroh, you get with your boss. Let's get busy. Oh, Commander. You might have Kat show your two men the best way to blow up a nuclear warhead with the least fallout."

"That's a Roger, sir."

A half hour later, Murdock couldn't help but grin.

"I don't like it at all, Murdock," said Kat. "How can I teach these two men in a few hours what should take weeks to learn? Sure, I can draw them some pictures and show them where to put the charges, but there's more to it than that."

"First we have to find the damn warheads," Murdock said. "I don't trust the CIA too much, especially in Afghanistan, where they have had a miserable record. There's a good chance those warheads are deep in a cave out in the desert somewhere and Osama bin Laden is sitting around his campfire chuckling, wondering how he can use the greatest of all terrorist weapons."

"Damnit, I still want to go."

"None of us might be going. We just have to wait and see. In the meantime, you take Khai and Franklin and teach them as much as you can about this kind of warhead, what they can do and shouldn't do, and keep it simple."

"I still don't like it." Her eyes flashed and her fists settled in on her hips.

"Join the club. Say you were in the middle of Afghanistan in the desert. It's a hundred and fifteen in the shade and no shade. There's a band of gunmen chasing you. Tell me, what would you do?"

"I wouldn't sit down and do my nails, I can tell you that. I'd use that twenty-millimeter weapon we have and blow them out of sight."

"Good answer. Here are Franklin and Khai. Make them into nuke demolition experts in four hours."

Murdock went back to the chair at the small table in the rooms NATO had made available to the SEALs, and stared at the maps the admiral had loaned him. How in hell could they get out of the damn country if they had to go in? Jump in on a HALO—High Altitude jump with a Low Opening of the chute. Fine free fall from thirty-three thousand feet to two thousand feet, and then open the chute for a fast trip to the ground.

The Navy didn't have a chopper that could travel even six hundred miles for a lift-out. The Sea Knight, their old work-horse, had a round-trip range of about 425 miles. That would dump them out somewhere in Pakistan, instead of in the wet of the Arabian Sea, where they could meet a boat or a chopper.

They could steal a couple of cars and try to fight their way out of the place. Hire a truck and head for the border. Yeah, sure. Maybe six men, two each day, could make it in and then out again by commercial air. Right now he didn't see any other way.

He and his father had lunched with the admiral that noon. It was authentic and the food was not all that good, but there was plenty of Greek atmosphere. Congressman Murdock had a meeting with the Greek defense minister later that afternoon, and he'd left in a NATO car shortly after they'd returned from the restaurant.

Now Don Stroh came in, flopped into a chair across the small table, and tipped up a can of Diet Coke.

"Well, a report from Kabul. Our lady there has nothing. Her best contact was just cut in half by the secret police. Not with bullets, with machetes. So she's starting over. She bristled when I told her we were sending in two Navy SEALs to help her. I'd guess your guys haven't done a lot of undercover spy work."

"Not lately. It's firm for us to send in two men?"

"Boss says it's a go. President and the CNO gave it a go. So it should come through Navy channels sometime tomorrow. Now all I have to do is figure out how to get papers and clothes and passports and everything they'll need so they don't get shot at the airport."

"Do it right, Stroh, or you'll have two SEAL ghosts haunting your every move for the rest of that miserable thumb-sucking thing you'll call a life."

"Yeah, and they probably would jerk every fish off my line that I hooked. Oh, yeah, I'll make certain all papers are up to date and absolutely authentic."

Jaybird made an entrance, sputtering and swearing about the Navy and the delays in getting him off the cruiser and back to Athens. Then he began asking questions to catch up on what he had missed.

"Hell, yes, my arm is okay for duty. Just don't ask me to make any rope climbs and I'll haul my weight. Now what the fuck do we have on the fire?" After he said it, Jaybird frowned and looked over at Senior Chief Dobler. He had been so careful lately around Dobler. If he was going to have any chance at all with the senior chief's daughter, Helen, he was going to have to be on his best ever behavior. A damn strain, but it would be worth it. Oh, yeah. He could picture her now and remember kissing her in the library. Just wait until he was back in Coronado.

Later Murdock watched as two makeup artists from town did a whole body-paint job on Khai and Franklin. They used some kind of water-based light stain that would wear off in a month or two. Both were given haircuts to conform to the Arab world, and then had their pictures taken for the slightly used passports.

Clothes came next, and small Old World suitcases for the trip with extra clothes and things Arabic inside. Their papers said that both men were from Saudi Arabia and they had been in Greece on business.

The two had Saudi passports, Saudi personal identification papers, an export-import license from Saudi Arabia, and two credit cards issued by Saudi banks.

"Best I can do," Stroh said. "They fly out tomorrow. They go to Ankara, Turkey, then directly to Tehran, Iran, and from there the long hop into Kabul. I've booked them on Iran Air, and they have return tickets to Riyadh, Saudi Arabia."

"They have an address or two to contact this lady spy once in Kabul?" DeWitt asked.

"They do, and no Western gear to give them away. That means no SATCOM. We'll have to rely on Jeru, our lady in Kabul, for all of our communications."

Stroh sat the two Arab-looking SEALs down at a table and began his in-country lecture.

"You should know something about Afghanistan. It's a highly unstable country. There have been about a dozen new governments, coups, and counter-coups in the past ten years. The Taliban is now in control of the nation. It's a country of about twenty-four million people who are eighty-five-percent Sunni Muslims. It is a mountainous country with most of the land over four thousand feet elevation. It has mountains that rise from sixteen thousand to twenty-five thousand feet. The famous Khyber Pass is located here. It's thirty-five miles long and is an ancient highway that runs from east to west.

"Kabul, where you'll start your search, is a city of just over two million people. So be ready for it. There is one doctor for each seven thousand people. Almost ninety percent of the adults have had no formal schooling.

"The most potent force in the country right now is the Taliban militia. They seized control of Kabul and the nation in 1996 and set up a government. Leader of this government is probably Mullah Mohammed Omar, who led the militia in its fight. There are few pictures of him, and he refuses to talk with journalists from any country.

"Some who have seen him say he is a determined man about thirty-seven years old who lost an eye fighting the Soviets. Some say that Omar is a nominal leader trained and controlled by the Pakistan intelligence agency, ISI. Others say that he is not even a mullah, a Muslim teacher of the sacred law. His opponents say he is illiterate and knows nothing about Islam.

"Remember, the Taliban is in total control. You'll be dealing with Taliban officials in the country.

"Money. You'll have plenty. The medium of exchange there is the afghani, easy to remember. It takes over fifty of them to make a dollar. So you'll be dealing in lots of paper. Each of you'll have over ten thousand dollars worth of the paper money in large bills in your pockets and your suitcases.

"Now, any questions?"

"Say we find out where one or more of these nuclear warheads are. Do we get some dynamite from somewhere and blow them up, or what?"

"First find them, then have Jeru tell us about it and we'll figure out what to do next. Getting explosives in that country will be damn near impossible."

"Anything else?"

Both men shook their heads.

"All right. You have two hours before boarding the plane here at the Athens airport. It's a long trip, but don't take any English books to read. Look at the pictures in Arab magazines is your best bet. Oh, and sleep a lot."

Murdock chimed in. "Franklin, you've got the con on this one. You two guys find the damn nukes and we'll come help you finish them off. But first, you have to find them."

# 18

## Airport
## Tehran, Iran

Guns Franklin had started to sweat when the Iranian Special Security Police prowled the plane as soon as it landed and before anyone left.

"Routine inspection," they had called it in Farsi. Franklin knew Farsi. The police at last let those get off who were stopping there. Through passengers were told to remain in their seats, that it would be a quick stop.

The police then checked on the ten passengers left. Those still on the plane were merely passing through the airport, not even touching Iranian ground. Franklin wondered what the police could want from these people.

The policeman looked down at Tran Khai and asked him in Farsi who he was and where he was going. Khai ducked his head and looked away as they had rehearsed.

"Sir, this is my cousin," Franklin said in Farsi. "He isn't exactly right in the head. He's never been out of Saudi Arabia before, so I am giving him a trip."

"You go to Afghanistan?"

"Yes, sir."

"Why doesn't he speak?"

"His mother has asked that question for twenty years. He just doesn't. Something happened in his head when he fell and hit it."

The policeman scowled, and kicked Khai's foot back under his seat. One of his feet had strayed into the aisle.

"Good riddance to get him out of Iran. We have no room here for the softheaded. If they can't work, we shoot them."

Franklin looked away.

"That bother you, Saudi Arabian man?"

"Sir, it's your country. I wouldn't comment on how you run it."

For a moment the policeman frowned. His hand moved toward the pistol on his hip. Then he grinned and laughed.

"Yes, Saudi, you will do well. You have the right outlook."

An old man lugging a suitcase stepped into the plane from the loading ramp, and the policeman barked something at him. The old man stopped. The cop hurried up the aisle and out the door before a sudden flood of oncoming passengers trapped him.

"Gone?" Khai whispered.

"Yeah, but keep quiet, mute boy. He could be back."

He didn't come back, and Franklin breathed easier once they lifted off the Iranian runway and headed cross-country for Kabul. Franklin tried to remember everything he had crammed into his skull about the area and about Afghanistan. It was a little smaller in size than Pakistan, had twenty-five million people and the lowest per-capita income of any nation in the area at the equivalent of $800 a year. To contrast it with Pakistan, the more southern nation had 142 million people and the per-capita income was $2,300.

It was almost exactly a thousand miles between Tehran and Kabul, as Franklin had found out by talking to one of the flight attendants. That meant a flight of just over two hours. Franklin had no idea what time it was. He asked the attendant again, and she set his watch for him. They would arrive slightly before 1500. Maybe they could find the address they needed before dark.

"Might be a better idea to go there after dark," Khai said. "We don't want to compromise the agent."

Customs in Kabul involved answering a question or two, and they didn't even have to open their suitcases. When they came into the main terminal with their luggage, Franklin was sure that someone was watching them. He was right. They hurried toward the taxi stands, but didn't make it.

A young man walked past them and turned slightly. "SEALs?" he said in English so only they could hear.

Franklin grinned. "Yes, the only easy day was yesterday," he said, giving the password.

The young man fell into step with them. "I must say they are doing a better job of getting the clothes and the skin tone right now than they used to," he said softly. "I have a car down about two blocks. You have any trouble getting through?"

"We could have carried in a nuke warhead and nobody would have checked," Khai said.

"Any news about where our babies might be?" Franklin asked.

"Almost nothing. We lost our best source. Now I'm scratching. I figure I have another six months here before the stupid police figure out who I am and I get bounced out of the country. A few regimes ago they would have shot me. But now Omar is taking a slightly different line."

"Is Osama bin Laden back in the country?" Franklin asked.

"Not that we know of. He did leave for a time, but there's word that he might have come back in across the border with Pakistan and to his old camps below Khowst. That's southwest of here about a hundred miles and almost on the border with Pakistan."

They crawled into the car he pointed at. Franklin had never seen one like it. French, Russian, maybe Polish. He didn't ask.

"My name is Jeru. I am dressed like a man since a woman can't be seen in public without being totally covered. A woman could not meet you here, own a car, or even drive a car. No woman can even ride in a car with a man not her husband or a close relative. That's why I am in this disguise. It is good, no?

"Yes, I grew up in the States when my father was with our embassy there. I am half Pashtun and half Hazara. But that does not make me a half breed."

She looked over at Franklin, who sat in the front seat. "Yes, I love my country, but it is bad times. Our government is in the hands of the militia. We don't know who is going to be killing our current president or prime minister and moving in to take his place. I do what I can to help. These warheads, if they are here, would be a disaster for our nation. Some hothead might actually use one and Kabul would be vaporized in retaliation. None of us want that."

"What can we do today, tonight?" Khai asked.

She turned to look at him. "I have nowhere to look. My one source is dead, my other not sure of my intentions."

"We could go see him right now," Khai said. "The quicker

we find that warhead, or more if they are here, the quicker we can put them out of commission."

Jeru frowned. Her face was triangular with strong brows over pale green eyes. Franklin figured that she was about five-eight and solidly built. Not a pretty woman but attractive. Competent looking.

"I'm not sure what we can do tonight. My next best contact is a businessman, an importer."

"Could we go see him tonight?" Khai asked.

"I'll phone him from my apartment. Maybe we can see him later tonight. He is often watched by the police."

"Let's do it. If we need explosives, can you get some for us?" Franklin asked.

"Now that will be tougher. I won't even try unless you say that you need them. Which means we'll know exactly where the warheads are and that you can destroy them. As I hear it, there is only one. There might have been two at one time, but the second one from the ship may have gone to someone else after the plane stopped in Iran."

"Iran has one of the warheads?" Khai asked.

"Not sure. The plane refueled there, but the warhead could have been flown out to any of a dozen other countries, some in Africa. We're working that angle."

"Jeru, if you just came into your own nuclear warhead that could be converted into a timed nuclear bomb, where would you store it for safekeeping in this country, until you picked out your target?" Franklin asked her.

She drove and considered it.

Kabul still showed the effects of the devastating civil war as first one side, then the other took control. There were blasted-apart and burned-out buildings on almost every block. The rubble had been cleared away, but the damage was still starkly evident.

"Where to hide it? If it's here, the militia must have it, and bought it from the Chinese. Yes, I know the whole story. Glad you boys didn't get shot up any worse than you did when you took on that Chinese destroyer all by yourselves. Pure guts."

"Would have been a gutsy move if we knew it was a destroyer," Franklin said. "Sure looked like a freighter to us."

"Still stands. You're goddamned heroes. Where to hide the bomb? Not at the outfit's GHQ. They would be afraid of leaking radiation and just scared stiff of all that potential power. Some of these people are not the brightest. So it would be outside of the city somewhere."

"Bin Laden's caves?" Khai asked.

"Certainly one possibility. I'm thinking more of a garrison of militia trainees on the outskirts of town, maybe forty miles from here. Far enough away so if the bomb goes off accidentally, it won't wipe out Kabul."

"We must know for sure, and how tough it will be to take over such an area long enough to destroy the warhead."

"Agreed." She parked in front of a four-level apartment building that had suffered some damage but looked as if it had been repaired.

"Home, sweet home. In Kabul this is upper-middle-class living. Wait until you see inside. As a man, I run a travel agency here in town. No one knows what I really do. I don't do a lot of business. It gives me good travel connections and I can move around without suspicion. Kabul is actually trying to stir up some interest in tourism."

She led them into the small hallway and up steps to the second floor. The second door on the right was Number 203. She used a key and they went inside.

"Four rooms and a bath. Absolute luxury accommodations for Kabul where housing is tight. Too many bombed-out buildings and no new construction. You'll stay here. I often have guests. Missed planes, no hotels. Even the Secret Police have stopped watching me. It lets me be more effective."

"After your family came back here, was your father still in politics?"

"Yes, for various presidents. The last one was President Najibullah, who was hanged, and twenty of his cabinet were shot, including my father. So, now I do what I can."

"Sorry about your father," Khai said. "We have money."

She took them to a door and opened it. "This will be your room. A double bed and dresser. You travel light, that's good. No weapons, I hope. A concealed weapon these days is cause for immediate execution."

"Not even a penknife," Franklin said.

"You rest up. I'll cook us something, then I'll call my business friend, but I can't guarantee anything."

After a simple meal, Jeru telephoned her importer friend. It was by then late in the afternoon. She arranged to meet Gulbi in the back of his store just after dark.

"We must be careful. Only three or four people in Kabul know who I am and that I am a woman. If the Taliban knew I was my father's daughter, they would at least throw me in prison."

A half hour after dark, they drove into the alley behind a row of small businesses. The woman told the SEALs to stay inside. "He may not say a word if you are along. I won't be long. Stay here and keep out of sight."

She slid out of the car and into the shadows behind the store, then vanished.

The SEALs waited. After twenty minutes, Franklin got worried. "What the hell do we do if she doesn't come back?"

A few minutes later a figure slipped out of the shadows and hurried to the car. Jeru stepped in and at once drove on through the alley. At the first street a police van with red lights flashing and siren wailing swept past.

"What happened," Franklin asked.

"We had talked for about five minutes when someone pounded on the front door. He went up there and opened it. Two men crashed into the store and without a word, shot Gulbi three times in the chest. He's dead. I've been hiding ever since."

# 19

Franklin stared at the woman. "Your contact is dead? I'm sorry. He was your friend?"

"An acquaintance. He will be missed. He only had time to tell me the name of someone before he was killed. The man who shot him wore a mask."

"So what can we do now?" Khai asked.

"We see this man Gulbi named. We do it tonight before the secret police find him."

They stopped at a dark corner where there was a public telephone booth. Jeru made three phone calls. She came away from the booth frowning.

"Nobody wanted to talk when I mentioned his name. They say he's a dangerous man and I shouldn't have anything to do with him. They say even the secret police do not mess with him."

"You have an address?" Franklin asked.

"Yes. One man said it is best to see him late at night. That way not so many eyes are on the visitor."

"Good, let's go," Khai said.

Jeru looked at him. Her frown vanished and she smiled. "Yes, if we are going to find those warheads we must take some chances. This will be a big one. You have no weapons. That's good."

She started the car and drove. It took fifteen minutes as they wound into the old section of town, where the streets were originally goat paths and the lanes were too narrow for a car. She looked at the notes she had taken and stopped the car.

"This is as close as we can drive to it. Down this way about three blocks."

The lane narrowed as they moved along, until it was little

wider than a sidewalk, with houses and buildings pressing in from both sides. A dog barked at them, but was quickly hushed. Franklin checked his watch. It was just after 0120. Should be late enough, he decided.

A man appeared in front of them, paused, then faded into a doorway and let them pass. A woman screamed somewhere ahead, but the sound cut off suddenly.

Franklin moved up beside Jeru and took her arm. She looked over in the darkness and nodded. He saw the tension on her face. Someone laughed. Music played out a window, then snapped off suddenly.

A woman walked toward them, slowly, with purpose. She held up her hand to stop them.

"Where are you going?" she asked.

Jeru answered. "We need to talk to Farrah. We have news for him."

"I know of no one by that name."

"You lie. Out of our way so we can find someone who will show us the way."

"All right, I do know him. Why should he see you?"

"To save Kabul from being vaporized by an atomic bomb."

The woman smiled. "Good enough. This way."

She led them another half block, then into a courtyard and up steps to a third floor. It was strangely quiet here. Franklin could sense moisture, as if there was a garden in this usually arid land.

They came into a large room only spotted with furniture. Someone sat behind an oblong desk at the far end of the room. Two men with submachine guns stepped forward, shielding the person behind the desk.

"Who are you?" one of the guards asked.

"I am called Jeru."

"Ah, yes," a woman's voice said. The two guards stepped aside and moved behind the woman at the desk. A spotlight snapped on highlighting the woman sitting there. Franklin's first impression was that she was topless with full breasts that had no sag. Her hair was dark and she wore eye makeup and rich, red lipstick, so unusual for the other women in this country.

Her frown was steady, eyes curious, yet wary.

"Yes, I am Farrah, but I didn't send for you."

"No," Jeru said. "How do we know you are Farrah?"

"I say so. I am."

"I am Jeru. We need to talk."

"Your bodyguards?"

"Yes."

"You are the lady who works for the American CIA. I know of you. Soon Omar will learn of you and you will vanish. Until then, why are you here?"

"With the hope that you and I can prevent Kabul from being vaporized by a nuclear weapon."

Farrah relaxed a little. Franklin couldn't stop looking at her breasts and the sleek torso under them.

"You know about the nuclear warhead. I should have expected it. In this case we can work together. It was a mistake for the leaders to bring the device here. No, it isn't in Kabul. Our leaders are not sophisticated enough to trust such a weapon. They fear it might explode without anyone's help and kill everyone in our city."

"Farrah, we would be pleased to work with you on this problem. We want to destroy the warhead so it can no longer be used as a nuclear weapon."

"How can you do that without releasing radiation?"

"There is a way. The actual radiation is minimal. The danger is even less. Much less than a retaliatory attack by some foreign power."

"We think along the same lines," Farrah said. "Please, sit down and relax. I will do you no harm. We must talk. I do not know exactly where the warhead has been taken."

"Is there just one warhead?" Jeru asked.

"Yes, one. My people are still a little frightened of such a device they do not understand. How can you split an atom? They don't even know what atoms are. Now, to the problem. Our intelligence shows us that the warhead landed at Kabul airport several days ago and was taken at once in a lead-shrouded van to the south and west."

"Near the caves of Khowst?" Jeru asked.

"We don't know. My men are good, but this is so top secret that not even the confidants of Omar know for sure. He trusts no one."

"Is Osama bin Laden back in the picture?" Jeru asked.

"We think he is, and that makes it all the more important to move swiftly. Mullah Mohammad Omar will negotiate with bin Laden a stiff price of some kind for the warhead. Perhaps money, perhaps where the bomb will be used."

"Like on Pakistan?" Jeru asked.

"Who knows." Farrah snapped her fingers, and a woman came up quickly and slipped a robe over Farrah's shoulders. "We must go now to our planning room. This is your entire force?"

"It is. They are specialists."

"Yes, SEALs. I know. This way." Farrah led them from the large room to a much smaller one with a desk, several computer readout screens, and a large, well-lighted wall map.

Farrah sat behind the desk and pressed two buzzers, and at once two men hurried in. Both were tall, sturdy, with briefcases and with submachine guns slung over their shoulders.

She went to the map, pointing out Kabul, then, to the southwest, the town of Khowst. "The caves that bin Laden once used are in this general area near the border. Our data show the transport used from the airport heading in this direction. Then it was seen in Khowst and moving south. My people are working now to determine the exact location. I have men and housing in Wazay, a short distance from the suspect caves."

"What type of protection does the warhead have?" Franklin asked.

"A company of regulars from the new Afghanistan Army. Their regulars are not really professionals, but have the uniforms, weapons, and trappings of such. My specialists have hit them several times to gather weapons and ammo, and they do not fight well."

"Then you have arms and explosives that we can use?" Franklin asked.

"Almost anything you want. Now, let me make some arrangements. We will leave in an hour. We can stop by your apartment, Jeru, and you can pick up what you and the men need."

"Will my two men be able to destroy the warhead, or will we need to call in the rest of our platoon to do the job?" Jeru asked.

Farrah smiled. "We will have to wait and see what facility they have, what protection, and what kind of arms. My first thought would be that we will need more than your two and a squad of my men to do the job. We will see. Shall we leave?"

An hour later they were on the road heading southwest out of the capital for Khowst. Franklin had no idea what kind of a vehicle they rode in. It was a sedan, but not American made, nor British. It could be a lesser-known make from Russia. The highway was paved, two lanes, and they rolled along at just over fifty miles an hour. It was a little over 120 miles the way they would travel to their first destination. It took three hours. The roads became worse the closer they came to the border. The last few miles were on gravel and not well maintained.

It was almost dawn when they stopped at a concrete block-house in the outskirts of the town of Khowst. They drove the sedan in back, and two more cars followed. Franklin hadn't known there were two more cars with them.

Inside, the house was sparsely furnished, with pallets on the floor for beds.

"Yes, not a lot of furniture," Farrah said in English. "We make sacrifices for our country. As soon as it's light we'll start our search. It shouldn't be hard. Omar and his gunmen will have a large security force around the bomb. They will point us right to it."

Most of those in the first car had slept during the three-hour ride. Now was no time to look for more sleep. Franklin felt as if he was wired. He couldn't wait to get into the search.

"Do we need weapons yet?" he asked Farrah. Franklin couldn't help it. As he said it, he looked down at her breasts and the thin fabric that covered them.

Farrah noticed and smiled. "No weapons yet. They would only get us in big trouble. And, Franklin, do not be embarrassed about looking at my breasts. It's only natural for a man to do so, and it also pleases me. Now, we should go."

They took only one car. Farrah, the driver, and Franklin sat in the front seat. It was a close fit, and her thigh pressed against his. In back were Jeru, Khai, and one of Farrah's bodyguards.

They drove about twenty miles through arid, near-desert conditions. Two sandstorms swirled across their path, and they fought to keep the car on the road. Past that, they came to a few small settlements. Franklin couldn't figure out why they were there. What sustained them? Where did they get water?

This was described as the Southern Plateau of Afghanistan, with a general elevation of three thousand feet. Franklin was glad that he didn't have to live in this area.

At the next small settlement, the car pulled off the road and drove behind a house made of mortar and local stones. It was two stories, and Franklin guessed that the walls at the base must be two feet thick and tapered upward.

They went inside and were welcomed. Farrah was treated as

a special person. She took it quietly, then began asking questions.

Yes, they had seen a group of soldiers pass through. Unusual for this area. There was a small border checkpoint another ten miles down near the border. Usually six men were there. More than two hundred passed by in trucks less than a week ago.

No, they did not know where the trucks went.

Yes, they could send along a man who knew the area, who could help them get through back roads if they needed to.

Then three women came in with trays of food and drink. There were sandwiches, cold beer, and three kinds of fruit that Khai did not recognize. He looked at the meat sandwich and hoped it wasn't dog meat. He was careful not to ask.

They left an hour later. Farrah's driver was replaced by the local man, who said he would show them what they had learned.

They didn't make it all the way. Less than five miles from where the driver said he wanted to go, they found a roadblock hidden from sight around a curve. A dozen Afghan soldiers all with new-looking rifles manned the block.

The driver rolled to an easy stop next to the soldier.

"Where are you going?" the soldier asked.

"To the Cave of the Prophet," the driver said. It was a tourist attraction, the only one in the whole area.

"Ah, too bad," the soldier said. "The cave has been closed to make repairs in the facility and to build a new entryway and restaurant. It will be open in two months."

"Ah, then we must make the return trip," the driver said. "Thank you for saving us the extra miles. We're in your debt." He turned the car around, drove past the curve, and Farrah looked at Franklin.

"The obvious lie by the soldier makes me more certain the bombs are in this area," Farrah said.

"Could I make a suggestion, Farrah?" Franklin asked.

She smiled, then sobered. "Yes, of course."

"We should put out some scouts and do a patrol and see what we can learn."

"Five miles?"

"We train in the desert, Farrah. All we need is one of those canteens we put on board and we'll be fine. You drive back down this road and check back with us along here every six hours. Five miles is about an hour for us to get in the area. Then slower finding out what we need to know. Khai and I will go."

"I will go too," the guard from the backseat said. "I grew up not far from here. I know the country. I must go."

Farrah scowled, then lifted her brows, and her pretty face smiled. "Yes. It seems the only way. The three of you go and we'll check along this road every six hours. It's now eight A.M. We'll be back here at two P.M."

The three men eased out of the car and each took a half-gallon canteen. All had hats, and the drab colors of their clothes would blend in well with the mostly barren ground. They could see no buildings in any direction.

Franklin held out his hand to the guard. "I'm Franklin," he said.

The man shook his hand. "I'm Syed Durali, former major in the Army. Now I work for Farrah."

"Good. This is Khai. He's a SEAL too. Let's get moving."

They went out a half mile from the road, then turned toward where the roadblock was. There was no cover whatsoever, so the men moved out another quarter mile before passing the roadblock. Then the SEALs settled into a ground-eating jog. The Afghan kept up with them. He nodded.

"You men are in good condition."

They jogged for what Franklin figured was four miles, then slowed to a walk. The low hills were bare, offering nowhere to hide. They moved more cautiously as they came over a small rise, and on the roadway saw another roadblock. As they watched while lying in the sand, two military vehicles came up the road, paused at the roadblock, then took the left-hand turn and proceeded down a dirt track that Franklin hadn't seen before. The trucks were coming their way, and would pass less than three hundred yards away from them. The men remained motionless until the rigs had passed.

"Looks like that is the direction," Khai said. The guard pointed the way the trucks had vanished, and they turned and ran that way.

There were more small gullies and some hills here. Once they climbed up the closest one, they came over the top and stopped.

Twenty yards in front of them stood a soldier with an automatic rifle aimed at the three of them.

# 20

"Halt," the Afghan soldier barked. "Do not move. Hands up. What are you doing here?"

"Frankly, we're lost," the local man, Syed, said. "We strayed off the road chasing a snake, and now we don't know where the hell we are. Can you help us?"

They waited. The soldier looked confused.

"I heard no vehicle. You didn't walk here twenty miles."

"Decoy him," Franklin whispered to Khai.

Syed waved. "Hey, soldier. We did drive in. Right over there behind that little dune. Our car. See it?"

Syed pointed and took several steps to the side. The soldier turned that way, confusion showing on his face.

"Hey, I said don't move," the soldier yelled. He looked at Khai, and in that instant, Franklin surged forward. By the time the soldier saw his mistake and tried to swing his rifle back to cover Franklin, the SEAL was on top of him, smashing him to the ground, jolting the rifle from his grasp. Franklin's hands went around the man's throat stifling his scream.

"Why are you on guard here?" Syed shouted at the man. He had come up and knelt in the dirt and sand beside the downed soldier.

"Orders. The captain told me to watch this area."

"Are there other guards along here?"

"For a mile or two, then the road leads to the caves."

"How many soldiers?"

"Fifty."

"What are you guarding?"

"They didn't tell us. Just said do it."

"Are there any scientists inside the caves?"

"Yes, but they don't tell us what they are doing."

"How far to the caves?"

"Two miles. There are guards all along the track of a road in the sand."

"Did trucks go in and come out?"

"Yes, at first. Now only the scientists, who go back to some town for the night."

"Is Osama bin Laden at the caves?"

The guard snorted. "No, he is an enemy of the state. He would not be here."

"That is what your officers have told you?"

"Yes, of course. They tell us what is important to know."

"Do you know anything more about the caves or what the truck brought in?"

"I know nothing of the caves."

"Then we don't need you anymore."

Before Franklin saw the intent, Syed drove a slender six-inch blade into the soldier's heart. His eyes glazed for a moment, then went wide. He tried to scream, but by then the nerve endings were collapsing. His heart stopped beating, and soon all nerve synapses ceased to function.

Franklin nodded. "Yes, now let's bury him somewhere out of sight. At least cover him up. He'll be missed on guard check. We need to get closer to those caves." Franklin had been surprised by Syed's move. But it was all they could do. No way the soldier could be tied up and left. He couldn't be a prisoner. He simply had to die.

Khai knelt beside the others. "How close are we to the caves? Sounds like they have a lot of firepower against our one rifle and forty rounds." Khai had stripped the ammo pouches from the soldier, and checked the magazines for the AK-74, the newer version of the old Kalashnikov rifle.

"All we have to do today is to get close enough to evaluate their guard force, check for a quick way into the cave, and figure out if we two can do the job or if we call in more of our men," said Franklin.

"Wish we had the Bull Pup and those twenty-mike-mike rounds," Khai said. "We could blow everybody up on the outside, put a dozen exploding rounds inside, and then mop up and blow the damn warhead and be out of this rat hole."

"Coulda, woulda, bubba. We don't got them, so let's move on up and see what we can find."

Franklin angled them a quarter mile away from the track of

a road to the north here, and kept a close watch for more guards. They spotted them every half mile, but had no trouble going around them at that distance.

Another twenty minutes of hiking, and they came to a slight rise. They bellied down and looked over the top. Below them, less than a mile away, was a small valley with a gleam of water from a stream. On the far side of the water they could see the black holes in the side of the cliffs that must be caves. In front of two of them were freshly erected combat wire fences. These antipersonnel fences were usually about three feet high in the center, and had series of laterals out six or seven feet on both sides. Hard to jump, impossible to crawl under, and tough to walk through.

Near the two active caves sat a truck that looked like it had the old quad-fifty machine guns mounted on it. In back of the quads and the fence were what looked at that distance to be a series of trenches connecting well-placed foxholes.

Khai snorted. "Hell, Franklin. We can take down those guys, get inside, and blow up the damn warhead without any help. Just you and me."

"Sure we can," Franklin said. He lay there wishing he'd brought some paper and a ballpoint pen. He stared at the layout again, memorizing it, then bellied back from the top of the rise, and they all began walking back to their pickup point. Khai carried the AK-74 and the ammo.

Again they circled around each spot where the Afghans had placed a guard. If they made it out of the area before the dead guard was missed, they would be lucky.

No such luck, Franklin decided as he lay in a small gully and looked over the top. It was about where they had killed the guard that he saw the truck stop. Twenty men poured out of it, ten moving to each side of the road and extending out thirty to forty yards apart so they covered more than a quarter of a mile on each side of the road.

A series of whistles sounded, and the troops began to work slowly toward the caves and directly at Franklin and his two men.

"Still a thousand yards away," Khai said. "We outflank them?"

"All we can do," Franklin said. "And fast."

They turned at right angles to the approaching soldiers and ran along a ten-foot-deep gully until it gave out, then found a new one in the same general direction and ran again. By the time the second wadi ended, Franklin figured they had covered more than a mile. They dropped flat on the ground and watched the closest of the pickets walk past them. He was a hundred yards away and when they stretched out in the gully, he had no chance to see them.

They waited twenty minutes, then continued their movement parallel to the road. Much later they went around the roadblock, and then angled more toward the road itself.

"Car coming," Khai said as he looked down the road. They were two miles from the roadblock by that time, and ran for the road. They made it before the car arrived, and sat down waiting for it.

Jeru was curious, and asked them exactly what happened as soon as they loaded into the car.

Franklin told her, and she made some notes in a small pad she carried.

"I was so worried about you three. I usually don't get this involved in the fieldwork. Now I know why. I was so nervous before back there that we had to stop the car so I could throw up. Honestly. Now. What do we do about contacting your people?"

"You have some communications with the CIA?" Franklin asked.

"Back in Kabul at my office."

"Then that's where we go. On the trip we can figure out how we take down those caves. Not much doubt that they have something highly important in there, and I can't think of what it would be except the warhead. We get some help and we take out the problem."

They stopped at their safe house in Khowst, where the women had a large meal for them. They served meat, fish, some kind of pasta, and three bowls of fruit, as well as three kinds of breads and dipping sauces.

They rested during the hot time of the day, then began their trip back to Kabul at dusk. They left Syed in the safe house, and their regular driver took the wheel for the return trip.

It was a little past 2100 when they arrived at Jeru's apartment. On the drive, Franklin and Khai had talked about the mission. They had at last come up with the size of the force they needed.

"The whole platoon with all of our regular weapons would be good, but not a chance we can get all the weapons and men into the country without attracting a lot of attention," Franklin told Jeru. "If we parachute in, how do we get out? If we come in by commercial air, there is a good chance we can get out the same way. We've decided that we need our first squad. Their eight men and Khai and me make ten. We should be able to do the job."

"Only ten, against fifty?" Jeru asked.

"Better odds than we usually get," Khai said. "Now, what about guns? We want them to bring in two Bull Pups with the twenty-mike-mike rounds. They should be able to break down the weapon into parts and put part of it in each of four checked bags. There wasn't any X-ray check of bags as we came in. Is that the usual system?"

"Usually. They do spot checks sometimes, or tougher examinations on luggage if they have any suspicions."

Franklin touched the CIA contact's shoulder. "Jeru, can you get the rest of the weapons we need? We'll want two sniper rifles with sound suppressors on them, six or seven submachine guns, and plenty of ammo."

"Around here that's enough firepower to start a coup. Yes, I can get them for you, but it will take two or three days. How soon can your eight men get here?"

"Papers and documents will be the slow part," Franklin said. "My guess would be at least three days."

"I have a SATCOM radio to my CIA contact. Your people in Athens should have the message within two hours after I send it. E-mail would be faster, but I don't have anyone's E-mail address in your Athens group."

"What do we do in the meantime?" Franklin asked.

"After I send the messages, you can help me shop for food. Somebody has to feed all of these people." She smiled. "Maybe tonight we can think of something else to do."

Franklin grinned at the double meaning. She smiled back.

"Yeah, maybe tonight," he said. "In that message you tell my CO exactly what we need. Alpha Squad and the two Bull Pups and ammo broken down and hidden in luggage."

She sent it exactly that way. It went through the crypto in the SATCOM and shot out in a burst of less than a second. Then into the voids of space and satellites.

They had an answer back in two hours.

"Evaluating your plan. Would come in over two days two by two. Alpha Squad seems right. What will the odds be? Hang tough and prepare the runway for us." The message was signed "Murdock."

That night after the meal, Khai left the group, saying he wanted to catch up on some sleep. Jeru's driver and the cook both checked out for the night. They didn't live in. Jeru turned to Franklin and frowned.

"Will your CO go along with your plan?"

"He will. It's all he has to work with, and my logic is brilliant."

"So it might be two or three days."

"Or four. They have to get papers for eight more men, and clothes and probably a haircut or two."

"So, we have lots of time. Tomorrow I'll start getting the weapons we'll need. Tonight we don't have to worry about that. Tell me about yourself. Where did you grow up?"

"Nebraska. York, Nebraska. Where the wind blows every day of the year. Where we had twelve feet of snow one winter. The next summer it was over a hundred degrees for ten days in a row and killed a forty-million-dollar corn crop. Then some years it really was tough."

They talked for an hour. Then she caught his hand, lifted him to his feet, and led him to her bedroom. She closed the door, and caught his face and kissed him roughly.

"Now, let me tell you about where I grew up and how I learned to make love in the most interesting ways." She smiled in the soft light of the single lamp. "No, I can't tell you. Why don't I show you, give you a complete demonstration."

She did.

With breakfast came a message on the SATCOM.

"Your basic plan looks good. Now in process of getting eight men ready to arrive Kabul by commercial air. Will advise date and time of arrival. No chance we can get two Bull Pups through. There are other customs besides Afghanistan. Believe we can get one broken down into enough components and mixed with other parts of a machine that we can get past. Refine your battle plan with one Bull Pup." It was signed "Murdock."

"So far, so good," Franklin said. He frowned as Jeru gasped when she saw a man walking up to the front door.

"Who is it?" Franklin asked.

"Quick, get into the kitchen. Don't make a sound. The man at the front door is with the Secret Police. He comes now and then to check on me. But so far it's been just a friendly hello and to let me know that they are watching me. It must be nothing or there would be two of them." Again she had dressed as a man.

Franklin hurried into the kitchen and left the door open a narrow crack so he could see. Nothing. Sure. Secret Police always meant trouble. He couldn't allow anything to disrupt their plans now. He picked up a butcher knife from the counter and held it as he watched through the door. Nothing was going to interfere with their plans for destroying the warhead. Nothing.

# 21

Franklin watched through the narrow space past the inside door as Jeru opened the outer one. He heard the words but didn't understand them. Franklin watched Jeru reluctantly step back and let the man come in. He was darker than Jeru and had black hair and a full beard. Jeru had dressed in her man's clothes, and with her short hair, horn rimmed glasses, and loose shirt passed easily as a man.

"I see that you are still unemployed."

"I have my travel agency."

"But not enough business to make a living."

"I have an inheritance from my late father."

"I don't know your father. He must have been wealthy."

"Of modest means, but thrifty. What do you want?"

"Just a regular visit. You sometimes have foreign customers. We are curious."

"Yet you encourage tourists."

"Only when they bring lots of money."

"Can I arrange a trip for you somewhere?"

"I am a working man."

"So am I."

"You look nervous today, should I be concerned?"

"Only if you are worried about my missing an appointment that could lead to a good customer for me. A merchant who does considerable traveling."

The man frowned, then laughed. "You are trying to get me to leave. Perhaps I should search your apartment?"

"Anytime, just don't touch anything."

They stared at each other, both grim faced. At last the bearded man nodded. "No, I won't look today, but we are watching you. If we have any suspicions we will simply eliminate you. Rcmember that." He turned, opened the door, and left.

Franklin rushed through the door and stood in front of her. She fell against him and he held her.

"He is an evil man. He doesn't like me, and hopes he can close down my business or simply shoot me."

"Maybe it's time you came in, quit this dangerous business. How long have you been with the Company?"

"Almost four years."

"When this is over, you should get away. The regime will make a lot of heads roll if we're successful. Yours could be one. Do you have identification papers in another name?"

She shook her head. "How can I leave my home, my country?"

"It's easy to decide if you face a firing squad if you stay. We'll talk more about it. Today you said we'd find some sub-machine guns."

"Give me a minute, and hold me tight. I need to forget about that terrible man."

He held her, and gradually her breathing slowed and she relaxed. She moved and came away from him, then bent back and kissed him lightly on the lips.

Jeru sighed. "Sometimes I want to forget all of this and travel somewhere so I can sit by the sea and drink a fine wine, and let the soft breezes billow over me. Then I go swimming in the warm water and I'll have no agenda, no worries, no danger."

"This will be your last mission. You'll come out with us. What you need are new identity papers. We'll change your look. We'll get you out. Now, let's concentrate on getting the weapons."

Jeru drove, and took only Franklin with her. They went to a shopping district, parked, and went inside a big store. Quickly she led him out the side entrance into a cab. They changed cabs twice.

"I must be certain none of the regime has followed us," she said. They walked two blocks in a part of town that would make Franklin nervous even if he had all of his weapons.

They went into a small corner store that sold a few food things and some clothing. A mom-and-pop-type place. The woman inside smiled at Jeru, and watched the front while Jeru and Franklin went through a beaded door and into a back room. From there Jeru led him down a series of steps, then along a tunnel he figured ran under the street, then back up steps to a third floor room where a man sat smoking a water pipe.

Franklin sniffed the smoke that layered heavily in the room. The man was on heroin. He didn't seem to notice them enter. Jeru reached out, gently removed the pipe from his mouth, and talked to him in gentle tones. Franklin couldn't catch what she said.

The man laughed softly. Franklin guessed he was in his seventies, with deep sunken eyes, cheekbones prominent under soft leather skin. His eyes were black marbles. He lounged on a recliner chair fully extended, and even in the warm weather had a blanket draped over his body. One bony hand came out and touched fingers with Jeru.

They spoke softly for a minute. Then she turned and introduced Franklin to the man she called only Gunner. He stared at Franklin for a moment, then smiled through his gaunt facial structure.

"Yes, an American. I lived once in San Francisco. Good town, plenty of rain. You want weapons to kill Mohammad Omar?"

"Gunner, I'm afraid that isn't our mission. At least this time. We're after the devil bomb, the holocaust-bringer, the vaporizer of whole cities in the blink of an eye."

"The warhead from the Russian ICBM," Gunner said. "You are surprised. I might be old and dying, but I'm not stupid. Yes, you can have any weapons you wish, no charge for such a noble mission. Qalat will show you the goods. You will need ammunition as well. I hear the caves are well protected."

"I saw fifty soldiers there and two quad fifties," Franklin said.

"Quad fifties? Were they mounted on a half-track?" Gunner asked.

"No, on the back of a half-ton truck."

Gunner nodded. "Even so, those four closely mounted fifty-caliber machine guns can plow up the ground you walk on. It's a murderous weapon."

"Those two quads will be the first thing we take out when we attack," Franklin said.

"First the driver, then the man firing the weapon," Gunner said. "The hardware itself is hard to harm."

Franklin smiled. "You sound like a soldier."

"Once, long ago and far away. Now, here is Qalat, he will help you. I am tired. Forgive me." He lay down fully and closed his eyes.

A tall thin man with flowing black hair and beard motioned

to them. The subbasement Qalat took them to was heated and temperature- and humidity-controlled. It was a room fifty feet square, filled with weapons and arms of all types.

"You want submachine guns," Qalat said. "Over here."

It felt more like a swap meet than a normal gun store, but they had the goods. Quickly Franklin picked out four H & K sub guns of the same basic design the SEALs normally used. He found four more weapons that used the same 9mm parabellum ammo, the Beretta 12S made in Italy. All four were used, but all had the forty-round magazines. Franklin tested the weapons and examined them and pronounced them fit for service.

The ammunition was a problem. How much would they need? At last Franklin decided on two hundred rounds per weapon. The sniper rifles were harder to find. In the far corner they discovered them: two brand-new Stoner SR-25's. The weapon is actually an M-16 modified to fire the NATO 7.62mm round for greater stopping power. These weapons had twenty-round magazines and a twenty-power scopes on top of the barrels.

All the guns and ammo went into three suitcases. Jeru tried to pick one up, and hurriedly lowered it back to the floor. Two men came to help them carry the goods out to their car. They stopped to speak to Gunner, who again refused payment.

"If it is something that strikes at this government, then I shall be well paid. When you're through with the weapons, you can return them if you wish."

Franklin said that sounded like a good plan, and they left. In the car, he noticed that Jeru kept looking behind them and twisting a strand of her hair. Her hands were trembling.

She drove back streets, and now and then she shivered. "You know if the Secret Police catch us with these weapons, we'll be shot on the spot?"

"Instant justice, or what they call justice," Franklin said. He took one of the submachine guns out of the suitcase and loaded a magazine and charged a round into the chamber. "Now we'll be ready for them if anyone tries to stop us," he said.

Jeru held her mouth tightly closed so her teeth wouldn't chatter. She almost sideswiped a car on a narrow street.

"Pull over and take a break," Franklin said. "This is really getting to you. Maybe I should drive."

"No, you don't have a license. That could cost you three months in jail. I'll drive." After a short stop she did better, and they made it back to her apartment without incident.

Upstairs, the two SEALs examined the weapons, and found them all in excellent condition. They loaded the magazines they had with the rounds and felt more ready to go.

A message had arrived for Jeru while they had been gone. It was from the Afghan Produce Company.

"That's one of the cover names for the CIA here," she said. She opened the envelope. They both read the letter.

"Have confirmation of plans for potato production. Special seed will arrive at the airport tomorrow just after 8 P.M. Please pick up the seed there. There will be eight cartons."

"Might seem like kid talk to you, but we found out this is the best way to fool the people here," Jeru said. "Anything that has to do with more food production is praised and promoted. We've been working on potatoes now for three years."

"So it's set. Murdock and his seven SEALs will be here Friday night about eight. We can go right from the airport, head southwest, and get to the first roadblock by midnight. Can you get two more cars to haul us?"

Jeru said no problem.

"Good. We take out the roadblock, then drive right up to a spot a thousand yards away and start hitting them in and out of the caves with the twenty-millimeter exploding rounds."

"Sounds good to me," Khai said. " 'Course Commander Murdock might want to make some changes when he gets here."

"Fast in and fast out is the best. Jeru," Franklin said. "Can we change our round-trip return tickets to catch an earlier plane? Several days earlier?"

"No problem."

It wasn't noon yet. Khai went from one window to another looking out.

"Would you like to take a walk, Mr. Khai?" Jeru asked.

"Hey, that would break up the day. I'm about slept out."

"Security, Jeru. He speaks no Afghan Persian."

"I'll send Jabal along with him. He's a good shepherd. No one will even notice Khai in this neighborhood."

Franklin hesitated. He had the con. A hundred things could happen. Relax. It would be fine. "Yeah, Khai, take a hike. Can't hurt you any."

"Thanks, Captain," Khai said. He checked his money. "Plenty of good Afghan cash. Where is Jabal? I'm ready."

Franklin watched them from his window when they walked down the street. They were supposed to be back in two hours.

When Franklin turned around, Jeru stood there watching him. She had taken off her blouse.

"Colt, there's something I want to show you."

"Hey, Jeru, I thought I saw everything last night."

She laughed and let her Western-style bra fall into her hands, showing her heavy breasts.

"Sometimes things look differently in the daylight," she said. She moved to the bedroom door and locked it, then walked back to him slowly, her breasts swaying, her hips pounding out an age-old rhythm.

"Looks like we have two hours to find out if anything is different," Franklin said.

On the street, Khai looked at everything. It was a new world to him that he hadn't seen much of. The people, the style of dress, the faces, the buildings. They all fascinated him. He wished he had his camera. He could get some amazing black and white shots to play around with in the base darkroom.

They walked down pathways labeled as streets that wound between buildings and around corners. Merchants, food vendors, and small business firms lined the streets. Then they came across a kind of farmer's market where many types of fruits and vegetables were for sale. There were also several kinds of bread, and here and there some goat cheese.

He took it all in, buying nothing. Jabal bought some fruit they munched on as they walked.

They came around a corner, and in the wider street they saw a police sedan stopped. Three officers were questioning everyone who came by. Too late Jabal saw them and started to turn. One of the policemen yelled at him. Jabal turned back and shrugged. "Go back the way we came," he whispered in English, not looking at Khai. Jabal walked to where the policeman was finishing questioning a woman. He looked up at Jabal.

"Where is the other one you were with," the policeman said.

"With? I was walking alone. Yes, someone was near me, but he wasn't with me, just walking past me."

"Liar. We saw you with him before. He may be the one we are looking for. You stay here. I'll find him."

Khai had turned away from Jabal the moment the cop yelled. He heard the whispered warning, and walked away slowly to the corner. Then once around it, he ran. He went through one small street after another, not sure where he was. Then he looked behind him and saw that there was no one chasing him.

He paused and looked around. Nothing seemed familiar. He'd never been here before. He started to retrace his steps. No. The cop might still be back there somewhere. What was the address where they had been? What was the name of the street? Khai searched his mind and then shook his head.

He was lost in a city of over two million people, he didn't speak a word of the language, and he didn't have the slightest idea how he could ever find Jeru's apartment.

# 22

Tran Khai leaned against a building and tried to slow his racing heart. Yeah, he was lost. So grab hold and get out of it. He was on a street with lots of businesses and some cars. Maybe someone spoke English.

Fat chance. Which direction had he run, south? Yes. So he had to move back north to find something familiar. He had no hope of finding Jabal again. Not in this crush and with his half-mile run. Yes, it felt like a half mile, no more. That gave him an initial point. So he would move that far back north and see if he recognized any streets.

Yes, now that he had a plan, he felt better. He had money, that was no problem. He could point and buy if he had to. Buy what? Food? He wouldn't be gone that long.

The first few blocks were disappointing. Nothing looked familiar. He saw another police car, and he dodged into a small store until it passed. He went back to the street and continued on. He hadn't felt so confused and alien since the first day he'd landed in the United States after coming from Vietnam. He would get through this, just as he had before.

At the next street corner he recognized a small stand where a woman sold live chickens. She would chop off their heads and pick off the feathers on any bird she sold. Yes, he'd seen it before, but which way had they come on the street?

He moved in one direction and his mind whirled. Had he seen the man lying in the street before or after the chickens? Yes, before. So he was heading the right way. He walked three more blocks, remembering things along the way. Then he came to the place where the buildings almost crowded out the sidewalk.

Jabal stood there waiting for him. He grinned, shook his hand, and said something that Khai didn't understand. Then he laughed. He bought two ice creams in paper wrappers with plastic spoons, and they strolled back the way they had come.

"Policemen?" Khai asked.

"They were just checking. No reason to hold me. Angry they lost you. Glad I found you. Longer walk?"

"Yes, if no more police."

They turned, and soon came to a river. On one side were luxury houses and apartment houses. On the near side it was a low-cost housing area, a slum, and Khai frowned at the contrast.

The two continued the walk for another hour, didn't encounter any more police, and came back to Jeru's apartment.

By that time, Franklin had the weapons all checked again, and had worked on a map of the cave area. He'd drawn what he remembered, and asked Khai for some input. Together they estimated distances and times require both walking and by car. They worked out two attack plans. One was with the use of two vehicles, either cars supplied by Jeru or captured transport onsite.

By three that afternoon they had the plans complete. Now all they had to do was show them to Murdock and get his okay.

Franklin found Jeru alone, and asked her if the Secret Policeman would come back tonight.

"He may. He is insistent. He hates me."

"We'll have to see if we can change his mind when he comes tonight. If you have decided to come out of country when we go."

"Yes, I must go. My usefulness here is at an end. I have a sister in Washington, D.C., I can stay with."

"Good. I'll have a small party planned for your Secret Police buddy."

The waiting began to drag at them. They received one more letter from the potato growers. The time of arrival of the potato seeds had been changed to 6 P.M., and there would be nine boxes of goods.

Khai frowned at the letter. "Nine? They bringing the J.G. too?"

"Doubt it," Franklin said. "My guess would be that Kat will be coming along with the others to be sure this warhead is nuked out of here right."

"Can she do the job?" Khai asked.

Franklin grinned. "Oh, yeah. I was with her in Iran when we had a long choggie out of that place. She did well. Saved the commander's life in a tough firefight. She's durable, smart, and pretty as well."

They had just finished dinner when a knock sounded on the door.

"It must be him," Jeru said. "Both of you, shoo out of here. I'll get rid of him. If I can't, I'll want some help."

"We'll be watching. Remember, you can stand up to him. You're leaving in two days."

They hurried out and Jeru went to the door.

"Well, you're slow," the Secret Policeman said. He walked in, pushed the door shut, and took off his jacket.

"Don't do that. You can't stay. I have nothing to say to you. Get out of my apartment. Now." Jeru drew a knife from her skirt. Jeru slashed, and brought blood where the blade cut through his shirt and the top of his forearm.

He gasped and reached for his weapon.

Franklin bolted from the near door, clamped his big hand on the cop's wrist, and forced it away from the holster.

"What? Who are you?" the cop asked.

"A friend." Franklin picked the weapon out of leather and threw it on the couch. The cop swung a fist at Franklin, who ducked it, let go of the wrist, and powered a right hand hard into the cop's cheek. He bellowed in pain and staggered to the side.

"You broke bones in my face," he cried.

"Good, next I'll break your neck. Is that clear? Or do I convince you some more?"

The cop shrank back. "I need to sit down." He flopped in a chair and bent over. The second he straightened, Franklin was there and kicked the hideout revolver out of his hand. Franklin heard a bone in the cop's wrist snap. The man sprawled in the chair, holding his right wrist with his other hand, keening in pain and rage.

Jeru looked up, amazed and pleased. "Yes, you did what I only dreamed I could do. Now I'll have to leave, no doubt about that."

"Unless this poor soul dies in a car crash, or maybe goes into the river."

Jeru stared at him. "That might be the best. He knows too much about me."

Khai came into the room. He pulled the cop upright and

bound his hands behind him with plastic cuffs. "As soon as it gets dark we'll find a good place for his accident."

"Now, Miss Jeru, it's time you began closing up shop here and winding up anything you don't want to leave open-ended. Within seventy-two hours you'll be in NATO headquarters with us in Greece."

She was shocked for a moment, her eyes going wide, and then her mouth coming open in a surprise "Oh." Then she nodded. "So quickly. Yes, you're right. I need to do several things. Friends mostly, so they won't think I'm dead in a sand dune somewhere. I'll tell my clients at the travel agency I have a long trip."

It was completely dark an hour later. The Secret Policeman had said only a few words.

Khai and Franklin had talked it over three times, and at last decided not to kill the secret cop. Rather, they would wait until the next day just before they headed for the airport and crash his car with him in it. He wouldn't have time to do anything about them before they were off and moving toward the caves.

The next day went slowly. They had watched the prisoner, unstrapped him enough so he could eat, then used the plastic cuffs again. At four that afternoon they drove his car to a sharp hillside with a barricade at the bottom. Franklin did the final bit.

He had the cop in the front seat with his cuffs off. Franklin clobbered him on the head with a tire iron and knocked him out. The car was parked at the top of the block-long hill. He opened the hand throttle, steered the car down the slope, then jumped free. The sedan rolled down, headed for the side of the street once, then veered back and crashed into the barricade with a glass-smashing, metal-tearing roar. Franklin walked away from the hill without anyone stopping him, and was a half mile away in the other car before they heard the police sirens.

The pickup at the airport went smoothly. They met the pairs of SEALs on different flights and ushered them out to the three cars. Murdock and Kat arrived last, and when they came to the cars, they all moved away from the airport down to a quiet industrial area, where they stopped and had a conference.

Murdock had the plans as soon as he stepped into the first car. He worked them over and digested them, and at the talk he told the troops about the hit.

"You men have heard the plans. We move in these cars down southwest about three hours and get in position, then work the plan. Weapons will be distributed when we come to the first objective. I agree that we should take down the roadblock and keep our vehicles as long as possible. If there still are only fifty men there defending, they will be no serious problem. Any questions?"

Kat had one. "Once we get in the caves and find the warhead, how much time will I have with it before we have to leave?"

"How much time will you need?" Murdock asked.

"Depends on what kind of a job you want. I can make certain changes that will lessen the radiation, or I can simply set in the charges where they will prevent the bomb from ever working."

"We'll go with the longer one if we have time."

"The caves themselves," Jaybird said. "When we set the charges on the bomb, why not also set some to bring down the front of the cave and seal the whole thing inside? That would negate any radiation. At least until somebody tried to open up the cave and see what was left of the warhead."

Murdock nodded. "Fine idea. If the configuration of the cave is right, we'll do that. Now, let's mount up and move out toward that funny-sounding town and then to the caves."

As they rode, Kat looked over at Murdock. "This is a lot easier than the last time we dropped in to work. Iran, as I remember." She spoke softly so those in the front seat wouldn't hear.

"Iran it was. You did good work there."

"I was baptized under fire."

"You did some firing of your own, as I will forever be thankful for."

"You never did properly thank me for that." She grinned.

He looked at her in the dim light of the car. "Well, now, that's a statement open to a lot of interpretation. And if I'm thinking about the right one at this moment, the chances of that kind of thanks are not too good."

"Never hurts to ask."

He flashed her a smile. "And what a beautiful option to have in my hip pocket . . . that is, in our hip pockets." He smiled and touched her arm. "Thank you for saving my life. Now, back to work. When we hit a firefight, I want you to keep your head down. That weapon you have is for defensive purposes only."

"Yeah, yeah, yeah, and a big SEAL hooorah to you, Commander. When I can help, I'll help. End of topic. We going to use the Bull Pup? Looks like it came through all the customs without a hitch."

"It did. The ammo was tougher, but we got it in, mostly in pockets. Nobody did a body search."

They were quiet a moment. Franklin had decided they should take three cars so they wouldn't be crowded. Kat and Murdock held down the back seat of a vintage Ziv.

They found little traffic, and with full darkness even less. It took then just two and a half hours to get to the town of Khowst. They did not stop at the safe house, instead pressed on toward the target. Fifteen miles down the gravel road, they could see lights ahead.

"Roadblock coming up," Murdock said into his Motorola mike. "Windows down and sub gun up. We'll take out whoever is there, but don't kill the trucks or sedans. We might need them later. I'd say we get into action in about five minutes."

The three cars set up a dust cloud that the second and third cars fought through. It wouldn't last long. They came within fifty yards of the roadblock, and could see two small trucks barricading the road, with a sedan to the side. Three soldiers stood in the glare of the headlights, and held up both hands in a stop gesture. Murdock had a submachine gun out his side window.

Fifty feet from the block the first car stopped, and the other two rolled up on each side of it. As soon as the three SEAL cars were abreast across the roadway, the men in them opened fire.

# 23

The moment the SEALs opened fire from the three cars on the roadway, the three guards at the roadblock went down like dominoes. Two men ran from a truck, and were killed at once by SEAL gunfire. Two more soldiers jumped out of the sedan where they evidently had been sleeping. One fired two rounds before both men were cut down by hot 9mm parabellums.

"Cease," Murdock said into his Motorola. The firing broke off like a cleaver chop.

"Lam, you and I'll make sure," Murdock said. He left the car, and saw Lam jump out of another one, and they ran to the roadblock. One Afghan tried to lift his rifle, but Lam sent him to Allah with a three-round burst. Another man behind the truck moaned. Murdock put a round through the side of his head. There were no guards at the roadblock left alive.

The two SEALs raced back to their cars. The little convoy moved faster now, with the SEALs hoping there had been no warning given about an attack from the guards by phone or radio before they died.

"How far?" Murdock asked on the radio.

"Should be about three or four miles," Franklin said. "Some day guards along here, but they won't bother vehicles, I'd guess."

Murdock had squelched the idea of using the twenties at long distance. "We have just one and I'd rather surprise them close-up," he said. There was no solid plan now. They would have to play it as it fell.

"We'll drive right up to the caves if we can," Murdock said now on the radio. "Everyone ready. If we take fire before we start shooting, we leave the cars and spread out as usual. Kat, hang on my shirttail. We want the caves. We don't know where they house the fifty troops, but my guess would be one of the caves. Probably they put up the troops in one cave, the warhead in the other."

"Dead ahead," Holt, who drove the first car, said.

"How far?" Murdock asked.

"Some lights on maybe two hundred yards. Must be from a generator."

"Head for the lights. Stop fifty yards out. Cars come up in a line same as at the block. Do it now."

The cars drove up on both sides of Murdock's on the wide roadway to form a line of skirmishers. Now they all could see the lights.

"Another fifty yards and we stop," Holt said.

"Lock and load and safeties off," Murdock ordered.

The three cars stopped a few seconds later, doors opened, and then the eleven guns opened fire on the lights and the two dark openings, which they all figured must be the caves.

The pair of floodlights bathing the opening of one cave shattered with the first volley of rounds. The SEALs had seen a few shapes of soldiers pawing around the light base, but no return shots came. The SEALs concentrated on the caves.

Murdock had the Bull Pup. He fired ten rounds into the two caves, watching the rounds explode on contact. It was like having a dozen grenades going off inside.

Men began to race out of the farthest cave. In the soft moonlight they made easy targets. Some had weapons, and fired as they ran. Many took slugs in legs and torsos and went down screaming.

No more firing came from the caves. Murdock pushed Kat behind the first car. "You stay here," he said. She nodded.

"Time to move up," Murdock said on the net. "We'll go running on assault fire. Single shots and keep them low and into that first cave. Let's go."

The SEALs lifted up and ran forward in a ragged line of ten, aiming at the first cave. When they were twenty yards away, Murdock called for them to hit the dirt.

"Anybody see anything?" Murdock asked on the Motorola.

"Saw one guy run away to the left," Bradford said. "He didn't have a weapon."

"Saw one shadow that must have been a man making a dash for the first cave," Senior Chief Dobler said. "He made it inside."

"Closest four men. Each of you put a grenade into that cave mouth. I'll do some more twenties."

Murdock fired five more rounds into the mouth of the cave, and heard the rounds explode inside during and after the grenades went off. Three of the hand bombs went inside the cave mouth, and one missed, rolling away to the other side.

"Move up," Murdock said. The men stood now and walked forward, using assault fire with single shots. A moment later a heavy machine gun opened up from the cave mouth. Two rounds jolted Ron Holt back a step and pitched him to the ground. The SEALs dug their noses into the ground as most of the rounds now went over their heads.

"Grenades," Murdock said. He fired three rounds at the front side of the entrance, hoping to get some shrapnel on the shooter. The man must be well protected from the front. The twenties exploded and rained down deadly shards of steel. Two grenades blasted just inside the entrance, and there was no more sound from the machine gun.

"Lam, take a look at whoever went down. I saw one of our men hit."

"It's Holt, Commander. He's hit bad, but I don't know where. He's out of action."

"Watch him. Jaybird, on me. Get extra grenades. Hands and knees and we work up front. Go now."

Murdock lifted to his hands and knees, then lowered and crawled, pushing with his toes in the sandy ground and dragging himself forward with his elbows. It was slow going, but kept his body close to the ground.

No more firing came from the cave.

Then to their right fifty feet away came the deep sound of AK-47's. More than a dozen weapons could be firing. "Return fire," Murdock said into his mike. "Jaybird, stay on course." Murdock could see a shape he figured was Jaybird inching closer to the cave mouth. When they were twenty feet from the cave mouth, Murdock said, "Grenades now, Jaybird." Both of them threw about the same time. They lobbed two of the hand bombs just over the lip of the cave, where the machine gunner must be positioned behind sandbags and rocks. The four blasts shattered the night and drowned out the firing from the right.

"Ready, Jaybird? Give me the word and we charge into that cave."

"I'm ready. Go."

The two SEALs lifted up and bolted straight ahead the twenty feet to the cave mouth. They found it had a four-foot wall across the front with a door to one side. They stopped in front of the wall. Jaybird held a grenade with the pin pulled, and edged it upward and then jolted up and looked over the wall. A scream billowed from inside, and then a shot blasted from inside the cave.

Jaybird pushed the grenade over the wall and ducked. Before the 4.2-second fuse cooked, Jaybird used the radio. "Saw just one man, looked wounded but had a rifle." The rest of the words were blotted out in a wave of crashing sound of the grenade exploding that was amplified by the cave.

Murdock wished for his night-vision goggles. But they were too dangerous to carry in the open. A customs suitcase check finding them would mean huge trouble. He waited. No more sounds came from the cave.

"Dobler, what do you have on the right? Move the rest of the men that way when you can."

"Looks like ten men or so with fire sticks. Maybe thirty yards away. We put some grenades into them. Still half a dozen firing. Don't think we've had any more casualties."

"Move over and take them out. We're about ready to go inside this one. Send me one man."

"Roger that. Bradford on his way."

A few breaths later, Bradford slid to the ground in front of the cave wall.

"We'll all lift up and fire over the wall at the interior," Murdock said. "Fifteen rounds each for you guys, then we go in on assault fire. We don't know how big this cave is. We play it by ear. Let's play the tune."

The three lifted up and fired over the wall, then darted to the doorway and charged inside. They couldn't see a thing. All three went to the ground instinctively.

"Green flare," Murdock said. He pulled one from the sleeve of his combat vest and ripped off the seal and threw it. It exploded into an eerie green light thirty feet inside the cave. They saw six bodies scattered around. One Afghan stood, his hands over his head. He had three wounds bleeding and seemed ready to drop.

Jaybird ran to him, pushed him to the ground, and cinched his hands together behind him with a plastic cuff.

"Flashlights," Murdock said. "Let's see what else is in this bastard of a cave."

Outside, Dobler looked at the men firing at them. His six SEALs had cover of sorts, a narrow ditch that gave them some protection. Grenades hadn't done the trick on routing the Afghans. Only one way.

"Franklin, Khai, and Lam, on me. We're going to crawl around to the left and outflank those fuckers. Let's go, crawl, now."

Dobler wondered why he kept going on these fun-filled field trips. He was thirty-seven damned years old and hurting in most places the way a seventy-year-old does. Crawling wasn't as easy as it had been twenty years ago. He held the submachine gun across his arms in front of him as he dug in toes and elbows and powered ahead.

They were halfway there when he heard a motor start. Then one of their sedans moved slowly toward the enemy rifles. "Hold," he said into the radio. He watched, fascinated. Who? Oh, damn, that had to be Kat. What was she doing? She had a weapon, a sub gun. Damn, she might just help. The Afghan rifles wouldn't stop the old Ziv.

He watched fascinated as the car covered the distance so it outflanked the enemy troops, then stopped. A moment later the stutter of her sub gun blasted from behind the Ziv.

"Fire, all fire," Dobler said. His men fired. They didn't have the best position, but they all shot up a storm. One Afghan lifted up and tried to run to the right. Four rounds hit him, dumping him into the dirt. The submachine gun behind the Ziv quieted. Then, seconds later, chattered again. Dobler grinned. He could just see Kat frowning and biting her lip as she quickly changed magazines.

Kat rammed a new magazine in the H & K sub gun, and aimed at the dark shadows that had been firing at the SEALs. She lay beside the front tire of the Ziv, mostly protected. Leaning out, she fired again, four three-round bursts. Two more men leaped up and tried to run. They took a few steps, then stumbled and went down. She fired again, aiming at the prone figures in the ditch that gave them frontal protection. Two of them jerked and tried to crawl away, then fell and didn't move again.

Oh, God! She had killed again. At least two. She flushed out the rest of them. Oh, God. She had killed again. She dropped her head on her hand on the weapon. Tears spilled down her cheeks. Had to be done. Had to. They'd hurt Holt. She'd heard it on the radio.

Where was Murdock? He had headed inside the cave. There was no more firing from the Afghans in the ditch. One man had escaped when he crawled away. She had missed him with her rounds. All was quiet again.

"Kat. Hey, Kat," Dobler said on the radio. "Thanks for the flanking job. You dug them out of there. Good shooting, Kat."

She shook her head and brushed back tears.

"Kat, you okay? Kat?" It was Murdock.

"Yes. Yes. Fine. Not even hit, I don't think. Well, maybe a little nick somewhere. It hurts, but I don't know where. Yeah, I guess. Oh, damn, Murdock. I killed those men again. I did it again. Oh, God, I'm so sorry. Oh, no. Now it does sting and . . . and hurts like hell. Hey, you found the warhead yet?"

"Kat, you get inside the car if you can, and stay there. Yes, we have the warhead. We'll let you know when this place is secure."

Murdock held the small flashlight at arm's length and turned it on. The powerful beam penetrated the cavern twenty feet deeper inside. Seconds after he snapped on the light, a pistol fired ahead of him, three rounds blasted off inside the cave before he could jerk down his hand. The light shattered as a bullet hit it and spun it out of his hand. He brought up the sub gun and pounded off three three-round bursts at the muzzle flashes that had burned into his eyes in front. There was a yell, then a scream, and at last a long final sigh.

"You hit, Cap?" Jaybird asked.

"No, but that flash is going to take some repair. I think I nailed the sniper. Let's try your flashes by the book." The other two men used their lights, held away from their bodies, and the three SEALs worked down the cave. It had a ten-foot ceiling, and was forty feet long. Another ten feet and they found the back wall. There, on a table with fold-out legs, lay two large packages still swathed in cardboard and bubble wrap for protection.

"First cave is clear," Murdock said, hoping the radio waves would find their way out of the cave. They did.

"Want us to work the second cave?" Dobler asked.

"No. Go see Kat and find out where she's hit and how bad it is. We have the warhead in the first cave. Check out Kat. Then find Holt and tend to him. You're our medic for the rest of this run."

As Dobler stood up to run to the car, four more soldiers blasted out of the second cave with their automatic rifles chattering. They were simply firing straight ahead. Four rounds went through the Ziv windshield. Then they swung away to the right, away from the second cave and the car, and all ran flat out into the blackness of the night.

"What was that?" Murdock asked on the net.

Dobler told him as he ran again for the Ziv. He found Kat in the backseat, unharmed by the second attack.

"Kat, where are you hit?"

"Not sure, it's all kind of fuzzy to me."

"Does either arm hurt?"

"No."

"How about your legs? Can you move them?"

"Yes, but I still hurt."

"Murdock has the warhead."

"What?"

"I said Murdock found the warhead in the first cave."

She sat up. "Good." She handed him the MP-5. "Then we certainly should get over there right away. Do you have the extra flashlights, the big ones?"

"In my pack." He edged out of the car and helped her to the edge of the seat.

Kat smiled at him in the darkness. "It's a good thing we found the warhead so quickly. Those last gunmen were accurate with their rounds."

"Too damn accurate. You sure you don't know where you're hit?"

"No, just fuzzy, fuzzy, fuzzy."

"Will you be able to work on the bomb?"

"Oh, that. No problem. Let's get over there. The first cave, you said?"

He told her it was, and moved back from the rear door. Kat put her feet out of the car to the ground, and stepped out of the backseat. She gave a little cry, and crumpled to the ground. Dobler swore. He knew the signs. She was either shot extremely bad, or she had fainted dead away.

He knelt beside her. "Murdock, you hear that? She wants to come work on the bomb but just collapsed beside the car. You better get over here and help me find out where she caught that bullet."

# 24

Murdock scowled. "Is Kat hit bad? Head shot? Anything visible?"

"Not that I can see in this light," Dobler said. "Hate to move her until we know. We're secure here?"

"Should be. Blink your light to let me spot you."

Dobler gave him three blinks of his small flashlight, then three more. He got two blinks back, and looked at Kat again. He pushed his hand under her back where she lay on the rear seat. No blood. He shone the light on her chest, then on her shoulder. Blood. It was high, upper arm just below the shoulder joint. Might not be that bad.

He felt self-conscious as he felt down each of her legs. No blood there. Wait. Yes. Her right calf was wet. He found the blood halfway down. Still bleeding. He took out his first-aid kit and tore it open. He cut open her pants leg, and then concentrated on getting a gauze pad on the wound and wrapping it tightly with a roller bandage. The leg didn't look too bad. An in-and-out wound. Must have picked it up while she was outside the car. He wished he had the aid man's kit.

He had just looked back at Kat's shoulder when Murdock shouldered into the sedan.

"Two hits, Cap. Left shoulder and right calf. Neither one looks too bad, but she passed out. Shock, I'd say."

"Let's get her into the cave, then we figure out what to do. Are we down to two vehicles?"

"Don't know. Rounds hit the windshield, maybe missed the engine. We'll have somebody check it."

They lifted Kat off the ground and Murdock carried her in his arms as they walked to the cave. One of the men had found candles, and had six of them burning around the nuclear warhead.

Kat mumbled something as Murdock sat her down in the cave and leaned her against the wall. There was no furniture except the table with fold-out legs.

Dobler used his knife and cut away part of her sleeve so he could bandage the shoulder hit. It was a ricochet of some kind, and hadn't penetrated too far, but must have hit her sideways. He treated it and bandaged it.

A moment later, Kat began moaning, then shook her head and woke up.

"Oh, yes, that hurts. What's going on?" She looked around.

"You were a hero, blasting those Afghan soldiers, and in the process you got shot in two places," Murdock said. "Neither life-threatening. That should make you feel better."

"Not much." She turned and looked at the candles. "Is that the warhead?"

"Yep. You feel like looking at it?"

"I didn't come all the way out here to ignore it."

Murdock put down a hand to help her up. She ignored it, and pushed down with her left hand to stand. Her arm crumpled and she whimpered with pain.

"Okay, help," she said. Murdock caught her shoulders and stood her up. Her face came close to his, and she smiled for a moment, then sobered.

"Can you walk?" he asked.

"Yes, and hobble and hop."

"Good. Dobler, find Holt and take a look at him."

Dobler left. Murdock served as a crutch as they moved across the cave fifteen feet to the table. She wobbled as she stood there looking at the packaging to one side.

"They protected it well enough." She turned to the warhead itself and nodded. "Yes, a duplicate of the ones we saw in Libya. No problem. Where are my tools?"

Murdock sent Lam to bring them. She turned and sat against the table, letting her left leg keep her in place.

"What kind of time?" Murdock asked.

"Fifteen minutes once I get started. You have out security?"

"Hey, I'm the SEAL here. We have four men on cover. Holt was hit, Lam is getting your kit from the car, and Bradford is checking out the Ziv to see if it will still run. Anything else you want to know?"

"Yes. How in hell did those bullets find me when I was in the backseat of that car?"

"Good question. What the hell were you doing outflanking those shooters? That's what we have SEALs for."

"Just seemed like a good idea at the time. It worked, didn't it?"

"Oh, yes, it worked, and it could have made you one dead GS-15 government employee."

Lam came running in with Kat's tool kit. Murdock moved two candles and pulled the warhead assembly over so Kat could work on it while sitting on the table.

"Weird," she said, but went to work.

"Skipper, Bradford says the Ziv will run, but the whole windshield is shot out and come daylight some cop is going to get damn curious about that."

"No way we can drive back into Kabul with it that way?"

"Not a chance."

"Have Bradford take you back to the roadblock and see if one of those Army sedans will run. If so, bring both rigs back here."

"Aye, aye, Skipper," Lam said, and ran out of the cave.

Murdock went to check on Holt.

He found Holt where he was hit on the assault. Dobler was bending over him in the darkness, the flash held in his mouth so he could see. He heard Murdock come up, and the second flash helped light the scene.

"Not too good, Commander. Took one high in his chest. Must have caught part of his lung, another one in his left shoulder."

"Not that bad, Skipper," Holt said, looking up. "Hell, I can still pull a trigger."

"Good, SEAL. You keep talking. Dobler. Drive one of the cars over here and get Holt in the backseat and shoot him up with some morphine. Two if he wants them. Kat is going to need one after she finishes the bomb."

"Kat get hit?" Holt asked. "Damnit, how did we let her take a slug?"

Dobler told him.

"What a fucking little trooper. She can be in my squad on any mission."

"Stay with him," Murdock told Dobler, and ran back to the first cave. He sent two men to clear the second cave. There could still be some hostiles in there. They came back five minutes later.

"Only four bodies in there, Skipper," Van Dyke said. "Must have been those sweethearts of twenties that did it."

Murdock nodded, and put him back on guard outside. Then Murdock watched Kat. She knew exactly what to take apart, what to leave intact, and where to slide in the charges. They were prepackaged and in with her tools.

Murdock looked at his watch. Kat saw him. "I know, I know. I'm slow working this way." She sagged, and Murdock caught her.

"I will not pass out, damnit. I will not faint dead away like some Southern belle. I fucking will not!" She looked at Murdock and grinned. "Talked myself through that one. Why does my damned shoulder hurt so much? Just a scratch, nothing to put a fucking SEAL down."

Murdock chuckled. "Hey, when you start talking dirty I know you're feeling better. No big rush. You've got the con on this one. We move when you tell us to move."

"Good. It's always nice to have control, as long as one does not throw up when one is bossing people around." She laughed. "Hey, I don't talk that way. Move me around a little more to face this devil. Another five minutes. These charges won't bring down the cave. It's solid rock in here, not sandstone or clay.

"Suggest we set charges to seal the front of the cave. We can set the timers on these for ten minutes, then set the timers for the front of the cave for twenty and drive off a ways and see what happens."

Murdock called to Franklin, and told him to position charges on the mouth of the cave.

"Leave the timer detonators off them until we get done in here. Another five minutes." Franklin jogged out to the front of the cave where they had left the TNAZ explosives. They had been sewn into their clothes in quarter-inch sheets six by four inches, and had come through the inspections in good shape.

Murdock went back to check on Holt. He sat up and sipped at one of the canteens.

"Hell, Skipper, I'm okay. Just have a little bit of trouble breathing is all. Just a couple of damn scratches. Be back in the pink in a day or two."

"Yeah, sure you will." Murdock looked at Dobler. "His shoulder is patched up and looks good. That puncture wound in his chest is bothering him a lot. He's got to get to a doctor."

"We'll see what kind of help Jeru can be on that score. Which means another day in her house. Hope the neighbors don't turn her in and the cops come. We don't need another shoot-out on this one."

By the time Murdock walked back into the cave, Kat leaned back, wiped her brow, and nodded.

"That should do it, Boss. No timers set yet. You give the word and I'll set them as you suggest."

"Let me check the guys at the mouth, and the transport." He ran out of the cave into the blackness of the night. It took him some time to get his eyes accustomed to the darkness. Then he saw the military sedan parked beside the other two cars twenty feet from the cave. The Ziv must not be in the best shape.

"Transport ready, Skipper," Bradford said. "We've put Holt in the Army sedan's back seat. The other cars are ready. We should have plenty of gas to get back to Kabul."

Murdock waved at Bradford, and looked at the charges set at the front of the cave. The sides and overhead here looked to be a softer stone than what was inside. He went back to Kat.

"Set them for ten minutes," he said. She watched him a moment, then pushed over and set the detonators and started the timers.

"I better give you a lift out of here," Murdock said. He picked her up in his arms and held her in front of him as he carried her out of the cave.

"Set your timers for fifteen minutes," he told Franklin. Murdock carried Kat to the second car, and put her in the backseat.

Franklin came running up. "Mouth charges set and activated on fifteen minutes," he said.

"Let's load up and move out of here," Murdock said. The men crawled into the cars, and they drove off five hundred yards and stopped.

Kat checked her countdown watch with her flash.

"A little over a minute left for the inside charges," she said. It was thirty seconds later that they heard the TNAZ go off inside the tunnel. A spume of dust billowed out of the cave's mouth.

"Good-bye, warhead," Jaybird said.

They waited.

"Thirty seconds," Franklin said on the radio. Almost before he finished the words, a cracking roar billowed across the desertlike country and a brilliant flash blossomed at the first tunnel. The slap of the shock wave from the blast pushed Murdock back a step where he stood beside the car.

He ducked inside the front seat. "First car will go take a look," he said. "The rest of you stay put."

They drove to the site through the thinning cloud of dust. What had been a cave mouth before now showed as a large rock pile with a small indentation near the top. It would take hundreds of hours of work with heavy equipment to open the cave.

"Let's get out of Dodge," Murdock said, and Bradford wheeled the sedan around and drove back to the others.

"All right, so far, so good," Murdock said on the net. "Now all we have to do is get home. We'll drive back, but not in a convoy. Keep the car in front of you in sight, but with a few cars between if possible. We'll close up more the closer we get to the big city. We go back to Jeru's place and park the cars a few blocks away. Most of us haven't been there yet. It should still be dark when we get there, but go in by ones and twos so we don't upset the neighbors.

"Our first job is to find a doctor for our wounded. Then we schedule our flights out of here two by two again. We'll leave all weapons and explosives here, except the twenty Bull Pup, which we'll break down the same way and put parts in ten suitcases.

"Better catch some sleep while you can. You may need it. The Afghans are going to be all over this one as soon as they find out. With any luck we'll be on planes and out of here before they discover that their baby has been blown into shrapnel."

They drove. They did not stop at the safe house in Khowst, but kept right on the road for the capital. They saw no unusual traffic and no military units racing toward the caves. That was good.

Murdock looked at Kat, who sat stiffly upright in the backseat beside him. "How's the shoulder?"

"Hurts," she said.

"You need a little help." He opened his first-aid kit on his belt, and took out an ampoule of morphine and injected it.

"Yes, thanks."

He put his arm around her, pulled her good shoulder against him, and eased her head down on his shoulder. Her eyes closed slowly.

"Now, relax, tough guy, and get some sleep. We'll get a sawbones to take a look at you as soon as we can."

They arrived back at Jeru's apartment with no problem. No additional military traffic was seen. They drove up, and Kat insisted on walking into the place. Then she collapsed on a cot. Holt walked slowly with a man on each side of him. He went down on another cot, and looked exhausted.

"We need a doctor," Murdock said.

Jeru frowned. "That's a problem. We had one man we could rely on, but he vanished and we think he simply left the country, fed up with the constant upheaval and chaos. Who else?"

She walked around the room, checked Kat's shoulder, and brought some supplies and rebandaged the wound there. Then Jeru brightened. "Yes, I have it. We'll call her 'Martha,' because that isn't her name. She's a medical doctor who went to school in Pakistan because they have better medical schools than we do. When she came back, the government wouldn't recognize her as a qualified M.D. and no women can work outside their home here anyway. She's a friend who helped me once before."

"Can you phone her?" Burdock asked.

"Oh, no. Her phone is tapped and constantly monitored. I'll drive over there and bring her back. I just hope she's home. What time is it?"

"A little after 0330. That's three-thirty A.M."

"Good, we know she'll be home. She lives alone."

"Want me to go with you?"

"No." She hesitated, and then frowned. "This is important to you. I don't want to let you down. Maybe you should send someone with me."

"I'll go. It's not only important, it's vital. We need both of these people." Murdock motioned to Dobler. "Have the men get some rest. As soon as it's light we'll have them head for the airport. Send Franklin along. Have him go to different airlines and change the tickets of two of his friends for earlier flights. Get them all out of here before noon if possible. Different flights or different airlines, so the counter people won't remember."

"Got it. We all have money if there are any more charges. We'll leave here about six. You be careful out there."

It was less than a half-hour drive into one of the poorer sections of town. Few street lights, litter in the streets. The houses and apartment buildings in poor repair. They parked, and went down a crooked street to a door that had a name on it and the word, evidently in Pashto, for "doctor."

Jeru didn't hesitate. She went past the door to a narrow walkway between two buildings and round to the back of the place. There were two doors. She knocked on one, then banged loudly. They saw through a window when a light came on. Jeru let out a held-in breath.

"Oh, good, she is home."

The door opened a crack against a chain, and the two women spoke quickly. Then the chain came off and Jeru and Murdock stepped inside. The woman wore a robe, her hair was mussed. She rubbed her eyes as she and Jeru talked. Murdock had no idea what they said. Then he heard the word SEALs and he frowned. Jeru turned to him.

"It's all right, she is one of us. We can trust her with our lives."

The woman smiled at Murdock, shook his hand, and said something.

"She said you're the most handsome man she's seen since she toured Washington, D.C., five years ago."

"Thank her for me. Can she come?"

"Yes. She needs her bag and some supplies." The doctor went into another room. She was back in five minutes, in traditional women dress, and with a medical bag and carrying a paper sack. She spoke to Jeru.

"Martha says she will do what she can and give you medications that you can use through the long flight back to Greece."

They went to the door. Martha looked out, nodded, and the three went out the door into the small alleyway next to the building behind her home.

They had moved only twenty feet when a man with a gun trained on them stepped out of the shadows. He barked something in Pashto and the women stopped suddenly. Murdock saw the weapon at once and froze.

Jeru whispered to Murdock as the man came closer, "He says not to move, we're all under arrest."

# 25

Murdock judged the man with the gun. A professional. He stayed six feet away when he came up to them.

"Faint," Murdock whispered to Jeru. She didn't look at him, but frowned.

"Oh, my," Jeru said. She put her hand to her head. Then her knees shook and a moment later she fell against Murdock, eyes closed, arms flapping as she went down. She was still dressed as a man.

"Now look what you've done," the doctor barked at the gunman. "You've scared him to death. He's fainted. We were going to his home for treatment. I'll have to give him some medication and some smelling salts. What in the world are you doing?"

The gunman, who Murdock figured was a Secret Policeman of some kind, hesitated. When he spoke, he stammered, then coughed. He touched his forehead, where sweat had appeared, and he cleared his throat.

"This person is on our list of subversives. He must be watched. All right, treat him. Then all four of us are going to my supervisor and get some answers."

Murdock didn't understand any of the talk. He had one chance with the gunman. He crouched beside Jeru, whose eyes fluttered, then stayed shut. The doctor stayed beside her, and took some pills from her black bag.

Murdock moved slowly, his left ankle out of sight of the gunman behind Jeru. He lifted the hideout from its leather holster and kept it behind Jeru.

"Hurry up," the Secret Policeman said.

Murdock started to stand.

"No," the cop snapped. He motioned down with his hand.

"Stay down, big man. I'll deal with you later. It is the tall one, Jeru, we are interested in."

"Cover is blown, Murdock," Jeru whispered. "Shoot him."

A siren sounded somewhere far behind them. The Secret Policeman turned, then looked back. Murdock pulled up the short-barreled .32 and fired four times with a point-and-shoot aim. Two of the four rounds hit the cop's chest and he went down. His trigger finger spasmed and fired two rounds into the pavement as he fell.

"Get the car," Murdock snapped. "We can't leave him here." He hurried to the Secret Policeman on the ground. He hadn't moved since he went down. Murdock checked him for a pulse. None. He lifted him over his shoulder and carried him into the shadows of a building at the near side of the alley.

No windows had opened when the shots came. No one had opened a door and looked out. No one wanted to be involved. Good, Murdock decided. The doctor was with him in the shadows as Jeru drove her car up to the mouth of the alley. Murdock carried the body to the car and pushed the body into the backseat. Then he stepped in after it.

A moment later the car turned around and Jeru drove it away.

"Where?" she asked Murdock.

"Landfill, garbage dump, river?"

"Nothing nearby."

"Any old wells, coal mines . . ."

"Wells. Yes, in an old section. Not used. Yes. About ten minutes away."

Murdock systematically stripped the body of all identification. There wasn't much, a wallet with some cards, a pin on the man's shirt. Murdock had brought the dropped gun. It would go down with the body.

By the time the car stopped, Murdock was ready.

"Let me look around a little," Jeru said. "We don't need any witnesses."

She was back quickly. She helped tug the body from her car. Then Murdock bent, lifted the man over his shoulder, and carried him where Jeru led. She had removed three old boards from the well top, and Murdock unceremoniously dumped the corpse off his shoulder down the hole. It didn't take long to hit. Thirty, forty feet deep, but it would do. They put the top boards back on the well top and hurried back to the car.

Twenty minutes later, Martha had examined Kat.

Jeru translated. "She says the lady is in good shape. The ricochet caused a lot of bleeding, but the wound isn't deep and should heal well. The bullet hole is a painful one, but Martha put on some antibiotics and treated both wounds. Kat will be fine on the plane ride."

Martha took longer with Ron Holt. She shook her head twice and looked up at Jeru. She talked to her for several minutes in Pashto then went back to checking his chest.

Jeru talked to Murdock and Dobler. "Martha says that the bullet definitely hit Holt's lung. She's not sure how bad it is. There's a danger his lung could collapse once he gets to altitude on the plane. The other problem is infection. That and the fact that the bullet did not exit his back. It's still in there, and will have to be found and removed. Three days, tops, for that. She will load him up with penicillin and antibiotics. He can walk with assistance. No hint of any health problem, or they won't let him on the plane. She says the shoulder wound was a graze that dug a half-inch groove. It will be fine in a month."

Murdock considered his options. He would send six men to the airport with first light. Franklin, who spoke Arabic, could get their tickets exchanged for flights going out today.

That would leave five more of them to get out. Jeru would be coming with them. Jeru would be their interpreter at the airport for the last five tickets. Yes, that part would work. Somehow they had to keep Holt on his feet and moving through the lines to the plane, and do it without attracting any notice.

Jeru came back. "Martha says she will go with us to the airport to guarantee Holt's health if there's any problem. She'll ditch my bloody car in the poorest part of town. It will be stripped and trashed within an hour after she leaves it. I have my passport and papers. I'll fly out with you. I've already phoned my control here in town, explaining as best I could over an open line."

"We could use some ampoules of morphine if Martha can spare any. It may be the only thing to keep Holt from screaming all the way across the continent."

Franklin left just after 0600. He took with him Khai, Jaybird, Bradford, Lampedusa, and Van Dyke. That left, for the second go, Murdock, Dobler, Kat, Holt, and Jeru. It should work.

It took Jeru two more hours to get her affairs in order, to check out with friends, and to decide what to do with the apart-

ment. It was furnished and rented by the CIA, but she had some
personal items as well. She sent the cook-housekeeper home as
soon as she arrived for work at 0700. They destroyed the SAT-
COM. Broke it up and trashed it in a three block area.

"Now, all I have to do is cut my apron strings and I'll be
gone from here while I'm still alive. That missing Secret Policeman is going to set off a firestorm here. His superiors must
have known he was watching either Martha or me. She will be
able to alibi her way out of it. I would be in Tolkif, the central
jail here in Kabul, before noon if I stay here."

It took Jeru a half hour at two different airline ticket counters
before she had their tickets exchanged. It cost extra, but they
had enough of the funny-looking money.

Murdock stayed right beside Holt every step. He was ready
to grab his arm if he wavered. He didn't. They sat in the seats
waiting. Murdock, Holt, and Kat took the first flight. They were
on Iran airlines. They had seats assigned. Holt stumbled on the
ramp, but Murdock caught him and they made it to their seats,
a three-across grouping with Kat on the window and Holt on
the aisle. Murdock sat between them, watching them both like
a mother hen.

Kat had yelped once as she walked into the airport, but had
been close-mouthed and quiet since then. Once in the seat, she
gave a long sigh. "Just a damn little scratch on my shoulder and
a small fratulogical hole in my leg," she whispered to Murdock.
"Sailor, there ain't no fucking way those little scratches are
gonna keep down a SEAL."

Murdock laughed softly, and reached over and kissed her
cheek.

"Hey, SEAL, you may win your gold trident yet" he said.
"Now settle down and try to get some sleep. Best way to pass
the time."

Kat grinned. "Yeah, you're right. 'Course, it depends on who
you're sleeping with." She reached over and kissed him on the
cheek, then turned away from him and closed her eyes.

Murdock tried to relax. He had checked both waiting areas
for planes leaving for Tehran, and hadn't found any SEALs
waiting. They must be on their way. Good.

The last five should be in the air within a half hour. Now, if
he could keep Holt from going critical, all would be fine. Anywhere but here, he would have requested a special doctor to be

on board in case Holt turned sour. Now he'd just have to take
his chances. SEAL lungs were always strong from all the underwater training they did. Still, lungs were tricky. They could
collapse for a dozen reasons. A bullet through one must be high
on the list.

Murdock watched the loading. He figured all of the passengers were on board. The attendants were closing overheads and
checking seat belts. Then two men in suits came on board, and
walked up and down the aisle staring at each person as they
passed.

A scream jolted through the air, and a man dove from his
seat and scrambled up, running full speed down the aisle. The
suit from the other way blocked his way, knocked him down,
and handcuffed him. They dragged him off the plane.

No notice was made of the incident, and no PA apology for
the delay. Moments later the doors closed and the plane rolled
out on the taxi strip.

Murdock watched Holt. The doctor said the decreased air
pressure of the cabin, set at about six thousand feet, might trigger a reaction by Holt. Murdock talked with him quietly.

"Look, Holt, this is the tough time. The cabin will be pres-
surized at the same as six thousand feet as we take off, and
remain that way until we land. You let me know if you have
any twinges, or if it's hard to breathe, anything at all."

"Yeah, sure, Cap. Hey, I'm a fucking SEAL, remember? No
little scratch like this gonna hurt old Ron Holt. You can count
on that."

He frowned.

"What, you hurt somewhere?"

"Yeah, my shoulder burns like hell. Not all that bad a hit
either. Doc told me it would hurt, but my buddy Morphine is a
big help."

Murdock could tell when the plane stopped climbing. Cruising altitude was maybe 31,000 feet or so. He looked over at
Kat. She was watching him.

"So far, so good," she said. "Ron seems to be making it fine."

"For now, just so he doesn't try a hundred-yard dash." He
watched her. "Pretty lady, how are you doing?"

"Better. That morphine did help."

"So will a Purple Heart. I don't see why we can't put you in
for one."

"Because we're covert, that's why. Where would I wear it, on my jogging bra?"

"Good place."

"We aren't done with this one yet, are we? There's that Chinese destroyer with all the rest of the warheads."

"True. And there was some worry that the chopper we missed in Athens airport might have been bringing in more than just one warhead for sale. It could have had four or five. That has to be checked out. NATO was running a trace on the chances."

"We might have three or four more Afghanistans to deal with?"

"We could."

It was the deluxe flight with lunch served. It came in the form of a plastic-wrapped sandwich, a cookie, and a cup of coffee.

They landed in Tehran, and Murdock watched Holt like he was a precious jewel. He never flinched or burped. Many passengers left the plane, but through passengers could not.

Murdock watched the usual two Iranian police work up and down the long aisle. They didn't talk, just stared at the people. Kat had gone back to sleep. Murdock tried, but couldn't. When the cops passed him, he stared back at them as fiercely as they looked at him. The plainclothesman eased up on his stare, grinned, and said something, then passed on by. Murdock let out a held-in breath. One more milepost passed.

They stopped in Ankara, Turkey, and as they came down, Holt wheezed and grabbed his chest. Murdock came alert at once and leaned over him. Holt could hold it only a few seconds before he began guffawing.

"Gotcha, Skipper," he said. Then he frowned and stopped laughing. "Hey, that laughing hurt more than anything. Remind me not to do that for a while."

"You must be feeling better if you can play the clown. Easy now, and we'll have you in white sheets within a few hours." The hop from Ankara to Athens wasn't that long. Murdock wished he had a cell phone or the SATCOM so he could have NATO meet them at the airport with an ambulance. There must be one on duty there close by. He'd raise all sorts of hell at Athens until he got an ambulance to that hospital they had used before.

On the last hop to Athens, Kat watched him. "Hey, this is the first time that I've slept with you." She grinned. "In a manner of speaking. I wanted to tell you it was extremely good for me."

Kat laughed. "I've always wanted to say that to a man. Yes. Now for your sparking comeback."

"Hey, it was good for me too."

They both laughed.

"I just hope the printing on the rain check I gave you doesn't fade out over the years."

"No chance. It's under lock and key in a humidity- and temperature-controlled environment, just like the Declaration of Independence."

"Good." She sobered. "What's going to happen to that Chinese destroyer with the other warheads?"

"Wish I knew. Depends on how tough NATO has been since we left. They might have it bottled up right now. We'll find out as soon as we get you two into the medics."

"Me? I'm all right."

"Hey, you're better than that. But you get checked over by the local medical guys anyway. They like working on pretty girls."

"Check me over and release me. I'm not staying there overnight."

They landed on schedule in Athens. Murdock told the attendant that they would need a wheelchair. They waited to be last off, and a chair was at the gate. Holt protested, but Murdock insisted. Kat could walk with only a slight limp.

Just forty minutes later both patients had been checked out in the Athens hospital. Kat was looked over quickly, the dressing on her shoulder changed and the leg wound treated, and she was released.

They waited for word from the doctors about Holt.

A harried-looking doctor came out of the operating room.

"Commander Murdock?" he asked.

"Right here."

"Your man, Holt, is not the best. His lung collapsed as we were examining him. Lucky it waited until now. We have to get that lung working again, patch up the hole in his lung, and find the slug that caused it. We don't know where the slug is. We're listing him as critical right now. We should know a lot more about his condition in twenty-four hours."

# 26

## Athens, Greece

Back in their quarters in the NATO base, the SEALs had showers, fresh uniforms, and various kinds of food service. Then it was sack time. It had been a long day.

After his shower, Murdock reported to his control, Admiral Tanning. The admiral was showing some wear and tear, Murdock decided. Not the usual zip. He wiped one hand across his face and waved Murdock into a chair.

"Good work in Kabul. That's one more down. Now we're worried about what else went on with that Athens relay. We've had a team of six men working the airport. By now we have chapter and verse on the terrorist chopper when it came in and what happened to the warheads. At least one of them went to Afghanistan. The word we have now is that there was one more warhead and we have three possibilities where it went. It was shipped out within minutes after it hit the airport here."

"Three different countries, Admiral?"

"As of this morning. We have since eliminated one of them, so we're down to two. Which doesn't help us one hell of a lot until we get down to the country who bought it from the smugglers.

"There was a lot of action by Libyan aircraft about that time, but we've ruled them out as participants. They were burned twice and must have decided to pass on chance three. Which leaves us with Syria and Lebanon. They had planes and agents all over that airport landing area. It could be either one. From what we have learned, it looked like both were supposed to get goods, but there was only one warhead available. One got it, one didn't."

"So how do we find out which is which?"

"Diplomacy, old man. Diplomacy."

"Which means spies. Do we have any in either of those countries?"

"NATO doesn't, but the CIA certainly does. Deep cover, way down there, and reliable. We've used them before. With any luck we'll have a report before breakfast call."

Murdock closed his eyes and shook his head. "Excuse me, Admiral, but it's been a long day. We had two casualties, a walking wounded and a more serious one. Kat took a round through her leg and picked up a ricochet scrape on her shoulder. She says she's operational, but we'll see."

"Commander, get out of here. You need some sack time. Sleep in tomorrow. I'll let you know if we have a definite on one country or the other. You have anyone who speaks Arabic?"

"Two of us, Admiral. We might need to go with just a pair. Talk more about it tomorrow. With the admiral's permission?"

"Good night, Commander. Sleep well."

Murdock did.

He slept in until almost seven the next morning, showered, and had breakfast before he headed to the admiral's office.

Admiral Tanning worked on some papers as Murdock came into his office. Murdock stood at attention until the admiral looked up.

"Murdock, yes. I sent a man looking for you. Sit down. Our spooks have found something. They can't say for sure, but they are ninety-percent positive that one warhead was taken into Syria. Those are not the most friendly folks."

"Do we have any kind of a location where the warhead might be?"

"Our people there say that anything of importance winds up in Damascus in southwestern Syria."

"When do we go in?"

"As soon as you're ready. Is Kat well enough to go?"

"She will think so. I'll have to decide."

"Look at this map. No good entry point except by air. We can fly you over Israel and the Golan Heights and into southern Syria. Exfiltration would be the same route except by land. No chance we can put a chopper in there to get you out."

"Looks like a long walk."

"Forty miles to the tip of Israel."

"Maybe we can find a camel. I better get the troops moving."

Murdock did a snappy about-face and hurried out to the SEALs' temporary dayroom.

Half the men were there, most clustered around Don Stroh, their CIA hand-holder.

"You already know," Murdock said, looking at Stroh.

"Hey, I'm CIA, I'm supposed to know. Syria. Only two of the guys speak Arabic. You want me to go along on this one?"

"Sure, Stroh. Check out your parachute and your H&K 21A1 machine gun."

Stroh grinned. "Hey, I was just kidding. You jumping in?"

"About the only way." Murdock looked for Ed Dewitt. The Bravo Squad leader was at a far table studying maps. He looked up and came over when Murdock signaled.

"We'll be going with Bravo Squad on this one," said Murdock, "with Kat, if she's able, and me. Khai and Franklin know the language, so they'll be our point men. We have a contact in Damascus who should give us some direction. Other than that, we're on our own. We hike out once we spike the warhead. Any questions?"

"Transport?" DeWitt asked.

"Admiral Tanning is having it arranged. It won't be our usual Black Duck, but some other C-130 that has been minimally outfitted for insertion work over hostile territory."

"Wonder where our Black Duck is," Jaybird asked.

"Probably swimming upstream without a paddle," Vincent Van Dyke chirped, and they all laughed. That broke some of the tension that had been building up since Stroh came in the room.

"So, how much time do we have," Senior Chief Dobler asked.

"We're calling it," Murdock said. "Whenever we're ready. Jaybird, see if you can find Kat. Don't tell her about the mission because I've decided she's not jumping on that shot-up leg."

"Everyone from Bravo Squad here?" Senior Chief Dobler asked. DeWitt looked around.

"I need two. Jefferson, flush them out wherever they are. Their bunks, or the PX. Move."

"Sounds like we better stick to regular ammo, so we don't bog down somewhere," DeWitt said. "Ostercamp, get your SATCOM and check it out. Just a quick run-through. Let's get our gear squared away, Bravo. I want you all ready to jump in an hour."

Murdock's watch read 0840. It would be a night jump, but

he wasn't sure when the plane would be on hand or how long the flight would take to Damascus. They would be ready. He spent the next half hour working on his gear, getting everything set and putting a new edge on his fighting knife with a stone.

Kat came in with her brown eyes blazing.

"What do you mean I'm not going along. Do you see me limping? Can I hold my arms over my head? Why the hell are you grounding me because of a little scratch?"

Murdock laughed. He couldn't help it. She stood there with her fists set on her slender hips, and that stretched her khaki shirt tight across her breasts. Her face was flushed and wreathed in a tight little frown.

"Don't laugh at me, Murdock. It makes me all the madder."

He recovered enough to get his voice working. "Hey, Kat, I'm not laughing at you. It's just that is exactly the same thing I've had a dozen SEALs say to me over the years. Which makes you a SEAL more than you know. You're thinking SEAL now, even with a shot-up leg and a shoulder wound that's going to leave a scar. Now, SEAL, drop and give me fifty push-ups."

Kat gave a long sigh. "Murdock, you know I can't do that with this fucking shoulder. But that doesn't mean I can't jump in with you to Damascus and spike that warhead just the way we did before."

"We are jumping, SEAL. It will be a HALO operation. That's a thirty-one-thousand-foot free fall, and it's going to be cold enough to freeze your nipples off. Why in hell would you want to go?"

"Sir, it's my job, sir." She shouted the words, and it made half the platoon turn and look at her. A cheer started halfway down the room, and then exploded all over the place.

"Come on, Cap, let the SEAL go and jump," somebody called.

"Yeah, besides, I don't want to be anywhere in Syria if you're gonna play with that nuke warhead," Canzoneri yelled.

Kat's frown faded. She turned and looked at the SEALs. A huge grin blossomed, and through the grin she felt tears rolling down her cheeks.

"Line up, you assholes, I want to hug all of you," Kat bellowed in a good imitation of a chief's parade-ground voice. The SEALs responded by cheering and clapping. At last, Murdock pushed up his fist into the air. The room quieted at once.

"Kat, walk over to the door and back."

She did, wiping away tears of pure joy and waving at the SEALs. She walked without a trace of a limp.

"Now, Kat. Run to the far end of the room and run back."

Kat did, with only as slight limp on the way back.

Murdock stood there frowning, his arms crossed protectively in front of him. Kat took up the same stance, staring hard at him.

"Kat, you promise me you won't get shot again, and you're on the manifest."

A whoop of delight came from the SEALs, and they waved at Kat and went back to getting their gear ready.

"Now, SEAL, you better get into the proper uniform for the jump. We only have another hour here. Move it."

Kat grinned and ran toward her quarters to change into desert cammies.

When Murdock had his gear ready, he went to talk to the admiral, who put down the phone as Murdock came to a braced attention in front of his desk.

"At ease, Commander. Sit. We have a C-130 from Rome. It took off twenty minutes ago and should be here in about two hours. We'll do turnaround service on it and she'll be ready to go. You'll want a night drop?"

"Yes, sir. As early after dark as possible. Flight time from here to our DZ should be about two and half hours."

"What our people figured. Dark this time of year in this zone is around seven o'clock. You'll be over hostile territory for about fifty miles or six or seven minutes."

"Let's have takeoff from here at 1630. That should work, sir."

"Sounds good to me, Commander. I'll issue the orders and we'll get you airborne."

"What about the Chinese ship, sir?"

"She's doing a turtle on us. She hasn't shown her true colors. She's anchored off a small island in the Aegean Sea about a hundred miles from here. Trying a waiting game. I don't know why, unless she's hoping we'll relax our CAP over her. No chance another chopper is going to get near her."

"Maybe by the time we're back from Syria things will have changed. If not we'll figure out what to do."

"Good hunting over there, Commander Murdock. I wish we had better intel for you, but you do have one contact. You'll be in a big-city situation again. Damascus has about two million people."

"We'll put on our city manners, sir." Murdock stood. "If there's nothing else, Admiral."

"Dismissed, Commander, and good luck."

Murdock charged back to the quarters that NATO had made available to them. They had plenty of time before liftoff.

Kat came back ten minutes later dressed and ready. She began to work on her gear, and at once four SEALs came to help her.

"Thanks, guys. I really need this." Her eyes had lost the anger, and now her face showed excitement, anticipation, and a little bit of fear.

"At least we won't be jumping into a combat zone," she said. "I mean, nobody is going to shoot at us as we come down in our chutes."

"If we're lucky," Jack Mahanani said.

Alpha Squad stood around kibitzing. They had just had their turn, and maybe lost a man doing it. Now Bravo would go in on a one-squad operation.

Murdock had changed the weapons assignments. He selected five Bull Pups, one sniper rifle, one 21-E machine gun, and three MP-S5D submachine guns.

An hour before flight time, DeWitt had the squad in formation in the workroom and checked them. He made sure the men had the right ammo for their weapons. The Bull Pup shooters each had thirty rounds, a real load of the huge 20mm rounds.

"Anybody not happy with his assigned weapon?" DeWitt asked. Murdock and Kat were at the end of the squad. Kat held up her hand.

"Sir, I'd rather have a Bull Pup," she said, grinning.

"Sure and two hundred rounds of ammo," somebody yelped. They all laughed.

"Any other real questions?" DeWitt asked. There were none. "Okay, take a break. We get on the bus to go to the airfield in twenty minutes."

A half hour later, the SEALs and Kat rattled around in the huge hold of the C-130 like ten peas in a giant peapod. Some of them sat in the fold-down seats along the sides. Three were sacked out on some moving padding blankets on the floor.

It was DeWitt's operation. Murdock would act as another gun for him, and give advice if asked for it. If they had to split up, he'd con half the force. DeWitt had just come back from the cockpit, where he'd talked with the Air Force captain flying the big plane.

"Captain Rothkind says he's been on this run before, but with just two CIA guys. He says the best place to jump is about twenty miles from Damascus. Any closer than that and there are suburbs all over the place. He suggests we come down in the countryside out a ways and then make our way into town. That way nobody should report our coming."

"Agreed," Murdock said.

"The loadmaster said we'd be using the side doors for jumping, not the fold-down hatch on the back. We'll hook up just the same and half the squad goes out each side door."

"Somehow it isn't the same," Murdock said, remembering that heart-throttling moment of the first step into space from the ramp.

"Gets the job done," DeWitt said, and went to check on a loose strap he saw on one of the men.

Kat sat beside Murdock. Her eyes still held the same snap and lightning charge they'd had when she was packing.

"This better than tearing down nose cones in some subbasement somewhere?" Murdock asked.

"A lot better, yes. This is so much more important, vital to the safety and well-being of the world."

"It's good to see that there are still some optimists in the world who believe that the good, not the most powerful, will win the day. Now, on the practical side, we'll be up all night. Might be a good idea to grab a couple hours of sleep." Murdock frowned. "Oh, you have done free fall before, haven't you?"

"Absolutely, in training. We went from twelve thousand down to five."

Murdock winced. "This one will be a little longer, and colder. Be sure you have your face mask, oxygen mask, and gloves on. And keep your glow stick lit so we can find each other. We'll use oxygen for the first twenty thousand feet or so."

"Real cold?"

"Extremely cold for about ten thousand feet, then it eases up. It will take us two to three minutes to get to two thousand feet, where our chutes open automatically. If yours doesn't, pull your emergency chute cord."

"Have you ever used your emergency?"

"Not so far. Now, get to sleep."

Murdock closed his eyes, and a moment later a hand touched his arm. He looked that way.

"Hey, super-SEAL. Is it all right if I'm just a little scared?"

Murdock grinned in the darkness of the plane. "Sure, you bet. Wouldn't be normal if you weren't."

"Good." She hesitated. "I don't suppose you could put your arm around me and hold me tight for a minute."

"Not if you're a SEAL. What would the other guys think?"

"Uh-oh, yeah. I forgot. Right now I'm a SEAL, not a woman. I'll remember that." She stopped again, then looked up at his face in the darkness. "Hey, you remember about that rain check?"

"I remember. One of my best memories."

She smiled. "Good. Now, good night."

Later, Murdock came awake in a flash. Somebody shook his shoulder.

"Hey, Cap, need some advice." DeWitt looked down at him. "You awake, Murdock?"

"Almost. What's the trouble?"

"We just entered Syrian airspace. The captain up front tells me he has some bogies showing on his radar that are headed our way but about fifty miles out. That means they will be keeping company with us in about seven minutes. Close enough for an ID in three when they can fire their missiles. What the hell can we do? The pilot wants to turn back into Israeli airspace."

# 27

**33,000 feet over Syria**

Murdock went forward to talk with the pilot.

"How far from our DZ?"

"Twenty miles, and I'm ready to turn back," the pilot said.

"Turn on the jump light," Murdock said. "We'll go out here. We can't turn back. Should give you time enough to get over the border before they fire their missiles."

"What if it doesn't?" the pilot asked.

"That's why you flyboys get the big paychecks. Let's move it, DeWitt."

It took them another minute to get everyone on their feet and at the jump doors. They turned on their oxygen and checked the eight-inch bottles on their harnesses, all were working. As soon as the loadmaster opened the doors, the SEALs jumped out. There was no time for anybody to even think about what was happening, let alone be afraid.

Kat hesitated at the door. She was next to last out on that side. Murdock touched her shoulder. She flashed him a smile, then stepped into the thin, cold, 33,000 feet of nonsupportive air.

Murdock went right behind her. He had his glow stick bent and working before he left the plane, as did the other SEALs.

The cold air hit him in the face right through the woolen protective mask and oxygen mask that left only his eyes uncovered. It jolted him like a bucket of ice water hitting him while he stood naked in the snow at twenty below zero. He spread out into a glide position with his arms and legs spread. Then he began to look around.

He craned his neck as he checked for the faint glow. He found two light sticks to the left, and moved his body to steer himself in that direction. By the time he got close enough to see the men in the thin, moonlit air, he counted three. There should be one more. All the SEALs had put on their Motorola personal radios before jumping and had radio-checked with DeWitt.

Murdock used his. "DeWitt. I have four of us on this side. One is astray somewhere."

"DeWitt here. I have four chicks and me. Where is your stray?"

"Left door jumpers, check in," Murdock said on the mike, hoping the words didn't freeze before they hit the airwaves.

Everyone responded but Kat. "Kat, can you hear me? Where are you?"

Nothing but silence came. He craned his neck, looking around. He thought he saw some faint glow in the far right. That would be DeWitt and his group. Where could she be? He stayed with his men, but looked behind and to the side and then up. She was smaller and lighter than the rest. Would that make a difference?

He checked his wrist altimeter. They were at 28,000 feet. Where was she?

He looked again to the side away from the others. For a moment he thought he saw a glow. Then it vanished. He left the group and sailed that direction.

"Kat, can you hear me? Maybe your mike froze up. Remember about laying out with your arms and legs spread so you can sail? Try it. If it works, turn a little so you move to your right. And keep that glow stick in your hand. Yes, now I can see it. Steer right, more to the right. You should see my glow stick soon."

He could see her glow plainly then as she worked her way toward him.

"Kat, if you can hear me, we're at twenty thousand feet and it's getting warmer. Try your mike again."

"Yes, I see you. Don't know if the mike is working. I'm coming your way."

"Good, Kat, your mike is working. Swing farther my way, then we'll join up with our group and DeWitt."

"I can see you!" Kat shrilled, her relief billowing into her voice. "Thank God. I thought I was alone in the whole universe. Really, I thought I was an astronaut cut loose from the tether in space. What a trip. What a ride. Just sail toward you?"

"Doing fine. We're at fifteen thousand. Won't be long now."

By the time she was close enough, Murdock realized that DeWitt's group had sailed over and joined with the rest of his party.

DeWitt came on the radio. "Okay, we have a full count, we're just passing ten thousand. Be down in a shake. Can anybody see a string of lights that might be cars on a road down there?"

"No damn road," Jefferson said.

"Batch of lights up north, I guess it is," Khai said. "Looks like a small town."

"Let's all turn that way," DeWitt said on the Motorola. "Maybe we can steal a car or a truck. What will hold ten bodies these days?"

"Maybe a van," Franklin said.

"Coming up on two thousand, grab those emergency chute cords just in case," DeWitt said. "Sound off when your chute opens."

"I'm open," Ostercamp said. He was followed by the rest of the Bravo Squad.

"Open," Kat said, then Murdock chimed in.

"We have ten open, let's turn the chutes toward those lights and see if we can find a soft landing," DeWitt ordered.

Murdock could see Kat to his left. Her chute had opened before his, so she was a little above him. She turned and he turned with her, steering closer so he was only fifty feet away. They were behind the rest of the squad now, and Murdock started to relax. There were lights around, but scattered, like maybe farming country with houses. The town was well ahead of them.

"Kat, watch it when you hit," Murdock warned. "Run forward if you can. It's a perfect jump if you can stay on your feet."

"Seems like we're going faster than that last night jump. My God, there it is, the ground."

Then Murdock stopped watching her and looked at his own LZ. He came down almost on top of a small building at the edge of a fenced field. He willed himself over the fence, then hit running in a plowed field and stumbled and fell. He jumped up, gathered in the parachute and lines according to the book, and ran with them ahead to where he had seen Kat land.

He realized they were almost at the back door of a small farmhouse and buildings. Kat had gathered her chute, and stood there looking down at a man sprawled on the ground. Even in the dim moonlight Murdock could see the man's penis outside his black trousers.

Kat had trouble to keep from laughing. She motioned to the man, then to the small outhouse, and giggled.

"He came out and stood there, legs spread taking a piss. I couldn't miss him. My boots whacked hard into his head. Did I kill him?"

Murdock looked at the man, then knelt down and touched his throat for the carotid artery. He stood.

"He'll live, but we better get out of here. Run, lady, run." They rushed ahead toward where they saw the others picking up their chutes in a field of newly mown hay.

"He isn't dead, just knocked out," Murdock told Kat. "Nobody will believe him when he tells his story tomorrow."

Just ahead they found another plowed field, and with the two entrenching tools they carried they dug out furrows, lined the chutes into them, and covered them up. Ten minutes later they were ready.

DeWitt had sent out Miguel Fernandez as scout as soon as they landed. He came jogging back as they finished digging.

"We've got a secondary road of some kind half a klick over here to the right. Not much traffic, but some. Damascus has to be north of us and a little to the east."

"Let's hit the road and see what we can find out from the next neighborly truck driver," DeWitt said. They moved out. Bravo Squad had its usual line of march. Fernandez out a hundred yards in front as scout, DeWitt next, with his radio man, Ostercamp, behind him with the SATCOM. Then came Franklin and Khai, who both could speak Arabic, followed by Mahanani, Canzoneri, Jefferson, Kat, and Murdock bringing up the rear.

They had landed in a small valley that had a water source of some kind to grow the crops. The surrounding hills were barren and desertlike, Murdock remembered from watching them as he came down.

They moved over another fence, then through a ditch, and went to ground as Franklin waited at the side of the road. Time was the important factor now. It was 1920, which left them roughly eight hours to complete their mission or find someplace to hide out during the day.

Franklin carried an MP-5 submachine gun. He waved two cars by in the glare of headlights. Then a small loaded truck went by. He stopped the next truck, holding the weapon in front of him but standing at the side of the road. He wasn't going to risk getting run down by a wild-eyed Syrian driver.

The truck stopped, and Franklin talked to the driver a moment, then ordered him out of the cab. It was a stake truck with canvas over the top, and would hold the whole squad.

"How far to the next town?" Franklin asked in Arabic.

"Five kilometers," the driver answered.

"How far to Damascus?"

"Fifty kilometers."

"You live around here?"

"Yes, next village."

Franklin put three silenced rounds from the sub gun through the man's heart. The Syrian farmer jolted off the roadway into the ditch. Franklin hurried after him, took off his hat and light jacket, and then went back to the truck.

Bravo Squad and guests were already inside, with DeWitt and Khai in the front seat.

"Can you drive this thing?" DeWitt asked Franklin.

"Can a duck fly?" He started the engine, pushed it into gear, and began backing up. The SEALs cheered. He ground the gears, found first, and moved forward.

They crept through the village at a modest pace, found nothing to hinder them, and gunned the rig to a faster speed once past the lights.

"Fuel?" DeWitt asked.

Khai stared at the small panel of instruments. "One gauge, but I'm not sure if it says almost full or almost empty." He pointed at it.

"Almost full," Franklin said.

In the back of the truck, Kat moved next to Murdock. He had just cut a hole in the front of the canvas top so they could push the machine gun out and fire in case of trouble.

"Murdock," she said softly. "About the driver?"

"Yes, an innocent man. But we couldn't leave a witness to run to the Army about a group of ten who hijacked his truck. He's a victim of war. His death could help save the lives of ten thousand people if Syria dropped that warhead on Haifa, Israel, say. I know when you look at it another way, it's shocking. But we're protecting our own backsides this way as well. We let him live, all ten of us could die before morning."

"I know, I know. I just had to hear you say it. Now, I'm all

SEAL again." He reached down and squeezed her hand. She clung to it. In the dark nobody could see.

Two miles out of the village the land changed back to desert. Wind whipped sand across the highway, and in places small dunes had built up a foot of sand on the ancient blacktop. They kept driving. For twenty miles they saw no lights anywhere in the surrounding area.

"Not a good place to run out of gas," Franklin said. "Hope to hell I'm reading that gauge right." Two autos passed them, whipping along at what Franklin said had to be seventy-five miles per hour. He kept the truck at a respectable fifty-five, and hoped the engine didn't blow up.

They came over a small rise and lights billowed ahead of them. The lights were situated well off the road, brilliantly illuminating some kind of facility.

"Limestone quarry," Franklin said. "They use a lot of limestone in buildings in some of their cities. We should be hitting more traffic now. They must have a rail line down here to move the stone to the north."

"Checkpoint ahead," DeWitt said. "Looks like just one man beside a jeep. He'll be on the driver's side." As they moved toward the checkpoint, they were sandwiched in between large closed truck trailers, moving slowly and evidently loaded.

The man at the checkpoint noted the truck in front of them, talked to the driver a moment, and made a note on the paper on his clipboard and waved him by.

The sentry had a revolver on a belt around his waist and the cap of an Army man. He only glanced at the farm truck, and waved it on through without a second look.

Everyone in the truck relaxed, and the people in back stayed low and out of sight until they were well down the road.

"Somebody from the quarry checking the goods coming out," Khai said.

Ahead they came to a wider, better road with signs. They could turn left or right. Khai studied the signs and when the truck was at the junction, he pointed to the left.

"Swings around and keeps going north," Khai said. "The sign says twenty-six kilometers to Damascus."

"Yeah, and that's probably the outskirts of the place," Franklin said. "How we going to find anybody in that big city?"

"We ask questions," DeWitt said. "When we get to the town, stop at the first little group of stores you see. You take the address inside, Franklin, and get directions to the street. Should work out well."

Five miles from Damascus, the traffic began to back up. Murdock looked out over the cab and saw the problem. He leaned under the canvas and yelled to Khai.

"There's a roadblock ahead. A real one. Looks like they're checking cars and trucks and cargo. How about a side street?"

They turned right at the next street, and a block down found a Syrian Army jeep parked sideways across the street. Two soldiers with rifles stood in front of the jeep.

"I see them," Murdock said. "I'll take the one on my side. Ed, you take the other one. We pull up and stop and they will come one on each side. We do them and push the jeep out of the way and drive on through. No chance for radio use. Got it?" DeWitt had a silenced MP-5. In back, Murdock grabbed a suppressed MP-5 and held it close to the hole in the canvas top over the hood. The rig came to a stop ten yards in front of the jeep, where one of the soldiers held up his hand. Then the Syrian soldiers began walking toward the truck.

Murdock pushed the MP-5 out the canvas and drilled three shots into the chest of the soldier on the left, slamming him backward into a quick death. At almost the same time, DeWitt shot the other soldier in the forehead with one round.

Franklin saw the left-hand man go down, pushed on the gas, and hit the rear end of the Jeep with the truck's left front bumper and jolted it out of the way. The truck rolled on through, down eight blocks, then over one, and back onto the main highway into town.

They stopped three miles down the road, which was now engulfed with houses and small businesses and what had to be small manufacturing buildings.

Franklin went into a food store, and came out a few minutes later with a sack of goods and a written note telling how to find the house they needed.

They had been supplied with funny-looking paper money before they boarded the plane. They were Syrian pound notes in denominations of twenty, fifty, and one hundred. Fifty-eight Syrian pounds were worth one U.S. dollar.

"Got the directions," Franklin said, passing the sack over to DeWitt. "Also some delicious sweet rolls that look like cinnamon rolls, and taste ten times as good. Hang on." They passed the rolls around. Khai leaned out and passed the sack to Oster-camp.

Franklin drove like he knew where he was going. He made several turns, backed up once and went in the other direction, then came to an unpaved street and grinned.

"Almost home to Mama," he said. He noted house numbers, and parked at the side of the street in front of a house. It was what the natives called an Old House, Khai told them. "It's made of unbaked bricks, often dried in the sun, and of wood and stone. Most of these are very old."

DeWitt and Khai left the truck and went to the rear of the house. They carried weapons, and hoped anyone watching in the darkness would mistake them for Syrian soldiers. At the rear of the house they found a door with a bell. DeWitt rang it and stepped back, giving the play to Khai.

A small panel in the door opened, and a face with two dark eyes looked out.

"Yes?" the woman asked in Arabic.

"We are looking for the one true believer."

The woman sucked in a breath, and they heard a bolt come free and latches open. Then the door swung outward, showing a shadowed narrow space. A woman in long flowing skirt and brilliantly colored blouse watched them with a frown.

"Come in quickly," she said in English. "Yes, you have found the right place. Get rid of the truck at once. Even though it is dark, bring in the others by twos. This side of the house. Then drive the truck down a mile and leave it. You stole it, right?"

DeWitt nodded. "I'm DeWitt, miss. We're grateful for your help."

"Hurry. If the neighbors see any of you, we all could die rather unpleasantly."

DeWitt went back to the truck, ushered the men inside, and told Franklin where to drive the truck and leave it.

"No trouble so far," DeWitt said. "Let's keep it that way."

The men slipped through the nighttime shadows and around the house, then inside. Murdock watched the truck drive away slowly, then went inside himself.

"Franklin should be back in fifteen minutes. Somebody keep the clock on him," DeWitt said. He turned to the woman. "I understand we are to call you Yasmin, which isn't your real name."

The woman was in her thirties, tall and graceful and a little on the full-figured side.

"Yes, Yasmin it is. I will do what I can. My sources say the warhead is here, but we're not exactly sure where."

"We'll need to know an exact location before we can do much," DeWitt said.

They had moved into a room from the entrance, and some of the men sat and some stood. Yasmin glanced at them, and paused when she came to Kat.

"One so young, he's just a boy," Yasmin said.

Kat laughed. "Not so, Yasmin. I'm twenty-eight, and as you can hear, I'm not a boy."

Yasmin put both hands over her face. "Oh, I'm so sorry. I had no idea. Dressed this way . . ."

"Yasmin, let me introduce you to Katherine Garnet," DeWitt said. "Kat works for the U.S. government the way you do, only Kat is our scientific expert on nuclear warheads. The rest of us are just delivery boys bringing her here to do her extremely sensitive work."

Murdock looked at his watch. Franklin had been gone almost twenty-five minutes. Where was he?

Four blocks down the street, Franklin stared at the two Syrian soldiers who had stopped him moments before.

"No one runs in Damascus unless they are criminals or enemies of Syria," one of the soldiers told Franklin.

Franklin looked at them, and saw two soldiers probably not out of their teens. They held their rifles slung over their shoulders and muzzles down.

One of them motioned with his free hand. "Come on, we're going to have to take you into headquarters if you won't talk. You could tell us what branch of special Army teams you're with, and we could let you go and finish our patrol. Going to be a lot of work for all of us."

Franklin understood every word they said in Arabic. He knew he had to do something fast. He just didn't know what.

# 28

Franklin had kept the MP-5 with him when he drove the truck down the street away from the safe house. Now, facing the two Syrian soldiers, he carried the weapon in his right hand by the hand-piece with his finger on the trigger.

He shrugged and screeched and pointed behind the two men. They turned to look, and he brought up the sub gun and sprayed the men with two bursts of three silenced rounds each. The soldiers went down, both dead or dying before they hit the ground.

Franklin turned and ran down the street, the MP-5 in both hands and held in front of him. He finished the rest of the mile in record time, and went to the back door of the safe house as they had told him to do. J.G. DeWitt stood there outside waiting for him.

"Any problems?" DeWitt asked.

"Two," Franklin said. "Couple of Syrian soldiers came out of nowhere and stopped me coming back from the truck."

He told the J.G. what happened, and they hurried inside and Franklin told their host.

Yasmin frowned when she heard the story. "This will make problems. What you must do is go back to the truck, put the bodies inside, and drive it five miles down the street. Then come back here. It is the only way. Otherwise we would have soldiers all over this area asking questions, looking for strangers."

"Franklin, you're up. You know where the bodies and the truck are," DeWitt said. "Take Jefferson with you. Then get back here without attracting any more attention."

The two men picked up their weapons and hurried out the door.

"There's not much we can do tonight," Yasmin said. "I know,

you want to do the job and get away, but it can't happen yet. I'm meeting two people tomorrow morning who should have some intel about where the Army has the warhead. Best I can do. Your men can sleep upstairs. Two rooms with mattresses on the floor. Not the best accommodations."

"We've slept on lots worse," DeWitt said.

"Any idea at all where the warhead might be?" Murdock asked. "Would it be on an Army base, here in town, out in the country somewhere they consider safe?"

Yasmin nodded. "Oh, yes, we know a little. It was flown here by commercial jet and taken at once to military headquarters near the edge of town. They were so afraid of it that they ordered it moved to a safe place until they could get engineers in to look it over and convert it into a drop bomb. My source said the top Army brass were almost paralyzed with fear of the warhead. They are afraid it might suddenly trigger itself and explode and kill most of the people in Damascus."

"So where did they move it?" DeWitt asked.

Yasmin sighed. "That, my friends, is what we have to find out. My sources say it must have been taken to one of two locations. Both are well outside of the city, but they are in opposite directions, so we must stay here."

"We'll do whatever we can," Murdock said.

Yasmin smiled. "Yes, I have been instructed. But you must be tired. The men can sleep upstairs. The lady will be with me. There are two beds in my room. Oh, I'm sorry. You also must be hungry. I have been stocking up on food."

"The men will be fine, Yasmin," Murdock said. "Something in the morning would be good. We know this is a lot of trouble for you. We and the government appreciate it."

Yasmin sat in a chair, and the two officers and Kat sat nearby.

"Yes, a bit of a problem," Yasmin said, "but that's why I'm here. I am a Syrian, but I grew up in Philadelphia. I've been here for eight years now, doing what I can. My cover is to teach math in one of the schools. My . . . my husband was also working with me for the Company, but he was killed three years ago in an operation that went sour. He was not suspected, just an unfortunate who was in the wrong place at the wrong time."

"No one suspects what you do?" DeWitt asked.

"So far. But I have been deep cover with no activity at all for the past two years. Now I have a chance to help. Yes, I am a trained field agent, as was my husband. We wanted to do something to help bring better relations between the Arab world and the West. We're not sure that we have."

"Every little bit helps," Murdock said. "If we can find that warhead and destroy it, we may be saving the lives of a hundred thousand people. That would be a real contribution."

Yasmin's eyes widened. "So many? I heard that the bomb in Chad killed almost thirty thousand. Unthinkable. How could the Russians let such a weapon loose on the world?"

"To our best understanding, the weapon had been stored and hidden in Ukraine, formerly part of Russia, now an independent nation," DeWitt said. "The government there probably didn't sell the missile. It probably went into the hands of an unscrupulous person who sold it to the Chinese."

"That helps me a little. At least a government didn't loose this terror. Tomorrow morning I will be up early to go meet with my source. I can't use the telephone. They are closely monitored. I am somewhat suspect since the government knows I was born in the U.S., but it's routine and thousands of people are monitored. I will be gone when you get up."

Jefferson and Franklin came in, both breathing hard. Franklin looked at DeWitt and gave a curt nod.

"Mission accomplished, J.G. We drove her six miles more and parked it in a lot with a bunch of other rigs."

"No problems coming back?"

"No, sir. All is cool," Jefferson said. "We uptight or on the pad?"

"Some sleeping places upstairs," DeWitt said. "Better hit them. We don't know what's up for tomorrow."

The two men vanished up a stairway that Yasmin pointed to.

Yasmin stared at Kat for a moment. "I think it's time for bed for everyone. Kat, that bandage on your leg probably needs to be changed. Let's go in and take a look." She waved at the men. "Stay up as long as you want to. Just turn out the lights when you go upstairs."

They did.

Murdock came awake at 0530 as usual. He had slept fully dressed, except for his boots, as the rest of the men did. He put on his boots, and saw that Ed DeWitt was up and staring out a window.

"She left in a black sedan about an hour ago," DeWitt said. "I couldn't sleep."

"How far do you think they took the warhead?" Murdock asked.

"Forty miles the other side of the suburbs," DeWitt said. "Figures. The government guys must be scared shitless by the hellish device."

"Might work to our advantage," Murdock said. "Might mean they wouldn't protect it with a lot of men, just some buildings and concrete and maybe a mine shaft. They do any mining here?"

"Not much. Some asphalt, gypsum, and phosphate."

"Hope they don't stick it down a mine somewhere."

An hour later downstairs, they discovered a woman in the kitchen ready to make breakfast. Franklin said she'd told him she was "cook" and was ready for their orders.

The SEALs had been warned to stay inside and away from all windows. They ate and then waited, stripping and oiling weapons, but only half of them at a time so they would be ready for any surprise.

Yasmin came back to the house just after 1000. She looked grim as she walked inside. Yasmin motioned for Murdock and DeWitt to come into a small room she used as an office. She wore a dark dress and a hat that she took off and threw across the room.

"Worse than I figured," she said. "My contact says he knows for sure that the warhead originally came into Damascus on the plane, but then was taken at once to a small munitions factory about thirty miles north of town."

"So we move again," Murdock said.

"The worst part is that the munitions plant is on the corner of an Army base used to train volunteers for hazardous duty. They have top-notch fighting men there. Usually about two hundred at a time in training."

DeWitt scowled. "You're right. It isn't a pretty picture. Is there a fence or barbed wire around the Army base?"

"I don't know. I had hoped it would be an easier target for you. How can you . . . I mean, with only small arms you have to take on maybe three hundred men."

"Yasmin," Murdock said. "Is there any way you could get us a dozen rocket-propelled grenades?"

"The shoulder-launched rockets?" She paused. "I know some counterrevolutionaries who have used them. Let me make a call and inquire about red posters. It's a key word we sometimes use. That one I can make on the phone."

While she phoned, Ostercamp set up the SATCOM and contacted Athens. He gave Murdock the handset.

"Yes, Athens. We arrived. Have located the package. Working on some local support. Will move as soon as it's dark."

"The contact working?" Admiral Tanning asked.

"Yes. She does a good job. Will contact you after our trip north to the candy factory. Murdock out."

Yasmin came back with Kat. The two were chattering away like old friends. Yasmin grinned. "Some good news at last. My friends say they can bring us ten, but if you can help them replace them, that would be good."

"Would money help?" DeWitt asked.

"Incredibly. They have to buy them. The going rate here is a hundred U.S. dollars each. You have Syrian pounds?"

"Right. At sixty pounds for the dollar, that's six thousand pounds per weapon," DeWitt said. "Each of our men was given fifteen thousand. So we can cover the cost of sixty thousand pounds."

"Kat," Murdock said. "Be our banker. Collect six thousand pounds from each of the men. Get the biggest notes they have." Murdock took off his thin cloth money belt and gave Kat his six thousand.

"Can they bring the weapons here just after dark?" DeWitt asked.

"I'll tell them to," said Yasmin. "Let me get a map and I'll show you where the munitions factory is to the north. Then we need to figure out some transport for you. We can't risk stealing another truck. We could all get blown away in a hurry if they caught us."

"Do you have any friends in the trucking business?" DeWitt asked.

Yasmin laughed. "Oh, yes. I do. And he owes me a big favor. One condition. I get to go along on the raid."

DeWitt looked at Murdock.

Yasmin smiled. "I can shoot, and I have my own weapon and ammo. An Uzi, as a matter of fact, and three hundred rounds."

"You just signed on," Murdock said.

That afternoon as the men slept, or worked on their weapons, Paul Jefferson and DeWitt played chess on a small peg board, and Kat and Yasmin began talking.

"Philadelphia, you told us," Kat said. "I spent several years in Philadelphia back in the late eighties."

"That's when I grew up there," Yasmin said. "We might even have been there at the same time."

They traded stories, and Kat told her how she had been on a job with the SEALs before. "Nobody will ever know about what we did. But when the President calls you and says he wants you to do something for him, not many people can turn him down."

"The President himself?" Yasmin asked. "From the White House?"

Kat nodded. "Not once, but twice now. But the SEALs take good care of me. I had to prove I could stay up with them hiking and swimming. They taught me to shoot. I like the MP-5 the best."

"My husband taught me to shoot. I'm not sure I learned well enough. It still haunts me that on the night he was killed I could have shot better and maybe saved him. I took two bullets, but I wasn't seriously wounded. They haven't let me go on any field missions since."

Her eyes turned misty and she dabbed at them. "I've had this one dream forever. I want to get my hands on a weapon and shoot down five or six Syrian soldiers. They were the ones who killed the love of my life. I deserve to get some revenge. Don't you think?"

Then she cried, and Kat held her until the sobbing stopped.

"This might be the time," Kat said. "If Murdock said you could go, you'll have to stay with us all the way. With that many troops up there, we can use an extra gun."

Yasmin dried her eyes and sniffed and then blew her nose. They took beers out of the refrigerator and popped the caps, and went on doing girl talk for another half hour.

Then Kat frowned. "Hey, you have any pants? Murdock is gonna flip if you show up for the shoot in that dress." They both laughed, and Yasmin assured Kat she would dress like a man for the fight.

Just before dark, a fifteen-foot moving van pulled up in front of the house and a man came to the door. He talked with Yasmin for a moment, then he and Kat carried a mattress out to the van. They went inside for more, and when it was fully dark, the SEALs began slipping out the back door and into the big door of the van. They went one by one at staggered intervals, until all ten of them were inside with their weapons and gear.

Yasmin had on black pants and a dark brown shirt. Her hair had been pinned up and covered with a brown floppy hat. They waited in the truck for ten minutes before a car pulled up and blinked its lights. The truck driver followed it for two blocks to a spot where there weren't any houses. The men in the car quickly delivered the ten shoulder-fired, rocket-propelled grenade weapons, and took the money in exchange.

Two minutes after the truck stopped, it moved ahead again, with Yasmin in front with the driver, and DeWitt in between them.

"Radio net check," DeWitt said.

All nine of the team checked in.

"So, we're up and operating," DeWitt said. "Rest and relax. Yasmin tells me it will take us about two hours to get through the outskirts of Damascus and then the thirty miles on north to the target. Time is now twenty-ten. We should be there by twenty-two ten, and check out the target for eval and planning. I hope we can hit it by midnight. Any questions?"

"Yeah, exfiltration," Manhanani said. "Can we use this same truck to get toward the border?"

DeWitt repeated the question for Yasmin. She spoke with the driver. They talked back and forth, and then she grinned in the darkness.

DeWitt held his mike toward the agent. "He says if we can get away from the area cleanly, without the truck being shot up or identified with the attack, he'll be glad to pick us up and take us as close to the border as possible. He is a businessman, and will need to be paid."

"Sounds reasonable," DeWitt said. "You know our cash position. Work out something with him."

To DeWitt it sounded like a haggling process. At last the two stopped talking and Yasmin smiled again. "He's part of the resistance here, but he has to make a living. He says he can get us almost to the border with Israel for fifteen thousand pounds. That's two hundred and fifty dollars."

"Sold," DeWitt said.

An hour and a half later the truck came to a stop a half mile from a brightly lit compound ahead. They were off the main road and on one that ran along the back of the Army base and the munitions factory. Lights seemed to be everywhere.

"Drive by so we can get a better look," DeWitt ordered. They drove at a normal speed along the dirt road, and when they were a half mile beyond the plant, they stopped and the driver turned off the lights.

"Let's hit the bricks," DeWitt said on the radio. The SEALs and two women helpers left the truck and went to ground in a shallow ditch next to an open field. Two hundred yards down the way a chain-link fence barred their way to the munitions factory.

"There it is," DeWitt said on the radio. "Now just how the hell do we get inside and find the fucking nuclear warhead?"

# 29

## North of Damascus, Syria

Murdock came to rest prone in the weeds of the ditch as he looked at the lighted target. DeWitt landed beside him, and made a futile gesture to his superior. Murdock shook his head and pointed back at DeWitt.

The J.G. took his field glasses and stared at the target. He shouldn't have shown any indecision. Damnit! What was the matter with him? It was a target, like any other. He'd find a way. He checked the near side of the chain-link fence through the glasses. At the corner he saw what looked to be a hole, or at least a section of the stiff fencing that could be bent back.

He grinned. Soldiers would be boys. When they wanted out without a pass, they could find a way. He used the Motorola.

"Looks like an entry point near the corner of the fence. Ostercamp, check it out. The rest of us will move up to fifty yards from the corner. Move, now."

Murdock had told Yasmin to stay right beside DeWitt. "You don't dare fire your weapon unless he does. When he does, it's a signal to the platoon also to open fire. Don't get excited and try to get the scalp on your belt before it's time. You could destroy the whole mission."

"I understand," she said.

Now she ran when DeWitt did, flopped on the ground when he did, always protecting her Uzi and her ammunition, kept in a shoulder bag slung at her back. All she wanted was one or two good shots at the enemy, at the soldiers who had killed her beloved.

Kat held close to Murdock. She carried an MP-5 and enough magazines of ammo to sink a battleship. This was crazy. What was she doing out here with these professional strike team guys? What was she trying to prove? Then she grinned in the dark. She had proved it already. Now she was just doing what her president had ordered her to do. Yeah, that was it.

Ostercamp's voice came on the radio. "Yeah, J.G., hole big enough for Mahanani to crawl through. Been used quite a bit. Don't see any kind of security on the other side of the fence where I am. Come on up."

"Let's go," DeWitt said into his mike, and the ten dark figures lifted off the ground and ran, bent over, toward the fence, then through the hole one at a time. Murdock and Kat went through last.

"Ostercamp?" DeWitt asked.

"Out front about fifty, J.G. There's a fucking track through the light grass and weeds where the AWOL guys have been walking. No guards, no rovers that I can see. Lights are another two hundred yards ahead."

"Go slow, watch on all sides, and keep moving up," J.G. told Ostercamp. Then he moved his squad forward.

Ten minutes later, DeWitt lay in the grass and weeds just outside the flare of the floodlights. The nearest building was open on the back and looked like a maintenance structure. They all hugged the ground as a small utility vehicle growled around the building, slowed as two men in the rig looked the area over, then speeded up, and went around the near side and toward the next building. A small-caliber machine gun was mounted on a pedestal between the seats.

The soldiers wore camouflaged fatigues much like those the SEALs had on. Their hats were different. DeWitt called Franklin up, and told him what he wanted him to do. Franklin grinned, and crawled back to Canzoneri and Ostercamp.

"We're gonna play soldier," he told them. "This is a Special Forces training area. Those guys must be running all over here on practice missions. We're gonna be one bunch of them. Follow my lead. If we hit any live Syrians out there, I'll do the talking. We'll go sneaky wherever we move. Now."

The three men lifted up and ran, bent half over, toward the first building. No one challenged them. They flattened out against the building, checked inside, then went around the near side and out of sight toward the next structure.

Franklin snorted as he saw how easy it was. Nobody around. Why no guards if this place was so damned important? He and his two men rested against the second building. At least the doors were closed. He read the sign over the small door. "Packing, Shipping." Not what he wanted. "Second building a dud," he said on the Motorola, and led the men toward the third one. All buildings were well lighted, and yet he saw no guards. Strange.

They had just come around the third building, which had a sign saying it was used to manufacture small arms, when a pair of soldiers came toward them. They walked with rifles on their shoulders as if on an interior guard post. The soldiers stared at the three SEALs, nodded and waved, and went on past.

The fourth building looked more promising to Franklin. About time they turned up something. His gut was tightening up the way it always did when he was in action. He held up his hand, and his men stopped behind a truck parked in front of the place. Two armed guards stood near a small man-sized door. Two large truck doors at the left were closed.

One of the guards said something to the other one, but Franklin couldn't hear what it was. One guard looked around carefully, then lit a cigarette and held it hidden in one hand.

"We go at them head-on like it was a target," Franklin said. "If we're lucky they'll only yell at us."

The three SEALs came out from behind the truck, held their weapons in front of them with both hands, and ran flat out toward the two guards twenty yards away.

"Hey, stop, you stupid assholes," one of the guards yelled in Arabic. The SEALs kept going until they were ten feet from the guards, who were fumbling with their weapons.

"You're both dead," Franklin shouted in Arabic. "We gunned you down while you were smoking."

"Damned goat-fuckers, this building is off limits to your play-acting. Go somewhere else and leave us alone. You don't even have real bullets, but we do. You get out of here."

"You're camel-shit stupid," Franklin shouted. He waved the SEALs to one side, and they ran behind another building. In the shadow of the overhang, Franklin used his radio.

"Might have something, J.G. Two real guards outside a building, fourth one in. Looks sealed up. Not as large as the others. No windows. Two truck doors, closed. Want us to take out the guards and check inside?"

"No, we're coming in. They believed you were Special Forces on maneuvers?"

"Worked well, J.G."

"Good. We'll use the same tactic if we are spotted. We'll have Khai out front if we need his Arabic. Stay out of sight. We should be there in about five."

DeWitt led his squad directly at the nearest building, swung around it, and headed for the second one. Well ahead he could see the smaller structure Franklin had described. They ran in spurts, then hid behind the wooden buildings. They had just rounded the corner of the third one when Khai stopped and lifted his Bull Pup. J.G. DeWitt nearly bumped into Khai, then saw the problem.

Directly ahead of them, no more than twenty feet, stood a squad of ten Syrian Special Forces troops, dressed in desert cammy uniforms and floppy hats. They had various kinds of weapons, and a young officer in front of them stared hard at the SEALs.

"We declare your unit captured or killed," Khai screeched in Arabic. "You are out of the maneuver. Sit down and take off your hats as a sign of surrender."

The officer leading the Syrians shook his head. "This isn't even your sector. You can't capture us. The referee will agree with us. I'm Captain Palmyra. I order you to return to your own sector."

"Call yourself a major," DeWitt whispered.

"I am Major Al Saad, with the division. I order you to sit down and remove the magazines from your weapons. You are hereby captured. I'll remember your name, Captain. Now we have to go capture our primary objective. Sit down!" The last command came as a thundering bellow, and the Syrian officer gave a quiet order and his men sat down, took off their caps, and took the magazines out of their weapons.

Khai nodded and waved his troops forward at a trot, past the surprised Syrians and on toward the fourth building.

"Nice work, Major," DeWitt said.

Khai grinned in the pale moonlight. "Hey, at least we're still alive. Good thing they had an exercise on."

Khai heard the roving jeep a moment later, and the SEALs slid into the deep moon shade next to a building and waited for the rig to pass. It turned and went around another building, and he took the men on toward the next structure.

Franklin and his detail came out of the night and met them. They could see the small target building fifty yards ahead. It was lit like the rest of them, and now there were three guards in front. One evidently was talking with the other two. They saluted him and he walked away into the night.

"Ostercamp, have you been around the building yet?"

"No, sir."

"Take a run, see if there are any other doors or any windows."

Ostercamp took off at a run to the end of the building that covered them. He looked around the corner, waved at them, then vanished.

"We need to keep this a quiet mission for as long as possible," DeWitt said in his mike. "If there are no other entrances, we'll charge forward in a no-shoot assault and capture the two guards as part of the maneuver games. It should work again."

The J.G. paused, then nodded to himself. "Any other bright ideas?" he asked the net.

Nobody had any.

"Murdock, any thoughts?"

"Sounds like a good move. We hustle the guards inside, replace them with Franklin and Khai with the Syrian weapons, and we see what they are protecting."

"Good."

Ostercamp was back five minutes later. "No back door, no windows anywhere."

"Let's move out at a trot. Then when we see the two Syrians, we sprint for them with weapons at port arms. Let's do it."

The nine SEALs, with Kat and Yasmin in the middle, charged the unsuspecting Syrians and overwhelmed them.

"Stop, stop," the Syrians shouted, but by then Khai had hit one with a shoulder block and slammed him to the ground. Mahanani put the second one in a bear hug and powered him backward three steps against the building. Their weapons were stripped away and Ostercamp worked on the door. The lock was too good. DeWitt fired twice with his silenced MP-5 into the lock, and the door jiggled open.

He went in first, fast and low, followed by the rest of the SEALs except for Khai and Franklin, who took the new Kalashnikov 74's and stood guard where the Syrians had been. The Syrians were hurried inside, then gagged and plastic bands cinched on their ankles and wrists.

Inside the lighted building, the SEALs found a short assembly line where large bombs were evidently loaded with their powder charge and the fuses attached. In the far corner, steps led downward. Ed DeWitt and Murdock charged down the steps with their flashlights on. Down ten steps they came to a concrete wall with a steel door firmly in place. It had a time lock on it.

"Fernandez, get down the steps with some primer cord, now," DeWitt said to his mike.

Fernandez arrived a few moments later, saw the problem, and unrolled two one-foot-long strings of the quarter-of-an-inch-thick pliable C-4 explosive. He pasted one strip against the door circling the lock, and then put an X across the lock itself with the other strip. He inserted a timer/detonator into the cord.

"Three minutes?" he asked, and looked at DeWitt. The officer nodded, and Fernandez activated the timer. All three SEALs ran up the steps and to the side, out of the way of the back-blast that would funnel up the steps.

The rest of the SEALs heard the talk, and faded to the sides away from the steps. The blast came on time with a muffled roar; the near side of the building next to the steps shook for a moment, but didn't come down.

Murdock and DeWitt hurried into the smoke down the stairs. They came right back up coughing and wiping their eyes.

"Check with the guards in front to see if there was any reaction outside," DeWitt said. Canzoneri slipped out the front door, and came back a moment later.

"No reaction," Canzoneri said on mike. "Our guys heard the blast, but didn't think the noise traveled far."

It was four minutes later before the SEALs could penetrate the fading smoke and get to the door. The lock had been blown right through the metal door, and it sagged outward on bent hinges. It took both men to pull the door open enough so they could get inside. There were no lights. Their flashes served as they checked the twenty-foot-square room.

In the middle stood a table with a sealed container on it.

"We've got our warhead," DeWitt radioed. "Kat, get down here with your kit of tools."

Kat came through the door with her kit and two flashlights she had borrowed from SEALs. She looked at the sealed container, and took out her issue fighting knife and began ripping it apart. It was made of hard and soft plastic, and soon she found the key and opened one seal that held the two halves together. She lifted the top half and looked inside.

"Yes, the same warhead as the one in Libya," she said. "Help me lift it out of there and then I can get to work."

They pulled it out, cut off the rest of the plastic, and Kat began to work.

"Jefferson," DeWitt said on mike. "Find Yasmin and stay with her. We don't want her doing anything weird."

"Aye, aye, sir," Jefferson said.

Murdock sent two more men downstairs to hold flashlights while Kat worked. They began to sweat when Kat did as she began the delicate operation to make sure the trigger device could not possibly work to set off the nuclear bomb.

"This one is different," Kat said. "No way I can kill this one without some radiation."

DeWitt checked with Murdock, who was topside.

"Do it," Murdock said. "Sometimes we have to crack a few eggs to get the job done."

"Hey, Cap, we've got trouble up here," Franklin said from the front of the building. "The damn patrol rig is coming up. What do we do?"

"If they get too curious, waste them and get the jeep out of sight around back somewhere. Keep it silent as possible."

"Got it," Franklin said.

In front of the building, Franklin watched the jeeplike rig come closer, turn away, then make a U-turn and come back straight for them. He was going to make a social call. Damn, Franklin thought. It might be the last U-turn that driver ever made. He lifted the AK-74 and wished to hell that he had his silenced H & K MP-5. Shit. A SEAL had to do what a SEAL had to do.

# 30

Franklin watched the utility vehicle come to a stop ten feet in front of them. The driver looked out and shook his head. From the other side of the rig a soldier came around with a marching step. He had chevrons on his sleeve, wore a floppy hat, and had a submachine gun slung over his shoulder, muzzle down. His face was a silent mask of anger.

"Soldier, what the hell are you doing here?"

"Guard duty, Sergeant," Franklin said in Arabic.

"You're not the men I assigned here two hours ago."

"Oh, yeah, we're from the supernumerary, replacements. The two guards here got food poisoning and they rushed them to the medics."

The sergeant came closer until he was only four feet away.

"Your uniform . . ." That was all he got out. Franklin had been holding the long rifle on his shoulder. He pivoted the butt downward suddenly and slammed the barrel into the side of the sergeant's head, jolting him to the ground like a head-shot deer.

The moment Franklin made his move, Khai leaped forward, swung down the Kalashnikov, and pushed the barrel into the driver's throat.

"Unless you want to die in five seconds, don't make a sound. Get out of the vehicle." Again all in Arabic.

The driver stared at his sergeant motionless on the ground, and slowly stepped out of the rig. Khai marched him to the side of the building in the shadows, where he tied his hands and feet with plastic strips, and then gagged him.

Franklin dragged the dead sergeant around to the side of the building. "No need to gag this one," Franklin said. "Can you drive the jeep?"

Khai said he could, and pulled the rig to the side of the building into the moon shadows.

The two went back to the front of the structure and resumed standing guard. Franklin told the net what had happened.

"Hope to hell nobody finds them. How much longer we have to stand like clay pigeons out here?"

"We found the device," DeWitt answered. "She's working on it. Hang tough."

Murdock went down to the basement to hold a flashlight and let one of the men go topside. He watched Kat work. She knew exactly what she was doing. No lost time, no waiting and wondering. She cut wires and pulled contacts and wiped sweat out of her eyes.

It took her fourteen minutes to get the warhead in the condition she wanted it to be. She leaned back. "Bring down the charges I made ready," she said to the mike.

Fernandez brought down the package, and she spent two more minutes placing them exactly where she wanted them, then inserted two timer/detonators, and looked at Murdock.

"That will take care of the bomb. Maybe we can seal this basement with some blasts at the sides of the stairway. They'll have to go off exactly the same time as the blast down here, or a fraction of a second later. I've set the charges so most of the blast will go against the back wall. Which should allow a half a second before it ricochets out the stairwell."

Murdock looked at the stairs and decided it would work. Fernandez brought more C-4 and TNAZ, and helped form the bombs and place them on each side of the steps low down.

"How long on the timers?" Kat asked.

Murdock used the mike. "DeWitt, ten minutes on the timers on the blasts?"

"Sounds right. I've got Ostercamp looking at that truck outside. If it will run, we can use that to blast back to the fence to the south. Ostercamp, do we have wheels?"

"That's a Roger, Mr. DeWitt."

"Ten minutes on the timers," DeWitt said.

Murdock, Kat, and Fernandez each set one of the bomb timers at ten minutes when Kat said, "Mark." Then they hurried up the steps and out the front door. The Syrian six-by stood at the door. The rest of the SEALs were inside. Murdock picked up Kat and tossed her up to the tailgate, then climbed in.

"Count?" DeWitt asked.

"That makes eleven bodies, J.G.," Mahanani said. "Let's roll it, Franklin."

They rolled back the way they had come. A block ahead they had to stop for a line of marching troops to cross the road.

Murdock looked at his countdown watch. "Less than two minutes to blast time," he said.

The troops kept coming.

"Must be a fucking battalion," DeWitt said, looking out the windshield. The road guard in front of the truck grinned at them. Then he turned and ran to catch up with the last squad of the formation.

A few seconds later they heard the blasts. Murdock figured the ones they heard were those in the open stairs. The other ones, deep inside the basement's concrete coffin, would be muffled.

"Hit the gas," DeWitt said. The truck leaped forward, and went past the second building just as sirens wailed and more lights came on. They drove past the end building, and then suddenly the truck came to an abrupt stop.

"Forgot about that damn ditch," Franklin said.

"Everyone out," DeWitt said on the mike. "We hoof it from here on if we're lucky."

The people in the back of the truck had been thrown around, but nobody was seriously injured. They dropped off the high tailgate and moved toward the hole in the fence.

"Company," Ostercamp said. Franklin had cut the lights on the truck. The SEALs crouched in the short grass just beyond the glow of the lights on the buildings.

Then they all saw them. A pair of armored personnel carriers raced along the sides of the boundary fence. One came to a stop at the far corner, and the other a hundred yards farther on. Both turned and aimed their mounted guns back toward the munitions complex.

The near armored rig, with its troops, was next to the fence a hundred yards ahead of the SEALs. A hundred yards down the fence, in the corner, was the escape hole, along with the other armored rig.

"What the hell?" DeWitt asked. "How did they know we're here?"

"Might just be a preplanned defense, I'd guess," Murdock said on the mike.

"They can't see us unless they have NVGs," DeWitt said.

"Let's move ahead and bypass that first APC and work on the second one. We go fast and keep low. Remember, Yasmin, no shooting. Go."

The eleven fanned out in a line of skirmishers and ran through the Syrian night. They were about fifty yards in from the fence where the first armored personnel carrier stood. They could see no men near it in the darkness.

Twenty yards past the first APC and still eighty yards from the next one, DeWitt dove to the ground. The rest of the SEALs did too. "I saw some movement down by that next APC," DeWitt said. "We swing in toward the fence so they can't get us in a cross fire. If either one shoots, they'll be shooting right into the other APC."

They raised up and ran again. Kat was sorry she had brought so much ammo. It was weighing her down, slowing her. She grimaced and ran harder to stay up with the men.

Fifty yards from the corner of the fence and the second armored rig, they went down again. DeWitt was on the radio.

"I can see six or eight troops around and behind the APC," DeWitt said. "That blocks our exit. Line of skirmishers and lay down ten seconds of fire on my first shot." He waited for ten seconds while the SEALs double-checked the field of fire in front of them. Then DeWitt sighted in with his Bull Pup set for the 5.56 barrel. He slammed out a three-shot burst, and the rest of the squad fired at the shapes and forms around the armored rig.

The first few seconds, there was no return fire. Then a shot or two came, then half a dozen, before someone screeched near the APC and the firing there stopped.

"Bull Pups. Let's each put three rounds of the twenty on the APC at the corner, no laser, just on contact. Fire when ready."

A moment later five of the big 20mm rounds slashed into the APC and exploded, bringing screams.

Kat moved over beside Yasmin and watched her. She had been firing her Uzi at the near APC with the rest of them. In the darkness, Kat could see a smile on the Syrian woman's face.

When the fifteen rounds of 20mm ended, DeWitt used his NVGs again, and saw four men running behind the rig. "Another ten-second welcome," DeWitt said, and fired three rounds from his 5.56 barrel, and the ten other guns with him chimed in the chorus.

Kat fired bursts of three at the vehicle, trying to graze along the side rather than hit it directly. She watched Yasmin firing the Uzi. She went through one magazine, then a second one before the weapons stopped.

"Now, Bull Pups, three rounds each of the twenties on the APC behind us. We need to discourage them as well."

When the firing stopped this time, they could hear the first APC start its motor and move quickly away toward the lights.

"Franklin, come back," DeWitt said on the net.

"Hoo-ya," Franklin said.

"Tell them they all don't have to die. They can pick up and roll out of there, following the fence the long way home."

"That's a Roger." In the quietness of the night, Franklin shouted his offer of a safe retreat in Arabic to the APC in the corner. They waited. Nothing happened.

"Three more rounds of the twenties," DeWitt said. They fired on and around the APC. Then quiet settled down again.

"J.G., we've got three sets of headlights coming from the rear, maybe four hundred yards off," Ostercamp said.

"Let's laser them with the airbursts and see what we can hit," DeWitt said. "Three rounds each."

It took the men a few seconds to get their lasers and range finders turned on and working. Then the first shots went out and they saw the airbursts over the moving trucks. The first salvo knocked out the lights of one truck and probably stopped it. The next rounds hit a truck, and a moment later it burst into flames. The third truck turned around, and they fired at its taillights.

Ahead of them, by the corner of the fence, the APC's motor started, and it drove forward along the fence away from the SEALs. When the rig was out of the area, Ostercamp ran forward and checked the position.

"Looks clear to me, J.G. Found one body they missed. They can get it in the morning. Ya'll come down."

Ten minutes later they were through the fence and running for the moving van three hundred yards down the road. The driver was pacing up and down.

"Friends coming in," Franklin called to him when the troops were thirty yards away. He gave a small cheer and started the truck engine.

The SEALs and friends jumped on board, and DeWitt took a head count. Then they drove away. The driver explained that he knew the area. They could go down four or five kilometers and turn back toward the city and not go past the Army base.

In the rear of the truck, Yasmin sat with her back against the side and smiled in the darkness. Kat moved over beside her.

"We did it, Yasmin. We exploded that warhead so it will never be any good as a bomb or even furnish parts or pieces for a bomb. The radiation should be minimal if they keep it in that basement and seal it inside."

Yasmin caught Kat's hand. "I'm glad it worked right, Kat. You were excellent. I'll put you in my report. I'm feeling better myself."

"You fired a lot of angry lead at those soldiers back there."

"Yes, it felt so good. I don't know if I killed any of them, but I might have. I hope that I did. I feel just great." She was silent for a minute. "Now, we should talk about getting you back to the Israeli border. It's about eighty or ninety miles. There's a chance there won't be any traffic checks, but there might be. Can you talk to the people in the front seat?"

"Yes. Talk to DeWitt?"

"The head man, yes. Tell him that the driver knows what he's supposed to do, where to go. He'll take some back roads so we'll be harder to find. They will be looking for us, especially after it gets light. But we should be near the border before then. Can you tell Mr. DeWitt that?"

"You just did, Yasmin. Did you copy that, J.G.?"

"Roger that, Kat. I want everyone to check weapons and be sure you have full magazines. We could find some more trouble before we hit the friendly lands."

"Have the driver tell you where we are now and then," Kat said into the mike. "We can't see anything from back here."

A few seconds later the radio earpiece came on again. "You folks in the cheap seats," DeWitt said. "We are now about five miles past the last turnoff to Damascus. We will stay on the back roads for another half hour, then hit the main highway south and make some time. More report later. Thank you for flying with Syrian Motor Transport."

Murdock moved over by Yasmin. "What are the odds that we'll get all the way without a roadblock or traffic check?"

"Not good. The Army does a lot of checking just to have something to do. No war to fight, so we civilians become the target."

"What kind of roadblocks do they use?"

"I've seen them with big trucks all the way across a street or a road. No way to bust through or go around. They get clever putting them in single-access areas."

Murdock had been holding his mike out to pick up what Yasmin said. "You hear that, DeWitt?"

"Every syllable. We're watching all the time. If we spot a block quickly enough, we will try to go around it. Might work. Otherwise we'll just have to blast through it. Will keep in touch."

"Do that." Murdock stretched out on the floor. "Good time for a half-hour nap. By then we might be busy again."

It turned out to be forty-five minutes before they hit trouble.

"We're on the main highway south," DeWitt said on the net. "Two lanes each way. Looks like trouble coming up. Lots of lights, some pointing our way. Headlights. Trucks. We've killed our lights and are parking at the side of the highway. No side roads along here, the driver says. No way around them. Suggestions?"

"How far ahead?" Murdock asked.

"Six hundred yards."

"What's your move, DeWitt?" Murdock asked.

"Damn. Dismount, split on both sides of the highway, work down by foot behind them, and take them out. Then radio the truck to come on through."

"Maybe signal the truck with a flashlight, then we keep all of our guns," Murdock said.

"Yeah, right. Let's dismount, people. Murdock, take the ladies, Ostercamp, and Jefferson on your side. I've got the rest. Let's do it."

They opened the back of the truck and the people jumped out, divided into two groups, and when no cars were coming, Murdock took his four guns across the road and away from it fifty yards. Then they walked forward.

When they were opposite the roadblock, they moved out another fifty yards, then checked with DeWitt. "We're even with the block," Murdock said. "Looks like three six-bys and two smaller rigs. They mean business."

"So do we," DeWitt said. "I count six men. We're opposite them too. Let's go another fifty and then get in firing positions. One volley should take them down. On my signal."

Three minutes later Murdock had his people in position. "Let's do it the first time," Murdock said. "When they get in front of their lights they make perfect targets. Let's do it when there is no traffic stopped."

DeWitt came on the net. "That's a Roger on the traffic. Just the bad guys. Traffic is clearing. Another minute or two. Everyone ready?"

The net check was completed, and they waited for the radio signal. Kat looked over at Yasmin through the darkness and nodded. Yasmin had her Uzi anchored on a small mound and sighted in on the nearest soldier beside one of the trucks.

"Now!" DeWitt ordered, and the night crackled with the small-arms fire from the eleven weapons. Kat thought she hit a man who went down, but it could have been another bullet.

Yasmin fired burst after burst, emptied a magazine, pushed a new one in, and fired again.

"Cease fire," the radio earpieces said. Yasmin kept firing since she had no radio. She heard the others stop, looked at Kat, who waved at her, and quit firing.

"Cover us," DeWitt said. "We'll move in and check the ground." It took five minutes before DeWitt came on the radio again. "Looks like a clean sweep. We find only five bodies. Might be a live one out there somewhere. Move up and maybe we can flush him out."

Murdock and his four stood and walked toward the trucks. Nothing moved. Then, when they were halfway there, a man screamed and began firing an automatic rifle. He was ten yards in front of Yasmin, firing at Kat. Yasmin lifted her Uzi and drilled the man with six rounds. He screamed, turned, and emptied his weapon at the Syrian woman as he fell. Yasmin spun around and fell hard.

Kat screamed, ran to the fallen woman, and knelt beside her. She could see blood on Yasmin's shoulder and chest. She cradled her head and shoulders in her lap.

"Yasmin, you're hit but you're going to be fine. They signaled for the truck to come up. Should be here soon. Then we'll get you inside and find a doctor. He'll patch you up. You're going to be fine."

"Did I get him?" Yasmin asked, her voice whispery, faint.

"Yes, he's dead. You saved my life, Yasmin. He had me in his sights. His next burst would have cut me in half. You saved my life!"

"Good. Finally I get some satisfaction for what they did to my beloved. They killed him. Now I've evened the score."

She coughed and turned her head as blood dribbled out of her mouth.

"Get that goddamned truck up here, now," Kat barked into her lip mike. "We've got a wounded lady here."

Murdock eased down beside Yasmin. He looked at the blood seeping into her shirt just below her right breast.

The big truck eased up to the first truck at the roadblock, and the driver gunned the motor. Its wheels spun on the blacktop a moment. Then it pushed the other truck to one side and slid through the opening.

Thirty yards down the highway, the truck stopped at the side. Murdock carried Yasmin across the road, and a dozen eager hands helped lift her into the truck. Everyone piled into the truck and the driver closed the door.

"Ed, tell Franklin to tell the driver to get us to a doctor," Murdock said. "I don't care where it is or who it is just so it's fast. We've got maybe a half hour to save this lady's life. So move it!"

# 31

They drove the moving van south on the main highway for twenty minutes. "We're in a desert situation here again," DeWitt said on the net. "Not a damn building, let alone a town and a doctor. How is our girl doing?"

"Not good," Murdock said. "She was talking for a while, thought she was back in Philadelphia. She's unconscious now. Not a good thing. Lost a lot of blood and that chest wound is bad."

"Doing what we can up here. Where is that next little town? We passed through lots of them on the way up."

Murdock scowled in the darkness. Damn shame. Yasmin must be chopped up inside. Unless they found a doctor in the next ten minutes, they would lose her.

"Anything out there, DeWitt?"

"Just sand and rocks and some scrub brush. I can't see anything but blackness down the road. Hey, yes, lights ahead. Some little burg. Another four or five miles."

"Have Franklin strip off his fighting gear, no weapon. Sic him on any live person you see and ask about a doctor."

"Will do. Coming up, another mile or two."

Murdock looked down at the woman with her head in Kat's lap. Her breathing had evened out, but when he shone his flashlight on her, her face looked too pale. He tried for a pulse. There was one on her carotid, but weak and slow. Not good.

He felt the truck turn off the highway and come to a stop. The front door slammed. *Go, Franklin, go, go, go.*

It was a small store at the side of the road, backed by half-a-dozen houses and one other store that had closed.

The store had an old woman behind the counter.

"Do you have a doctor here?" Franklin asked in Arabic.

The woman shook her head. "Ten kilometers south. Good doctor. You hurt?"

"No, a friend. Thanks." Franklin ran back to the truck. "No medics here," he said to the mike. "A good doctor down ten kilometers. Can she hold on?"

"Doubt it, but we'll give it a try," Murdock said. "Tell the driver to put his foot through the floor."

Franklin jumped back in the truck next to DeWitt and told the driver to crank it up. "Drive this thing as fast as it will go," he said. The driver knew the problem. When he heard where the doctor was, he nodded and they raced down the highway.

Murdock checked on Yasmin again. Her face looked pasty now, as if it wasn't getting enough blood. Her breathing had turned ragged and slow. He was afraid to check her pulse. He'd seen people die before. If they didn't find a doctor in another five minutes, it could be too late.

In the cab, Franklin scanned the buildings in the small village. No hospital, for sure. Then he saw a sign that had the medical symbol. The driver stopped the truck, and Franklin ran to the door of the dark building and pounded hard. DeWitt opened the back doors of the van.

Franklin yelled and pounded on the door again. A light came on inside, and Franklin kicked on the door. A minute later, it opened a crack.

"What do you want?" a man's voice asked in Arabic.

"We have a woman who's almost dead. She needs a doctor's help at once. We need to bring her inside."

"It's too late, too late," the man said.

"Are you the doctor?"

"Yes."

"Then you must help us."

Franklin shouted at the truck, but they had heard him on the radio. Three of them carried Yasmin, careful not to harm her any more. They brought her through the door, to a waiting room, and into a surgery. There was a table with a light over it. They put Yasmin down and stepped back.

The doctor checked her chest wound and shook his head. He tested her pulse and shook his head again.

"Give her a shot of morphine, something to keep her alive," Franklin yelled at the doctor. He frowned at Franklin, took out a package, and unwrapped a needle and filled it, and gave her a shot, then began examining the chest wound. He shook his head again.

"Too much blood lost. Bullet wound?"

Franklin nodded. "Accident," he said.

The doctor snorted and put a probe into the wound, searching for the bullet. He didn't find it. He started a saline solution drip in her arm, and then went to a refrigerator and brought out a package of blood. He typed her blood, nodded, and started the blood transfusion. He gave her another shot he told Franklin was an antibiotic.

Franklin told the SEALs to dig out their cash. He collected twenty thousand pounds and pushed it into the medic's hands.

"Make her well," he said. "She is an important person from Damascus. Make her well. We have to leave. Make her well." He shook the doctor's hand and they hurried back to the truck. Franklin talked to the driver.

It was about an hour more to where he would leave them near the border. "When you drop us off, we'll give you the rest of our money. You go back and check on Yasmin, and do everything you can for her. You help her get well and you'll be rewarded. You understand me?"

"She's a friend. I'll help her all I can. The doctor seemed better than some in our country. I hope she can make it."

It was nearly 0400 when the driver pulled to the side of a dirt road. They had been off the main highway for most of the past half hour. Now he stopped. "End of the road," the driver said. "This is as far as I can take you. The border is about five miles across these hills. No more roads."

Franklin told DeWitt what the driver said.

"Okay, guys. Ante-up time. We need the rest of your cash for the driver. He'll go back and stay with Yasmin. He's a friend and will do everything he can for her." Nobody counted the money. It was a lot more than he'd asked for to make the trip.

The SEALs saddled up with their gear and weapons, and watched the truck drive back the way it had come. DeWitt led them out on the hike due west, where they should find the tongue of Israel that extended north between Lebanon and Syria.

"I can't imagine any section of this border without guards on both sides," DeWitt said on the mike. "So we'll walk light and keep our eyes open. We have any more casualties after that little firefight?"

Nobody spoke up.

They hiked to the west through the sand and scrub growth of
an apprentice desert. Five miles. DeWitt figured it could be more
like eight or ten.

Kat settled in beside Murdock as they hiked. "Think she'll
make it?" she asked.

"The medic looked like he knew what he was doing. He put
fluids in her and started a transfusion. If he has enough blood,
she has a chance. We'll check with CIA later and find out for
sure."

"She saved my life," Kat said. "That Syrian would have
chopped me in half a second or two later."

"But he didn't. Thank God for that. How's that leg of yours?"

"Still working. It should have another ten miles or so before
it collapses."

She was quiet for a few minutes.

"Will we have trouble getting over the border?"

"Could, depending what kind of border guards both countries
have. Be a damn shame to come this far and get whacked by
some friendly fire from the Israelis."

The land rose quickly. Ahead they could make out the slopes
of mountains. From somewhere Murdock remembered that the
Anti-Lebanon mountain range defined the border between Lebanon and Syria. They would be at the lower end of the range
with, he hoped, much smaller mountains.

An hour later the upward slopes had turned into nasty little
hills that climbed upward one after another. There seemed to be
no top to them. The time was working quickly toward 0600,
and Murdock was wondering if they could get over the border
before daylight. That could be anywhere from a half hour from
then to two hours.

They kept walking. Slowly the brightening sky ate up the last
of the night, and it was dawn.

Ostercamp led the way as scout. He used his radio now.
"Let's hold it right here a minute. J.G., you need to look at
this."

The SEALs hit the dirt. Murdock almost went forward, but
held back. This was DeWitt's operation. Let him finish it.

DeWitt bellied up to the top of a small ridge they had been
climbing and looked over. Halfway down the reverse slope, and
not more than two hundred yards away, lay a communications
tower and a collection of ten to fifteen six-man tents, several
vehicles, and what had to be a cooking tent.

At last they might have found the border, but were the soldiers he saw walking around below Syrians or Israelis? He used his binoculars. There must be something to identify the troops. He kept searching. Vehicle numbers? He tried to find some. The rigs he could see were parked sideways, so there was no exposure of the numbers painted on the rear and front bumpers.

It was on one of the tents, over the door. He looked again, adjusted the focus, and tried once more.

"Ostercamp, take a look at this. That second tent from the end. What do you see?" He gave the scout the binoculars. Ostercamp adjusted the focus and stared. He pulled down the glasses.

"What do I see? Just a tent showing a door and a Star of David over the door. Damn, that's Jewish. They must be Israelis."

How to get close enough to yell at them? There were no gullies, no ditches, no cover. Nothing but sand and rocks. The hell of it was, the SEALs' uniforms looked almost like the Syrians'.

"Murdock, can you get up here and take a gander?"

"Be right there."

Murdock checked the tent, saw the Star of David, and agreed. "Israeli, but how do we let them know who we are without getting our heads blown off?"

"I was about to ask you the same question," DeWitt said.

"White flag?" Ostercamp suggested.

"Who has anything white?" DeWitt asked.

"Curiosity," Murdock said. "We pique their curiosity into getting them to come to us."

"How?" DeWitt asked.

"Range to subjects?" Murdock asked.

"Two hundred yards."

"Bad spot for a border guard unit, wouldn't you think? With the bad guys on a reverse slope right in your backyard where they could shoot the hell out of you."

"Tremendously bad planning," DeWitt agreed.

"Unless we're not on the border, but a mile or two inside Israeli territory."

"A WP grenade," Ostercamp suggested. "Roll it down about halfway and stay out of sight. They will have to send out a patrol."

Murdock had a WP in his vest. He agreed, pulled the pin, and tossed it twenty yards down the slope. They edged back so only their eyes and tops of their floppies showed over the ridge as the WP exploded in a Fourth of July shower of furiously burning white phosphorus.

Nothing happened for ten seconds. Then a whistle shrilled and six troopers came out of a tent in battle gear and stared at the grenade's smoke pall.

An officer barked out an order, and the six men split fifteen yards apart and charged up the hill, holding their weapons at port arms.

"Everyone move up within a few feet of the crest of this ridge," DeWitt said on the radio. "We have some Israeli visitors, so no shooting."

The run by the troopers below slowed to a slogging walk as they advanced up the sharp slope with their weapons now aimed forward and fingers on triggers.

When they were twenty feet down the hill, the SEALs all began to shout and yell that they were Americans and not to shoot. The SEALs kept yelling up a storm.

The Israeli soldiers stopped, and one of them held up his hand. The SEALs quieted.

"Who the hell is Beavis's buddy?" one of the Israelis shouted.

"Butthead." The word came back from all along the line.

"Hey, you must be Yanks," the Israeli noncom said. "Come on out, we won't shoot. Where the hell did you guys come from?"

After that it was a short ride in American-made armored personnel carriers to a group headquarters. Ostercamp warmed up the SATCOM, and DeWitt reported to Admiral Tanning in Athens. The admiral said there would be air transport for them from Haifa. Next came a truck ride to Haifa. A U.S. Airforce Gulfstream business jet, the VC-11, met them at Haifa. The SEALs swarmed on board the VIP plane, usually reserved for generals and admirals, and an hour and a half later landed back in Athens.

Murdock took Kat to the medics to check her shoulder and her leg. The doctor admitted her to watch her leg, which had become infected.

"I'm fit for duty," Kat kept telling him. The doctor pretended that he didn't speak English, and pampered her and kissed her hand, and the nurse said the doctor would come by and see her the next day.

"Get me out of here," Kat hissed at Murdock. He grinned, kissed her hand, and told her he'd see her the next day. He had an after-action report to make to Admiral Tanning.

Before he left the hospital, he stopped by to check on Ron Holt. The doctor told him the chest wound was better. They had dug out most of the shattered bullet from his chest. Now the left shoulder was not responding well. He would be out of any physical action for at least two months. Murdock and DeWitt talked to the radio operator and longtime SEAL. He asked about the mission. Murdock asked him if he'd like a ride home.

"Oh, God, yes. Give a month's pay to be back in Coronado where they at least speak English."

Murdock made arrangements to have Holt sent to Balboa Navy Hospital in San Diego.

Murdock and DeWitt's next stop was the admiral's office. The tanned ex-ship driver already knew the good news about the mission being accomplished. Murdock told him about the CIA agent and how she'd saved Kat's life but was shot down for her trouble.

"We don't know if she'll make it or not. The Syrian doctor didn't know. He said he would do his best."

"Yes, we've heard from the Company about her. They will get her off her station as soon as she's able to travel. We're counting on her beating that chest shot."

The admiral paused and shook his head. "Now our next job is to take care of that damned Chinese destroyer disguised as a freighter. She's still anchored off that uninhabited Greek island. We have all sorts of plans, but nobody is satisfied. I suggested we wait for your input on the problem. What do you suggest we do about the rest of those forty-seven nuclear warheads in that destroyer?"

# 32

Admiral Tanning had coffee brought in for the SEALs, then got down to business.

"Some updating for you since you blew three holes in the hull of that Chinese destroyer masquerading as a freighter. We've had a picket fence around her for the past four days. She's still anchored near a small Greek island about a hundred miles southeast of us. The AWACS boys have spotted two different helicopters making a run for the ship, but our gunship choppers outflew them and turned them back with a pair of missiles across their bows.

"Our guess is the Chinese tried to sell some more of the warheads with chopper pickup. If that was the plan, it didn't work. Since then, nothing. No exceptional radio transmissions. We're monitoring their frequencies, but their messages are encrypted.

"That's it up to date. We have no grand strategy. There are five or six attack plans set up, but nobody will say that we should simply blow the ship out of the water and sink her with the missiles and the warheads on board. That would raise a stink. Now, do you have any ideas for us?"

Murdock took the lead. "I had some time flying back to think on this, Admiral. I knew the work wasn't done. A vertical assault on the ship would result in at least fifty-percent casualties. Not practical.

"One of our smaller Navy missiles into the ship would probably be too much for her to stay afloat. The Chinese would probably meet any missile attack with return fire on the ship.

"Any kind of a military attack on the ship, by missile, aircraft, or surface ship, is going to result in large Chinese casualties. A destroyer of that class has from two hundred and sixty to three hundred men on board.

"The longer we wait, the more time the Chinese have to dismantle the missiles, remove the warheads, and dispose of the missile bodies themselves. Then it would be fairly simple to seal off a compartment and hide the warheads there. Forty-seven of them, even with their rockets and guidance systems attached, would not take up a lot of room in a destroyer."

"You've just shot down three generals, two admirals, and a captain, Commander. So what is your suggestion about what we can do?"

"Wait," Murdock said.

"Wait? Give the terrorists time to dismantle the missiles and hide the warheads?"

"Yes, sir. I began thinking what I would do if I had command of a ship like that in the same situation. It was quickly evident what I couldn't do, steam home making five knots with three big holes in my hull. I also could not choggie into Athens for repair work on my hull with all of NATO and the rest of the world gunning for me.

"What was left? Yank the warheads out of those missiles and dump the useless carcasses overboard, then hide the warheads, welding shut the compartments required.

"Then I would stagger into port, asking for clearance to repair three holes where I had hit rogue mines left over from World War II. Once in port, I would be searched under some pretext, but I would win the day with my welded-shut compartments."

"Better than anything else I've heard so far," Admiral Tanning said. "This way, by waiting, we can't lose and we might win. Will that Chinese ship-driver do it that way?"

"The destroyer captain probably isn't in charge. I'd guess a civilian high in the government from Beijing is on board calling the shots with plenty of radio directions. He's had four days to dismantle the missiles. Depends how many engineers he has and how afraid of the warheads they are."

"That means how many more days, Commander?"

"My guess is three or four."

Admiral Tanning had been making some notes. He stopped and frowned, picked up a pipe and filled it, then looked at Murdock.

"So, let's say this boss Chinese does what you say, and comes into port here in Athens. International shipping laws being what they are, how do we board a foreign man-of-war and take off those warheads."

"The Greek National Health Commissioner," Murdock said.

"What? How could the health commissioner have anything to do with this ship?"

"The plague, the Black Death. We have strong evidence that one of the sailors on the ship has the plague, and he must be found and treated before he spreads the disease to the rest of the ship's men and before it breaks out in Athens itself.

"In this case the health laws far outweigh the maritime laws, and the search could be carried out in an orderly fashion, or with Greek police and military backing them up. Along with the medical search parties would be your men with Geiger counters and other sniffers looking for the barest hint of radiation. Every warhead is going to leak a little. The most sensitive instruments can pick up the scent through steel walls."

Admiral Tanning sat back in his chair and lit his pipe. He puffed two or three times, then blew a wobbly smoke ring at the ceiling and laughed softly.

"By George, Murdock, I think you might have something here. It's a no-risk plan for three days or a week. We have nothing to lose and forty-seven nuclear warheads to gain."

"Admiral, is Don Stroh still in the compound?"

"That he is. He was here earlier looking for you. My suggestion would be the officers' mess." The admiral puffed on his pipe and smiled. "Yes, Murdock, I think you have an idea that will work, and there shouldn't be a single drop of blood spilled."

Outside, DeWitt slapped Murdock on the shoulder. "When did you work out that neat little plan?"

"About the time he asked me for my suggestion. I just jammed myself in that Chinese guy's shoes and tried to figure out what I could do with all of that military firepower aimed right down my throat."

"The plague part?"

"The same time. It's the most feared of the most deadly diseases. People hear about the days when it wiped out millions. Might work with the Greeks."

"You hungry?" DeWitt asked. "I think it's steak time."

They found Stroh in the mess finishing a third cup of coffee. He beamed when he saw them.

"Heard the good news about the Syrian affair. You'll ask

about Yasmin. I don't know yet. We've talked to our embassy there. They have sent an ambulance to that little town to transport her to a hospital. Last we heard, she was still alive and doing better."

"Good news," DeWitt said. "You keep us informed about her progress. Now, Stroh, I hear this is the day you buy us dinner. I'm having a steak and maybe lobster."

Stroh looked confused. "This is the day? Did I lose a bet or something?"

"Yeah, a bet, you lost a bet," Murdock said. "So sit tight and we'll order. Then we can do our after-action report right here."

"No, the admiral will want to be in on it. Dinner? I lost a bet?" He threw up his hands. "Okay, okay. I give. Order anything you want, I'm on an expense account. The CIA will never miss a few bucks. Speaking of cash, did you spend all of your Syrian pounds?"

"All gone," Murdock said. "To the truck-driver friend of Yasmin."

"Right, so order. I'll just have a salad. I'm trying to cut back a little."

The next three days the SEALs shuffled around their quarters, worked on weapons, and killed time. Then DeWitt took the platoon on a ten-mile hike just to keep them busy.

Kat showed up on the third day, furious at the doctors. "They finally let me out of jail," she said. "Told me to stay off the leg and no marching and not much walking. My leg is fine."

She wore the khakis of a Navy lieutenant, skirt and all, and had a new bandage on her right leg.

"Where's Murdock? I have a couple of bones to pick with him."

Nobody could find the commander.

"I'll wait," Kat said, and went over to talk to Senior Chief Dobler.

### Star of Asia
### In the Aegean Sea

Chen Takung watched the men working on the last missile. They had the nose cone off, and were extracting the individual warheads with the utmost caution. They were so cautious, it seemed that they would never get the job done. Seven more warheads to remove and that part of the job would be done.

For days they had been stacking the warheads in three different compartments in the 528-foot-long warship. They buried the bulkhead in front of one of the compartments with stacks of supplies. A second compartment was filled with the warheads and their missiles and guidance system, and then the door was welded shut.

The third compartment was ready for the final ten warheads. They had taken more time on these, and separated the guidance systems and small rockets from them. They were placed in containers and positioned at the far end of the powder magazine, where the ship's big shells and ammunition were stored.

Chen expected that there would be some kind of a search of his vessel once he docked. He had checked his plan with Beijing and it had been approved. It was the only thing he could do. He told his superiors that the holes in the hull were the result of frogmen planting mines there. He was not sure of this, but no one could prove otherwise. That had gained him more respect in Beijing. He had been aware from the first that he was hemmed in by U.S. warships. The closest cruiser was now less than four-thousand yards away, working a lazy box course to stay in close contact. He was sure that when the last warhead was sealed away and he pulled anchor for his three-knot move into Athens, the U.S. warships would shadow him, perhaps even escort him.

He had his schedule worked out. It would take a day in port to set up the repairs. Then a week for the repair work to close up the holes in the hull and make her seaworthy again. Then, on the eighth day after docking, his ship would once more be on the way back to China and with the load of forty-seven nuclear warheads intact. Yes, what a great day it would be when he docked in Tiantjin harbor.

He went to the bridge.

"We should be ready to sail in two hours," he told the ship's captain. "We will dock in Athens for repairs. Yes, Captain, we will be inspected. By whom, we don't know. But it is my certainty that they will not find what they are looking for. The last of the missile bodies will be dumped overboard just before we sail."

"Aye, aye, sir," the regular Navy captain said. His irritation and dislike for this civilian he had to take orders from had not improved over the past few days, with his ship wounded and anchored, awaiting the whim of this self-important politician. But to move to port for repairs, that would be good. He could be home in Tsingtao in time for his family's celebration yet.

## Athens, Greece

Murdock and the SEALs, minus Kat, had just returned from a ten-mile run without their fighting gear, weapons only. Murdock paused to talk to the men for a minute before he headed for his shower. The phone rang and Mahanani answered it, listened a moment, and pointed at Murdock.

"Murdock here."

"Good, I found you. This is Admiral Tanning. The Chinese destroyer is moving. It lifted anchor and is now steaming along at three knots on a generally northwest course, which could mean it's heading for Athens."

"Good. Are the health authorities alerted?"

"They have been waiting for three days. We have two teams on the dock with the sniffer equipment. It's so sensitive that it can pick up a glowing wristwatch dial from across the room. If there are any warheads on that bucket of bolts, we'll find them. Then the Greeks will decide what to do with the ship. They could confiscate it for violating Greek nuclear weapons laws."

"Good. I hope it all works."

"Their ETA is about thirty-two more hours, which makes it sometime tomorrow afternoon. I'll send a car over to give you and your party a lift to the dock. I'm sure you'll want to be in on the final kill of the campaign."

The next day at 1615, Murdock, DeWitt, Kat, and Dobler watched the two "medical" teams swarm on board the Chinese destroyer that still looked like a freighter. Admiral Tanning's car drove up, and he went to Murdock's group to watch.

"Should be a good show," the admiral said. He held a civilian Handie-Talkie radio, and used it.

"Medical One, how goes the search?"

"Admiral Tanning. We've found traces of radiation in a large work area that is long enough to accommodate the eighty-foot Russian missiles. One of our men says he has a trail of radiation traces that could lead us to the prize."

An hour later it was all over. The "medical" investigators had found the three stashes of warheads. Greek military units stormed the ship and carried out the nuclear bombs in special sealed containers. The final count: forty-seven warheads. They were quickly transported to the NATO compound, where arrangements would be made for their destruction.

"I don't want that job," Kat said. "I've done enough of that for one trip."

It took two days to get all of their gear sorted out and ready to travel. Kat asked to be sent home with the SEALs, but she was overruled and booked on commercial first-class the next day. She had one last beer bust with the SEALs at the noncom club that night. Two hours into the fest, she held up her beer for quiet.

"Just a little drunk, but ready to take on any of you shitheads who want to try to outswim me." She took a long breath and held on to the table for balance. "Going home tomorrow. Probably never see you fuckers again. Been good shooting up people with you. You ever in D.C. and need an overnight, give me a call. 'Course you don't have my number. I can give it to you." She frowned. "Yeah, I could if I remembered it." The troops cheered and laughed.

Kat began to cry. Tears rolled down her cheeks. She went down the line of SEALs and punched each one in the shoulder, then kissed him on the cheek. At the end of the line she punched Murdock, then kissed him on the lips and grabbed his hand, and led him out of the place with hoots and hollers following them.

Outside, Kat stopped and looked at Murdock.

"Oh, shit," she said. "He's still a one-woman guy. My fucking luck." She giggled. "Actually that should be my no-fucking luck. No, no, don't walk me to quarters. I'm not that drunk that I can't find them. Get back in there with your men so I don't ruin your rep."

She turned and walked away with only a slight list to port.

Murdock grinned and went back into the bar for another round of drinks with the best damn SEALs in the Navy.

# 33

## NAVSPECWARGRUP-ONE
## Coronado, California

Third Platoon of SEAL Team Seven had been back at base for three days. The jet lag was over. Their weapons had been scrubbed, cleaned, repaired, oiled, and readied. Those who wanted them were off on a three-day liberty, and Murdock was trying to find Ardith Manchester at her office in D.C. She wasn't in, and her secretary didn't know where she was or when she would be back. "But then, sir, it is Friday at two and some of the offices around here don't do much work on Friday afternoons."

Murdock left a message. He was home. Call him.

Jaybird stood near the Coronado public library at a telephone booth. He had called Senior Chief Dobler's home twice now. Once the chief had answered, and Jaybird had hung up without a word. The next time, ten minutes later, Mrs. Dobler had answered, and Jaybird had mumbled something about a wrong number.

Did he dare call again hoping that Helen would answer? He'd been trying to get up nerve to call her since they came home. Just before they left for Athens, he'd had two delightful meetings with her. The one at the library had been delicious and thrilling, and he had to admit, he'd never even seen a girl like Helen Dobler, much less had the fun of talking with her and trying to get to know her.

Yeah, the big problem. Her old man was his top chief in the platoon. Senior Chief Dobler could make life so miserable for Jaybird that he would want to ask for a transfer. He'd seen a senior chief chase one guy out of the platoon, not because the kid didn't belong there, and wasn't good enough. No, the chief had just taken a dislike for the guy, and in two months the poor sod was begging to get transferred to another platoon.

What the hell could he do now?

Another call?

He took a deep breath, walked up the block and back down, taking his time, getting up his courage. Facing enemy fire was child's play compared to this. He stopped at the phone and reached for the handset. He hit the first three numbers, then the last four. Before the instrument could ring, somebody pushed down the turnoff button.

"She isn't home," a voice said close behind him.

He still held the phone and turned.

"Helen!"

"Yep, me, gonna stay that way all day. When I heard the second phone call was a wrong number, I just knew it was you. So I came to the library. Want to look in the stacks for some books?"

"Oh, yeah. I love those stacks. Let's go look there first." He held her hand as they walked into the library and into the tall shelves of books all in a row. In the far corner they stopped and looked at each other. There were books all around them. Nobody could see them unless they came right into the aisle. She moved closer to him until their thighs touched, then their chests, almost. He reached out and brushed her lips with his, then came back and kissed her firmly. Their hands were at their sides.

When their lips parted, Helen let out a sigh. "Oh, my," she said. "Wow, I mean, I've never felt anything like that before."

"That wasn't your first kiss, Helen, was it?"

"Well, no. I mean I've kissed boys lots of times." She hesitated. "Just not . . . just none of them felt as wonderful as that time."

"One more," Jaybird said.

Helen smiled and backed away. "No, not right now. I think we better find two books I can take home."

They found the books and checked them out, then went back to a reading room and sat and stared at each other for a minute. The talk came then, both anxious to learn more about each other.

"So, on my fifteenth birthday I got a new portable CD player and ten CDs. But I've never even tried to play them. Some kind of a package deal and the discs were gloppy. I have my own set of CDs I play. You have a CD player?"

The talk went on until she checked her watch and they hurried

the six blocks toward the Dobler house. Half a block before
they came to the house, a big liquidambar tree shadowed the
sidewalk from the streetlight nearby. They stopped in the darkness and kissed gently, then again with more feeling.

"Oh, oh, yes, but that is fine, Jaybird. But no more. You stay
here until I get in the front door. When you call me, try to make
it at five o'clock. Daddy isn't home yet and Mom is getting
dinner and I can usually answer the phone first."

"Done," Jaybird said, watching her walk away. What a fine
little body, so neat, compact, so . . . just right. Jaybird turned to
walk the mile and a half back to the apartment he shared with
another SEAL.

Oh, yeah! Only now he had to major in sneaky. One slip and
the senior chief would simply fillet him and hang his two slabs
of meat out to dry in the California sun.

The next three days they had training exercises as if they were
just off the boat and hitting BUD/S for the first time.

Jaybird's dislocated shoulder had become strong again. He
was second fastest on the OC rope climb. Canzoneri had full
use of both his lungs now, and showed no ill effects from the
last mission when he'd nearly drowned.

Ron Holt was still in Balboa Naval Hospital there in San
Diego. They set up a schedule so at least one of the platoon
went to see him every day they had enough time off. Usually it
was in the evening. They all knew that Ron would never get
back in the SEALs, not with his bad wound.

The next day Senior Chief Dobler interrupted their OC work-
out. The platoon gathered around him on the obstacle course.
"We picked up some special duty. All right, I volunteered you.
There's a thirteen-year-old girl missing down on the strand.
She's been missing for four hours from a swim with her family.
Her name is Janice and she's the daughter of a SEAL, a guy in
First Platoon. I know how this guy feels.

"I have a daughter, and if anything happened to her . . ." The
senior chief looked away as his voice caught and he dabbed at
his eyes. "Anyway. Any monster who attacks a thirteen-year-
old girl should be eating his balls for lunch just before somebody
empties a whole clip of 9mm rounds into his goddamned head.
Yeah, I get emotional about this. My daughter Helen was missing for an hour once. She was with friends. Her mother and I
almost went out of our minds. Hey, not so much of a problem
now, she's fifteen and damned responsible.

"Okay, give me a line of ducks. We move out to the start of the shoreline and go to a line of skirmishers, and we search every square inch of the sand and grass until we find her. Janice. Her name is Janice."

Jaybird felt like somebody had kicked him in the head and then in the balls. He'd heard right. Senior Chief Dobler wouldn't lie about something like that. Helen was fifteen years old. Oh, damn. How could he have missed it? She was still in high school. She didn't have a driver's license because she was too young. Oh, damn! He'd almost blown his whole career in the SEALs.

They jogged to the end of the sand, where the grass started along the strand, and spread out. He was near the highway and watched every blade of grass growing in the sand.

Jaybird shook his head in wonder. That was an almost. He would call her today or tomorrow at five o'clock and ease out of their little innocent affair. Friends. Yes, they could still be friends, but not kissing friends. He valued his head too much for that.

The platoon worked the rest of the afternoon. They searched their side of the road, then the other side. They sloshed along knee-deep in the edge of San Diego Bay on the other side of the strand, watching the water. Nothing.

Dobler led them back to the platoon area about 1730. Master Chief Gordon MacKenzie met them.

"Thanks for your good work, lads. We have a happy ending. The girl has just been found. She's been with a young lady friend. The girls thought they told Janice's mother, but evidently not. She's well and safe, and the family thanks you one and all."

That night Jaybird stayed home, watched TV, and read a thriller about a biological weapon attack on New York City.

In his apartment, that same night, Murdock tried to be patient. "Yes, yes, big-city girl. You can buy salsa in a half-dozen different types. But none of it is as good as the special Murdock Salsa. Watch and learn, young lady."

Ardith Manchester leaned over the table, knowing full well what it did to the neckline of her silk blouse. Murdock saw the sagging silk material and the two marvelous revelations behind it, and chuckled.

He kissed her gently. "Lady Ardith. If you ever want to have the fabulous Mexican feast I'm fixing, you'll have to restrain yourself.

"Salsa, for instance. First I chop up these dead ripe tomatoes into quarter-inch chunks. Then I do the same with half a medium green bell pepper. No, you don't need to use jalapeno peppers for good salsa. Next I add an equal amount of chopped onions. Same as the tomatoes. Next a pair of pinches of finely ground black pepper, a half-teaspoon of salt, and a teaspoon of grated lemon peel. Then we top it off with two tablespoons of lemon juice. Mix well and let sit for ten minutes to blend. Then you have Murdock Salsa."

"What about the cilantro," Ardith asked.

"Hate the stuff. Tastes like sinkhole water. Now test this with some absolutely plain taco strips."

She dipped one in, captured the lumps of tomato and onion, and ate it. "Yes, good. I'll take a gallon. Now, I had a talk with Don Stroh today. He's all excited about a new mission coming up, but he wouldn't tell me what it was.

"I talked with my dad, and then your dad, and we have an idea what it might be. They know what's hot out there right now."

Murdock pushed a loaded taco into her mouth.

"Stop, stop. I don't want to hear about it. I'm off duty now. I just want to play house with this beautiful lady I lured up here with my salsa. Do you think it's going to work?"

Ardith unbuttoned the silk blouse. She wore nothing under it. "I don't know about the salsa. Maybe the burritos you told me about would do it. In the meantime, between courses, let's see what else we can become involved with."

Murdock smiled, then chuckled as the blouse hit the floor. "Oh, yes, I do enjoy the negotiations. My first suggestion is that we move from the kitchen down a ways to that next door, the one with the king-sized bed right behind it."

Later, Ardith Manchester decided she loved the bean burritos almost as much as the Murdock Salsa.

# *SEAL TALK*

## *MILITARY GLOSSARY*

**Aalvin:** Small U.S. two-man submarine.

**Admin:** Short for administration.

**Aegis:** Advanced Naval air defense radar system.

**AH-1W Super Cobra:** Has M179 undernose turret with 20mm Gatling gun.

**AK-47:** 7.63-round Russian Kalashnikov automatic rifle. Most widely used assault rifle in the world.

**AK-74:** New, improved version of the Kalashnikov. Fires the 5.45mm round. Has 30-round magazine. Rate of fire: 600 rounds per minute. Many slight variations made for many different nations.

**AN/PRC-117D:** Radio, also called SATCOM. Works with Milstar satellite in 22,300-mile equatorial orbit for instant worldwide radio, voice, or video communications. Size: 15 inches high, 3 inches wide, 3 inches deep. Weighs 15 pounds. Microphone and voice output. Has encrypter, capable of burst transmissions of less than a second.

**AN/PUS-7:** Night-Vision Goggles. Weighs 1.5 pounds.

**ANVIS-6:** Night-Vision Goggles on air crewmen's helmets.

**APC:** Armored Personnel Carrier.

**ASROC:** Nuclear-tipped antisubmarine rocket torpedoes launched by Navy ships.

**Assault Vest:** Combat vest with full loadouts of ammo, gear.

**ASW:** Anti-Submarine Warfare.

**Attack Board:** Molded plastic with two handgrips with bubble compass on it. Also depth gauge and Cyalume chemical lights with twist knob to regulate amount of light. Used for underwater guidance on long swim.

**Aurora:** Air Force recon plane. Can circle at 90,000 feet. Can't be seen or heard from ground. Used for thermal imaging.

**AWACS:** Airborne Warning And Control System. Radar units in high-flying aircraft to scan for planes at any altitude out 200 miles. Controls air-to-air engagements with enemy forces. Planes have a mass of communication and electronic equipment.

**Balaclavas:** Headgear worn by some SEALs.

**Bent Spear:** Less serious nuclear violation of safety.

**BKA, Bundeskriminant:** Germany's federal investigation unit.

**Black Talon:** Lethal hollow-point ammunition made by Winchester. Outlawed some places.

**Blivet:** A collapsible fuel container. SEALs sometimes use it.

**BLU-43B:** Antipersonnel mine used by SEALs.

**BLU-96:** A fuel-air explosive bomb. It disperses a fuel oil into the air, then explodes the cloud. Many times more powerful than conventional bombs because it doesn't carry its own chemical oxidizers.

**BMP-1:** Soviet armored fighting vehicle (AFV), low, boxy, crew of 3 and 8 combat troops. Has tracks and a 73mm cannon. Also an AT-3 Sagger antitank missile and coaxial machine gun.

**Body Armor:** Far too heavy for SEAL use in the water.

**Bogey:** Pilots' word for an unidentified aircraft.

**Boghammar Boat:** Long, narrow, low dagger boat; high-speed patrol craft. Swedish make. Iran had 40 of them in 1993.

**Boomer:** A nuclear-powered missile submarine.

**Bought It:** A man has been killed. Also "bought the farm."

**Bow Cat:** The bow catapult on a carrier to launch jets.

**Broken Arrow:** Any accident with nuclear weapons, or any incident of nuclear material lost, shot down, crashed, stolen, hijacked.

**Browning 9mm High Power:** A Belgium 9mm pistol, 13 rounds in magazine. First made 1935.

**Buddy Line:** 6 feet long, ties 2 SEALs together in the water for control and help if needed.

**BUD/S:** Coronado, California, nickname for SEAL training facility for six months' course.

**Bull Pup.** Still in testing; new soldier's rifle. SEALs have a dozen of them for regular use. Army gets them in 2005. Has a 5.56 kinetic round, 30-shot clip. Also 20mm high-explosive round and 5-shot magazine. Twenties can be fused for proximity airbursts with use of video camera, laser range finder, and laser targeting. Fuses by number of turns the round needs to reach laser spot. Max range: 1200 yards. Twenty round can also detonate on contact, and has delay fuse. Weapon weighs 14 pounds. SEALs love it. Can in effect "shoot around corners" with the airburst feature.

**BUPERS:** BUreau of PERSonnel.

**C-2A Greyhound:** 2-engine turboprop cargo plane that lands on carriers. Also called COD, Carrier Onboard Delivery. Two pilots and engineer. Rear fuselage loading ramp. Cruise speed 300 mph, range 1,000 miles. Will hold 39 combat troops. Lands on CVN carriers at sea.

**C-4:** Plastic explosive. A claylike explosive that can be molded and shaped. It will burn. Fairly stable.

**C-6 Plastique:** Plastic explosive. Developed from C-4 and C-5. Is often used in bombs with radio detonator or digital timer.

**C-9 Nightingale:** Douglas DC-9 fitted as a medical-evacuation transport plane.

**C-130 Hercules:** Air Force transporter for long haul. 4 engines.

**C-141 Starlifter:** Airlift transport for cargo, paratroops, evac for long distances. Top speed 566 mph. Range with payload 2,935 miles. Ceiling 41,600 feet.

**Caltrops:** Small four-pointed spikes used to flatten tires. Used in the Crusades to disable horses.

**Camel Back:** Used with drinking tube for 70 ounces of water attached to vest.

**Cammies:** Working camouflaged wear for SEALs. Two different patterns and colors. Jungle and desert.

**Cannon Fodder:** Old term for soldiers in line of fire destined to die in the grand scheme of warfare.

**Capped:** Killed, shot, or otherwise snuffed.

**CAR-15:** The Colt M-4A1. Sliding-stock carbine with grenade launcher under barrel. Knight sound-suppressor. Can have AN/PAQ-4 laser aiming light under the carrying handle. .223 round. 20- or 30-round magazine. Rate of fire: 700 to 1,000 rounds per minute.

**Cascade Radiation:** U-235 triggers secondary radiation in other dense materials.

**Cast Off:** Leave a dock, port, land. Get lost. Navy: long, then short signal of horn, whistle, or light.

**Castle Keep:** The main tower in any castle.

**Caving Ladder:** Roll-up ladder that can be let down to climb.

**CH-46E:** Sea Knight chopper. Twin rotors, transport. Can carry

25 combat troops. Has a crew of 3. Cruise speed 154 mph. Range 420 miles.

**CH-53D Sea Stallion:** Big Chopper. Not used much anymore.

**Chaff:** A small cloud of thin pieces of metal, such as tinsel, that can be picked up by enemy radar and that can attract a radar-guided missile away from the plane to hit the chaff.

**Charlie-Mike:** Code words for continue the mission.

**Chief to Chief:** Bad conduct by EM handled by chiefs so no record shows or is passed up the chain of command.

**Chocolate Mountains:** Land training center for SEALs near these mountains in the California desert.

**Christians In Action:** SEAL talk for not-always-friendly CIA.

**CIA:** Central Intelligence Agency.

**CIC:** Combat Information Center. The place on a ship where communications and control areas are situated to open and control combat fire.

**CINC:** Commander IN Chief.

**CINCLANT:** Navy Commander IN Chief, atLANTtic.

**CINCPAC:** Commander-IN-Chief, PACific.

**Class of 1978:** Not a single man finished BUD/S training in this class. All-time record.

**Claymore:** An antipersonnel mine carried by SEALs on many of their missions.

**Cluster Bombs:** A canister bomb that explodes and spreads small bomblets over a great area. Used against parked aircraft, massed troops, and unarmored vehicles.

**CNO:** Chief of Naval Operations.

**CO-2 Poisoning:** During deep dives. Abort dive at once and surface.

**COD:** Carrier Onboard Delivery plane.

**Cold Pack Rations:** Food carried by SEALs to use if needed.

**Combat Harness:** American Body Armor nylon-mesh special-operations vest. 6 2-magazine pouches for drum-fed belts, other pouches for other weapons, waterproof pouch for Motorola.

**CONUS:** The Continental United States.

**Corfams:** Dress shoes for SEALs.

**Covert Action Staff:** A CIA group that handles all covert action by the SEALs.

**CQB:** Close Quarters Battle house. Training facility near Nyland in the desert training area. Also called the Kill House.

**CQB:** Close Quarters Battle. A fight that's up close, hand-to-hand, whites-of-his-eyes, blood all over you.

**CRRC Bundle:** Roll it off plane, sub, boat. The assault boat for 8 SEALs. Also the IBS, Inflatable Boat Small.

**Cutting Charge:** Lead-sheathed explosive. Triangular strip of high-velocity explosive sheathed in metal. Point of the triangle focuses a shaped-charge effect. Cuts a pencil-line-wide hole to slice a steel girder in half.

**CVN:** A U.S. aircraft carrier with nuclear power. Largest that we have in fleet.

**CYA:** Cover Your Ass, protect yourself from friendlies or officers above you and JAG people.

**Damfino:** Damned if I know. SEAL talk.

**DDS:** Dry Dock Shelter. A clamshell unit on subs to deliver SEALs and SDVs to a mission.

**DEFCON:** DEFense CONdition. How serious is the threat?

**Delta Forces:** Army special forces, much like SEALs.

**Desert Cammies:** Three-color, desert tan and pale green with streaks of pink. For use on land.

**DIA:** Defense Intelligence Agency.

**Dilos Class Patrol Boat:** Greek, 29 feet long, 75 tons displacement.

**Dirty Shirt Mess:** Officers can eat there in flying suits on board a carrier.

**DNS:** Doppler Navigation System.

**Draegr LAR V:** Rebreather that SEALs use. No bubbles.

**DREC:** Digitally Reconnoiterable Electronic Component. Top-secret computer chip from NSA that lets it decipher any U.S. military electronic code.

**E-2C Hawkeye:** Navy, carrier-based, Airborne Early Warning craft for long-range early warning and threat-assessment and fighter-direction. Has a 24-foot saucer-like rotodome over the wing. Crew 5, max speed 326 knots, ceiling 30,800 feet, radius 175 nautical miles with 4 hours on station.

**E-3A Skywarrior:** Old electronic intelligence craft. Replaced by the newer ES-3A.

**E-4B NEACP:** Called Kneecap. National Emergency Airborne Command Post. A greatly modified Boeing 747 used as a communications base for the President of the United States and other high-ranking officials in an emergency and in wartime.

**E & E:** SEAL talk for escape and evasion.

**EA-6B Prowler:** Navy plane with electronic countermeasures. Crew of 4, max speed 566 knots, ceiling 41,200 feet, range with max load 955 nautical miles.

**EAR:** Enhanced Acoustic Rifle. Fires not bullets, but a high-impact blast of sound that puts the target down and unconscious for up to six hours. Leaves him with almost no aftereffects. Used as a non-lethal weapon. The sound blast will bounce around inside a building, vehicle, or ship and knock out anyone who is within range. Ten shots before the weapon must be electrically charged. Range: about 200 yards.

**Easy:** The only easy day was yesterday. SEAL talk.

**ELINT:** Electronic INTelligence. Often from satellite in orbit, picture-taker, or other electronic communications.

**EOD:** Navy experts in nuclear material and radioactivity who do Explosive Ordnance Disposal.

**Equatorial Satellite Pointing Guide:** To aim antenna for radio to pick up satellite signals.

**ES-3A:** Electronic Intelligence (ELINT) intercept craft. The platform for the battle group Passive Horizon Extension System. Stays up for long patrol periods, has comprehensive set of sensors, lands and takes off from a carrier. Has 63 antennas.

**ETA:** Estimated Time of Arrival.

**Executive Order 12333:** By President Reagan authorizing Special Warfare units such as the SEALs.

**Exfil:** Exfiltrate, to get out of an area.

**F/A-18 Hornet:** Carrier-based interceptor that can change from air-to-air to air-to-ground attack mode while in flight.

**Fitrep:** Fitness Report.

**Flashbang Grenade:** Non-lethal grenade that gives off a series of piercing explosive sounds and a series of brilliant strobe-type lights to disable an enemy.

**Flotation Bag:** To hold equipment, ammo, gear on a wet operation.

**Fort Fumble:** SEALs' name for the Pentagon.

**Forty-mm Rifle Grenade:** The M576 multipurpose round, contains 20 large lead balls. SEALs use on Colt M-4A1.

**Four-Striper:** A Navy captain.

**Fox Three:** In air warfare, a code phrase showing that a Navy F-14 has launched a Phoenix air-to-air missile.

**FUBAR:** SEAL talk. Fucked Up Beyond All Repair.

**Full Helmet Masks:** For high-altitude jumps. Oxygen in mask.

**G-3:** German-made assault rifle.

**Gloves:** SEALs wear sage-green, fire-resistant Nomex flight gloves.

**GMT:** Greenwich Mean Time. Where it's all measured from.

**GPS:** Global Positioning System. A program with satellites around Earth to pinpoint precisely aircraft, ships, vehicles, and ground troops. Position information is to a plus or minus ten feet. Also can give speed of a plane or ship to one quarter of a mile per hour.

**GPSL:** A radio antenna with floating wire that pops to the surface. Antenna picks up positioning from the closest 4 global positioning satellites and gives an exact position within 10 feet.

**Green Tape:** Green sticky ordnance tape that has a hundred uses for a SEAL.

**GSG-9:** Flashbang grenade developed by Germans. A cardboard tube filled with 5 separate charges timed to burst in rapid succession. Blinding and giving concussion to enemy, leaving targets stunned, easy to kill or capture. Usually nonlethal.

**GSG9:** Grenzschutzgruppe Nine. Germany's best special warfare unit, counterterrorist group.

**Gulfstream II (VCII):** Large executive jet used by services for transport of small groups quickly. Crew of 3 and 18 passengers. Cruises at 581 mph. Maximum range 4,275 miles.

**H & K 21A1:** Machine gun with 7.62 NATO round. Replaces the older, more fragile M-60 E3. Fires 900 rounds per minute. Range 1,100 meters. All types of NATO rounds, ball, incendiary, tracer.

**H & K G-11:** Automatic rifle, new type. 4.7mm caseless ammunition. 50-round magazine. The bullet is in a sleeve of solid propellant with a special thin plastic coating around it. Fires 600 rounds per minute. Single-shot, three-round burst, or fully automatic.

**H & K MP-5SD:** 9mm submachine gun with integral silenced barrel, single-shot, three-shot, or fully automatic. Rate 800 rds/min.

**H & K P9S:** Heckler & Koch's 9mm Parabellum double-action semiauto pistol with 9-round magazine.

**H & K PSG1:** 7.62 NATO round. High-precision, bolt-action, sniping rifle. 5- to 20-round magazine. Roller lock delayed blowback breech system. Fully adjustable stock. 6 × 42 telescopic sights. Sound suppressor.

**HAHO:** High Altitude jump, High Opening. From 30,000 feet, open chute for glide up to 15 miles to ground. Up to 75 minutes in glide. To enter enemy territory or enemy position unheard.

**Half-Track:** Military vehicle with tracked rear drive and wheels in front, usually armed and armored.

**HALO:** High Altitude jump, Low Opening. From 30,000 feet. Free fall in 2 minutes to 2,000 feet and open chute. Little forward movement. Get to ground quickly, silently.

**Hamburgers:** Often called sliders on a Navy carrier.

**Handie-Talkie:** Small, handheld personal radio. Short range.

**HELO:** SEAL talk for helicopter.

**Herky Bird:** C-130 Hercules transport. Most-flown military transport in the world. For cargo or passengers, paratroops, aerial refueling, search and rescue, communications, and as a gunship. Has flown from a Navy carrier deck without use of catapult. Four turboprop engines, max speed 325 knots, range at max payload 2,356 miles.

**Hezbollah:** Lebanese Shiite Moslem militia. Party of God.

**HMMWU:** The Humvee, U.S. light utility truck, replaced the honored Jeep. Multipurpose wheeled vehicle, 4 × 4, automatic transmission, power steering. Engine: Detroit Diesel 150-hp diesel V-8 air-cooled. Top speed 65 mph. Range 300 miles.

**Hotels:** SEAL talk for hostages.

**Humint:** Human Intelligence. Acquired on the ground; a person as opposed to satellite or photo recon.

**Hydra-Shock:** Lethal hollow-point ammunition made by Federal Cartridge Company. Outlawed in some areas.

**Hypothermia:** Danger to SEALs. A drop in body temperature that can be fatal.

**IBS:** Inflatable Boat Small. 12 × 6 feet. Carries 8 men and 1,000 pounds of weapons and gear. Hard to sink. Quiet motor. Used for silent beach, bay, lake landings.

**IR Beacon:** Infrared beacon. For silent nighttime signaling.

**IR Goggles:** "Sees" heat instead of light.

**Islamic Jihad:** Arab holy war.

**Isothermal layer:** A colder layer of ocean water that deflects sonar rays. Submarines can hide below it, but then are also blind to what's going on above them since their sonar will not penetrate the layer.

**IV Pack:** Intravenous fluid that you can drink if out of water.

**JAG:** Judge Advocate General. The Navy's legal investigating arm that is independent of any Navy command.

**JNA:** Yugoslav National Army.

**JP-4:** Normal military jet fuel.

**JSOC:** Joint Special Operations Command.

**JSOCCOMCENT:** Joint Special Operations Command Center in the Pentagon.

**KA-BAR:** SEALs' combat, fighting knife.

**KATN:** Kick Ass and Take Names. SEAL talk, get the mission in gear.

**KH-11:** Spy satellite, takes pictures of ground, IR photos, etc.

**KIA:** Killed In Action.

**KISS:** Keep It Simple, Stupid. SEAL talk for streamlined operations.

**Klick:** A kilometer of distance. Often used as a mile. From Vietnam era, but still widely used in military.

**Krytrons:** Complicated, intricate timers used in making nuclear explosive detonators.

**KV-57:** Encoder for messages, scrambles.

**LT:** Short for lieutenant in SEAL talk.

**Laser Pistol:** The SIW pinpoint of ruby light emitted on any pistol for aiming. Usually a silenced weapon.

**Left Behind:** In 30 years SEALs have seldom left behind a dead comrade, never a wounded one. Never been taken prisoner.

**Let's Get the Hell out of Dodge:** SEAL talk for leaving a place, bugging out, hauling ass.

**Liaison:** Close-connection, cooperating person from one unit or service to another. Military liaison.

**Light Sticks:** Chemical units that make light after twisting to release chemicals that phosphoresce.

**Loot & Shoot:** SEAL talk for getting into action on a mission.

**LZ:** Landing Zone.

**M1-8:** Russian Chopper.

**M1A1 M-14:** Match rifle upgraded for SEAL snipers.

**M-3 Submachine gun:** WWII grease gun, .45-caliber. Cheap. Introduced in 1942.

**M-16:** Automatic U.S. rifle. 5.56 round. Magazine 20 or 30, rate of fire 700 to 950 rds/min. Can attach M203 40mm grenade launcher under barrel.

**M-18 Claymore:** Antipersonnel mine. A slab of C-4 with 200 small ball bearings. Set off electrically or by trip wire. Can be positioned and aimed. Sprays out a cloud of balls. Kill zone 50 meters.

**M60 Machine Gun:** Can use 100-round ammo box snapped onto the gun's receiver. Not used much now by SEALs.

**M-60E3:** Lightweight handheld machine gun. Not used now by the SEALs.

**M61A1:** The usual 20mm cannon used on many American fighter planes.

**M61(j):** Machine Pistol. Yugoslav make.

**M662:** A red flare for signaling.

**M-86:** Pursuit Deterrent Munitions. Various types of mines, grenades, trip-wire explosives, and other devices in antipersonnel use.

**M-203:** A 40mm grenade launcher fitted under an M-16 or the M-4A1 Commando. Can fire a variety of grenade types up to 200 yards.

**MagSafe:** Lethal ammunition that fragments in human body and does not exit. Favored by some police units to cut down on second kill from regular ammunition exiting a body.

**Make a Peek:** A quick look, usually out of the water, to check your position or tactical situation.

**Mark 23 Mod O:** Special operations offensive handgun system. Double-action, 12-round magazine. Ambidextrous safety and mag-release catches. Knight screw-on suppressor. Snap-on laser for sighting. .45-caliber. Weighs 4 pounds loaded. 9.5 inches long; with silencer, 16.5 inches long.

**Mark II Knife:** Navy-issue combat knife.

**Mark VIII SDV:** Swimmer Delivery Vehicle. A bus, SEAL talk. 21 feet long, beam and draft 4 feet, 6 knots for 6 hours.

**Master-at-Arms:** Military police commander on board a ship.

**MAVRIC Lance:** A nuclear alert for stolen nukes or radioactive goods.

**MC-130 Combat Talon:** A specially equipped Hercules for covert missions in enemy or unfriendly territory.

**McMillan M87R:** Bolt-action sniper rifle. .50-caliber. 53 inches long. Bipod, fixed 5- or 10-round magazine. Bulbous muzzle brake on end of barrel. Deadly up to a mile. All types .50-caliber ammo.

**MGS:** Modified Grooming Standards. So SEALs don't all look like military, to enable them to do undercover work in mufti.

**MH-53J:** Chopper, updated CH053 from Nam days. 200 mph, called the Pave Low III.

**MH-60K Black Hawk:** Navy chopper. Forward infrared system for low-level night flight. Radar for terra follow/avoidance. Crew of 3, takes 12 troops. Top speed 225 mph. Ceiling 4,000 feet. Range radius 230 miles. Arms: 2 12.7mm machine guns.

**MIDEASTFOR:** Middle East Force.

**MiG:** Russian-built fighter, many versions, used in many nations around the world.

**Mike Boat:** Liberty boat off a large ship.

**Mike-Mike:** Short for mm, millimeter, as 9 mike-mike.

**Milstar:** Communications satellite for pickup and bouncing from SATCOM and other radio transmitters. Used by SEALs.

**Minigun:** In choppers. Can fire 2,000 rounds per minute. Gatling gun-type.

**Mitrajez M80:** Machine gun from Yugoslavia.

**MI-15:** British domestic intelligence agency.

**MI-16:** British foreign intelligence and espionage.

**Mocha:** Food energy bar SEALs carry in vest pockets.

**Mossberg:** Pump-action, pistol-grip, 5-round magazine. SEALs use it for close-in work.

**Motorola Radio:** Personal radio, short range, lip mike, earpiece, belt pack.

**MRE:** Meals Ready to Eat. Field rations used by most of U.S. Armed Forces and the SEALs as well. Long-lasting.

**MSPF:** Maritime Special Purpose Force.

**Mugger:** MUGR, Miniature Underwater Global locator device. Sends up antenna for pickup on positioning satellites. Works under water or above. Gives location within 10 feet.

**Mujahideen:** A soldier of Allah in Muslim nations.

**NAVAIR:** NAVy AIR command.

**NAVSPECWARGRUP-ONE:** Naval Special Warfare Group One Based on Calmoloi Cal. SEALs are in this command.

**NAVSPECWARGRUP-TWO:** Naval Special Warfare Group Two based at Norfolk.

**NCIS:** Naval Criminal Investigative Service. A civilian operation not reporting to any Navy authority to make it more responsible and responsive. Replaces the old NIS, Naval Investigation Service, that did report to the closest admiral.

**NEST:** Nuclear Energy Search Team. Non-military unit that reports at once to any spill, problem, or Broken Arrow to determine the extent of the radiation problem.

**NEWBIE:** A new man, officer, or commander of an established military unit.

**NKSF:** North Korean Special Forces.

**NLA:** Iranian National Liberation Army. About 4,500 men in South Iraq, helped by Iraq for possible use against Iran.

**Nomex:** The type of material used for flight suits and hoods.

**NPIC:** National Photographic Interpretation Center in D.C.

**NRO:** National Reconnaissance Office. To run and coordinate satellite development and operations for the intelligence community.

**NSA:** National Security Agency.

**NSC:** National Security Council. Meets in Situation Room, support facility in the Executive Office Building in D.C. Main security group in the nation.

**NSVHURAWN:** Iranian Marines.

**NUCFLASH:** An alert for any nuclear problem.

**NVG One Eye:** Litton single-eyepiece Night-Vision Goggles. Prevents NVG blindness in both eyes if a flare goes off. Scope shows green-tinted field at night.

**NVGs:** Night-Vision Goggles. One eye or two. Give good night vision in the dark with a greenish view.

**OAS:** Obstacle Avoidance Sonar. Used on many low-flying attack aircraft.

**OIC:** Officer In Charge.

**Oil Tanker:** One is: 885 feet long, 140 feet beam, 121,000 tons, 13 cargo tanks that hold 35.8 million gallons of fuel, oil, or gas. 24 in the crew. This is a regular-sized tanker. Not a supertanker.

**OOD:** Officer Of the Deck.

**Orion P-3:** Navy's long-range patrol and antisub aircraft. Some adapted to ELINT roles. Crew of 10. Max speed loaded 473 mph. Ceiling 28,300 feet. Arms: internal weapons bay and 10 external weapons stations for a mix of torpedoes, mines, rockets, and bombs.

**Passive Sonar:** Listening for engine noise of a ship or sub. It doesn't give away the hunter's presence as an active sonar would.

**Pave Low III:** A Navy chopper.

**PBR:** Patrol Boat River. U.S. has many shapes, sizes, and with various types of armament.

**PC-170:** Patrol Coastal-Class 170-foot SEAL delivery vehicle. Powered by 4 3,350 hp diesel engines, beam of 25 feet and draft of 7.8 feet. Top speed 35 knots, range 2,000 nautical miles. Fixed swimmer platform on stern. Crew of 4 officers and 24 EM, carries 8 SEALs.

**Plank Owners:** Original men in the start-up of a new military unit.

**Polycarbonate material:** Bullet-proof glass.

**PRF:** People's Revolutionary Front. Fictional group in *NUC-FLASH*, a SEAL Team Seven book.

**Prowl & Growl:** SEAL talk for moving into a combat mission.

**Quitting Bell:** In BUD/S training. Ring it and you quit the SEAL unit. Helmets of men who quit the class are lined up below the bell in Coronado. (Recently they have stopped ringing the bell. Dropouts simply place their helmet below the bell and go.)

**RAF:** Red Army Faction. A once-powerful German terrorist group, not so active now.

**Remington 200:** Sniper Rifle. Not used by SEALs now.

**Remington 700:** Sniper rifle with Starlight Scope. Can extend night vision to 400 meters.

**RIB:** Rigid Inflatable Boat. 3 sizes, one 10 meters, 40 knots.

**Ring Knocker:** An Annapolis graduate with the ring.

**RIO:** Radar Intercept Officer. The officer who sits in the backseat of an F-14 Tomcat off a carrier. The job: find enemy targets in the air and on the sea.

**Roger That:** A yes, an affirmative, a go answer to a command or statement.

**RPG:** Rocket Propelled Grenade. Quick and easy, shoulder-fired. Favorite weapon of terrorists, insurgents.

**SAS:** British Special Air Service. Commandos. Special warfare men. Best that Britain has. Works with SEALs.

**SATCOM:** Satellite-based communications system for instant contact with anyone anywhere in the world. SEALs rely on it.

**SAW:** Squad's Automatic Weapon. Usually a machine gun or automatic rifle.

**SBS:** Special Boat Squadron. On-site Navy unit that transports SEALs to many of their missions. Located across the street from the SEALs' Coronado, California, headquarters.

**SD3:** Sound-suppression system on the H & K MP5 weapon.

**SDV:** Swimmer Delivery Vehicle. SEALs use a variety of them.

**Seahawk SH-60:** Navy chopper for ASW and SAR. Top speed 180 knots, ceiling 13,800 feet, range 503 miles, arms: 2 Mark 46 torpedoes.

**SEAL Headgear:** Boonie hat, wool balaclava, green scarf, watch cap, bandanna roll.

**Second in Command:** Also 2IC for short in SEAL talk.

**SERE:** Survival, Evasion, Resistance, and Escape training.

**Shipped for Six:** Enlisted for six more years in the Navy.

**Shit City:** Coronado SEALs' name for Norfolk.

**Show Colors:** In combat put U.S. flag or other identification on back for easy identification by friendly air or ground units.

**Sierra Charlie:** SEAL talk for everything on schedule.

**Simunition:** Canadian product for training that uses paint balls instead of lead for bullets.

**Sixteen-Man Platoon:** Basic SEAL combat force. Up from 14 men a few years ago.

**Sked:** SEAL talk for schedule.

**Sonobuoy:** Small underwater device that detects sounds and transmits them by radio to plane or ship.

**Space Blanket:** Green foil blanket to keep troops warm. Vacuum-packed and folded to a cigarette-sized package.

**Sprayers and Prayers:** Not the SEAL way. These men spray bullets all over the place hoping for hits. SEALs do more aimed firing for sure kills.

**SS-19:** Russian ICBM missile.

**STABO:** Use harness and lines under chopper to get down to the ground.

**STAR:** Surface To Air Recovery operation.

**Starflash Round:** Shotgun round that shoots out sparkling fireballs that ricochet wildly around a room, confusing and terrifying the occupants. Non-lethal.

**Stasi:** Old-time East German secret police.

**Stick:** British terminology: 2 4-man SAS teams. 8 men.

**Stokes:** A kind of Navy stretcher. Open coffin shaped of wire mesh and white canvas for emergency patient transport.

**STOL:** Short TakeOff and Landing. Aircraft with high-lift wings and vectored-thrust engines to produced extremely short takeoffs and landings.

**Sub Gun:** Submachine gun, often the suppressed H & K MP5.

**Suits:** Civilians, usually government officials wearing suits.

**Sweat:** The more SEALs sweat in peacetime, the less they bleed in war.

**Sykes-Fairbairn:** A commando fighting knife.

**Syrette:** Small syringe for field administration often filled with morphine. Can be self-administered.

**Tango:** SEAL talk for a terrorist.

**TDY:** Temporary duty assigned outside of normal job designation.

**Terr:** Another term for terrorist. Shorthand SEAL talk.

**Tetrahedral reflectors:** Show up on multi-mode radar like tiny suns.

**Thermal Imager:** Device to detect warmth, as a human body, at night or through light cover.

**Thermal Tape:** ID for night-vision-goggle user to see. Used on friendlies.

**TNAZ:** Trinittroaze Tidine. Explosive to replace C-4. 15% stronger than C-4 and 20% lighter.

**TO&E:** Table showing organization and equipment of a military unit.

**Top SEAL Tribute:** "You sweet motherfucker, don't you never die!"

**Trailing Array:** A group of antennas for sonar pickup trailed out of a submarine.

**Train:** For contact in smoke, no light, fog, etc. Men directly behind each other. Right hand on weapon, left hand on shoulder of man ahead. Squeeze shoulder to signal.

**Trident:** SEALs' emblem. An eagle with talons clutching a Revolutionary War pistol, and Neptune's trident superimposed on the Navy's traditional anchor.

**TRW:** A camera's digital record that is sent by SATCOM.

**TT33:** Tokarev, a Russian pistol.

**UAZ:** A Soviet 1-ton truck.

**UBA Mark XV:** Underwater life support with computer to regulate the rebreather's gas mixture.

**UGS:** Unmanned Ground Sensors. Can be used to explode booby traps and claymore mines.

**UNODIR:** Unless otherwise directed. The unit will start the operation unless they are told not to.

**VBSS:** Orders to "visit, board, search, and seize."

**Wadi:** A gully or ravine, usually in a desert.

**White Shirt:** Man responsible for safety on carrier deck as he leads around civilians and personnel unfamiliar with the flight deck.

**WIA:** Wounded In Action.

**Zodiac:** Also called an IBS, Inflatable Boat Small. 15 × 6 feet, weighs 265 pounds. The "rubber duck" can carry 8 fully equipped SEALs. Can do 18 knots with a range of 65 nautical miles.

**Zulu:** Means Greenwich Mean Time, GMT. Used in all formal military communications.